Lion of the Balkans

A Novel by
Vladimir Chernozemsky

Triumvirate **P**ublications
Los Angeles, California

Lion of the Balkans
by Vladimir Chernozemsky

Published by: Triumvirate Publications
497 West Avenue 44
Los Angeles, CA 90065-3917
Phone/Fax: (818) 340-6770
E-Mail: Triumpub@aol.com
SAN: 255-6480

ISBN: 1-932656-01-4

Library of Congress Control Number: 2004105199

First Edition. Printed in the United States of America
0 9 8 7 6 5 4 3 2 1

Cover and Page Design by Carolyn Porter, One-On-One Book
    Production, West Hills, California
Cover Illustration by Borislav Zdraebev
Production: Nancy Gadney
Editing: Carolyn Porter, Steve Hobson

Dedication

To Colonel Vladimir Seraphimov
and his wife, Ellena.

—The Author

Special thanks to my one and only collaborator
in all aspects of life,
Charlotte Friedman-Chernozemsky.

—The Author

Prologue

LION OF THE BALKANS is based upon a little known conflict in 1912, between the countries situated in that distant part of Europe. It started as a liberation war; it ended as a predators fight. The initial enemies, Bulgaria and Turkey, were joined in this 'Dance Macabre' by the rest of the Balkan kingdoms and that became the infamous Balkan War.

Most everybody has read at one time or another about the First World War. Many historians have tried to explain it; scores of authors have written about it. The Balkan War, though a prelude to World War One, has been left obscure and unknown. Was that *miniature* war just another quarrel of unruly neighbors, or the first tremor of a devastating earthquake, ready to set the world in turmoil for the rest of the century and into the present? Was the Bulgarian experience of 1912-13 a vague and dark chapter in the history of a small nation, or had God chosen to warn us through that 'world in a drop of water' example, for the future to come?

Who was to blame that we never got the message?

LION OF THE BALKANS is a concise narrative of those turbulent times. All characters, but a few, had existed in the past. I grew up with tales about their lives; many of them told me their piece of the story in person. Slowly the past materialized in my mind as an immediate reality. I felt the spreading of the sinister cobweb that had closed over their destiny to a point of no return.

The life of my grandfather, Colonel Vladimir Seraphimov, and his family, the mighty shadow that he opposed—Tzar Ferdinand I, his sycophant court and unpredictable mistress; the 'Sick Man,' an agonizing Turkish Empire under a weak and whimsical Sultan, a puppet in the crafty hands of the British, ruling him and the Balkans from behind the sets; and the ordinary people caught up in that deadly game of blind ambitions, paying the ultimate price for it. As usually happens, that *Inferno* brings out not only the worst in human nature, but a lot of love, self-sacrifice and generosity, surfacing in a period of crises as proof that God hasn't turned His face away from our race.

The two nations in war overcome the hatred and misunderstanding of the past, to find their real enemies. By reading *LION OF THE BALKANS* we might learn one more time to discern those universal foes and maybe... just maybe... drive them from our embittered planet forever!

Vladimir Chernozemsky

Principal Characters

In Sofia
Capital of Bulgaria

Ferdinand I, Tzar of Bulgaria
Prince Boris, Heir to the Throne
Prince Cyril, his younger brother
General Borislav Robev, Adjutant to the Tzar and their Tutor
Nayden Hadgylvanov, Minister of Justice
Sultana Hadgylvanova, his wife and mistress to the Tzar
General Jallov, Member of the War Council and the Diplomatic Corps
General Ghenev, Commander of Second Army
Colonel Semerdgiev, a special assistant to the Tzar
Lieutenant Semerdgiev, his son and secretary to the Tzar

In Istanbul
(Formerly Constantinople)
Capital of the Turkish Empire,
called by the Bulgarians, Tzarygrad

Sultan Mehmed, Padishah, Ruler of the Empire, Topkapi is his favorite palace
Avzy Bey, the Commander of his personal guards
Yaver Pasha, famous general and Sultan's favorite
Zyumbul, his mistress
Lord Covington, British Ambassador

In Plovdiv
Second City in Bulgaria,
called Phulbee by the Turks

Lieutenant Colonel Vladimir Seraphimov, asst. commander of 21st regiment
Ellena Seraphimova, his wife
Rayna, their eldest daughter
Jeanna, Elsa, Jivca, Lily, younger daughters of the Seraphimovs
Assen Mitackov, houseboy
Donca, the cook
Ivan Zemsky, a young actor from a rich family that disowned him
Colonel Nedelev, commander of 21st regiment
Colonel Voznessensky, head of the Military School
Captain Dimmitriev and
Captain Dennev, adjutants to 21st regiment
Dr. Michailov, Public Health Official in Plovdiv

Pashmakly

Rhodopy Region: partially in Turkey, later liberated by the Bulgarians. It covers the Rhodopy Mountains. Villages: Progled, Chepellare, Arda, Moguilitza, Derrekioy, Allamy Derre, Chamgass, Smollian, Ustovo, also Station Bouk and Catoun.

White Sea Region: includes cities: Tessalonica and Ksanty; villages: Memmee and Saksalla

The Rhodopians:
Gavril Kademov (Gavro)
Radoul Boev (Radco) from Progled
Stryna Nonna, Radco's mother
Haydouk Dimmitar, Radco's father
Ermin Droumev, a soldier and noted flute player

Arrif Agha, mahmour or customs master of the Turkish border garrison at mount Rhojen, also a temporary commander

Ismail, Arrif Agha's son

Delly Hassan Caursky, a young smith in Progled, also a village bully

Dannail Marrin (Danco), also known as Ibrahim, from Derrekioy

Medco Marrinoglou, Danco's father

Magda and **Bogdana,** Danco's sisters

Ignat, Bogdana's husband

Metyo and **Mourco Bachovy,** brothers from Progled

Ivan Sullinadgiev, notable from Ustovo

Rossitza Podgorska, from Derrekioy, later in Progled

Goran Podgorsky, her father

Pope Stoyco, a priest in Derrekioy

Humayun and **Agoush,** brothers and the beys of Moguilitza

Mehmed Agoushev, their son and nephew

Ahmed, Mehmed's son who was later killed

Roustan, Chief of the Guards in the castle of Moguilitza

Rammadan, hodga or priest of Catoun

Sadak, mayor of Catoun

Nickola Vassilev, mayor of Arda

Dinno, Nickola Vassilev's son

Gavrail, Nickola Vassilev's youngest brother

Tenyo Voyvoda, leader of the extramilitary force in Arda

Kell Addem, a miller of Turkish origins

The Vampire (Major Kerrim Abdoullah) from Istanbul Headquarters

Rashid Babba, landowner in Chamgas

Azimee and **Fatima,** Rashid Babba's daughters

Sergeant Jellyo Jetchev, gunsmith master

Sergeant Ranghel Sabev, commander of a special cavalry detachment

Sallih and **Radgeb,** deserters from the Turkish army, cousins

Diado Ivvo Chichellaky, a Carracachan shepherd

Costaky and **Idris,** Ivvo Chichellaky's sons

Ghana from Chepellare, Ivvo Chichellaky's daughter

Orrania (Orry), Ivvo Chichellaky's granddaughter

Lieutenant Vrannev, later Lt. Colonel, the officer that burned Moguilitza

Part One

Prelude

Vladimir Chernozemsky

The Shifting Borders of Bulgaria

The Ottoman Turkish Empire had occupied and oppressed Bulgaria for five centuries. After the Bulgarian Uprising and the resulting massacre of 30,000 Bulgarians by the Turks in 1876, the major nations of Europe attempted to arbitrarily establish Bulgarian boundaries at the Constantinople Conference (see historic map above).

Bulgaria was liberated by the Russians during the Russo-Turkish War (1877-78), and became an autonomous principality within the Ottoman Empire — however to maintain status quo, Bulgaria's borders were again constricted by the Great Powers of Europe (Berlin Congress, 1878). Bulgaria restored some historic territory in 1885 and formally claimed independence in 1908. (Map above shows the Balkans at about the time of the First Balkan War, 1912.)

In the First Balkan War (1912), Bulgaria and its neighboring nations (the Balkan League) liberated the Balkans from the Ottoman Turks. Victorious Bulgaria, the "Lion of the Balkans," restored much of Macedonia and Thrace to its kingdom and established an important outlet to the Aegean Sea (as shown on map above).

However, at the London Conference (1913) the Great Powers of Europe again attempted to readjust boundaries and restrict the size of Bulgaria and its neighbors (map above), thus setting in motion the Second Balkan War, a brief war between Bulgaria and its former allies to re-divide the Balkans and eliminate Bulgaria.

TERRITORIAL MODIFICATIONS
IN THE BALKANS
TREATY OF BUKAREST

With the Bucharest Treaty at the end of the Second Balkan War (1913), Bulgaria had lost part of Macedonia (to Greece and Serbia), part of Thrace (to Turkey) and Southern Dobruja (to Romania), but still retained their territory to the Aegean Sea (historic map above).

In an effort to reclaim those lands taken by Greece and Serbia, in 1915 Bulgaria joined Germany/Austria-Hungry in World War I. By the end of the war Bulgaria had further lost most of its territory in the Balkans, including its gateway to the Aegean Sea. It also had to pay enormous war reparations to the victors. (The map above shows Bulgaria today.)

Chapter One

In the fall of 1911, the capital city of Bulgaria, Sofia, was in a rather festive mood. Banners and garlands of paper flowers were everywhere, as well as portraits of the visiting kings under their own flags and coats of arms.

The three kings of Romania, Greece and Serbia, along with their families and courts, were paying a ceremonial visit to the Tzar of Bulgaria. The agitation and commotion were practically everywhere. The sleepy, quiet city with oriental overtones, had suddenly been turned into a bubbling European capital. All hotels were booked months ahead; even the private houses and apartments were crowded with relatives from all over the country. Adventurers, prostitutes, thieves and merchants from all parts of Europe and the Orient had their meeting place in Sofia for the occasion. Murders, rapes, even a bank robbery had overtaxed the relatively small and inefficient police force. The palace guard had been called out to help, but, having their own hands full, the army came to the rescue. Fires roared throughout the overcrowded city, and the fire department proved inadequate.

In the palace itself, everything was far from perfect.

A bloody row had erupted between the young princes on the subject of horses and a controversial race. At a gala presentation in the opera house, a golden ornament had fallen on the head of the Romanian queen. A Greek princess had accused a Serbian counterpart of stealing a brooch from her. The brother of the Bulgarian heir to the throne, young Prince Cyril, had knocked out his Serbian counterpart in a dispute over a tennis match, not to mention the three duels between minor courtiers and the numerous cases of inebriation and overeating.

But this night, the palace was brightly lit. Winter had yet to come but the light breeze coming from Vitosha Mountain was simply freezing. Phaetons and coaches waited in a long line extending out of the gates down Tzar Liberator Boulevard. Crowds of onlookers pressed alongside the narrow sidewalks, full of curiosity and impatience.

"Did you see the kings?"

"I had a glimpse of the King of Serbia."

"I saw the Greek and the Romanian King, too."

"God Almighty! What an honor; this city has never seen that many luminaries in a single day. If they sign a treaty with our Tzar, the Balkans will be invincible forever."

Inside the palace, on the marble steps of the atrium, a line of the most handsome cadets, dressed in parade uniforms, formally escorted the invited ladies, flushed with pleasure, all the way to the ballroom. Their husbands trotted behind, looking rather ungainly.

Ferdinand I, Maximilian Karl Leopold Maria Sax-Coburg-Gotha, by the Lord's Grace Tzar of Bulgaria, had a word of welcome for all new arrivals. Further on in the great reception hall, the kings of Greece, Serbia and Romania held their own courts surrounded by their families, courtiers and respective members of their governments. Ferdinand had only his favorite adjutant, General Borislav Robev, standing by.

"Tell me, General, how is the spirit in my old city of Philipopulis?"

"The spirit in the garrison of Plovdiv is high. It simply couldn't be better, Your Majesty."

The Tzar looked at him half ironically, half cynically and droned on in his nasal, foreign accented voice, "Did you break the news of the upcoming war to the staff officers?"

"Of course, Your Majesty," Robev answered pleasantly in his most servile, velvety way, "they were simply ecstatic. They hardly can wait for the outbreak. I would say, all…but one."

Ferdinand let out a moan, his eyes heavenward. "How could I ever guess who!"

"Fortunately, Lieutenant Colonel Seraphimov's abhorrence of war is far from being typical—the rest, very patriotic, Majesty, ver-r-ry patriotic. Will it be soon?"

"Soon enough, my dear Robev, soon enough." He then pointed discreetly at the three kings, "What is vital for us is this formidable alliance with our Christian neighbors."

At the same time, in the midst of the high and mighty guests, the conversation was following a different trend. The Serbian King sounded quite conspiratorial.

"Messieurs, permettez-moi de vous donner promptement mon avis. Je ne voudrais pas vous l'imposer, ni vous contradire, mais La Bulgarie n'a auqune chance dans cette guerre contre l'Empire de Turquie."

"Parbleu!" exclaimed his Romanian counterpart, "La Bulgarie sera aneantie."

The Greek was rubbing his hands. "Et c'est le moment que nous arrivons."

Tzar Ferdinand kept a shrewd eye on them. "We'll talk more some other time, dear General. Now if you'll excuse me, I'll try to pry my son, Boris, from the grip of the Turkish Ambassador. You know how vulnerable our heir to the throne is."

Robev withdrew in his reptilian way and made his way through the glittering crowd toward his heavy-set wife, who was still panting after a waltz.

"I saw you talking to the Tzar," she bubbled hurriedly. "Everyone was green with envy. Was it about the war?"

"It's none of your business," her husband said in a hissing voice. He could hardly stand to view her loose perspiring flesh. "Find another handsome youngster to dance with…or go and stuff yourself with champagne and caviar."

She mused without a trace of malice or vexation. "I'd like to dance with you, Bouby."

Robev swallowed his ever growing irritation. Her father had too much money and the young General was living far beyond his means.

"I am sorry, darling," he mumbled, forcing himself to kiss her pudgy hand, "Please, excuse my stupid outburst."

Engaged in a superficial conversation in one corner of the ballroom, the famous beauty, Sultana Hadgyl-vanova, wife of the ailing justice Minister, had attentively watched the movement of the Tzar for the last half hour. She looked upon him with both love and hatred in her heart, outraged at His Majesty's deliberate lack of interest in her presence at the ball. It was not the death of his wife. He never loved her, Sultana knew this better than anyone. Besides, her death had happened quite some time back. Sultana and he had spent a happy time in the seclusion of His Majesty's retreat, Tzarska Bistritza, right after the funeral ceremonies. But Sultana was just as sure that the lofty Monarch didn't love her either. It seemed impossible that he would ever admit to loving anybody. Oh, she knew him very well! He would consider any feeling of love toward someone else a crime against his own person.

There was always intrigue in a royal court, but he was not susceptible to it. A person as snobbish as he would never degrade himself by mixing with the lower ranks. What then? Isadora Duncan had turned down Ferdinand's generous invitation to open a dancing school for maidens of gentle birth at his palace by the sea. He wouldn't consent to anything less. The "friendship" between those two had cooled quickly after the world famous dancer had turned him down. His relationship with Sultana was built entirely on a different basis—convenience—convenience for both of them. Then why, Dear Lord, why? Her husband caused no trouble at all. He was happy with the royal favoritism he received in spite of his obvious mediocrity.

Could it be that handsome nonentity, General Robev? The general didn't have a pretty wife to keep him floating in His Majesty's sea of plenty. His mind was only capable of choosing the right people to perform for him and leave the impression that he was a good officer. She knew from reliable sources who the military man was that kept the garrison in Plovdiv thriving. The prevailing opinion in the War Ministry was that Lieutenant Colonel Vladimir Seraphimov was the best strategist and drill instructor in the army. And yet, the Tzar talked to General Robev as if he were a luminary, even disregarding the ambassadors and his own staff and guests. The ministers of the cabinet, even the prime minister, were always treated by Ferdinand like little more than house servants, but not so with the young, handpicked officers of the court.

Oh, my God! Was it even remotely possible, that His Majesty...? Sultana was afraid to pursue that any further, even in her thoughts.

In another part of the spacious room Tzar Ferdinand had accosted his son and heir. He spoke in a low but nagging voice. "You could've found better company than that old fox Zewlmer Pasha."

"But, father, nobody was talking to him."

"Stop playing with the handle of your sword. Mingle with the guests, for goodness sake, but leave the Turkish Ambassador to himself. Talk to the Romanian Princess, compliment her on her gaudy tiara, say a word or two to the Serbian Crown Prince, but not about botanical specimens, please."

Boris stuttered nervously. "I have a headache, Father… a terrible one. Please, permit me to retire."

"No. Of course not. Take hold of yourself. This is my night, son. I have waited for it all my life. It might seem strange to you, but one day you'll be a witness to my true grandeur…"

At that moment, the young Crown Prince's sword, under the nervous pressure of his hands, dropped to the floor with a clatter that attracted everyone's attention. The heir to the throne bent over and awkwardly picked it up, face pale and eyes filled with confusion.

"Sorry, Father. The sash broke," Boris apologized feebly.

Ferdinand looked at him with a mixture of pity and scorn. "Just like your mother. No ambition, no vigor, no brilliance. Only a big heart…and who needs that?"

After the festivities and the glittering ball, the Grand Council was scheduled. The communiqué issued by the Balkan kings was vague: full of praise and compliments, mentioning at the end an alliance against the common enemy, generally noncommittal and unbinding. Afterward, in Tzar Ferdinand's hunting lodge at Chamkurria, the three visiting kings held a secret session, excluding their host, in which they decided not to permit a powerful Bulgaria to rise up after winning the war against Turkey, something they considered very doubtful.

Tzar Ferdinand walked slowly along the mountain path, rifle under his arm. His older son, Boris, was with him. Tall pine trees waved under the slight touch of wind, silver dust flying in the crystal air. The sun had broken through the ragged clouds, but its light did nothing to banish the uneasiness between the two. The snow under their boots produced funny squeaky sounds that made the silence even thicker.

"Listen, my son," said the Tzar in German, "I might be a dreamer, but I am realistic as well. Bulgarians are tough: I would say, rude and idealistic, a nation of peasants, often given to heroics. They'll hand a beautiful port at the warm White Sea over to me. They'll open the gates of Tzarygrad for me and make me the Emperor of the Balkans." He stopped, slightly flushed and panting from the long walk in the snow, or because of his sweet vision of glory. "I see myself in a magnificent procession filing through the splendors of the newly rendered Christian Saint Sofia, and the trembling hands of the patriarch crowning me. "

He ceased his long-winded speech abruptly, his clever foxy eyes focusing on his son's face. Boris had paled, mouth open a bit, his keen, intelligent eyes evading his father's. Ferdinand sighed. No, the heir to the throne was not the glamorous type, far from it. The scholarly type, yes. What kind of monarch will he make? And the other son was temperamental, unbalanced, hardly any brains. God Almighty, to whom should he leave his empire? "You don't approve of me, do you, son?"

"I don't know, father," said Boris, in his quiet gentle way. "I thought we were going into this war to unite the nation, to give freedom, to liberate the still enslaved people. I think that's what Bulgarians will fight for."

Ferdinand looked at him with a mixture of disappointment and sarcasm. A thin, sardonic smile lingered on his lips making his expression even haughtier and more snobbish.

Just like his mother, he thought for the hundredth time, but much worse, because he happens to be a man and moreover, the heir to my throne.

"Let's go back to the lodge. It's getting colder."

Lieutenant Colonel Vladimir Seraphimov was slightly bent over against the bursts of wind and the penetrating drizzle that fell over the open drill-square all morning. From the back of his horse, wrapped tightly in his "magic" mantle that, according to his troops, shielded him from the enemy's bullet, he closely searched the faces of the young soldiers for any signs of fatigue or demoralization. There were none. Rumors of a coming war had electrified everybody. A war against the Turks—the age-old oppressor that still held the Rhodopy Mountains and its population under tyranny—was anticipated by the Bulgarian youths on both sides of the border like a wedding celebration. The mountain people, separated from their kinfolk for years, could hardly wait to be united with the young kingdom.

On the other hand, a young generation of Turks, even after the radical changes in their crumbling empire, still held a grudge against the newly liberated country. Their hot blood boiled and violent tempers soared. "Damn it," they would say in the cool Turkish pub, sipping on the strong coffee, "Let's tangle with the rebels again. The next day we'll be in Phulbee, in three days we'll be drinking our coffee in Sofia. This time there won't be any Moscovites to help them out. It will be between us two: The Great Ottoman Empire and a handful of rebels." Bulgarians and Turks, as well, looked upon this coming clash of the two nations more as a sporting event, flexing muscles and exchanging insults and challenges. However, Vladimir Seraphimov knew what war meant to the common people. He could foresee death, innumerable sufferings, hunger and epidemics coming to victors and defeated as well.

Shortly before noon recess an officer of the guard came to relieve him from duty. An urgent message had come for the lieutenant colonel. Seraphimov threw a last look at the exercises on the square and galloped his horse toward the garrison's quarters. It was warm inside with the persistent smell of wet clothes drying. The little tin stove, red hot, seemed to be booming with delight. Assen Mitackov, his houseboy soldier, jumped to attention. Seraphimov searched the open peasant face for something alarming, but read nothing.

"Is it about my wife, Assen?"

"Yes, sir, Colonel!"

Seraphimov led him away from the gawking clerks. "What is it?"

"She's all right, but the baby is hungry."

"What do you mean? Doesn't she feed her?"

"No, sir, Colonel, she does not."

Seraphimov visibly paled with anger. "What is happening at my home?"

The young man looked confusedly at his boots. "For the second day in a row, the baby is crying and madam says she doesn't want to see her, 'cause the baby is another girl and five of them is enough under the same roof..."

Seraphimov caught himself shouting. "She said that?" then he remembered the presence of the clerks and toned down, "I can't believe it. Did she really say that?"

The boy stepped back speechless with fright; then regained his voice and whispered, his innocent blue eyes wide open, pleading. "For Christ sake...I didn't invent it, it's true..."

Vladimir felt ashamed. He had to learn to cope with his temper if he ever wanted to be a good commander.

"It's all right. You've done the right thing. Thank you. Now go home and I'll come as soon as possible," Seraphimov ordered.

The houseboy left promptly and Seraphimov waited for the general. Permission was granted. In less than an hour he confronted his rebellious wife. Ellena's unusual beauty had faded after giving birth to the last baby. Her face was swollen and there were slight bluish pouches under her large green eyes. She had a sullen and stubborn expression, but she evaded the hard stare of her husband.

"I don't want to see her," Ellena reiterated.

Seraphimov said nothing. He just kept staring at her in his hard way.

"You don't frighten me. I am not one of your soldiers," she pouted.

The man went around the bed slowly, and at this point, she had to look at him and she was frightened.

"Ellena," he said in a low and husky voice, "I have never laid a hand on your hind parts. Pray that this never happens."

Then he stepped back and opened the door. "Bring in the baby."

Ellena cried softly. "I wanted so badly for it to be a boy this time...to make you a proud father..."

For the first time in days Seraphimov smiled. He took the baby from the hands of a confused and flushed Assen, looked at the small reddish face for a moment, then gave her to his wife with a kiss on the forehead.

"I am the proudest father of my Amazon Tribe. Proudest in the whole wide world," he beamed.

Sultana was leaning against the window when the long magnificent coach drew along the side of the house. The day was dark, wintry, swept by a piercing, hostile wind. The suave greyhound pricked up his ears, then sprang gracefully and stood erect, whining softly. Though all the lamps had been lit in the elegant town house, they only seemed to make the shadows in the corners darker. The blaze in the marble fireplace flickered over the smoothly polished mahogany. A quick summary look proved everything to be in its place, the way a refined aesthetic like Ferdinand would like: the rare unseasonable flowers in the Porcelain vase from Dresden, the exotic fish in the crystal container next to the silver tray full of nuts, tangerines and grapes. Some of the Little Hollanders would have loved to paint it in this light, thought the young exquisite woman on her way to the sofa. The greyhound moved behind Sultana and settled at her feet.

Pale faced, with his aristocratic beard and prominent Hapsburg's nose, in hunting clothes that gave a hint of his enormous wealth, the middle-aged Tzar of Bulgaria entered pompously.

What a garish actor his Majesty is, thought Sultana while she made an elaborate curtsy.

"Bad weather for hunting, Your Majesty."

"Outside, my dear lady, only outside," he crooned. "Great weather for hunting inside."

The monarch looked down at her sarcastically with his sharp eyes.

Sultana stood motionless for a moment, shocked by the grossness of the remark. She took possession of herself and pointed to the sofa. The Tzar sat down heavily and the greyhound moved immediately beside him, the fingers of his well manicured right hand restlessly stroked the hound's smooth coat.

Sultana's voice seemed to ebb away: "I am sure; my husband will be terribly disappointed..."

"Stop acting, Sultana." The sovereign cut her short. "You know very well who called for him this morning, don't you? I can see him at this very moment patiently waiting in my anteroom."

The beautiful face of the still youngish lady blushed profusely. Ferdinand went on, "I saw you at the window. You were expecting me."

Sultana walked around and sat on the other side of the dog. "I was simply trying to save face," she said in a dismal voice.

The man pushed the hound out and took her delicate hand, piercing her with his cold imperative eyes: "Save us from hypocrisy, my dear. You'll feel much better. Besides, it isn't our first time, is it? We don't need special vestiges to impress each other. Spare me the vaudeville songs, please. I am not in the right mood for such."

On New Year's Day 1912, the deep blue sky over Rhojen was clear and the sun reflected off the dazzlingly white snow cover. A small group of boys, between twelve and fourteen years of age, burdened with survatchnitzy (decorated branches from a cornel tree) gaily trimmed with ribbons and paper flowers, struggled in the snow drifts toward the fortifications of the Bulgarian frontier post.

The morning air was crystal clear and one could see from that point the mighty spread of the ancient mountain, far beyond the area still occupied by the Turks, to the warm and enticing White Sea. It was extremely cold and the freezing boys had no eyes for the fabulous panoramic view. They doggedly went on ahead, panting and reeling about in the deep snow, as if they were intoxicated.

Radco, the eldest of the group—who got the idea in the first place to go and visit the lonely outpost on New Year's Day—had been met by all the parents without enthusiasm. Though the tiny village of Progled was less than a mile and a half away from the border, to allow young kids to go out by themselves in the cold snow seemed to them an utterly crazy idea. One that would only be thought of by a freedom fighter's (haydouk's) son. It was well known by them how lonesome the soldiers were up there, restricted to the post. What a joy it would be for sourvacary children to swat their backs with the cornel branches for good health and prosperity throughout the New Year. So, after a long discussion, the decision was reached just to end the debate: no girls or younger boys, only a few husky lads might go, with Radco as a leader.

Struggling in the snow, he was grateful to the old folks. Even for him, an unusually big and strong lad for his age, this was proving to be a tough endeavor.

The boys from the village were always welcome at the post. They felt at home there and everybody was their friend. The soldiers were all country boys from the plains and homesick in this isolated place. They laughed and played with the youngsters as if they were the same age. They would ask about the pretty girls that they had seen at the annual fair at Rhojen, about house parties and dances. One of them—maybe seventeen or eighteen years old—a lanky guy with big, sad eyes was a masterful player of the long shepherd flute called a cavall. Some songs he played were full of melancholy, others joyful and lovely. Listening to his music was like coming out of a beautiful dream. A sigh, a silence that nobody was willing to break. His name was Ermin and he was Radco's best friend. He happened to be the first who saw them coming. He left the patrol booth and squinted against the blazing whiteness. He spat out his cigarette, a sign of unusual emotion, and fired a shot in the air with his old berdana, a Turkish-made rifle.

"Hey, men, the sourvacary are coming! Happy New Year!"

There was real joy in the fort that morning!

The village boys beat the soldiers' backs with their survatchnitzy and recieved some small change for it according to the age-old tradition. They all ate a hearty meal together, sang old songs and listened enraptured to

Ermin's cavall. The choro and the rutchenitza dancing at the end made this a day to remember.

At parting time, Radco and Ermin embraced each other like brothers. "Happy New Year to you, Ermin!"

"Same to you, Radco! God bless you for not forgetting the lonely men at this forsaken post."

"My soul was hungry for your magic flute."

A deep sigh came from the young soldier's chest. "How's Rossitza doing?"

"Same as ever."

"Is she still pining after that lad in Tursko?"

"I've seen her all by herself, at the end of the road, looking and looking beyond the border...play me something to keep my soul warm until I reach home...please... forget about Rossitza."

Ermin smiled with sadness. "What else can I do? What else am I good at?" mused Ermin.

"Don't talk like that brother, just play." encouraged Radco.

"No, Rad. My heart is broken. One day you might come to know what that means...not now. Your band is waiting. You have to deliver them back to their parents before dark, don't you?"

Radco took a quick look at the sun.

"Bah...there is still plenty of time. This time we'll make our way downward, using our footpath in the snowdrifts. Don't mind me for being a pest. I never have my fill of your music. God bless you, brother."

The boys were really anxious to go, counting and recounting their gain. Money in those parts was scarce and not easy to come by. But Radco had a devil dancing in his eye. "I know a way we can easily double our money."

Gavril Kademov, jealous of Radco's leadership, would never stop trying to rile him in front of the other guys.

"Are you suggesting that we go and look for Haydouk Dimmitar's treasure?"

Radco knotted his eyebrows threateningly. "Let my father rest in peace, I'll take no jokes about him. Take your silly jibe back, Gavril, or stand up to it like a man."

Another boy stepped between the two. "Cool it Radco. Don't start a fight on the first day of the New Year."

"Let him take it back!" demanded Radco.

"Don't be an ass, Gavril," said the mediator, "you can't beat Radco when he's mad. You know better than that."

"Hell's fire! I don't want him to think I am afraid of him—just because his father was a freedom fighter. He's no stronger than me."

Radco spat on his large hands. "Step back, Boyco. You tried," he said to the mediator. "Come, Gavril. Let's have it."

Now Gavril Kademov was reluctant to really face Radco as the rest of the band bunched up to hold back the raging lad. Boyco tried again.

"Calm down, Rad, Everyone knows what a big mouth Gavril has, tell us about your idea."

"Not until he takes it back."

"All right, all right...I take it back, we'll straighten this out some other time, when there aren't any soldiers around to break up the fight."

"They won't break it up. They'll be eager to watch. Are you yellow? Ain't ya stronger than me?"

Gavril lost ground. "I took my words back, wasn't that what you wanted of me? How can we double our money?"

Finally Radco settled down. "Next time, I'll shove your face in the snow. Now, let's go up to the Turkish Fort and beat the backs of the Turkish soldiers there with our survatch-nitzy."

There was dead silence for some time, the boys staring at him openmouthed. Then Boyco swallowed and uttered very quietly: "You don't really mean it."

One of the younger boys cried in terror. "My father'll skin me alive! To wish good health and wealth to those Turkish bastards?!? I'd rather send them to hell!"

"Why, Petyo? They are human too."

Gavril seized the opportunity to gain some of the lost terrain.

"Yuk..." and he spat in the snow on Radco's side, "vampires!"

Radco bristled. "Are you afraid of them, Gavril?"

"Who, me? I'm not afraid of anybody. I hate them, but if the rest agree with you, I'll come too."

Boyco wanted to be sure that they all stayed together.

"There are no yellow bellies here, Radco. We'll all follow...though all hell will break loose if someone squeals on us."

Now the younger boy, Petyo, found his courage.

"Mum's the word! It will be our secret," he said, all fired up, " If we take the short cut, even our soldiers won't see where we're headed...that is, if we really decide on..."

"Don't be afraid of your own courage, Petyo," Radco smiled at him, "Follow me everyone!"

He led his small group to the Turkish fort, some 200 meters across from the Bulgarian post. The soldiers were milling around inside the walled square; not even a dog at the gaping portal. They were pleasantly surprised by the arrival of the kids. Radco stepped out first and hit the back of the senior officer with the cornel branch.

> *Sourva zdrava! Sourva zdrava!*
> *God bless you with kismet*
> *this year and ahead,*
> *all, through life*
> *in good heath,*
> *—berrechet and big wealth!*

The Turkish officer smiled broadly and gave Radco a large silver coin. The boldness of their leader and the fortune he received for it encouraged the rest of the boys. They quickly spread out among the soldiers with their survatchnitzy. The Turks proved themselves more generous than the Bulgarians. In a short time the young boys gathered more money than they had ever seen in their lives. They were generously fed sweet cakes and halvah and got their first taste of coffee.

There was real joy in the fort that day.

"Let's go to the customs house now!" Radco offered in a matter-of-fact voice. The boys looked at him as if he had hit them in the heads. It was bad enough that they had to explain their visit to the Turkish Post when they got back home.

Then Boyco spoke up, "Are you out of your mind? It's bad enough what we've already done."

"Wait until we get back. You'll get the daylights beat out of you," cried out little Petyo. "You're really gonna get it!"

"And us along with you," added Boyco.

Radco looked at them humorously. "Did you eat the halvah?" he asked them.

"Yeah…" his friends mumbled.

"And sweet cakes?" "Yeah, but…"

"And had your coffee with marshmallow locoum… Then, what are you crying about? All right, all right! If you are chicken, I'll go by myself to the custom-master's residence. You can wait for me around the corner. What about you, Gavril?"

Gavril hesitated a bit. "Go to hell! I'm not gonna put my neck under the ax for you."

"Fiddle-faddle," Radco said smugly and crossed the courtyard with a firm step and up the staircase leading to the private quarters of the custom-master. The boys watched him openmouthed and disbelieving as he knocked at the door and disappeared behind it.

The custom-master, mahmour-onbashy, was with his family, two young girls and a boy about Radco's age and size. What struck Radco immediately was that they were all smoking cigarettes. Not even in his wildest imagination could he see himself smoking a cigarette in front of his mother. His father would've killed him on the spot for much less, if he were alive today. To hide his embarrassment, Radco spoke out cheerfully; "Chock selliam, Mahmour Chorbadgy! Happy New Year to you and your family!"

The old man patted his grizzled beard and smiled.

"Happy New Year to you! Bouiroom, chodgouk, hosh geldin."

Radco performed the ritual with his survatchnitza to the backs of the master of the house and his children, reciting the little poem. The kids were ecstatic. Their father gave him a golden coin. Then he was invited to sit down at the their sofra, a low round table, and share their meal. The kids piled sugar plums, dates, tangerines and chocolates in front of him, none of which he had ever dreamt of before. The two giggling girls brought more sweets and were feeding him out of their hands. Radco had heard about Ismail, the son of the Turkish official, but had never laid eyes on him. He was an extremely handsome lad with sharp dark eyes, well-chiseled face and broad square shoulders in contrast to his narrow waist. The boy came to him and offered his own tin box of cigarettes.

After a brief hesitation, Radco took one and with the first inhalation, he choked and tears ran down his face. "I am sor...ry...never had one...before."

In his heavily accented Bulgarian the custom-master tried to save the situation.

"I know your customs, son. Nothing to be ashamed of. You don't speak Turkish either."

"Only a few words, sir," replied Radco respectfully.

It was obvious that the only son in the family had been deprived of a playmate of his own age for a long time. There was also a struggle within Ismail. He was torn between his pride and manliness and his desire to befriend the Christian boy. He said something in fast Turkish and blushed. His father had to serve as a translator. "My son, Ismail, asks for your name and your age."

Radco blushed, "How impolite of me! My name is Radoul Boev, but everybody calls me Radco and I am fourteen. Going on fifteen, next month" he quickly added.

"Mashallah! Glory to your father! Such a big and handsome lad. Ismail is fifteen and he likes you very much. Let's see who's the taller of you two guys. Get up here next to each other; straighten up. Let's see now... well...I'll be darned if you two are not exactly the same height and build."

Ismail started talking again, looking at Radco from time to time. His father stroked his gray beard and he too looked at the Bulgarian boy with a mixture of doubt and hope.

"My boy asks if you would come by again. He wants to show you around and go hunting with you."

Radco looked at Ismail openly and smiled.

"I'd be glad to, though I have no rifle of my own."

Ismail could hardly wait for the end of his father's translation. He went quickly to the wall, took down a priceless Arabian rifle, richly adorned with silver and mother of pearl and handed it to Radco. The poor boy looked at the treasure as if it was just a dream that would dissolve into thin air.

"I can't, effendi, sir, I really cannot..." he almost whispered. "This isn't for real, it's just a joke...isn't it?"

Ismail's father looked at him with delight. He put his hand around his broad shoulders and said warmly, "It's all yours, son. I'd consider it an honor if you accept this present from Ismail."

Now Radco embraced the rifle—his rifle, his dearest possession in life.

"Thank you, effendi... Thank you, Ismail. Tell him we have a lot of game around our village, too. I want him to come and be my guest."

The moment he said it, he bit his lips. Such a visit would be like setting the village on fire. The son of Dimmitar, the legendary Freedom fighter, *commita*, killed in an ambush by the Turks, accepting a fabulous present from the son of the custom-master and inviting him to his home! His poor mother would die of shame; his mother, who would never even allow him to get near a gun.

Ismail's father watched closely as the deep flush spread over Radco's face, down to his neck. He knew very well the inner struggle going on within him, but Radco's voice came across clear and steady: "He may come as often as he wishes. My home will always be open to him."

Radco's mother was seated on the low sofa facing the door when her son entered from the porch carrying an armload of wood for the fire. She looked up as if she were waiting for him a long time and spoke in a low, toneless voice; "Sit down, my boy, I'd like to talk to you."

"In a minute, mother...just let me throw some wood in the stove."

His mother shook her head impatiently. "Now, son, right now!"

Radco dropped the firewood in the corner and obediently sat next to her. She stood for a while, erect and distant, as if she had forgotten about him. Soon, the wrinkles on her still youngish face became more pronounced, her age more visible than ever, and she spoke with desolation.

"I have sat here for hours. I have thought about everything you told me. I did not listen to what other people were saying about you around the village. I listened only to what you said and nothing else. I know that the son of haydouk Dimmitar cannot be a traitor. I know it better than anybody else. I gave you birth; I held you for your first steps; your father bore you on his shoulders; he taught you to sing 'Dear Fatherland,' 'He's Still Alive up in the Mountain…' You swore with him in front of this icon to live and die for your country. Maybe I was wrong to keep you away from guns and rifles. Maybe it was my fault asking you not to kill…not to be killed. I thought God forbade that. There was too much hate and violence around. I wanted you to grow up clean and fair. I believed that you could live without bloodshed; your father had done enough of it for you and for all to come. He paid for it…dearly."

Now she broke into tears, crying softly, helplessly.

"I was wrong, dear boy, dead wrong. There are other things that people cannot live without…big, powerful words, dangerous and violent. Men love them. Men die for them. Freedom, pride, happiness. I thought one could have them without taking up arms. And I forbade you to so much as touch one of those murderous things. Is that why you took that rifle? Made friends with the enemy? Invited them into your own home…where your father…" Her voice trailed off.

Radco swung his big arm around his mother's fragile frame and kissed her fading curls lovingly.

"Mama, those people out there are not our enemies. They are nobody's enemies. Enemies are made…don't you understand? It's up to us to make them our enemies *or our friends.*"

His mother stiffened. "I never told you how your dad looked when they brought him here dead."

Radco shook his head.

"His nose, ears and lips were cut…all his fingers, toes, his genitals…one at a time…and he was still alive. Then his arms and legs were separated from his body…then, finally his head."

Radco felt sick to his stomach. He almost shouted out, but took control over his voice. "Please, ma...I...I know. What you said is true. It's horrible. I wish I could explain it to you..." Radco tried to comfort his mother.

His mother's whole body shook uncontrollably.

"You cannot, my son. You can't explain five centuries of slavery, humiliation, lawlessness and barbarism. You can't erase all the memories, the bitterness, the suffering of our people in the name of any God. It just has to be forgotten, buried in the past." She smiled vainly, her fingers still trembling, touching the side of Radco's face in a caress, "Give us some time," she begged.

There was a slight tremor in the high and clear voice of the boy.

"You just tell me, ma, and I'll do whatever you say. Do you want me to do to that Turkish lad, what they did to my father? Is that gonna make it easier for you...for all of you? I can do it when we go hunting alone in the woods. I can carve him up with my father's knife."

She put her hands, disfigured by hard labor, in her lap and did not answer for a long time, two hard lines forming along her mouth; then quite unexpectedly she said in a firm metallic voice: "Let him come."

"Seraphimov!"

It was General Robev coming after him.

The hallway in the headquarters was full of staff officers walking along in couples or gathering in groups, talking excitedly, hands moving in agitation, raspy voices, nervous laughs, flushed faces.

"Are you going home for dinner, Colonel?" the general asked.

"Yes, sir."

"Let's go together. We're in the same neighborhood. I'd like to talk to you."

The day was cold and gray, but the fresh air felt good after the overheated atmosphere in the building. They both took a deep breath and smiled involuntarily. As they walked down toward the stables, the general was silent; yet it was clear that he had something on his mind. A junior officer came to him with some papers for signing. Robev waved them aside.

"Later," he grumbled.

Finally, while waiting for their horses, Robev commented "You don't seem to share the excitement."

Seraphimov looked into the handsome, energetic face of the general. He was quite a bit younger than himself, and people close to the palace had spread the word about the special treatment he was getting from the monarch. Special attention for special favors, the bad tongues were saying.

"Different persons have different ways of expressing their emotions."

"What's your way, Seraphimov? To suppress them?"

The face of the older man remained dispassionate. He looked tiredly into the bold eyes of his superior and coughed to clear his throat.

"To better carry out the orders of my commander, I try not to get emotionally involved."

The horses were brought out and the two officers mounted them in silence. They rode for a while in silence. Soon the young general opened up again.

"Your reaction is strange to me because—pardon me if I am wrong—but the only way for a self-made officer to get promoted quickly is during a war. At your age, with a large family like yours, you should consider yourself rather, shall I say, lucky at the upcoming opportunity. The high ranking officers in the War Ministry have reservations about you. The prevailing opinion is that under battle circumstances you might not be able to make a courageous decision. On those grounds your promotion was postponed again. And now…"

"What do you mean by a self-made officer, sir?"

"Uh…I meant your situation, of course, no hard feelings, eh? I just want to be helpful, Seraphimov."

"I certainly appreciate that, sir, but I still don't understand the meaning of 'self-made' as applied to my case. I went through military school like everyone else," Seraphimov protested.

"But, of course, Seraphimov, of course. Only somehow you were accepted without the prerequisite education. You've been many things, an apprentice tailor in Anatolia, a waiter in this town, to mention just a few, but never a scholar, to my knowledge. Correct me if I am wrong."

Lieutenant Colonel Seraphimov concentrated on a spot between the ears of his horse as blood rushed to the back of his neck. His large gray eyes bore a cool, steely expression that he did not care to share with his superior.

"No, sir, your information is perfectly correct. I was accepted on the recommendation of the Russian officer that I met when I was a waiter."

"But how did you have the audacity to confront him under the circumstances. I mean…"

Seraphimov inhaled the clean invigorating air deeply as he avoided a street vendor, masterfully balancing a huge tray of baklava and collache on his head. The man had almost gotten himself run down by the colonel's horse.

"You really mean I was brazen, I guess. Well, at the time, during the day, I would work in an attorney's office as a clerk copying papers for the court. The master liked my handwriting pretty much. So you see, I wasn't entirely without education. At night, I worked in that fancy restaurant so I could pay my private tutor in mathematics."

"But when did you manage to get the time for those lessons?"

"In between the two jobs. There were exactly two hours left," offered Seraphimov.

In front of Courshoum Han, an overturned wagon had created considerable congestion. The wagon had collided with another cart and had broken all to pieces. A huge crowd of idle people had gathered instantly. Some of them were trying to subdue the frightened horses; others were busy separating the fighting drivers, and a third group were helping themselves to the loads of potatoes and earthenware pots that had not been shattered by the collision and now spread all over the cobblestone street. After the two horsemen managed to guide their nervous animals around to the open space of Djumaya Djammia Square and the uncongested Main Street, the general picked up the conversation again. "But how in heaven and earth did they ever admit you to the entrance examinations without any diploma?"

"Those Russians were seated at another waiter's table. The head waiter knew of my aspirations and told me that this would be the perfect opportunity for me. The officers were in charge of the new military school in the city. So I offered them my services and in the ensuing conversation, I asked if anyone could be accepted at their school without a high school diploma? The answer, of course, was negative. I still remember the tone of the senior officer, jocular and inquisitive at the same time, "Might that 'anyone' be you, by any chance, young man?" I nodded, and then he asked me, "What makes you think that you might qualify as a cadet?" I thought for a moment; then answered: "If I had a diploma and failed the examinations, would you accept me?"

"No, of course not."

"Then, what would you do, if I didn't have one, but passed all exams successfully?"

The officer squinted and with a little smile under his huge moustache, amidst the laughter of his comrades, he exclaimed loudly: "Molodetz! Fill out your application and bring it to me in person. Ask for Colonel Voznessensky."

The two officers rode through some side streets in silence until they came to the general's residence on the other side of the City Park.

"So, all your life you dreamt of being a military man, and now you dislike even a patriotic war for the liberation of our territory and fellow countrymen still under slavery. I really don't understand you, Seraphimov."

The older man shrugged his heavy shoulders.

"There is no mystery to it. What is there to like in a war? But to help and protect people in need; that's what makes me love and respect the military profession."

It was quiet at dinner time in the rented first floor of a private two story house that the Seraphimovs called home. Vladimir presided over the table and his womenfolk with simple dignity. The food was good and healthy, the discipline perfect. His oldest daughter, Rayna, an unusual beauty at eighteen, had been spotted by the voluptuous monarch at the Eastern Procession and next day a young officer had brought her a gold and porcelain egg bearing his initials, with a pearl necklace inside it. At first Seraphimov was furious. He wanted to return the present to the sender immediately, but his wife finally convinced him that it was merely a token of admiration on the part of a well known aesthete. "Some aesthete he is; I know what he is looking for!" he grumbled, yet the present was accepted and his wife wrote a thank you letter. Even with lofty principles like his, he could not afford to provoke the wrath of the Tzar. Not with a large family and his sole income being his officer's salary. But that was not the end of the story. Ten days later Lieutenant Colonel Vladimir Seraphimov was officially invited to join the court in Sofia.

As a courtier he would automatically get his long overdue promotion to colonel; his road to diplomatic service as military attaché would be paved and many other benefits would be open to him. Even so, Seraphimov was adamant. He would not sell his daughter even if he had to be a street sweeper for the rest of his life.

That night, the green eyes of his beautiful daughter, that had cost him so many sleepless nights, were blood-shot and puffed. He waited until Assen, the houseboy, had brought the fruit and the big "samovar." While his wife, Ellena, was serving the tea, he looked at the girl with his imperative gray eyes and asked matter-of-factly, "Why have you been crying?"

There was general commotion around the table.

"I wasn't crying, papa...I was...just helping in the kitchen...the onions..." Her voice trailed off.

"Just because you go to a French school, it does not mean..." He was annoyed, "All right, call me what you wish; just tell me why you've been crying?"

Rayna dropped her eyes and started to cry bitterly. Her father stiffened. For a moment he was speechless. Then his eyes turned angrily toward the lady of the house.

"Ellena, there's not a man at the bottom of this, is there?"

Ellena brushed her plate aside and almost spilled her cup of tea. "No, of course not. For goodness sake, you are getting obsessed with that theme. It's the silliest thing you can imagine."

"I want to know what's going on."

"All right, all right. You'll get it all. You know that shawl Rayna has been knitting for the past three years? No...I shouldn't start with that. Jeanna and Elsa, you know they always play together, they're inseparable."

"Mamma!" cried Jeanna.

"Mamma!" copied Elsa.

"Quiet, both of you! I've had enough! Quite enough! So they are about the same age and though at the age of twelve, or thereabouts, other kids have some brains, study their lessons and play the piano, these two still play silly games."

"What games?" asked the father, rather at a loss.

Ellena waved her hand, "Oh, games, like stupid girls play..."

"Mamma!" begged Elsa.

"Mamma!" Jeanna interjected.

"They are the two princesses, Evdokia and Nadejda, the Tzar's daughters. They're about the same age, too. They talk to each other about their clothes, what kind of diadem they'll wear today, what necklaces they'll wear to the ball, their toilettes that arrived from Paris, is the carriage ready...things like that."

"But what has that to do with Rayna? She is a grown up girl."

Ellena looked at her eldest with some reproach. "Well, not quite. At least, she doesn't behave like one at times."

"Mamma!" This time from Rayna.

Jivca, the youngest girl next to the baby, giggled and spoke, her mouth still full of orange she had been eating during the dialogue. "Elder sister Rayna hid under the table, listened to them and then suddenly burst out laughing."

Her mother was dumbfounded with indignation. When she retrieved her voice, she spoke sternly, "First, one never talks with a full mouth. Second, it is not permissible for a child to butt into a conversation of grown ups. Third..."

Jivca gulped her orange hurriedly. "But, mother, I was just trying to help. You kept talking and talking, and it was such a simple thing."

Now her mother was furious. "Jivca! You forget yourself. You are not a little baby any more. There is a real one in the family now. Your age is no longer an excuse for taking liberties like that. Go to bed immediately!"

"May I have an apple for bed...please?"

"No!"

"As a matter of fact, I don't see why not," the father scratched the back of his neck, "She's the only one that will tell me loud and clear what happened."

His wife was mad, but somehow she managed to keep her voice down. "I don't interfere with your soldiers; don't you destroy my authority in front of my daughters."

"Well...our daughters."

"All right...our daughters. Just let me handle this," Ellena demanded.

"Well, for God's sake, why did Rayna cry?"

"Well, she cried because, in retaliation, the 'Tzar's daughters' took her knitting that was almost finished, after so many years of work, and ripped it out completely."

There was a long pause after this final statement. Everyone except the venerable father was consumed by the drama. The father laughed. A jovial, roaring laugh that shook the lamp above the table. Rayna was shocked. Her mother, after a moment of hesitation, was ready to join her husband.

"So...ha...ha... So that was all...ha...ha...ha..."

"Well, yes...what did you expect?"

"Most anything, the way you started out."

"Never mind. I am glad at least you got your laugh out of it." She chuckled, kissing her flushed and confused daughter, Rayna.

"Then, why did we get punished?" asked Elsa, her voice bitter with accusation.

"Yes, why were we imprisoned in the dusty closet full of mice for a whole hour if everyone laughs at it?" protested the usually silent Jeanna, "We brought on those laughs, and it was not a bit of fun for us two, staying in the closet. It was horrible!"

Now Ellena could no longer suppress her laughter. The melodious sound of it spread through the whole room.

"I am sorry, you were the victims as usual. I'll try to make it up to you." And she kissed them heartily, even if they still chose to play sullen.

That was the moment when Jivca intervened again.

"Is anybody going to answer me? May I have an apple before going to bed, as I was rudely told to do?"

Chapter Two

The winter of 1912 was unusually cold and long on Rhojen. The tiny village of Progled was almost lost in the snowdrifts coming from the mount above. The heavy February winds brought most of the snow and the village was practically paralyzed. Even the traditional winter socials, the so-called "sedianky," were postponed. Very few of the hotheads, refugees from occupied territory, had their headquarters in the local *mehana* or pub. During spring and fall they worked in the lime kilns or as woodcutters. In the summer they would gather in the forest, armed as well as they could afford on their own. They'd form "chetty," little fighting groups with a well known local freedom fighter as the leader and in the dark of the night would go through Turkey to bring a vendetta to all Turkish authorities and wealthy landowners, called *chorbadgee,* who had wronged the Bulgarian population.

The pub was low-ceilinged with beams darkened by smoke, coarsely made chairs and tables. The owner improvised the long bar by using the old closet door from a burned down mill. The two kerosene lamps provided a dim light that created a mysterious mask over the faces, no matter what time of day or night it was. Daytime made little difference. The little window panes had never been washed and the frost piled over the dirt gave the sun very little chance. So the lamps burned around the clock.

The regular customers were the brothers Mourad and Mehmed Bachov from Baroutin, Delly Husseinov from the hamlet of Rechany, Assen Shcodrov and Roussy Rousev from Arda and Delly Hassan Caursky from Ustovo. Some of them had Turkish names, forced on their ancestors by the Islamic religion under the blade of a sword. Although those people were quite willing to change their religious beliefs, changing their names was a more complicated matter.

"There are another seven youngsters from Shyroca Lucca." said Mourad Bachov, playing with moustache sharpened like the end of a pencil. "They were supposed to report at Ksanty last week and they never bothered to go. If things continue that way, the Turks..." and he spat on the floor fiercely, "let them all go to hell, the damn Turks will soon run out of soldiers."

Mehmed Bachov, or Metyo as he was usually called by his friends, giggled loudly. "I just don't see how those rascals are going to make war with us, unless the big shots from Stanbul come out to fight in person."

Delly Hassan didn't share the roaring laughter. He sipped his brandy and smacked his full lips. "And when will that war start? For three years it has been, aha...aha...this summer, next spring, in the fall..." he executed a dirty gesture with his forearm and his other hand, "on fools day, I am telling you!"

Assen Shcodrov scratched his head, buried under an enormous fur cap, called a *calpack*. "Hold your wild horses, Delly, it takes time for the gentlemen in Stanbul and Sofia to make up their minds."

"God help 'em 'cause...because...I'm running out of breath," stuttered the younger brother, Metyo Bachov.

Another roar of laughter made the bottles and the glasses on the shelves tinkle.

"Na zdrave!" "To war!" and "Bay Stanko, be a brother, give us another round!" shouted the men.

The round-bellied, ruddy-cheeked owner of the pub brought them the drinks and pleaded, pointing with his fleshy chin at the rifles leaning over the table. "That's on the house, gentlemen...just don't start shooting now, eh?"

"I wish I had a Turkish bastard in front of me at this very moment," Delly Hassan muttered somberly.

"Hey, guys, let's go and look for one!"

"Nuts, they're scared stiff now. You can't find a real Turk anywhere but at their frontier post."

Delly banged the table and spilled the brandy.

"Let's go late in the night and kidnap the mahmour's bastard son!"

"Oh, come on...better wait until summer," protested one of the men.

"Go to hell! Why wait until summer? The weather is warming up."

"Snow is melting a little during the day, but it up freezes in the night. Why the hurry? War may start any moment now!"

"You know what that fucking mahmour did to my cousin?" persisted Delly Hassan drunkenly, "On the afternoon before Christmas Eve, he had him over to chop wood for him, so my cousin was late to join his family for celebration. We both swore to chop his head off for that!"

"I thought your cousin still sticks with the old faith," said Assen Shcodrov who was a bit lost in the religious maze of his own people.

"No," Delly Hassan shook his head a little gruffly, "we both got christened together. You know his wife is from a Christian family."

"Don't you like it better?"

Delly Hassan shrugged his massive shoulders.

"Why...yes, of course. You can drink as much brandy as you want, there is more fun for the kids, *sourvaky* and

Christmas. They have all those saints, you know, there is more chance to be heard than by only Allah and Mohammed." He finished his drink in one gulp, smacked his lips again and added, "We may go out and look for a Turk to kill later. Let's have another round now."

"Meet Ismail, mother!" rang the clear young voice of Radco Boev from the doorway, where stood a stalwart figure erect against the bright sunlight.

"Chock selliam, hannum!" said Ismail in his deep, velvety way. Radco's mother paled a bit, but answered in fluent Turkish.

"Chock selliam, chodgouk…be at home, come in, don't stand out in the cold. I'll make something good for you two to eat. You must be starved, boys. All the way from Rhojen…"

And while the lads were brushing off the snow from their moccasins and pants, she had some sausage sizzling in the frying pan. Radco said, "bouiroom," one of the few Turkish words that he knew, inviting his new friend to sit down on the soft low sofa called a *minder* alongside the windows. Ismail's gleaming teeth flashed in a smile, but he shook his head pointing to his wet moccasins and sat down at the edge of the carpet, his legs crossed in front of him. Nonna, Radco's mother, or stryna Nonna, as they called her around the village, didn't miss a thing.

"Glory to your mother, Ismail! She has brought up a fine lad. A thing like that wouldn't enter my Radco's head even if I were alive to teach him for the next fifty years. Shame him now so hopefully he'll remember."

Radco got the message, even though it was spoken in Turkish. He looked at his feet guiltily and there they were, two wide pools of muddy water, gathering on the thick Rhodopian rug. He stepped out on the flagstones around the entrance, kneeled down and started taking off his moccasins with a mischievous grin on his face.

"Sorry, mother. It won't happen again," and he winked at Ismail.

"Go ahead, kids," said stryna Nonna gaily, "make yourselves at home."

Ismail didn't wait for a second invitation. He quickly took off his own moccasins and followed Radco. It was so comfortable sitting cross legged on the low, soft sofa. Radco made a mock ugly face at him, waving a fist under Ismail's nose. He was a good performer.

"So, you're gonna shame me, eh?"

He grabbed the other boy's neck and they tousled happily amidst the brightly colored pillows, then tumbled tightly wrapped in a ball over the shaggy rug.

"I see! You do understand some Turkish, arcadash!" said Ismail gaining the upper hand.

Radco wriggled vigorously under him, giggling.

"Enough to know when somebody is putting me down in front of my own mother. You do understand some Bulgarian, don't ya?"

"Yes I do! Now say 'I give up!' "

"No... I won't say give up. You're gonna get it, brother. I'll roll you down, just wait and see what's gonna happen to you..." and, with some huffing and puffing, he toppled his opponent under and got on top of him.

"Now I'll teach ya some Bulgarian!"

Stryna Nonna, her hands full, stopped to watch them roll all over the rug. She had always dreamed of a house full of rowdy kids, but after Radco's birth something happened to her. She knew how disappointed her young and virile husband was. In the mountains, not having a nice large family was a fault usually pinned on the man. Over time, they both got used to living with it.

She laughed heartily at the earnest eagerness of the young wrestlers. "That fellow seems to be giving you a hard time, Ismail," she chimed.

"Indeed he does..." puffed Ismail, "strong as me... almost..."

"Almost? Who's on top, buster? Look at me, mom, I mopped the floor with him!" Radco shouted with pride.

"Knock it off, boys. It's time to eat."

"Uhh...ma...now that I've got him, let him holler uncle..." demanded Radco.

But the Turkish lad was no less stubborn than the young Bulgarian. "I don't give up...we'll finish it later."

"No. Say enough now!"

Stryna Nonna pulled the heavy mop of Radco's hair. "I say enough now! And enough is enough! Let me find you both at the table when I come back with the sausages."

The two ruffled boys got up on their feet, tucked their shirts in, tried to smooth thatchy hair. Their faces were flushed, eyes sparkling.

"Well, it's a draw, now." said Radco, panting, " But, we'll try it again another time to the finish."

"Oh, I'd love to..." smiled Ismail broadly, "I haven't had such a good time for years. At the fort I wrestle the young soldiers, but they don't take me seriously."

"I am taking you seriously. See...now we started talking the same language," laughed Radco boisterously.

They both sat down at the low round table called parralya, piled with tidbits, pickled green tomatoes, cabbage, peppers, eggplant and pickles. There were home-made cheese, cookies, butter and halvah. Soon stryna Nonna brought out the sizzling sausages and freshly baked bread. The two young lads ate as if they had not seen food for ten days. Nonna enjoyed just watching them eat with such a great appetite, but she did not join them. It might have been embarrassing for the young Muslim. A woman doesn't sit and eat side by side with men even if she is the lady of the house. Finally, they both slowed down. Ismail gave a deep belch to honor the meal, as good manners in his fatherland required, and said jovially, "Binn berrecket versin, hanumm. I've had plenty!"

"You're quite welcome, Ismail. I am glad you enjoyed it."

"In Allah's name, I did. Living at that isolated fort with my father and sisters isn't much fun. I haven't had a playmate of my age since we moved out there four years ago. Father won't let us go to Derrekioy without an escort, and who in the village would want to play with you when there are soldiers hanging around?" added the boy sadly.

"But what about your mother?" asked Nonna.

Ismail withdrew in silence for awhile; then said quietly, "Mother died seven years ago in an ambush meant for my father. He won't trust his younger wives with my safety. I am his only son."

"I don't understand how he ever trusted you with Radco. Does he know whose son Radoul Boev is?"

Ismail nodded slowly, his large dark blue eyes were full of premature wisdom. "Yes, ma'am...he knows."

Stryna Nonna was amazed. "I...don't get it," she stammered.

The boy smiled sorrowfully.

"He said, somebody that has been down the same road knows what pain is. He can be your brother."

"But there are other people, armed fanatics," Nonna reminded him.

"If we are two together, we can watch out for each other's backs. Turks are mostly fatalists. One cannot forever remain a prisoner of his own hatred, can he?"

Stryna Nonna lowered her head and said very quietly.

"No, I believe not..." and she looked at him openly, "I wish you'd both stay home instead of going out hunting in this cold. Besides you can hardly find anything in the snow."

"Don't worry, mom. We'll be all right," said Radco cheerfully.

"I wish I had some coffee to give you boys."

Ismail hit his forehead with the palm of his hand. "Boudallah! What a dumbbell I am. I completely forgot. Father gave me a present for you." He jumped up and brought a package from the corner where he had left his things. There were at least three pounds of aromatic, freshly-baked and ground coffee inside and a large quantity of lemons and oranges.

"He really shouldn't...I simply don't know how to thank you anyway. We haven't seen such luxury...since my husband's death. You just wait a bit. It won't take me long," and she set off to brew the coffee.

But the boys were impatient, already tightening the strings of their moccasins.

"No time for coffee."

"It's past noon already, mother, and I want to show him the village, too. You don't want us to be late, do you?"

"No, by all means, no! Get back before dark."

Ismail bowed to her. "Thank you for the good meal, ma'am...and for your hospitality."

Stryna Nonna felt as if somebody had a hold on her throat. She involuntarily made the sign of the cross over him. Her voice sounded raspy. "Take good care of your-selves, you two."

When Ismail was on his way out, Radco came to her and whispered with a mischievous smile playing on his lips, "Do you want me to kill him, mother?"

She pushed the unruly curly blond forelock under the fur cap and kissed his forehead. "You fool. At least this one time, you proved right. God bless your heart."

For some reason the picture of his mother waving at them from the doorstep, with the old dog Mourdgo at her feet, stuck in Radco's mind forever.

Radco whistled softly and bent over the prints again. He stared in disappointment. The rising wind had blown so much of the powdery snow into them that the patterns of the deer's hooves were filled. The prints that led them here were practically useless to follow. Ismail tried on his own, but to no avail.

Radco rose to his feet with a short sigh. "God damn it! Such bad luck for my new gun."

They set out, but a minute later Ismail pointed down at the snow again. The prints were clearly discernible for another fifty meters. As they emerged from the shelter of the trees, the wind racing downhill from the north struck them with all its force, cutting right through their clothes to their bones. Blasts piled the snow into drifts that they had to stumble across on the trail. In other places the ground was swept bare. The tracks vanished entirely. On both sides, gusts of wind lifted the snow in whirling wreaths. As each of these appeared, the boys jerked their rifles in place, only to recognize them for what they were, and each cursed them in his own language. Radco began to fear that they might mistake each other for a deer and let go with the rifles. Besides, they had been playing this game over and over for three hours and both were getting pretty sick of it. Only their stubbornness kept them at it. Each of them expected his partner to give up first. But now darkness was coming on and to persist was a dangerous risk. They squared and looked each other in the eye, seeking a sign of resignation. There was none.

Radco laughed huskily. "Holler 'nough, damn it!" He tried to drown out the wind, "Say evallah, you Turkish mule!" and he extended his right hand.

Ismail took his hand firmly and smiled. "Evallah... let's go back and look around the village while there's still some light."

He swung an arm around Radco's shoulders. Their frustration ebbed and they even tried to sing a song together. Their voices, tenor and baritone, mixed well. Though the words were in different languages, the melody was the same. That encouraged them and they tried other songs too, challenging the howl of the freezing wind. If one of them didn't know the words, he learned the tune fast, and joined his friend by humming. When dissonance occurred, they'd both burst out laughing and throw a handful of snow in each other's face. With that kind of fun, the substantial distance to the village was covered; it seemed to them in no time at all.

The two lads had not strolled the length of the village of Progled long before Ismail realized that there was an atmosphere here quite strange to him. Yet he had visited unfamiliar and hostile towns and villages before in the multinational Turkish Empire. Following his father in assignments all along the borders was a good lesson in geography and politics for him.

The village was about half a mile long, spread out on two sides of the road, graduating from large houses of stone and wood in the center to flimsy frame structures along the outskirts. Radco had told him, partly in Turkish, partly in sign language, that the population was in the vicinity of five hundred.

It was almost dark and there were no street lamps. Only a few yellow lights from some windows fell upon the road covered with snow and ice like bright patches on a dirty shirt.

Radco eventually led them to the pub. Ismail's still boyish curiosity made him look through the window. He saw a long wide room and some figures sitting around one of the tables. Thin wreaths of blue smoke floating in the glaring pale lamplight made the scene surreal. One could hear the clink of glasses, the murmur of hoarse voices and the sound of tiles on the backgammon board.

Radco felt uneasy. He knew about "patriotic" sentiment, especially around saloon tables. He tugged at the sleeve of his friend and repeatedly said: "Let's go home, man, let's go home!"

At that moment the backgammon game at the center table broke and Radco saw one of the men get up, unsteady on his legs. His young chiseled face was red-hot with the alcohol he had consumed; a large sensual mouth, bold eyes, and a broad, low brow, bloody veins sticking out on it like angry serpents. His rocky voice filled the room, "I wanna kill me a Turk!" he shouted in Turkish, wildly brandishing a pistol, his beastly eyes bulging.

For a moment Radco was paralyzed. He tried to move, he tried to say something, but nothing came out. As if in a dream, he saw Ismail in full possession of himself, walk calmly toward the door and open it. That shock brought Radco out of his numbness and he quickly followed him.

Ismail stopped half way through the room, hands resting over the barrel of his rifle, tall and handsome, all eyes focused on him. His voice was firm and manly without a trace of strain or nervousness. "I am a Turk."

The side of the bar behind Delly Hassan had been vacated by drinkers sliding out toward the rear. There was a short stir, then silence. Delly Hassan's face grew frightful, distorted with rage, dark and ugly, his moustache dripped with perspiration and mucous, his eyes bulged with hatred.

"Hell's fire!" he shrieked, saliva flying from his heavy lips, and he aimed his pistol at Ismail's chest.

A thunderous report beside Radco nearly deafened him. Delly Hassan uttered a beastly scream as he dropped his gun, convulsively grasping his blood soaked arm with his other hand.

"Anybody else want to kill himself a Turk?" Ismail asked in a deadly calm voice, inserting another bullet in his still smoking rifle. Radco moved closer to him, his rifle steady in his hands. Delly Hassan raved in fury.

"Kill them both, hear me! A traitor is no better than a Turk, no matter whose son he is. Shoot them both!" pleaded Delly Hassan.

There was little reaction from the others except for a few doleful stares fixed upon the two husky lads. They retreated in silence, guarding each other's backs as they left the saloon. There was no immediate action.

The moon had broken through the flying clouds, but its feeble light did very little to disperse the darkness. The boys traversed an unbroken expanse of snow behind the house. Even under normal conditions a flight up the steep hill in the dark would have been a test of strength, but the snow and the blinding wind turned it into a nightmare. Under the snowdrift, the hill was frozen solid. After every attempt to climb up, they slipped back. No place to hide. The boys stood out like sitting ducks. They had no protection whatsoever. Anybody might swoop around a corner or from behind the trees to strike at them without warning.

The drunken voices behind were easy to detect in the gusts of wind, but there could be others waiting for them in an ambush. Every few meters the gnarled shape of some tree would suddenly appear, straining their shaken nerves. As they moved forward with caution, Radco became conscious of a plan growing in his mind. They had been struggling through the deepening drifts for about ten minutes before he realized what it was. There was a hiding place! Their persecutors were gaining on them. They probably knew some short cuts around those backyards. Some random shots were fired. Ismail and Radco crept forward silently. The young Turk had put himself entirely in the hands of his new friend. He would not know where to go in these unfamiliar surroundings. A dark blur appeared, grew more distinct, and a moment later Ismail made out the snow streaked logs of a cabin.

"It's ours," whispered Radco, "my father used to keep his grain inside before the old house was burned down."

Motioning Ismail to stay where he was, Radco moved to the window and peered in. It was empty. He waved to the other boy to follow him and walked through the front door. They had hardly gotten in the door when their bloodthirsty pursuers caught up with them and went ahead, cursing and panting heavily.

"Hurray! We made it!" whispered Radco huskily, still laboring to breathe, yet he did manage a short laugh. "You really gave that mad dog, Delly Hassan, what he deserves. As a matter of fact, I would've killed him if I were in your shoes."

Ismail didn't understand much of that speech, but he smiled and embraced his partner. "Thank you, brother... Thank you for staying with me against your folk. Now I believe you are as much of an outlaw in this village as I am."

Radco responded, "Don't worry about anything, pal. I wish my mother knew we were safe and out of danger. She's heard the shooting for sure and now is praying for us. She won't get much sleep tonight, especially if those jerks go looking for us at home."

Ismail looked into Radco's eyes, more guessing than understanding the meaning of those words. "Anything you say, Radco."

"It is all right. She's a haydouk's bride. She's had lots of nights like this in her life, and another one on my account won't kill her. We'll make it through first thing in the morning, while those loonies are in bed fast asleep." Radco said this as much to convince himself.

They investigated the cabin in the dark trying to accommodate themselves for the night. There was plenty of hay, but nothing else and it was as cold as an ice box. The boys plunged into the hay and tried to roll close to each other as tightly as possible. The cold was still piercing. Radco laughed drowsily, trying to ignore the pangs of growing hunger. "Great time for a wrestling bout, partner. It'll keep us warm."

Ismail slugged him in the ribs and they both giggled for awhile, jabbing at each other, but the activities of the day soon took over. They were sound asleep, impervious to the cold and the mortal danger they had just escaped.

The intense cold, accompanied by the distant barking of dogs and the nearby howling of wolves, woke them at dawn. With groans and grunts and curses, the boys rolled out of the hay, heavy with sleep, stiff in their joints, vacant of mind. They both felt terrible hunger, but had no time nor desire to talk about it. The morning star was going down in the immense blue sky. The wind had chased away all the clouds.

As the two stalwart lads walked outside, Ismail became aware that something around them had changed. Then it came to him… the wind had stopped! All night he had grown accustomed to its presence. Now the air was utterly still. There was no sound anywhere, except for the distant barking. Even their moccasins seemed to fall noiselessly in the snow. They crossed, climbing over a fence and were close to the ridge of the hill. Daylight came slowly. The valley below cleared of darkness. In the east, over the horizon, the pink light deepened to rose, and then to red. A disc of gold appeared above the mountains. The sun had risen on this memorable day for Radco and Ismail—the day, unbeknownst to themselves, that would lead them into manhood.

Chapter Three

"Do you know what time it is, darling?"

Ellena had come up behind her husband, who was drowned in his military drills, stratagems, charts and favorite masterminds of war history. He rubbed his eyes, made heavy by the inadequate light and the long vigil, then moved his massive shoulders and smiled when he felt the loving touch of her hands.

"Tell me dear, what time is it?"

"It is well past our time, Vlad…and you and the kids, that's all I have. My only touch with the outside world. We've stopped going to the officer's club. I know, you can't stand the endless patriotic speeches. Nor can I. I don't go to any of the women's circles, not even to the Red Cross. I turn down all invitations to parties and 'Jourfix.' But, dear, don't you see how isolated we've become and how difficult it is to go on living in this self-inflicted vacuum. Don't get me wrong. I am not complaining. It's just that I need you more than ever. You have your vocation, your daily chores…your modus vivendi. I have you and only you. I love the kids because you gave them to me. If anything were to happen to you…"

Vladimir Seraphimov took her in his strong arms, and Ellena felt the familiar prickle of his moustache on her face.

"I know, Ellena, darling. It is not easy to be the wife of a failure. No, don't say a thing. I know, too. For all I promised you, you got nothing. We don't even have a house of our own. We keep moving from one provincial city to another, garrison after garrison, daughter after daughter. And we are not young anymore.

Now listen to me. The end of May, I am getting ten days leave. We are going to rent a house in Hissara and we'll go there—lock, stock and barrel. You can stay there all summer long. I'll come to see you whenever possible. The brigade will be engaged in extensive summer maneuvers, but I'll be coming to see you anyhow."

He took her chin in his cupped hands. "That's an order. You have to listen to me. You are my best soldier."

Ellena rested her head in the hollow of his shoulder and her wonderful golden hair spread in ripples all over his chest. Her voice was soft and murmuring. "Anything you say, Vlad."

Theatre Luxembourg was full to the last seat for the opening night of Maxim Gorky's latest play, *The Lower Depths*. Though many people were a bit of uneasy about his works, his enormous popularity with students and the so-called intelligentsia piqued the curiosity of the good solid citizens enough to pay for the opening night. On the other hand, this was one of the rare occasions in a provincial city when you could make a show of your newly acquired wealth: the new clothes of your wife and your own shiny top hat.

Sultana was engrossed in her own thoughts and paid little attention to the audience, who gaped at the minister's box and the fabulous diamonds of his young wife. She didn't listen to what her husband was saying, either, until he mentioned the name Seraphimov.

"Are they here tonight?" she asked, trying to conceal her excitement.

The man, much older than she, was so unused to her attention that it took him some time to find his voice. "Of course they are here, my dear. Maxim Gorky is Vladimir's favorite writer. As a matter of fact, they have very much in common. Neither of them had any formal schooling. They both led restless, nomadic lives in their youth, changing many trades among the 'lower depths.' He wouldn't miss this play for anything in the world."

"How do you know him so well?" she inquired, interest piqued.

The minister laughed a bit, and nervously played with his gold chains. "He was an errand boy in my office. Of course, he's changed a lot. I, too. He and his wife are in the tenth row, about the center. You can't miss them. The most beautiful girl in the theatre is seated between them."

Sultana focused her golden lorgnette and uttered almost indistinctly: "So...that is Rayna."

Rayna felt the almost physical touch of the eyes through the lorgnette.

"Father, who is the elegant lady in the box up there?" Rayna asked, tugging on his sleeve.

Vladimir Seraphimov followed her eyes. "The man beside her is the Minister of Justice. The lady, I presume, is his wife."

Ellena squinted at her husband with amusement. "You don't know Sultana?"

Seraphimov coughed unnecessarily. "Yes, I do, but Rayna is too young to know the likes of her."

Sultana drew back from the parapet deep into the velvet armchair. Her thoughts racing, her mouth dry and full of bitterness: "Yes, she is prettier than I, and much younger too. Now I know why Ferdinand invited my husband, along with me, to the festivities in Plovdiv. It's never happened before." She laughed inwardly, "I'd like to see how in the world he can get hold of her with that Cerberus, watch dog, around. Her father seems to be an impregnable fortress, or I don't know anything about men."

She waved her exquisite fan in her usual nonchalant manner. "Why don't you introduce me to Madame Seraphimov some time?" she coquettishly asked her husband.

The minister couldn't hide the fleeting expression of surprise on his deeply wrinkled face. He looked at her sparkling diamonds, Brussels lace and Parisian gloves, and thoughtfully stroked his gray beard, which she had made him cut in that absurd Napoleon III way.

The minister replied, "Madame Seraphimov is a very ordinary lady. I really don't see why…"

She stopped him with the coolness in her voice that he feared most. "Need I explain such a simple request to you?"

The poor minister felt like falling down on his knees. "Oh, no, nooo. Of course not, darling. I'll do whatever is possible…even impossible…to please you. That family is not very much interested in social life, but I'll find some good excuse."

Sultana smiled at him condescendingly. "I know, darling. You were just a lawyer before marrying me, weren't you?"

The play proved to be far too intellectual for the majority of the audience, who were more appreciative of simple vaudevilles than a plot about the underprivileged. The "depths" remained untouched by their shallow minds and vice versa. For the well-to-do classes, all the misery of desperately poor people was beyond any feeling of social conscience or good will, especially after dinner. There was quite a bit of coughing, chairs squeaking and feet thumping. Very few took the trouble to applaud. The Seraphimovs, with brooding eyes, still full of tears and minds bursting with questions and controversial sentiments, were the last to leave.

"I like the young man that played the part of the artist," said Ellena to her husband on their way out, "what is his name?"

"The name of the character?" asked Vladimir.

"No, the actor," answered Ellena.

Raising his eyebrows, Vladimir looked in the program. "It's a minor part...anyway, the name is Ivan Zemsky."

"The part is of no importance. What I like in that character is his natural goodness, naiveté...a basic honesty, the way he..."

Rayna interrupted her mother. "The way he said, 'my hands are always dirty.' "

Ellena was surprised by the sudden flow of good memory, from an otherwise scatterbrained Rayna, but waved it aside. "Oh, never mind. Let's go!"

How could she have known at that moment, for the first time, she had approved of a prospective son-in-law.

The covered wagon wound slowly up Merchants Street toward the old bridge over Maritza River. Vladimir Seraphimov, riding on his favorite mare, Sanya, held to the rear. The ringing voices of his overjoyed girls were like fine music to his ears. They would roll on the mattresses, amidst the furniture, the omnipresent samovar, the frying pans, casseroles and baskets of food, then run to the open flaps to see the crowded street, eyes wide open, faces flushed with excitement. The little baby was asleep in a beam crib fastened to the ceiling, her mother beside her, and a happy Assen driving the oxen. Soon they reached the outskirts of the city and were headed west toward the ancient, walled town of Hissara, some fifty kilometers from Plovdiv. Seraphimov planned to do it slowly, making camp along the road, sleeping in the wagon, making of it an adventure to remember. The kids would certainly remember, and so would he. Who knows? That might have been the last time he'd spend with his family. Sanya, that beautiful white mare, turned her head, as if she sensed his thoughts. The man patted her on the neck lovingly, and whispered, "Shush, dear, whatever happens we'll be in it together."

They followed the road across the field of the rich and fertile Tracian Plains, full of fruit and vegetables, the vast spaces filled with wheat and rye already swaying in the breeze. It was early morning and the air still felt chilly, but invigorating. The larks glided high up in the almost dark blue sky, through a few puffy clouds traveling to nowhere.

Toward evening they started ascending the first slope. From that point on the terrain got hilly and slowed them down considerably. Tired villagers were heading back home from the fields, their faces burned by the sun, yet masked with a happy expression of fulfillment lingering over them. They would smile broadly, bidding farewell to the travelers, the little boys and girls running barefoot, waving their hands.

The night came on like a blessing.

It was quite late in the evening, but the day still lingered, reluctant to let the night come on. The oxen slowly climbed up and across the hill in their quiet dispassionate way, as if going uphill or downhill little mattered to them. Beyond it rose the range of mountains, enveloped in dusk, mysterious as a kingdom of fairy tales. Finally they came to the waterhole that their "commander-in-chief" had decided should be the night camp. The spring was surrounded by age-old trees and a pasture around it thick and rich.

The tired travelers drank from the stream. The water was cold and sweet. The animals trooped in below and drank thirstily. After they had their fill, the oxen pawed the mud and rolled in the water, Sanya looking at them with a sneer, raising her noble head over the long graceful neck, her silky mane falling on both sides evenly. Assen took loving care of her, bathing and drying her while the cook was busy around the fire.

At last everybody had gone to bed—Ellena and the girls in the wagon, the orderly and the cook under it. Vladimir Seraphimov remained seated next to the dying fire, leaning back on the huge trunk of an old oak, smoking his pipe. The cold night wind reminded him that he had not rolled out his blanket. He went toward the wagon, but did not feel like getting in. All seemed sound asleep. Somebody under the wagon, the cook, he thought, was snoring sonorously. He took his indispensable black mantle, hanging by the wagon flaps, threw it over his shoulders and found a fine spot near some flowering bushes, whose delicate aroma came to him like a forgotten memory. He emptied his pipe and lay under the immense, crystal sky with its millions of scintillating stars. How many nights had he lain under them, trying to read their secret message? He was sure they were watching him from above, sometimes sad, sometimes laughing.

His horse was restless. She might be having bad dreams, he thought, or an evil spirit's prowling about.

He closed his eyes and he was back to his boyhood in the village of Adjar. He had just come home. He heard those many strong voices from behind the door to his father's room which was slightly ajar. He could not resist the temptation. The room was full of men seated around his father, Gheno Seraphimov, a teacher and a young handsome man with a thin moustache and fiery eyes. He wore a monk's cassock over his broad shoulders and under it, bullet clips crisscrossed his deep chest, and two huge pistols were tucked into his belt. His voice was loud and clear. "That's the reason we gathered here, brothers in arms!" He deftly took out his two pistols and crossed them. "Swear to God!"

Vladimir's father first extended his hand over this strange cross, looking at the steely eyes of the stranger. "To life and death, cousin!"

At this moment, young Vladimir felt two strong fingers take hold of his ear and he was led, promptly and silently, to the adjoining bedroom.

"Spying, eh?" said his mother in a hushed voice. "Spying on your own father!"

"Uh, ma, I wasn't spying. I just looked in." But his natural curiosity took over, "What kind of a monk is that with guns in his belt?" asked the six-year-old Vlad.

His mother paled. "Shush, big mouth! If your father ever finds out that you saw this monk, he'll cut out your tongue with his own hands."

Then suddenly, in Vladimir's dream, came the day when the Turkish soldiers burst into their house to arrest his father. They rushed all over and didn't find him, but never thought of looking behind the entrance door where he was hidden. He simply didn't have the time to go under the fireplace to the special hiding spot between the walls. Anyway, of all places it never occurred to them to look for his father behind a door. Unfortunately, that wasn't the case with one of the three Turkish urchins who followed the soldiers inside. The first place that kids look in a game of hide and seek is behind the doors. And that's what one of them did.

"Here is your man, effendilar!" he shouted at the soldiers as they started to leave.

"Run after them and see what they're going to do to your father, Vlady!" said mother Rayca to her young son, in a voice strangely unfamiliar under the strain.

He was able to keep up with the detachment without being seen. They arrested two more men and headed toward a quarry out of the village. There, the three men were asked the whereabouts of Vassil Levsky, the leader of the liberation movement.

When his father's turn came, the youngish, good looking officer was sarcastic. "And you never heard of your first cousin, the so-called Apostle of Freedom?"

His father, Gheno boldly looked into his eyes and replied in the same tone, "Even if I knew his whereabouts, do you think I'd tell you?"

The young officer nodded thoughtfully at the waiting soldiers and turned his back. The soldiers undressed the three men to the waist and started cutting their heads off. Vlady tried to detach his eyes from that horrible scene, but it did not work. He was transfixed.

When his father knelt down, the ax surprised everyone. His head flew off at the first try—no agony whatsoever. The din of metal on stone filled the ears of the small boy, and he screamed at the top of his lungs then lost his senses.

He opened his eyes to find himself on the lap of the commanding officer. He was pouring the contents of a canteen over the deadly pale face of the boy—a mixture of sadness and pain in his eyes. When he realized that the child was watching him, his face turned blank, but his voice was still soft and kind.

"Ha, youngster, go back home now."

In the fall of 1910, the time had come for Dannail (Danco) Marrin (also known as Ibrahim) to make up his mind. The choice was simple in a village like Derrekioy still under the

Turkish rule; be drafted into the Turkish army, or cross the border and join the Bulgarian army. His father at that time, had very good rapport with the Ottoman authorities and didn't want to get on any blacklist because of his only son's deeds. To be on the safe side, he had changed the family name to Marrinoglou, but Danco stubbornly kept his Bulgarian name and never called himself Ibrahim.

"The world is wide and rich, Ibrahim," said his father, "go ahead and see it while you are young. In my trade as a prosperous merchantman I learned my lesson well. There is always time to shift to the winning side. Who knows? You might do better service to Bulgaria just where you are. Sometimes, one man, at the right time and place, can decide the outcome of a decisive battle."

That did it for young Danco. He was sent to Istanbul. Being a good looking fellow, big and well built, he was taken into the palace guard at Dolmabahche, a very special unit to protect the life of the sultan and to guard the gates of the enormous palace and its numerous other buildings. The guardsmen enjoyed "royal treatment" in the complicated hierarchy of the Turkish court. They were considered to be sultan's youths, dressed in elegant uniforms with tall fur caps, richly decorated with golden braids and a beautifully ornate dagger hanging from their belts. They always had the best food and even pocket money for their private pleasures. Hand-picked to the last, they were all stalwart and handsome young men.

The garrison was at Yaldazkioshck, next to the old palace of Sultan Hammid. The present sultan, Mehmed, was a frightened little man. He wouldn't dare cross the city without a special detachment of his guardsmen surrounding him on all sides. And even those trips grew fewer and fewer, except to visit and pray in the Blue Mosque, his favorite place of worship. Usually the palace mosque was as far as he would go. That was the reason why, besides the harem, the palace guard was his main source of entertainment. He loved to watch their parades, drills and physical exercises. But most of all, the sultan enjoyed their "gurresh," a peculiar kind of Turkish wrestling in which the participants smear their naked bodies with oil that makes them slippery as an eel. The competitions were held on a wide grassy spot behind the stables, with no time limit and no holds barred, which sometimes led to serious injuries and even to the death of one of the participants. There was a special band that followed the movements and the rhythm of the wrestlers. Sultan Mehmed would get so emotionally involved in the outcome that he'd grant almost anything to the winner.

That was on the mind of Dannail Marrin when, at the end of the second year, he entered the tournament. The usual ten days leave wasn't enough even to travel back home. What he needed was at least a month and a half. For awhile he hoped that the sultan's guardsmen would be permitted to take part in the war with Italy as volunteers, and he could earn the battle leave to go home. But the Guard stayed for protection of the sultan at Dolmabahche on full alert. Even the usual leaves had been cancelled.

Anxious as Dannail was to go home and see his family and his sweetheart Rossitza, there remained just one alternative, a very difficult one, but not impossible. Of course, he wasn't the only one with high hopes. There were eighteen fellows of his size and might competing for the championship, which meant he had to wrestle with half of them in the system of elimination before he could face the winner of the other half in the final match.

At the end of a seemingly endless string of bouts, he made it to the championship round. He hardly remembered anything except what seemed to him a massive line of gleaming muscular bodies that he had to somehow dispose of. The bunch of faces distorted with pain, twisted, puckered, eyes bulging with hate and determination, did not relate to the comrades-in-arms he had shared food and lodging with for two long years. They were obstacles to his way home and had to be overcome.

And he did it.

By the last match, he was hurting almost everywhere and dog tired. But, so is that buster fighting me, flashed through his mind before he became tangled with a husky guy about his height and build. He knew him well. His name was Iscander. Together they used to go to the whorehouses at Chogoun Sockak, sharing stories with each other about home and their loved ones...and now they started a battle that dwarfed all of the preceding ones.

After more than an hour of gruesome predator wrestling, Dannail stepped over the broad laboring chest of his rival and was proclaimed Champion of the Guards. His defeated opponent, according to the ancient tradition, had to kneel down in front of him and kiss his hand.

The next day, he was summoned to the private apartment of the commanding officer. Dannail made the best he could of his appearance and reported to the adjutant right on time. He was ushered into a large room filled with the fading light of a late afternoon sun. Avzy Bey was smoking a water pipe, cross-legged on a low sofa. Opposite him someone else was lying on a pile of richly embroidered pillows drinking coffee from a golden cup. Avzy Bey did something very unusual for him. He smiled.

"Ashcolsoum, bash babbait...mashallah! You distinguished yourself."

"Thank you, effendi. I am trying to do my best for the pleasure of the Padishah," countered Dannail.

"Iscander from Anatolia is a tiger, but you, young man, you are the best I've seen, bash pehlivan! Afferim, afferim, onbashy!" Avzy Bey took another long pull on his *chobouck* water pipe, "Allah has given you the strength of a lion. A man like you can go far in our ranks." At these words he looked for a moment at the face of the man across from him. Dannail saw a fleeting expression of servility in his slanty eyes, but he didn't have time to think about it. "I have here," Avzy Bey went on, "your personal request to be transferred to Tripoli against the Italians. Your request is granted. If you fight them the way you fought the Anatolian yesterday, you'll soon be promoted to colonel."

Dannail was taken by surprise. He had completely forgotten about his earlier request. He blushed, broke out in sweat, then paled. To turn down a great opportunity like this would not only be foolish; it was like spitting in the face of his superiors, high and low...

"Anything wrong, young soldier?"

Dannail closed his eyes for a moment, "Allah, have mercy on me, and You God Almighty, and all the saints around You, help me, please!" Then he blurted out, "I've changed my mind, Pasha Effendi, I would like to go back home to my native village in the Rhodopian Mountain. I haven't seen my people for over two years."

Now it was Avzy Bey's turn to get flushed. It spread from the back of his neck, to his ears and rawboned face, all the way to the dome of his bald head under the red cap with black tassel called a fez.

"You'd trade the great benevolence of the padishah for a measly ten days leave!?!"

"One month, Pasha Effendi. Then I could still go and fight like a lion for the glory of the Padishah."

Avzy Bey was about to have an attack of apoplexy when a thin laugh came from the richly turbaned silent man, laying on the pillows with his back to Danco.

"One month and a half, young soldier!"

It was the Sultan himself.

Dannail Marrin spent the night with some fellow country-men from the city garrison. They read and reread his papers and still could not quite believe it. A month and a half leave at a time when tension along the Bulgarian border was at its peak was more than anyone of them could assimilate. They listened to the account of his wrestling ordeal, then of his personal meeting with the padishah. Dannail's compatriots were open-mouthed, eyes wide open with astonishment, and looking at him as if he were a mythical hero just escaped from a story book. Gradually, with more glasses of fiery Stanbul brandy, they came to believe his tale and gave him a hero's welcome that lasted until morning, with more drinking and singing. Musical instruments came into play—a tambourine, a flute, a violin and a drum. There was kiocheck dancing, *choro* and *rutchenitza*. When morning came and the bridge over Gallata opened, they all accompanied him to the control point with songs and music, bearing him on their shoulders, under the curious scrutiny of the passersby. At parting, his friends gave him letters to their families, messages and presents. He ended up with quite a load on his back. On top of it all, a merry, heavy-set fellow pushed into his hand a demijohn with Stanbul's brandy, saying: "Let those suckers out there get a taste of what we're drinking in Tzarygrad!"

The short cut to the station, Sirkedgiskellessy, was along the sea shore. Dannail knew about the numerous cannon asker or military patrols out there, but he had little choice. He had spent too much time with his countrymen and the train was due to depart in less than fifteen minutes. He approached the station from the opposite side with no difficulties and saw the locomotive puffing, ready to take off, when a voice behind him stopped him from crossing the railway tracks.

"You cannot cross here, fancy fellow. Go roundabout to the station."

He was a medium size soldier, stocky and mean looking, but he was alone.

"Come on, partner," Danco smiled at him good-naturedly, "can't you see how late I am? My train is about to leave."

The sentry advanced toward him and smelled his breath, hot and spicy after the run.

"You are drunk, young soldier!" and he started to arrest him. There was no time to waste. A quick look around assured Dannail that nobody was watching, only the engineers in the locomotive. He left the demijohn on the parapet and, drunk as he was, grabbed the thick neck of the sentry and whirled him around. The man, though no match for a champ, proved to be a tough cookie. He put up quite a bit of resistance for awhile. So they fought, grunting and cursing each other under the encouraging shouts of the engine drivers who were having a whale of a time watching them. Finally, Danco wrestled his man toward an open water tank and threw him in, gun, ammunition and all. While the soldier splashed and thrashed in the tank, our hero picked up his brandy and ran for the train. By the time he got to the locomotive, the sentry, spitting water and more curses, had blown his whistle and several patrolmen ran toward him. At that moment, the laughing engineers called to Danco. Without hesitation, Danco joined them. They smeared his face and threw a dirty, torn cloth over his shiny uniform.

The angry patrolmen held up the train for ten minutes rushing from one end to the other, to the great delight of Danco's companions. At last they got permission to take off with a detachment still looking for the culprit. The detachment stayed on the train until San Steffano, where bristling with fury and frustration, they left, checking everyone's papers including the bystanders on the station platform.

"Your enemies are gone for good, soldier," shouted one of the stokers over the roar of the engine.

"God bless you, men," Danco shouted back, delivering the demijohn with the brandy to them, "it's all yours, boys!"

While the train ran through the endless waste of Stanbulcur, the men took care of the excellent brandy, complimenting him for bringing it along. The conductor joined them in time to get his share and was so pleased with the drink that he insisted that Danco take a first class compartment to catch up on his sleep.

"Berecketversin, effendi, thank you, men." said the young man, his voice a bit shaky from the brandy and a flow of real affection, "I'll remember your kindness."

Soon, face neatly washed from the soot, he sprawled on a soft velvet couch in first class and slept the sleep of a twenty-year-old.

Little Jivca was in bed with a sore throat.

The day was nice and warm yet she felt defeated. She could hear the voices of her elder sisters playing outside. It wasn't fair. Just a little sip from the spring water spout after a game of hide and seek and now—well—she didn't feel lonely. She loved the little old house rented by them in the city of Hissara, with its huge garden and many curious wall paintings. The four corners of the bedroom ceiling were painted to portray the different seasons. On one side of the wall it was winter in the mountains, pine trees heavy with the fallen snow, a tiny village far away and a horse-drawn sled speeding toward it. Jivca was in the sled. She was the daughter of the silver queen and the two horses suddenly changed to a magnificent team of reindeer...and now on the other side, it was spring time: blooming trees congratulated her as they waved their branches; happy birds brought her silky red and white tassels that had been woven in March for good health, and the flowers, the kind and shy snow drops, the cocky crocuses, the graceful tulips...

"Psst! Hey, Jivca, it's me." The beaming face of Assen hung through the slightly open door like half a moon, "Want me to bring you something to eat?"

The little girl was sulky. That stupid, stupid Assen. He had no right to chase away her beautiful dreams! She whispered as if she were on her death bed, "I can't eat...my throat hurts."

Assen came to her and squatted down. "Come on, sweetheart, eat something. You are so frail. Sometimes when the wind is too strong, I worry about you. Honest to God...it might just blow you off like a dandelion. Poufff!! Nothing left of little Jivca."

That funny Assen! But on the other hand, who else was there? Her elder sisters kept to themselves...and the baby was, just a baby. Assen was her only friend. For better or worse, she was stuck with him. She sighed and coquettishly arranged her golden curls on the pillow.

"I don't know, but I might eat something...one or two bites. Let's see what you have to offer." At this point she felt really hungry, "I wouldn't mind some, er...some ice cream. There is a street vendor right around the corner at this time of the day. Of course. that's if you really love me," she teased.

Assen made a funny face. "Little princess, anything in the world, but not that, not with your sore throat."

"Even if I tell you my dreams?"

"Even if you tell me the tallest of your tales," Assen replied.

"Well, you may be right. But if it's not ice cream, it doesn't really matter. Bring whatever you wish. Wait, first tell me one of your poems."

"If that is what the little princess wishes...let me see...

This summer
is a bummer.
In spite,
or just for that,
Jivca has
a bad kismet.
She lays in bed
And
no weather wise
spins
her little lies.
Up and down
all around,
aloof
on the roof,
dance a thriller
with the caterpillar!"

Jivca clapped her hands.

"Oh, what a silly little poem! Besides, for your information, I don't lie...er...sometimes, just a tiny bit...and it is only an excess of imagination, as mamma says."

"That just could be the case, well, never mind," Assen said.

"Anyway, where is everybody else?" asked little Jivca.

"As you can hear, Jeanna and Elsa are playing in the yard. Your parents took Rayna with them to the park. They'll drink mineral water from the spring and listen to the brass band."

"How come they didn't take Jeanna and Elsa along with them?"

Assen scratched his closely cropped head. "I really don't know. They probably did something wrong. Wait a minute—now, I remember."

"What? Please, Assen, do tell me quickly!"

Assen smiled and a little devil danced in his merry blue eyes. "When they were ready to go, your sister Elsa started to cry. She said her mother and elder sister, Rayna, had their silk dresses on and she and her playmate were dressed all in cotton. So, they were left behind."

Jivca sighed again, this time with satisfaction. She murmured to herself, "Good, it makes me feel better to know that I am not the only one left behind."

"That's not nice, Miss Jivca!" Her faithful Assen shook his head, "You'll go straight to hell for words like that. A young Christian does not think like...like..."

Jivca interrupted, "Who said I am one?"

"Oh, come on, miss..." Assen started.

"If you must know," said the girl, glancing at the open window and the door, her voice brought down to a conspiratorial whisper, "the real me is a heathen, and that's the very truth about me."

"God Almighty..." exclaimed Assen. Jivca pointed with her chin toward the door, making a quick sign to keep silent. When the young man looked over his shoulder, he saw the heavy-set cook enter the room.

"What is it, Donca?" Assen asked.

"A messenger just dropped a telegram for the master. He says it's urgent."

Assen walked to her and took the piece of paper. "All right, let me see. You haven't opened it by any chance, have you?"

Donca made the sign of the cross. "God forbid! Just a little bit."

Assen scratched his head again. "Jesus Christ! This house is full of pagans. What's in it?"

The cook scowled. "See for yourself."

"What do you take me for? I wouldn't do anything like that...but since you've already done it..."

Jivca pricked up her ears. Donca hesitated a moment, then her gossipy nature prevailed.

"They're calling him back immediately."

"Nonsense. He hasn't been here even for three days and his leave is for ten," said Jivca, with an air of importance. "You haven't read it properly. Let me see it."

Assen was reluctant. "Why not give it to the town announcer to read it all over the city?"

Jivca pouted. "I am his daughter, and the cook has read it."

Assen shook his head again. "You are an eleven-year-old girl with a sore throat. Next one to read it is going to be the master. You can take my word for that."

Life had not changed dramatically for Radco Boev. Some of his friends avoided him for awhile, but nobody dared to call him traitor. They all knew his bad temper when he was piqued.

Delly Hassan met him on the street once, and his right arm was all bandaged. Delly blushed profusely, bit his lips and muttered a hollow good day over his shoulder. But Radco accosted him.

"How's your arm, Delly Hassan?" The young man looked bewildered. He shifted from one foot to another and brushed his nose with the back of his left hand. "Nothing very much. It's just a flesh wound. It'll be good as new in a month's time. Even now I help in the smith shop with my left hand."

"Aw...that will make it stronger," promised Radco.

They stayed there in silence for half a minute or so, neither one wanting to leave. Delly Hassan picked up little stones with the tip of his hard moccasin and hurled them in the side stream of melting snow running down the narrow winding street called a sockak.

"How's your friend?" he asked finally, in a hoarse voice.

Now it was Radco's turn to become bewildered, but he got over that in a moment and laughed, "Wait a minute, Delly, which one of my friends? I've got many."

Now Delly Hassan laughed too, shaking a finger at the youth. "You know goddam well which one."

"You mean the one that gave you a stiff hand?" Radco feigned ignorance.

Delly Hassan tipped his cocky black moustache and sighed, somehow funny and sad at the same time.

"I shouldn't drink so much...drinking..." he didn't finish whatever was on his mind. Instead, he coughed a bit and said, "Tell him I bear no grudge against him, but his father had many enemies that have sworn to kill him on sight when fighting begins. Tell him to pack and go to Istanbul. It won't be long now."

Radco looked at him as if seeing him for the first time in his life. Then an unexpected warmth was reflected in his eyes and voice. "Is it going to be that bad?"

The man met Radco's eyes with straightforwardness. "A massacre."

Radco and Ismail, legs crossed, sitting on the sofa, were sipping hot coffee and making low purring sounds. As stryna Nonna watched them, she passed a prematurely dry and wasted hand over her faded cheek, and a tiny smile colored her lips. So young, so handsome, so much alike in spirit and heart, she thought. Only God knows what is in store for them...

"Berecketversin, stryna Nonna," said Ismail finishing the last of his coffee with delight. "I'll miss your coffee. You make it exactly like my mother used to. Not sugary like my sisters and most of my people prefer. That was just the right amount of sugar and you never over boil it, not an instant too long on the fire. That preserves all the aroma."

"Thank you, Ismail. You seem to know a lot about coffee making."

Ismail smiled broadly. "More about drinking it. I've been drinking coffee with my father ever since I can remember...Allah Acbar! Maybe we'll meet sometime, somewhere again. All roads are in His Hands."

Radco interrupted. "Did you tell him, mom?"

"Yes, son. I told him quite awhile ago that he should leave the fort with the whole family, that there will be atrocities and that the best thing for his father would be..."

"What was his answer?" he asked anxiously.

"He says his father is an officer under the supreme command of the padishah, that his life and that of his family belong to him. Besides, he is convinced that this war will be won by them and we are in the same danger."

For a moment Radco was dumbfounded. That possibility had never entered his mind. Then he rejected it, shaking the idea off as if it were a hateful Turkish fez planted on his head.

"Nooooo...that can't be!" he almost shouted, grabbing Ismail's shoulder and spilling his coffee. "That can't be. You have no chance of winning this war!"

Obviously Ismail understood what he was saying. He laughed without malice and banged his broad chest, speaking in broken Bulgarian.

"We have the strongest army in the world. We are big, you are small. You will cry evallah."

Radco withdrew his hand slowly. "Have you ever heard me say, I give up?"

Ismail felt uneasy. Two small vertical lines formed between his beautifully shaped eyebrows in an effort to compose another sentence.

"We were just wrestling. If faced with death, you might say it."

Radco shook his head so vigorously that a shiny tuft of blond hair fell over his forehead like a wing. "Never! My father never did; I won't either."

Ismail understood. There was sadness and pain in his large eyes, veiled by the long, sooty eyelashes. "Life is life...and death is death."

Radco met his eyes and they looked at each other as if for the first time. When Radco spoke, his clear voice had changed; it was rocky and dark. "If we were to meet out there, Ismail, would you kill me?"

Radco could almost hear the minutes ticking away. It was a long time before Ismail dropped his head on his chest, so that the black helmet of his curly hair was the only visible thing, and said so quietly that stryna Nonna had to strain to hear what he was saying.

"I don't know... Would you?"

Radco smiled. Through all those months since they first met, like two evenly matched athletes, a silent rivalry had developed between them. They had to find out who was king of the mountain—running up the hills, shooting, hunting or wrestling. Everything turned into a wild competition meant to bring one of them to submission. Now Radco knew he had won. He was the stronger.

"No, Ismail," he said and his voice sounded young and clear as ever. "I would not kill you for anything in the world!"

On his way to the Tzar's residence in Plovdiv, the hooves of General Robev's horse slipped over the cobblestone street. The general was deep in thought and almost hit an old woman walking by. Fortunately neither one was hurt and the old woman spit in her bosom to chase the fright away and went on up the street. The general silently cursed the monarch's leaning toward romantic places. He could have built himself a new palace for his visits to Plovdiv instead of using this age old structure in the ancient city, with its maze of tiny alleys where transportation was practically impossible.

"No, I am not hurt," he said to the preoccupied adjutant, clearly agitated. "Take care of my horse, and I'll walk to that ramshackle old building. If Alexander the Great could tramp on those stones I can do it, too. Besides it's just around the corner."

"You are three minutes late, General," said Ferdinand at his entrance. "No excuses, please. I will not tolerate that in the future."

"It won't happen again, Your Majesty," Robev bowed a bit shakily, "Is the great news at the door, Majesty?"

"Humdrum." The Tzar took a few steps, hands behind his back, his royal profile outlined his prominent nose and well kept beard more. "I thought so..." he droned through his nose. "Unfortunately, the British are making waves, indicating that my uncle, the Kaiser, will calm down. It will take some time, of course. Meanwhile, soon the best time to launch a campaign in the mountains will be gone. Summer is the right season for this kind of action and now we're just coming into it. What a waste!?!"

His impeccable uniform, glittering with its countless medals and decorations, seemed for a moment to give way under the strain of a royal sigh. But the portly monarch became aware of what could happen to his tightly fitted coat and eased his corpulent torso. Robev, knowing well the vanity of his master, turned his head to hide a smile. But Ferdinand, as usual, had eyes behind his back.

"What are you laughing at?" He huffed.

Robev was at a loss, but just for a second. "I just saw the face of Lieutenant Colonel Seraphimov in my mind's eye receiving the news that his vacation has been cut short on the basis of a false alarm. He hasn't been on leave for over two years."

The Tzar turned slowly to face his favorite general with an expression of scorn and amusement lingering at the corners of his mouth. "It's not a false alarm. I want to see that man in person, General. As soon as possible."

Crown Prince Boris looked at Vladimir Seraphimov with open admiration. "I witnessed, in person, the way you handled the maneuvers at Stanimaka. Being fascinated by the science of contemporary war tactics, I was rather impressed with your masterly—permit me to say virtuoso—orchestration of the attack."

Seraphimov felt uneasy. He never knew how to react when paid a compliment. "Thank you, Your Highness."

"Parbleu! Why don't you sit down, Colonel?"

"Colonel?" asked Vladimir, perplexed.

Boris smiled pleasantly. "I am sure you'll be a full colonel after this audience with my father."

The prince sat down and Seraphimov followed, still stunned.

"I don't know what to offer you, Colonel," said the youngster, fighting his natural shyness. "You don't drink or smoke either, or so I am told."

"Sometimes. Anyway, you've offered me enough, Your Highness, are you sure...?"

Prince Boris anticipated his question, "Am I sure my father won't be mad that I'm keeping you company while he intentionally keeps you waiting?"

"Yes, in a way," Seraphimov replied, revealing an uncommon shyness.

On a sudden impulse, the young prince put his hand on the older man's shoulder and told him with boyish straight-forwardness, "One day, *I'll* make you a general, sir."

The door flung open and Tzar Ferdinand hurriedly burst in. "I hate to be late, as you probably know, Seraphimov, but even a sovereign isn't always able to stick to his principles," his tone changed imperceptibly, "but I see you are in good hands. I can hardly believe my own eyes. This is the first time he has sought the company of a guest of mine on his own. You're making progress, my boy. Why don't we skip the protocol and sit down like old friends." He chose for himself a comfortable armchair and pointed to a chair next to his for Seraphimov, "Let the young man stand. It's good for his muscles. He definitely does not get enough exercise. You know what his latest passion is? Machines! When his grandma asked his foremost wish, his answer was to drive a locomotive."

The laughter that followed was strangely hollow. "Now, young man, go out and get some fresh air and…" he pointed an autocratic finger at the blushing prince, "…and none of those books under your arm. Now march!"

Prince Boris bowed formally and left.

"I believe my son has already broken the news to you?" asked the Tzar, his sharp penetrating eyes delving into Seraphimov's mind. "He was so excited about it. I try to keep him involved in my decisions in spite of his youth. At our age, my friend, one never knows…" He closed his eyes, "I am tired, Seraphimov, very tired, and nobody seems to appreciate what I am doing. You think I am blind. The whole chorus that now sings *Hosanna* at the first sign of a shift will all turn against me."

There was no bitterness in his smile, only deep enormous scorn. Seraphimov shuddered involuntarily, and the thought ran through his mind, "That man certainly doesn't like humanity. He wouldn't hesitate to sacrifice a million lives to fulfill a dream. But what if his life was at stake…?"

The Tzar leaned over and lowered his voice, "Robev is a fool. You know that as well as I, but you would never say it out loud. Loyalty, I understand. But I am left with a bunch of conspirators and opportunists to face a war on which depends the liberation of the rest of my people. It's a holy war, don't you think so, my friend?"

Seraphimov nodded, though his broad rugged face was void of emotion. Ferdinand did not miss that, but didn't turn off the thin smile still hanging on his lips. "In a time of crisis like this, the presence of a man like you, Seraphimov, is invaluable. Your place is next to me, in the palace."

"I am a field officer, your Majesty," Vladimir protested.

"You are a strategist," the Tzar countered.

Vladimir persisted, "I have bad manners, a hot temper and am a stranger to society. I am a peasant, Your Majesty, and am not ashamed of it."

"Your father was a teacher and his grandfather a revered monk in the famous monastery of Atton. A seraphim!" the Tzar reminded him.

Vladimir Seraphimov shrugged his shoulders and, for the first time, a smile lighted up his austere face. "That doesn't change a thing, sir. They were peasants at heart, as I will be until my last day. I chose the military profession because I could live and die for the Earth my people worked from time immemorial. I don't have to get away from it and, in a sense, I still earn my daily bread by working for it. If you separate me from my earth and my people, I'll be as dull as anybody else around you."

Ferdinand drew back from him as if he had suddenly gotten a whiff of a very bad odor. His face paled, his eyes grew distant and lonely. There was unmistakable finality in his words.

"Thank you, Lieutenant Colonel. Your sincerity has been appreciated." When Seraphimov prepared to leave, the Tzar said, "Give my regards to your wife and…Rayna. She is a beauty, isn't she?"

By the time Dannail Marrin reached Derrekioy on the fifteenth day of his leave, his story had grown even more astonishing than at the start. He had been arrested in a little railway station while walking up and down to stretch his legs—just because nobody had ever seen a uniform as resplendent as his and the local reserves weren't able to read his papers. He was taken to the jail, and spent two days in that filthy prison cell, until it was proven by a priest that, according to what was written in his passport, he was a member of the palace guard and not a spy of a foreign power. Finally, he was released with many apologies and even more bugs that he had gotten from the infested cell mattress. From that point on, he had to walk through the mountain since he didn't have enough money to buy another ticket and the old one had been lost. In a dark and isolated canyon, bandits ambushed him and took the few presents he was carrying home to his mother and sisters. Bleeding and bruised, he was found in the morning by a shepherd who knew his father and helped him reach the village.

In a week's time, his youth and strength served to put him back on his feet. He visited old friends and relatives, laughing and joking, telling them his unbelievable adventures. Old people shook their heads, young ones smiled in open disbelief.

When he asked his mother why the house of his old-time sweetheart was all boarded, locked and abandoned to the elements, she answered rather hastily that they had moved across the border into Progled.

"You know, son, they had a hard time, being one of the few Christian families left around here. Daur Bey was always after them and Rossitza's father had no choice." She paused for an instant, wiping her tearful old eyes and appeared to dread disclosing any more.

Dannail was restless. She knew how much he loved that girl, and none of her children was as close to her heart as her only boy. She lifted an appealing hand to him, but Dannail shook his head.

"Tell me everything, mother. Please, don't make me hear it from others."

Danco's mother carefully straightened the embroidered apron on her lap and somehow found the courage. "Rossitza's father never seemed to like you because of your faith," she faltered, "but when you became a sultan's guardsman, he was really mad. He let it be known everywhere that he would shoot you between the eyes if you came near his new home in Bulgaria."

Dannail slowly sank down on the soft cushions of the sofa, and his brooding eyes fastened on the old rifle over the fireplace. He had deliberately gone far away to forget about Rossitza and her fanatical father and, in a way, he thought he had. The strange city, the new friends and military routine, the adventures helped, but, back here, the past came back. It was just temporarily buried in his heart and now Rossitza's lovely face bloomed in front of his eyes, more alive and coveted than ever. The powerful feeling of love swept through his being like wind.

His mother read his flushed face like an open book. She implored him, "You are not going out there, son, are you?"

"How old is she now, mom?" asked Dannail, forcing himself to remain calm.

"She's still too young to make a decision against the will of her father, if that's what you're thinking."

Danco buried his burning face in his big hands. "I'll try to forget, mamma…I'll try very hard…"

The spring evening was filled with a thousand fragrances. The air, still cold, carried the invisible presence of something warm and promising. Ermin was playing his flute. His music was light and changeable like the breath of awakened life in the bosom of the old mountain. He played a snatch of one tune and then interpolated a piece of another—a melody as eerie as the light patches of mist between the young pine trees. After playing for awhile with those melodies, he would scramble them and come up with a new one—joyful or sad, filled with the melancholy of the coming night, or following the songs of the morning birds.

The interpretation of a melody was entirely dependent on his mood. The same tune would sound different in rhythm and color if the moon was full, or the wind was blowing from the north. His feelings were easily affected by everything around him, so it was almost like nature itself playing that magic cavall of his. The soldiers on the post were convinced there was truth in the story about the young boy Ermin, lost in the woods and taught by the bewitched spirits to play that musical instrument like they do.

Whether that was true or not mattered little to Radco. He listened to Ermin, completely enchanted, lost in the centuries old forest, prisoner of the magic and beauty that only songs, forgotten with age, can bring to a young soul. When the sound of the cavall faded into the falling darkness, Radco still kept hearing it deeply within himself as if the night were talking to him. For a long time, they both remained enveloped in silence, Ermin's long delicate fingers resting on the simple wooden instrument.

"Do you begrudge me my friendship with Ismail?" Radco asked suddenly.

In the thickening darkness Ermin's huge light blue eyes had a fluorescent effect. "No. Why should I?"

Radco sat closer to the older youth. His voice, bereaved of its usual clear vigor, sounded hollow and dull.

"Everyone does."

Ermin flung his arm around Radco's hunched shoulders.

"And how do you feel about it?"

Radco's shoulders trembled as if a cold outburst of the night breeze had touched him. "I don't know. Sometimes, I think they may be right. The past is a living part in all of us. It can condemn you, it can blast you to pieces if you try to rub against the grain, against what is expected. I thought I was strong enough to love Ismail for what he is, a part of myself, lonely and proud." He closed his eyes somewhat tiredly, "It wasn't love," he added, resigned.

Ermin smiled sadly. "If it wasn't love, what is it?"

A wry smile touched Radco's dry lips. "A desire to excel, to prove manliness in the face of an adversary—good and strong."

"Do you still want to see him?"

Radco didn't answer right away. "Yes, I do. Because I must cut the final link between us two."

"The rifle?" asked Ermin.

"The rifle. Could you find a way to meet him and give it back to him. And tell Ismail I lied, I would kill him! I don't want to use this rifle against his people, and using it against him would be like...killing myself."

Ermin looked at the brightest star in the darkened sky.

"I cannot do it. I am a soldier. But I'll find somebody trustworthy for the commission. Now tell me about Rossitza. Is she still waiting for her stranger?"

Dannail gingerly climbed up the steep street, eaten away by many torrents of rain. Just a few houses before his sister's, he came face to face with the priest from the small church of Sveta Bogoroditza, Pope Stoyco. Being a Christian priest, he was barely known by the young Mohammedan, but whenever they met there was a short exchange of greetings and sometimes a few words about the weather and the crops, something they both rather enjoyed. Danco was getting ready to bid him good day and ask about his young daughters, when suddenly he became aware of the strange, distorted face that hardly looked like the ruddy cheeked cheerful and gentle Pope Stoyco.

"Chock selliam, Pope Stoyco. What is the matter?" queried a bewildered Danco.

The priest avoided his keen eyes. "Chock selliam, chodgouk...nothing...we just...we ran out of brandy...I have to go and buy some..."

Dannail knew from his father that Pope Stoyco had never had a drop of brandy in his whole life.

"Got some guests, I presume," he mused curiously.

The man paled even more and muttered, "Right, some guests. Good day, Danco." And he continued down the street, looking sort of dazed and glassy eyed. If ever Dannail had seen a man in trouble, it was right now. He ran after him.

"Wait a minute, Pope Stoyco. I wanted to ask about your daughters. You know, they were Rossitza's best friends and...is it anything about the girls, Pope Stoyco?"

The priest kept silent, looking at Dannail's uniform with a mixture of distrust and anguish, then suddenly sobbed, his reddened eyes swimming in tears, he blubbered incoherently, "An officer from the Turkish army and his junior officer from the fort..."

Dannail needed no further explanation. Several days ago the Turks had called the village notables to the outpost. His father was one of them. They wanted them to identify a corpse. Nobody had the courage to say who the dead man was, though each and everyone of them knew him quite well. He was a young man from a neighboring village, who prospered in the wool trade, who had gone, with official permission to Bulgaria on a business trip. He was due to come back some day with lots of money in his belt. The soldiers said the man had tried to cross the border illegally, so had been arrested and shot on the spot when he attempted to escape. No money or passport were found on the dead body. The customs officer, Arrif Agha (Ismail's father), was silent and evaded the eyes of his guests. Everybody, including Dannail's father, had shaken their heads and sworn that they had never seen or heard of the dead man. The next day the officer and his junior went on a drunken spree, spending golden coins throughout the village as if they had located the horn of plenty. Danco had seen enough of these dirty tricks in the glorious army of the padishah and this seemed to be the very last straw.

His big hands tightened into huge fists, red veins like angry serpents popped out on his neck and over his forehead, his face became purply red and ugly, his eyes filled with blood. Pope Stoyco kneeled down in horror, his long black cassock spread in the mud, his beard blown all over his face by the wind, eyes full of pain and desperation, hands outstretched in a silent plea. When he finally found his voice, it was more of a wail than human speech.

"Do o on't…in God's name…they said they'd kill them if I ever tell anybody. They'll cut their throats, Danco, and yours too. Don't make them angry, please. Have mercy, you can't fight the two of them—they're big and strong and armed to the teeth. Don't go, please…don't goooo…" His voice trailed off in a crescendo and left him in an animal scream.

Shrouded in the last purple rays of the fading sun the figures of the two men seemed like visions out of a nightmare. In desperation, Pope Stoyco tried to grab at the knees of the young man, but Dannail shook off his trembling hands as if they were dead branches, let out a low primeval roar that came deep from his chest and sprang like a beast after his prey.

Dannail ran at top speed through the Christian stockade, where the small church faced Pope Stoyco's home. For a moment he listened, heard desperate screams from inside, then broke down the door with his heavy body.

Laughing and cursing, the two drunken, half-naked brutes, had torn the dresses of the horrified girls.

Dannail yelled at them, "Freeze, you bastards!"

The men turned to him totally caught by surprise, and Danco attacked them barehanded. Later, he had little recollection of what had happened. He vaguely remembered dragging their bodies toward the canyon, helped by a stunned Pope Stoyco.

The young man sent them flying to the very bottom.

"What are you going to do now, Danco?" the priest asked him shakily.

Danco pointed with his chin toward Bulgaria. Pope Stoyco embraced him. "God be with you, young man!"

Danco descended the steep, rocky hillside. His instinct told him that he had to reach Progled earlier than daybreak, but before arriving on the other side, a gray mist already foretold the coming of dawn. For most of the night, he had to play hide-and-seek with the Turkish patrols. To fool the dogs, he went through the marshes, soaked to the bone. Only his knowledge of every nook and cranny, and his daredevil courage, coupled with his animal instincts, saved him from capture.

Dannail ran, walked and crawled for hours, his ragged uniform hanging in ribbons. He washed off the smeared blood in the stream, then drank thirstily, still followed by the screams of the terrified young girls, and by the horrified, glassy eyes of his victims. As far as he remembered, he had killed the Turks with his bare dagger. One thing stuck with him—the downpour of golden coins that had fallen from the Turks' belts. When he came across the corpses at the canyon's bottom, he buried them in shallow graves.

Dannail had little recollection of what had happened after he found the two drunk, half naked soldiers over the girls who were screaming in terror. All that remained in him was his atavistivstic instincts.

To the exhausted young man, the road to Progled seemed endless, and the line of stone houses and wooden shacks got no closer. The land gave a different picture from what he had seen on the other side of the border. Grassy hills gleamed in the soft morning light. The upper part of the mountain range was hard and rocky, but the lowland was suitable enough for pasture and cultivation. And the farmland all around was well cared for, treated with love by people of their own free will.

At last he entered the outskirts of the village, reeling and drunk with exhaustion. He crossed it cautiously and without seeing a living soul, passed the first farm house. Cattle and mules grazed in pasture. Further down an early shepherd had opened the gates of the fold, letting the sheep out. He paid little attention to the young man in spite of his ruffled appearance and answered his question quite politely.

The road turned to the right around the slope of a hill covered with low bushes. Danco's eyes caught a column of curling blue smoke that rose from a thicket of pine trees. Rossitza's house would be in there. Suddenly hordes of memories besieged his mind. He shook his head and looked around for dogs; there seemed to be none. Climbing over the low stone fence, he cut across the orchard, hiding behind the trees. Inadvertantly, he spotted the figure of a girl, lithe, full of grace, coming around the corner of the little stone house. Danco's heart swelled in his heaving chest. Rossitza!

He hurled himself to meet her, stepping from behind the tree in her path. She dropped a basket, put a trembling hand over her mouth, stifling a rising cry, her amber eyes wide open with a mixture of terror and recognition.

"Don't be scared, Rossitza. I am not a waylay man, though I might look like one," he begged.

"Danco..." whispered the girl, her rosy cheeks turning pale.

He flung his arms wide open and Rossitza leaped into them like a bird into its nest. She swung her arms around his burly neck and for a while they kissed each other in frenzy. Finally the girl shuddered and her head, covered with a shiny helmet of hair the color of honey, fell forward on his broad chest, a stream of rusty gold spilling all over him. Danco held her pressed tightly with that enormous strength of his, but gently enough to let her breathe.

"Danco, Danco..." she sobbed uncontrollably, digging her fingers into his back as if to keep him at least a minute more, "Run away from here, my dearest...for you, only death and hatred grow in this place... Run if you love me! I want you alive even if I never see you again in this wretched world!"

Danco felt himself choking with the mighty beating of his heart. He had to call upon all the self-control he could muster not to lay her down in response to the urge of the hot wave that was devastating him inside. He strived to restrain himself, shaken to his very depths by the revelation that she still loved him.

In ecstasy, Dannail gazed out into the trees with blurred eyes. Between the still bare branches, he saw the outline of a tall, bony man with a big salt and pepper moustache hanging down his cruel mouth. The man moved to face him, a long deadly rifle aimed at his forehead. "Leave us alone, Rossitza," uttered the man through clenched teeth.

Rossitza turned around and screamed. "NO, father… nooooo!!!"

Instead of being shot by the crazed Goran Podgorsky, Rossitza's despotic father, Dannail was locked in an empty stone house for several days and nights. The young man muttered through his teeth, "I should have killed him. But then Goran is Rossitza's father, how could I, damn it? Of all people, me, arrested as a Turkish spy! Where can I run now, *Allah*? Where?

Later, a Military Tribunal sentenced him to forced hard labor for a period of ten years and one day.

The military tutor to the young princes, General Robev, had just finished his lecture when the successor to the throne asked him for a private conversation. Robev was surprised. The shy, elusive prince had rarely asked him a question before, although his occasional outbursts about war and battle strategy never lacked imagination and were well founded. Unlike his younger brother, Cyril, who acted solely on emotion, Boris would offer a solution formed from a lucid mind and solid knowledge. In spite of his open sympathy toward the younger brother, the general had to admit to him that he had the talents of a good politician and an outstanding diplomat, even if he might not have the best components for a military man.

While Prince Cyril went for a joyride on his bicycle, the general accompanied the elder brother to the garden. During their walk, Boris, without losing his train of thought, would stop to closely examine a tree or flowering bush. Knowing of His Highness' botanical interests, Robev waited for him with a slight smile on his lips.

The prince offered very little in the way of overture to what he really wanted to talk about, "How is Colonel Seraphimov? I haven't seen him around for a long time. Is there anything wrong with his family?"

The older man studied the face of the youth, but it was impossible to guess how much the prince really knew. "Oh, nothing is the matter. The lieutenant colonel keeps himself busy, as usual, and afterwards blames his superiors for giving him too much to do."

In the greenhouse Prince Boris looked at the petals of a rare flower with the help of a magnifying glass.

"Very unlikely. I never heard the colonel complaining of anything."

"That, of course, was a joke!" intimated the general.

"Sorry, General. Everybody knows I have a poor sense of humor." He moved to the shrubbery next in their path and with the same loving care studied its buds, ready to bloom. "What I heard about him is quite different. There seems to be some talk of moving Seraphimov to Yamboll, away from the eventual theatre of war. How much do you know of that matter, General?"

Robev was lost for awhile, then he decided to try to gain some time. "Your Highness seems to have better sources than I."

The prince straightened up and for the first time came face to face with Robev. There was unconcealed anger in his young voice. "My father wouldn't reach any decision on that subject without informing you."

The general didn't answer at once and thought to himself, *Would that pup allow me my honors if something happened to his August father? Never! I have the feeling he despises me for some reason. He may know too much. Anyway my chances with him are very slim.* Outwardly he smiled. "Why don't you ask His Majesty? He wouldn't withhold anything from you unless he really didn't want you to know. And that, I am sure, would only be in the best interests of this country's policies."

Boris paled, a slight nervous tic formed in the corner of his mouth. He tried to conceal it behind the case of the magnifying glass, his sense of helplessness proved too difficult for his young idealism. "I can see why you are so indispensable to my father," he said with real bitterness ringing in his voice, "Will you at least tell me one last thing: did he arrive at this decision on your advice?"

General Robev made a desperate face. "You don't think very, highly of me, Your Highness, do you?"

The prince blushed but stood firm. "I think you are an opportunist, General."

The Prince's tutor nodded thoughtfully. "Candor for candor, Your Highness. Your August father's response to the war ministry council's request for removal of the second-in-command of the 21st Srednogorsky Regiment in Plovdiv was negative. He said that under battle conditions, the presence of Lieutenant Colonel Vladimir Seraphimov is most needed."

Boris' eyes lit up. "Thank you, General."

That night nobody slept in the garrison barracks in Plovdiv. Soldiers of the regular army that had never met before now embraced and kissed each other as if they were old buddies.

"The new recruits are coming tomorrow, did you hear?"

"Finally! Long live the Tzar!"

"Mobilization! Total mobilization!"

"The war can't be more than a few days away."

"You'd better take along your rifle."

"My old berdana is the best in the regiment. I'm gonna take it to bed tonight...to keep any of the new-comers from grabbing her and running to the front."

The rifles were locked up for the night. Somebody threw a stone. Many followed. The windows of the army depot were smashed to smithereens. After taking the rifles, most of the soldiers slept with rifles between their legs. It was as if in a strange ritual they had gotten married to the arms...and their own death.

The next morning, from the very break of dawn, the garrison's band started playing the national anthem and the one dedicated to the Tzar. Crowds of smiling youths covered with garlands of flowers came from the nearby villages. The elders were accompanied by spouses carrying babies at their bosoms, singing along with the bagpipes, laughing and drinking as if this was the best thing that could happen to their families.

And above all that joyful celebration, a sunny autumn sky seemed to give an extra festive mood, a generous approval of peoples' foolishness.

The hot wave of patriotism and regular drunkenness reached its peak at noon, when General Robev, young and handsome, appeared riding a magnificent Arabian stallion. The ovations bordered on frenzy.

Robev lifted up his arm, the silver blade of a priceless sword reflecting the sun like lightning, his powerful voice drowning out the noise of the hushed crowds.

"In the name of the Tzar and the Fatherland, I'll lead you to the liberation of your brothers and sisters! God be with us!"

As if from one single throat the crowd roared, "AMEN!"

Chapter Four

"Ellena."

"I am not asleep, dear. Is it time?"

"Yes. I have to be back at the garrison at 5:00 a.m. Now listen to me. I don't want you to come along the road with the kids throwing flowers and waving goodbye. We can live without that…I want to remember you exactly the way you look now, your long golden hair spread on the pillow and those eyes with tiny stars in them, full of tears and love. No, don't say anything, just look at me as I leave. And, one more thing. When you kiss our kids in the morning, long after I am gone, tell them that Vladimir Seraphimov, um, their papa, will be back no matter what happens—and that's a promise!"

The march of the 21st Field Regiment through the streets of Plovdiv was a real march of triumph. All autumn flowers from the gardens of the city were gone—either on the young heroes chests, hanging over the jubilant faces of the soldiers, forming a thick carpet under their boots, tucked into the barrels of their rifles or still trembling in the hands of their dear ones seeing them off. The music and crowd followed the marching troops through Main Street, then to Stanzionna, the railway station and to the very outskirts of the city, on and on, toward the Rhodopa Mountain. The morning was crystal clear, one of those beautiful fall days that makes it impossible to believe that winter is on the way, and even harder to think that many of those youths, full of merriment and pranks, might never return.

"We'll send you postcards from the White Sea."

"Don't wait for a line from me before taking over Tzarygrad!"

"Next address—Dolmabahche, Istanbul!"

Then, there was a hush in the crowd.

"That one, on the white mare with the black cloak over his shoulders, he's Commander Seraphimov, and the mantle itself is magic. No bullet can strike him through it. It has been proven throughout the Serbian War."

"What an austere and noble face. Envy of those who serve under him."

"Long live Commander Seraphimov!"

The appointed commander, Colonel Nedelev, riding next to Seraphimov, was the last minute substitution for General Robev, detained at the palace by a matter of state priorities. He smiled good-naturedly. "They've already given you the promotion, Lieutenant Colonel. Anyway, nobody seems to miss Robev. You're a real crowd pleaser."

"People don't see as much of the general as they do of me. I think they've seen more than they really wanted. It's only natural to rejoice seeing my back," he chuckled.

Nedelev shook his head still in good humor. "They most certainly have a lot of respect for you. That doesn't come easy. Nobody ever notices me...except for my tremendous bulk."

The shouts grew weaker as the troops marched toward the mountains and the last of the followers faded away. "God bless you. Come back to us with victory..."

The festive mood persisted amidst the soldiers until they passed the city of Stanimaka, where a similar party awaited them. Already in the canyons, even after a short break and a snack, the feeling of euphoria and the rush of adrenalin was replaced by ordinary fatigue. Dust and an unusually hot sun for this time of the year erased the smiles, and rough terrain gave them their first sore feet. Boys from the plains were ill prepared for a prolonged march, and badly equipped as well. Very few of them had real boots on. Most wore soft field moccasins for walking on smooth ground but offered little protection against rocks and gravel. Mountain people wore a different kind of footwear: hard moccasins that gave them maximum protection on tough roads.

Gradually the march slowed down.

No songs were heard anymore, just moaning and groaning, and now and then, some swearing. There was a work outfit of prisoners along the road that stopped working to watch the passing soldiers with mixed feelings. Seraphimov's trained eye spotted a magnificent specimen among them—a young man in his prime, good looking, an athletic figure bronzed by the free exposure to the sun and cut to perfect proportions. He owned hard muscles under silky smooth skin that could explode with energy.

The commander stopped his horse right in front of him and looked deeply into his bold eyes. The clear blue eyes under the sandy forelock didn't flinch under the scrutiny. He continued to stand erect and proud, in all his awesome height, though slightly bent over the handle of the shovel.

"Are you a Bulgarian?" asked the officer.

The clever eyes remained fixed.

"Yes, sir." The voice was deep and melodious.

"You've been in the army?" asked Seraphimov.

"Yes, sir, Lieutenant Colonel."

"What rank?"

"Corporal, sir."

Vladimir Seraphimov paused a bit. "What crime have you committed?"

"Escaped from Turkey to fight on my own side, sir," he answered.

"That isn't a crime," Seraphimov was taken aback.

"That's all I have done, sir."

Colonel Nedelev, who was listening to the dialogue, sullenly spoke up, "The Turks have tried to spread a net of informers within the army. That man has a soft accent."

Seraphimov did not even look at him. "That is the way mountain people talk in this part of the country."

"The man might still be a traitor and a spy," protested Nedelev.

Now the junior in rank averted his eyes from the prisoner and looked straight into Colonel Nedelev's face. "Can't you see it in his eyes? That lad is telling the truth!"

Nedelev waved his hand as if to make peace. "Do whatever you find necessary, Seraphimov," he said as he galloped his horse ahead.

Seraphimov took out his indispensable black notebook. "Name and work detachment."

The young man dropped his shovel and stood at attention.

"Dannail Marrin from Derrekioy Tenth Work Detachment, the prison of Stanimaka."

Without any further words the officer rode ahead in a cloud of dust. The prisoner looked after him, eyes wide open, then uttered unbelieving, "Seraphimov! The black mantle commander!"

In the last few weeks, life in the village of Progled had changed drastically. More and more troops were coming, wagons, horses, artillery, mobile kitchens, field hospitals.

Every house, barn, even the school, was full of soldiers. They built barracks and spread tents all over. Refugees from the other side said the same thing was happening in their villages. The local people had never been so excited, except for a few days in the spring when *bay* Goran Podgorsky, Rossitza's father, had caught a Turkish spy right in his orchard. A group headed by bay Goran wanted to hang him on the spot; others led by the village teacher insisted that the young man should be sent to the district jail. It was against the law to sentence anyone to death without a competent judge.

"We didn't free ourselves from Turkish oppression just to commit the same shameful crimes ourselves!" said the youthful teacher, and most of the crowd agreed with him. So *bay* Goran and the few from the pub gang, who had not been drafted yet, grudgingly went along with the majority.

After the final decision, everyone seemed to be satisfied except for a desperate Rossitza, who took it very hard. Her father said that it was just her tender age, but many women thought it was *ochtica*, as they called infatuation or love sickness in villages. She lost her appetite; her healthy tan disappeared; she would sit for hours in a sunny spot, her wide amber eyes staring at the road leading to the plains, one day with hope, the next in total desperation.

Radco Boev liked the change in the formerly sleepy village—the loud noise of passing wagons and artillery, the racing dispatch carriers, the soldiers milling around the main street. He would pass the day going from one command post to another, pleading with the officers to take him on as a volunteer. At first they were willing, because of his muscular build and powerful shoulders, he looked the right age. But then someone from the village told them that he was not yet sixteen and he was sent home, followed by catcalls and laughter. Radco was enraged. When one of the junior officers said, "Go home, young'un; you're not a man yet," Radco shook his forelock angrily and yelled back: "Okay, sarge, show me someone you consider a man and if I can't beat him in ten minutes, I'll admit you're right and you won't see me around anymore!"

Just for the fun of it, the sergeant agreed, and selected a husky fellow about Radco's size and build and set them up to wrestle, stripped to the waist. Radco put him down, not in ten, but in five minutes. A bigger, strapping youth stepped out, and Radco took care of him as well in the time frame he'd promised. When he looked at the rest of them with his fiery eyes and said, "Anyone else want to test me?" there were neither laughs nor catcalls. They all accepted the sturdy mountain boy as an equal. He was enlisted...but kept out of sight of the superiors.

Volunteer private Radco Boev was in his glory.

Early in the morning on the 5th of October 1912, Arrif Agha, the highest officer at the Turkish outpost at Rhojen, was awakened by rheumatic pains in his left knee. He was wounded in the same ambush where Aysha, his most beloved wife, was killed. Since then, his leg was never the same, and he was moved from active service to an administrative job as a customs master. Of course, he had dreams of his younger days. As a rather handsome and physically strong officer with an open mind and noble character, he was expected to go far in the army of the Great Padishah.

It didn't happen quite that way. He lacked a very important element for advancement: cruelty. He remembered the day when he had to execute three Bulgarians in the small village of Adjar. The young teacher's head didn't come off right away. His soldiers had to chop it again and again with that dull axe—and the man's little boy was watching. Many nights afterward he had prayed to Allah for forgiveness. He lost sleep and became indifferent to duty. Another thing that hurt his career was his first marriage to a poor girl from an insignificant family—a peasant family. Aysha! How they loved each other! The fact that they had no kids for many years marred their happiness and his stubborn refusal to take other wives made him suspect in the eyes of his superiors. Ismail came to them later in life. Maybe too late, but Arrif Agha thought Allah had forgiven him for the martyr's death of the young teacher that left behind many orphans. After which he had taken two younger wives. Neither one of them filled the shoes of Aysha though they gave him beautiful cuddly daughters. He was ecstatic! But that was, he was certain, just to make Allah's last punishment more enduring, because in the ambush set for him, Aysha had to pay with her life.

Arrif Agha tried to go back to sleep. It didn't work. In bed, he tossed from one side to the other. Why, Allah, why should his only son, Ismail, the light of his old eyes, be a sensitive and goodhearted boy like himself? Why wasn't he brutal and forceful, going through life like a devastating storm for the glory of the Padishah? What kind of a chance would he have against the enmity and unfair rivalry in life?

The corporal and the man under him had been killed in the spring like mad dogs. They had fully deserved it. Arrif Agha knew only too well what kind of cut-throats and no-good bastards both of them were. But superiors never paid any attention to his plea for substitutes, so they remained short of trained officers. He was transferred back to active service.

Now, when the damage was done, the local population didn't trust the military. The Bulgarians hated him fervently. What will happen if their army isn't victorious in this imminent war, and the Bulgarians get the upper hand? Everyone seemed so cocksure that small Bulgaria would be easily defeated. He wasn't. None of those cookies will be drinking his coffee in Phulbee (Plovdiv) on the next day.

Now he knew he wouldn't be able to go back to sleep. Under his bedroom window, the young rooster in the chicken house raised his untrained voice. Soon daylight would come.

Stifling a moan, Arrif Agha got out of his bedding and, favoring his bad leg, limped down the hallway. The girls were sleeping with his wives in the women's quarters—*haremlak*. He stopped for a moment to look at the fresh, happy looks on their sleeping faces. In the light of the little oil lamp they seemed pretty as visions from another world. There was not a glimmer that this would be the last time he'd see them alive.

He stopped in his son's bedroom. The youth slept, as usual, stark naked. The cover had fallen and his beautifully sculptured body gleamed softly in the moonlight. How much he has grown up this summer! marveled his father to himself, placing the cover back on Ismail's broad muscular shoulders. By all measures, a man. Only his character and the expression on his face was still somewhat boyish...or was it? Ismail woke up instantly.

"Are you in pain, father?" he asked.

"Just the usual, my boy. It's too early yet. Go back to sleep. I'm gonna have a cup of coffee."

He left and went to the kitchen in the side wing of the house. Some of the charcoals in the brazier were still alive. Soon Arrif Agha had the fire going and a copper *djezve*, a small, long-handled, metal cup, warming up. He heard barefooted steps and saw Ismail coming down the stairs. He was still half naked, a gentle smile on his handsome face.

"I want some coffee, too," croaked Ismail, half asleep.

He took another *djezve* and sat cross legged on the other side of the brazier, setting the small brass container over the blazing charcoal.

"One of these days you'll catch your death of cold," mumbled his father, "put something around your shoulders."

"It won't be from cold, babba. I am hot, believe me."

Arrif Agha shivered. Maybe the boy was right. Many years ago, young Arrif probably went naked on a cold autumn morning without feeling any chill. Maybe, it was long ago. He stroked the back of the old tomcat that had joined them.

The coffee was ready. They poured it into tiny *flidgans,* cups with no handles, and sipped it in silence.

"Are you still sore about that Christian boy Radco?" the old man asked unexpectedly.

Ismail nodded. "He was the only friend I had...or thought I had. He shouldn't have given back my present, should he?"

Arrif Agha shrugged his shoulders under the heavy woolen mantle. "Another faith, different upbringing... How can one tell? While we don't return a woman, a gun or a horse, to them it might be perfectly acceptable. For them a present probably is not a living thing, but just an object they exchange, turn over, or send back just as they wish."

It was at that moment that the first mortar shell found its target in the women's quarters, next to Ismail's room.

The war had started.

At that hour, batteries from the surrounding heights started firing at the Turkish outposts. Heavy guns from above Progled, on Ballaban Hill and Dliogoto Bortze, attacked the fort of Rhojen, and rifle volleys followed the cannonade. There was a strange wild music in the complicated orchestration of different firearms. The cannons were the heavy drums, the lighter guns and hand grenades played the supporting part, and the handguns and rifles were the violins, bearing the sinister melody of death.

The main Turkish strongholds in the area were the forts at Rhojen, Couroucalle, Kallachboroun and Carramandga. The fort of Rhojen was by far the most secure. Sturdily built, well armed, extra soldiers on the fortifications and fanatic commanders—all contributed to make it the primary concern of the Bulgarian forces. The lucky salvo of artillery that hit right in the middle of the fort and the surprise attack that followed pushed the Turks into panic and flight. In absolute chaos, they ran downhill for dear life, abandoning all their heavy arms, ammunition and provisions. Empty handed, half naked, faces smeared with blood, they crossed the villages of Derrekioy, Bostina and some smaller hamlets where they regrouped with the Army forces from Cavgadgick and Ustinna.

The Bulgarian troops didn't follow them. One of the forts had not yet fallen. It held the whole front line. Vladimir Seraphimov was mad, but there was very little he could do about it. The order came from the palace, signed by General Robev.

"I can't believe it," he roared, walking back and forth in one of the few rooms left intact in Rhojen's fort—the kitchen, "we could make a clean sweep all the way to Smollian and maybe further; instead we wait here like fools, just because a handful of men still hold Carramandga."

"I know, Seraphimov, I know perfectly well," Colonel Nedelev tried to pacify him, "and even if I didn't know anything about momentum in war, you've explained it to me so many times that it would take a real dummy not to understand it by now."

Seraphimov dug his fingers into his thick gray hair. "I am sorry, Nedelev. I know I am getting impatient, but this is one chance in a million. Here we are throwing the whole effect of the surprise attack to the winds and…and how can you sit there so calmly, sipping your coffee and talking so casually as if we were having a discussion on the weather? You know how many soldiers will die taking over the same terrain that we could have had by now without shedding a drop of blood?"

"Calm down, my friend. Have a cup of coffee, or lie down on this couch for half an hour. You haven't slept for two nights. See, when you get to be my age and my 250 pounds, you'll know that there will always be somebody at the top to spoil the drive of a whole campaign and, in the end, hold you responsible for the failure. His failure. And you have to take the blame if you want to move up."

"Why don't you move up?" asked Seraphimov sarcastically.

"Because I'm way too heavy. They like good looking men in the palace, and me and my enormous pot belly… How old are you, Seraphimov?" He switched the subject.

"Fifty-two," Vladimir replied.

"You look older."

"I have not had an easy life."

" I can assure you it won't get any easier. You can take it from me.

"For the past two days, while you were worrying yourself to death, I looked through the papers of the Mahmour Arrif Agha. The Turks left in such a hurry they didn't burn any of the archives. That gentleman is 66 years old and has not advanced higher than a damn customs officer in this God forsaken outpost. He certainly was a noble man, if you know what I mean."

Seraphimov sat dejectedly on a small three legged chair. "I know what you mean, and probably with my big mouth, I'll go no higher either. You've been very comforting. Thanks a million." He got out his short pipe and filled it with tobacco from a tin box. While he was lighting it, Nedelev got up to his feet with a sigh. "I don't know about you, but I am getting hungry…and cold. See if you can find somebody to stoke up this brazier. There is no heat left in it. I'll go and look in the private pantry of Arrif Agha. There's still a bit of food left. I don't know anything better to fight depression than some sugary dates, halvah, or delightful *locoum* from Stanbul."

He climbed the steps, moaning softly and disappeared into the hallway by clearing his way through the debris.

Vladimir Seraphimov smoked his pipe trying to drive away his nagging thoughts when he heard steps coming from the courtyard. There was a short conversation, then Nedelev's orderly entered the low-ceilinged kitchen. Seraphimov had left Assen Mitackov at home and still had not gotten around to finding an orderly of his own, so they shared the same tight-lipped and spare man.

"What is it, Gancho?" questioned Seraphimov.

"There is a private outside. He has been waiting since yesterday to see you—has some papers for you to sign, sir." The soldier looked uneasy.

"Anything else, Gancho?"

"Well, that man is a big fellow, sir. Don't you want me to come back with him?" the orderly offered.

"No. Take this brazier and revive it. Your master is getting cold," ordered Seraphimov.

The orderly took the brazier and left. An old tom cat came to the feet of Seraphimov and, purring loudly, rubbed his head on the officer's boots. For a moment their eyes met and there was a silent understanding. The cat jumped up into his lap and cuddled there, happily.

A firm deep voice came from the dark. "Allow me to approach, sir."

Seraphimov peered into the darkness, but saw only the silhouette of a tall strapping man. "Permission granted. Step into the light."

The man approached the yellowish light of the oil lamp rather diffidently. Vladimir Seraphimov looked hard at the face, and a fleeting smile crossed his lips, "Ah, the jail bird. Marrin...Dannail Marrin, if I am not mistaken."

The young man looked at him with surprise. "You remembered!"

"Of course, I remember," said Seraphimov a bit impatiently, "What kind of commander would I be if I didn't remember the names of my soldiers?"

"I am not your soldier, sir," Danco protested.

"Then what are you?" demanded Seraphimov.

"That's exactly what I'd like to know, sir."

"Has someone told you that you are too hardnosed for a private?"

"No, sir."

"I don't blame them," laughed Seraphimov. "With those awesome muscles of yours not many would dare to tell you the truth to your face. The orderly told me you had some papers to be signed."

Danco dropped his head and shifted his weight from one leg to the other. His voice was almost inaudible. "I don't. The officer on duty signed them the day I was brought here."

"So you lied. Why?"

Now Dannail looked straight into the colonel's eyes without any trace of embarrassment. "They wouldn't let me see you, sir."

"Why is it so important that you see me, in particular?"

"Because I like you, sir. There is nothing in the whole world I would not do for you."

Seraphimov was aghast. "I like you too. That's why you are here. I trust you. If you don't measure up to my expectations, my reputation could suffer considerably."

The young man stuck out his mighty chest. "You don't have to worry about that, sir. Just give me a chance. I know every inch of this area like my own pocket...and I hate the Turks."

Seraphimov looked at his open good looking face, long and hard.

"We'll see about that. Did you have a rank in the nizam?"

"Corporal, sir."

"Yes...I asked you about it at our first chance meeting." The officer stroked the sleeping cat's head thoughtfully, "You realize that I cannot give you the equivalent rank in our army...though there might be a solution: I have no orderly. Would that be good for you?"

Dannail's face lit up as if he had just been promised the riches of the padishah. "Yessss, sirrr, Colonel!!!"

"All right. In that case, go to the sergeant major and tell him to give you brand new clothes and boots. Take Gancho with you. I don't have to tell him. He's listening at the door anyway."

Danco, all flushed, shifted again nervously from one foot to the other.

"What's wrong now?" asked Seraphimov with a frown.

"I have a girl in the village of Progled," he mumbled. "May I go see her after I get the new uniform?"

Seraphimov didn't laugh, but his eyes became soft and relaxed as they had not been for days.

"Yes, by all means, go and see her. We might not come back to this area for months...who knows? A soldier's life. Now go, you'll have all day tomorrow off."

"Yes, sir!" shouted Danco, snapping a perfect salute. The next moment he was gone.

From the landing above, Colonel Nedelev roared with laughter. "You might just be right, Seraphimov. That guy is something else. It would have been a shame to keep him in prison and away from the front. He is a born warrior."

Hidden behind a clump of pine trees, Danco had watched the slim figure of the girl for ten minutes. Clad in his new uniform, clean shaven and well rested, he looked like a different man, though something strange held him back, a nagging feeling that something had changed within Rossitza. She stood straight, motionless, gazing at the zigzagging road, her hands clenched to her breast, as if listening to some music deep within herself. That was a lonely spot with a fallen pine tree across the uneven banks of a swift and noisy stream.

Danco slipped closer to get a better look at her face. Close to the bed of the stream he crouched down, restraining the storm raging within him, feasting his eyes on the sight of her in silent adoration. The heavy braids of honey gold hair, the tender outline of her profile, and those big amber eyes and tiny golden freckles under them…and… that little nose of hers with such sensitive nostrils trembling from her own tumult…the mouth slightly open, lips forming a gleaming rosebud…

He could wait no longer. A quick jump over the stream took him right in front of her. Rossitza cried out, startled, stepping back.

Danco smiled broadly, throwing his arms open. "Don't be scared, my darling! I am not coming from the nether world."

She came to him slowly as if afraid that he might disappear any moment.

"Danco! You are alive? Am I dreaming?"

"Why not try me, my love?" he said, still aching to hold her.

She nearly collapsed in his powerful arms. "Where did you come from?"

"Not from the grave, as you can see. Am I not hot enough for you? I was hiding because I wanted to see you first."

She locked her still trembling hands behind his sturdy neck. "You...waylay man...have me...have all of me! Then, even if you go again, I'll be forever yours!"

Time had no value for them anymore. Neither one knew if it was night or day. They were blind to the beautiful surroundings—the dark blue sky covered with the broken lace of the white feathered clouds. All was wasted on them. They could not even hear the distant fusillade from the outpost on Carramandga.

When they were back to themselves, Danco set her tenderly on the fine carpet of new grass and told her all his story. She listened rapturously to him, wide eyes, following him as he spoke of the long years in this fabulous city of Tzarygrad, known to her only from songs and fairy tales, a foreign city of strange customs and untold riches. His description of violent encounters didn't abate her admiration, though it left her breathless, eyes full of both fright and pride.

Her story was that much poorer. She began at the time she had seen him last, before going to Istanbul. She didn't leave anything out, every single detail was there. Where they met, the way he was clothed...her father's blind, fanatic hatred. A Mohammedan! A Turkish soldier! A guard of the most despicable ruler on earth!!! Bastard to his own fatherland! She had suffered, too. She confided in him about the endless hours of solitude and the haunting dreams of mostly sleepless nights. She told of days at the isolated farm while Danco was far away, and there was not a living soul around to trust with her love. No, there was one—a young flute player, Ermin. He was able to understand it all, even the singing of the birds.

When she finished, she was awash with tears.

"Don't cry, dear heart. Here we are together again," Danco pressed her closer to himself, "Don't trouble your heart over the past."

"I can't help it, Danco. It's just how I feel."

"All right then, have my shoulder." He felt the convulsions of her most-desired body gradually calm down, relieved of the burden of what she had been feeling, a wave of relief took its place. "Oh, Danco, Danco…"

The young man felt the same effect, but was concerned with something much different.

"That guy," he mumbled, "The flute player, I mean… was he appealing to you? Was he big and handsome?"

"Oh, Danco!"

"Was he giving you all this music just for the hell of it? Damn it! Was he in love with you? And where can I find him for a little chat?"

With tears still running down her cheeks, Rossitza laughed, bringing back memories of that swift laughter she'd had in the past. "For all your size and muscles, you are still a child, Danco. My love for you was so overwhelming, even if he was in love with me, I would not have known about it."

Danco crushed her to his starved body, kissing her with all that fiery thirst stored for the two long years they spent apart.

Suddenly, the pounding of hooves crashing pell-mell through the branches forced them brutally from their embrace. They hardly had time to leap up before a horse and rider were upon them.

The face of Rossitza's father was distorted with disbelief and astonishment. His eyes bulged and his jaw dropped. He stared at Dannail and Rossitza as if he were seeing ghosts. Slowly he was able to grasp the reality. Red splotches burned his rough cheeks as crimson rage possessed him.

"So...they were right. You...you...Turkish bastard... You are back!" he yelled, instinctively groping for his rifle across his back. Dannail beat him to the punch as his hands were already swiftly handling his new carbine.

"I wouldn't try if I were you, *Bay* Gorane," he said in a cool and detached voice.

"You've escaped, mangy cur...hell's fire! Why didn't I finish you on the spot before! Why did I have to listen to those crazy people?" he bellowed, baleful eyes nailed to the impassive face of the youth behind the steady barrel, "Why didn't I kill her to cure her for good of that shameful passion of hers?"

His initial wrath, however, had suffered an obvious setback. Something like sobbing cut his harsh biting voice. More people came up behind him, curious eyes staring at the young couple. Someone shouted impudently, "Give 'em your blessing, *bubayco*! Anyway, that lad is going to be your son-in-law."

"Soften your heart," added someone else, "see what a nice couple they make, *Bay* Gorane."

Rossitza's father bit his lips until he drew blood from them. "Are you going out of your minds!?! Give my only daughter to a traitor to the Christian faith and his own native land? Is that what you're asking me to do, people?"

"Are you blind? He's in the Bulgarian Army now. Look at his uniform!"

Dannail came forward and extended his hand to the angry man. "Let's forget the past, *bubayco*. Tomorrow, I might be killed. Look at my good side."

"Go to hell!" shrieked Goran Podgorsky.

Now Rossitza joined Danco.

"Please, father! In mother's name, if you ever loved her, say yes!"

All eyes were centered on him, pleading, hopeful, while he saw nothing but his daughter. He was transfixed, ugly. His face grew frightful to see. Beastly. Full of desperation.

"Like mother, like daughter. Never! Never! Over my dead body! Damnation to both of you! Be damned! Damned forever!" He urged his steed ahead and rode off.

On the third day of the war, the fort at Carramandga fell. The same gunner battalion that destroyed Rhojen, Kallachboroun and Couroucalle on Mount Saint Georghy, now moved their cannons to the opposite hill, almost into enemy territory, and with several precise hits had set the building on fire. It burned all through the night, sporadic explosions sending up debris and sparks in the air. The entire population of the nearby villages gathered up on the hills to enjoy the fireworks. The Turks had stored enough ammunition to keep the entertainment going until the early morning hours.

Meanwhile, the whole regiment started moving in two main directions. The first brigade with colonel Nedelev and Vladimir Seraphimov, toward Smollian; the second one advancing toward the village of Arda.

The hills and the roads were free.

One thing was obvious. The number of dead Turks was far greater than the regular army had killed. Some of the corpses were badly mutilated, a sure sign that a personal vendetta had taken place. There was not the slightest manifestation of organized resistance. The Turks had retreated in a riot. Only days ago they were beating their chests with declarations that on the next day, they'd be drinking coffee in Plovdiv, the largest city of Bulgaria. Those same heroes abandoned their positions even before there were any Bulgarian soldiers in sight.

The Ottoman Empire was based on the courage and strength of its Great Army. There is no doubt about the heroic exploits and victories of its men. But what had happened? The Empire had lost touch with everything natural and vital to Islam, and was constructed entirely of fragments of the nations heretofore enslaved by its power. Now all of those nations were claiming their freedom.

On the other hand, the Empire had nothing to offer its own people but systematic acquisition and plunder. The "Holy War" had degenerated into small scale skirmishes and massacres. There was nothing holy left to die for, and people were unwilling to die without a cause.

And that precisely, was the strength of the small and badly equipped Bulgarian Army. People were willing to die for freedom. They were fighting the ignoble Turkish yoke—peasants with new found strength, beating their plow shares into swords. That was their battle of Sempach.

"Make way for liberty!" he cried,
made way for liberty…and died.

The spirit of Arnold de Winkleried had come to the Rhodopian Mountains. It's small wonder that in the centuries-long fight for freedom that small Balkan country had created more known and unknown heroes than any other nation in the same period of time.

Chapter Five

The meeting of the Bulgarian troops in the liberated region was extremely touching. Church bells peeled, men and women wept with joy and pushed their kids forward to see "our own soldiers." There were long processions meeting the army at the liberated villages. At the head, carried by an old man, was a silver church tray containing bread and salt for the traditional welcome. Then the local priest said a prayer and blessed the flag. The village mayor, choked by tears, kissed it. Then the army troops and the whole congregation joined in singing patriotic songs and hymns. The troops showed themselves at their best, too. Only in one village, the bread served was so dark that one of the officers exclaimed, without thinking, "How can one eat this black mess?" The soldiers around him threw him dirty looks, and one of them said, "You'll eat it, sir, and you might ask for more if you're hungry." The officer bit his tongue and got lost in the crowd.

After the official ceremony there was a hearty meal on a field by the village where everyone brought what he had actually saved from the Turks. Food, wine and *rakia* (the strong peasant brandy) were never short. More often than not there was the traditional *cheverme*, roasted lamb and *banitza*, a kind of strudel filled with feta cheese. After the meal, people and troops milled around together. That was the time for Ermin's flute and *gayda* bagpipe players. The *chorro* dance chain, hand-in-hand, sometimes grew a mile long and the young soldiers' hearts started beating stronger than the drums whenever they happened to be dancing next to a pretty girl. There was the swift *rutchenitza* for the best dancers, a sort of marathon dance to see who would last longer, the girl or the boy.

There were stone throwing competitions and wrestling. That's where Danco excelled and made himself known throughout the brigade. The soldiers' pride in Radco's unit was piqued by the fact that a stranger, from out of nowhere, was able to run over all their champs. It was decided that, in spite of his youth, Radco Boev was the only one that had a chance to win. He was quick as a weasel and knew how to use not only his muscles, but his brain as well. Only that powerful combination could bring the domination of the stranger to a halt. Ermin was against it and pleaded with his young friend to stay away from the giant, but Radco's ambitious nature and fighting spirit were ignited by the faith his comrades had for him, and he challenged the older youth.

Fortunately, there weren't any serious injuries, but a few minor bruises that Radco Boev had to put up with along with his battered self-confidence and slightly tarnished record. But in the end, he did not regret his defeat at all.

Danco generously offered a hand to help Radco up. "You made me sweat, young brother. What's your name?"

The youth took Danco's hand and struggled to his feet grimacing. "Radoul Boev from Progled, but my friends call me Radco. And what is yours?"

The young man looked at him seriously. "Danco... Dannail Marrin from Derrekioy."

Ermin was relieved.

Lieutenant Colonel Seraphimov's new orderly had found two friends for life. From that day on, Danco, Ermin and Radco were inseparable.

Though, fate had its own games.

The hallway was poorly lit in the direction the voice came from, and Ellena's tired eyes tried to adjust. No, she didn't know the face. She went on toward the volunteer nurses room to change, when the same voice followed her again, "Madame Seraphimova!"

Ellena stopped at the door and turned back. It had been a long, tiring day—the first load of wounded from Rhojen had arrived and there was much to be done in the new wing. Everyone talked about the upcoming war, but not as reality. Very few thought of offering themselves as Red Cross volunteers. Most of the women recoiled at the idea of treating wounded soldiers, and felt that there were enough doctors and professional nurses. There won't be that many wounded anyway; it was going to be a short war, at least that's what everyone believed. *But to treat enemy soldiers*—that was way beyond their grasp.

Ellena tried to explain to her befuddled audience of indignant matrons that the whole idea of the worldwide organization of the Red Cross was a noble one—to protect and care for *all* casualties—to help everybody in need. That seemed to them to be unpatriotic, if not suspicious, but if she cared that much, there were a few old barracks at the back of the hospital. Madame Seraphimova could open a new wing there if some of the doctors and nurses donated their time. It remained highly doubtful that any of the ladies would volunteer to care for those filthy Turks.

When the first transport arrived, there were twelve Bulgarians and eighty-three Turks. In the hospital rooms, all the professional staff and fifty lady volunteers took care of the few Bulgarians. For the Turks, there was one doctor, two nurses and three volunteers. The two women, besides Ellena, were retired teachers from a high school, quite reliable, but tiring fast. The medications and instruments for that part of the hospital were thrown in as an afterthought. Most of the needles and syringes were too dull and unsanitary to be used on human beings—so much for the humanitarian impulse of the "society" of Plovdiv. Ellena had a difficult time just finding beds for all those young men who seemed to be grateful just to have a roof over their heads. Many were surprised that someone was taking care of them at all. There was a painful look in their eyes, as if at any moment they expected someone to accuse them of being the enemy, to punish them for that. The ladies, smiling and kind, were a miracle sent to them in their misery by Allah Himself—a blessing they felt they didn't deserve at all. Many of them were fluent in Bulgarian, and they wouldn't stop repeating how grateful they were until Madame Seraphimova , in her sweet way, forbade them to talk, "Just rest now…and everything will be okay."

But everything wasn't okay. She was dog tired. Now another of the society ladies was about to reproach her for wasting her time on their enemy the Turks. She turned to face the woman with a sigh. Instead, she gasped. It was Sultana!

"I am sorry; we have never been introduced to each other and it's entirely my husband's fault. He knows Colonel Seraphimov very well, but always seems to find some pretext for putting off our meeting. Now that you are in charge of this wing, I will introduce myself." She extended her hand with natural cordiality, "My name is Sultana Hadgylvanova. If you accept me, I'd like to work with you as a volunteer."

Ellena was speechless.

Ferdinand 1st, King of Bulgaria, was often at his desk as early as seven o'clock a.m. in the little room at the south end of the palace. He used to call it his "working den." There were many important telegrams from the past night he had not read, and still other urgent papers for signature. His young secretary stood at attention at the door, covering a large stain on his breeches with a portfolio. He had spilled coffee on them when the monarch rang for him. Ferdinand had that quality of making everybody around him nervous and jumpy. Now he looked over his shoulder and arched his eyebrows. "You still here, Symo? What is the matter?" he demanded.

"General Robev is waiting in the ante chamber and so is the Minister of Justice."

"Oh, I remember. Let the general in."

Robev came in, a dazzling smile on his handsome face. "Good morning, Your Majesty."

"Good morning, good morning, Robev. You should be an actor in vaudeville. I've never seen such a good stage entrance. Did you bring me the materials?"

"It's all in this folder, Your Majesty" replied the general.

"All right. You have my attention."

The young general filled his lungs with air like a prep school student preparing to recite a poem in the presence of the dean.

"Wait a minute," the Tzar cut in with a scornful little smile at the corners of his mouth, "call the Minister of Justice. He should not miss the show."

The old man came in, bowing lowly.

"That's all right, Hadgylvanov. Listen to what Robev has to say about the Turkish atrocities found by our Army during the liberation of Pashmakly and vicinity. I want it to be heard throughout the world—and especially by my cousin, the King of England, who harbors a rather soft spot for our enemies. Sit down. The general is young. He can stand."

They listened for a quarter of an hour to his tale of people tortured to death, eyes gouged, noses and ears cut off, hands in disemboweled stomachs—unbelievable cruelties for which Turks are known throughout history. When the reading was over, Ferdinand took the file and put it on his desk.

"Give the minister a copy, Robev. By tomorrow morning, I want the whole Army to know about this. Exhibit the cadavers and let the available troops file in to see the martyrs. Same with the local population. Spontaneous meetings afterwards. Speeches. Show them some of the captured Turkish officers. Blame the Padishah and Islam in particular. Let them know it's a shame to be a Muslim. Instruct the Christian priests to treat the martyrs for Christendom like saints. As soon as we liberate the mountain area, we will start a campaign of converting the Bulgaro-Muslims to Christianity. Hadgylvanov, talk on that matter to the Saint-Sinnode, and the representative of the Patriarch. For the time being keep the campaign quiet from the world at large. Let the newspapers prepare public opinion all over Europe. We'll make the *Sick Man* even sicker, leading him forcefully to imminent death."

Ferdinand was referring to the Turkish Empire, which, at all international conference tables, was referred to as "the sick man." It was feared that the steady disintegration would start a chain reaction through the entire continent and around the globe. The crafty plan of the Bulgarian Tzar was to create a powerful new empire, built on the ruins of the old one to keep the balance. He imagined this state to spill not only over the Turkish boundaries, but extend across the Balkans as well. This made him Enemy Number Two, after the Padishah, to all local monarchs. Above all else, they did not want to see him emperor, and they secretly prepared for his downfall.

"Send copies of this report to my brothers, the Kings of Greece, Serbia and Romania," the Tzar commanded.

General Robev bowed and left immediately. The Tzar looked at Hadgylvanov with a flicker of mockery in his eyes. "I heard your wife went to Plovdiv—with your permission, I presume."

The old man evaded the Tzar's quizzical eyes.

"Yes…of course," he said in a feeble voice, "General Robev's spouse is her second cousin. They love each other dearly."

"But the General's wife is here with him," remarked Ferdinand.

The wrinkled face blushed slightly, drops of sweat dripping down. "She is, Your Majesty, naturally," he stammered pitifully, "She…Sultana, I mean, is using the premises. She'll be back shortly."

The monarch leaned back in his chair with a dry laugh. "Not too shortly, I believe. For the time being, she's enlisted as a volunteer nurse in the Alexandrov Hospital."

The minister made a miserable effort to smile.

"That's enough for today, Hadgylvanov. You can go," Ferdinand said dismissively and turned to his desk.

The Great Padishah—Sultan of all Turks, Sovereign of the United Empire and Commander-in-Chief of the Invincible Army—had the flu. He felt absolutely miserable and lay on the huge bed tending a stuffy nose and sore throat. He had little fever, but the aching in his bones was driving him crazy. His sallow complexion combined with his lean and leathery face, was never much to look at, now his expression of helplessness and boredom made it unbearable.

Standing on their aching feet in a semi-circle, for the last half hour or so, were the Great Vizier, Yaver Pasha, Avzy Bey and the British Ambassador. The weak squeaky voice of the Sultan sounded plaintive. "I don't understand, effendilar. Are you trying to tell me that our Army in the Rhodopy Mountain is in retreat?"

The Minister of War, who was half hiding behind the shapely figure of Avzy Bey, shifted nervously and muttered, "Worse, Great Master. Our troops are fleeing. If the enemy had not stopped pursuing them for some unknown reason, the Bulgarians would've been by now in the White Sea area"

The Sultan looked at all their faces helplessly; then suddenly started shouting—out of control and void of common sense. The shrieking voice produced the same effect of scraping a fork over a china plate. The luminaries around him felt it in their teeth and made sour grimaces.

"Well, do something! Don't stand around like idiots!"

The British Ambassador coughed.

"Oh, never mind, Ambassador. The Queen ought to do something, too."

"The Queen, I am afraid, can do very little, Your Majesty," the Ambassador uttered in disbelief, "She has been dead for a long time. We have a king now."

"Whoever is on the throne. I don't care. Do you expect me to go and fight the rebels in person? I am sick. Besides I don't think it's your wish to see the Bulgarians in here. Their friend, the Kaiser, would be delighted. But you'll never see the Bosporus or the Dardanelles again. So it's your problem. That's what my father used to say, and he was never wrong."

The English Ambassador, Lord Covington swallowed his mounting anger but said nothing. Now the little man in the bed was shrieking again at Yaver Pasha. "You go in person. Take all the troops and go."

"With Your Majesty's permission, we have trouble in Asia Minor and more still with Italy and Greece. A lot of our forces were trapped by the Bulgarians at Odrin. The Army in the White Sea Region is in bad condition…"

The Sultan interrupted, "I couldn't care less! That's your problem. Take all the troops from Istanbul! Take my guards…no…don't take my guards. I need them. Draw up all the papers you need and I'll sign them. Now go, all of you. I have no friends. So, attend to your business and leave me alone!"

The men looked at each other and began filing out. "You, Avzy Bey, stay here!" screeched the Sultan.

Avzy Bey approached His Majesty's bed and kneeled down.

When they were alone, his master said gruffly, "I have a headache."

"I am sorry to hear that, Great Master. Shall I send for a doctor?"

"No doctors! They only want to poison me with their good-for-nothing medicines. My government is giving me the headache. They all want me to die. At the time of my Great Father, heads would've been rolling by the score. But now, with this new silly set of laws, I can do nothing. I cannot cut off even one single head without the approval of I don't know how many sonofabitches…" he burst into a coughing fit, wriggling pitifully under the silk covers. When the fit abated, he added mournfully, "… that's why everything goes to the dogs. The British insisted on making the Christians equal to us, and now the slaves are rioting while their Ambassador shrugs his shoulders and loads everything on me."

"I wish I could help, Great Master," mumbled Avzy Bey servilely, touching the floor with his forehead.

The Sultan was silent for a few moments, then suddenly his exhausted face became animated.

"Go, find that big young soldier of my guards with those blue eyes and shiny forelock that falls like a wing over them…that Marrin, or…you know. I remember him very well. Don't look at me like an idiot. The one that took the championship last spring. Make him wrestle my new African bodyguard. Let 'em maul each other to death!"

For awhile, Avzy Bey was at a complete loss. Finally he banged his head on the marble floor and wailed, "I don't know what happened to that man, Great Master… he never came back. He has disappeared."

The Sultan's mouth twisted with bitterness. "Don't quail, Avzy Bey. I almost forgot. I have no friends. Men don't disappear nowadays. They simply run away. Get out of here. I want to be left alone."

Sultana's presence in the prisoners' ward proved incalculable. She was born and raised in Ksanty, the only daughter of a very rich merchant. The city was populated partly by Greeks, the Bulgarians made up another substantial part and the Turks, although fewer, were the dominant group. At this time, the whole White Sea region was ruled rather evenhandedly by a governor appointed by the sultan. These three groups living peacefully together enabled the children in Ksanty to speak three languages fluently.

Madame Hadgylvanova was disciplined and a fast learner. The young men instantly fell in love with her and were ready to do anything just to please her. Besides her personal charms, Sultana was extremely wealthy, thanks to her father. Since her arrival, there were no shortages of anything that money could buy. Ellena didn't know what she would have done without her. Sultana had hired two private doctors and five nurses and, as someone who was well placed in Catholic circles, had recruited a few nuns who were doing a great job.

That night, as usual, Ellena Seraphimova was late. The rain fell in a real downpour. In this weather, all the roads around the barracks turned into swamps. She was watching the falling rain helplessly when Sultana's phaeton pulled up in front.

"Come with me, Madame Seraphimova," said the young woman cheerfully, and she took Ellena by the arm, "we'll share your umbrella to the cab, and take my phaeton to your house. Is that a deal?"

As a greatly relieved Ellena struggled to open her umbrella, one of the nuns hurried in.

"Le jeun Ahmed va mourir, Madame Sultana. Il vous en prie de venir!"

"I'll come with you," said Ellena and the three of them ran down the corridor. Ahmed's bed was in the furthest room next to the window. When he saw them coming, a tired smile lingered over his bluish lips for a moment. He was a lean, seventeen-year-old boy from the far away region of Smollian, whose abdominal wound had turned worse. The doctor stepped back and Sultana sat on the edge of his bed.

"My, my." whispered Ahmed, "Madame Seraphimova too...what an honor! Tell her Allah will pay her and her whole family...for...everything she's done for us..."

"I'll tell her, Ahmed, don't worry."

The pale, still boyish face tightened, hiding his pain manfully with clenched teeth and tense jaw.

"Will you write a letter...to my family in the Castle of Moguilitza?"

"Yes, Ahmed. I will."

"Write in Turkish...my grandpa and uncle don't read Bulgarian."

"I'll write in Turkish, Ahmed."

"Tell 'em...I was a good soldier...only I don't know why I have to die...it was such a short time...it was like yester...day..." His voice became inaudible.

The rain drummed on the roof of the phaeton. The two women rode in complete silence all the way to Ellena's residence. When the cab stopped at the gate, Ellena put her hand on the shoulder of her companion. "Come with me, Sultana. Let's have a cup of tea together."

Assen met them at the door. "The children are in bed. Miss Rayna is reading in her room." He took the umbrella and the wet mantles.

"Very good, Assen. Is there any hot tea in the kitchen?"

"Yes, ma'am, your supper is ready."

"Supper for two, Assen. And tell Miss Rayna to join us in the parlor."

"I'm sorry, ma'am, the parlor hasn't been heated for days. It's damp," Assen advised.

"In the living room then," she said as she waved him away.

"Yes, ma'am." Assen bowed slightly as left the room.

The living room was warm and cozy. Ellena motioned her guest to one of the chairs at the table.

"We move a lot...you know, *famme d'un officier*. Everything is mismatched," Ellena apologized.

Sultana sat down with a short sigh. "It's a home. May I call you Ellena?"

"I'd like that very much."

"I'll remember this, Ellena. Of course, Colonel Seraphimov doesn't have to know about it."

Ellena blushed and took both her hands into her own. "Colonel Seraphimov will come out of this war much wiser, as will we all."

Rayna was surprised to find them in such intimacy. For a moment she felt like leaving, but her mother was quick enough to notice her. "And this is my eldest daughter, Rayna."

At the village of Ustovo, the rain became so heavy that Vladimir Seraphimov issued an order to the regiment to gather at the central square. Nedelev, with a bad head cold, came up from behind with a train of oxcarts carrying the ammunition. The mayor and the priest of the village met the troops with real enthusiasm. Ustovo was large and there was room for everyone.

Seraphimov, with forty of his soldiers, was taken into the spacious house of a cloth merchant. There was plenty of hot food for the hungry men in the kitchen; the tables were improvised from planks and kegs in the basement. A supper for the commander and his officers was served in the huge parlor on the second floor. Colonel Nedelev waived the invitation and retired after a light meal. Seraphimov presided at the dinner table and spoke to the local notables in the adjoining room after the meal.

There were also the children of the family, fascinated by the glittering medals on the chest of the commander. They had never before even seen a picture of a Bulgarian officer, though taught by their father that everything Bulgarian was the best in the world, now for the first time, they had a real test of it.

Late in the night Vladimir Seraphimov retired to his room, exhausted. He had just undressed when Danco knocked at his door. It was a message with an urgent dispatch. Headquarters had gotten information about movement of a Turkish army in the direction of the village of Arda. He was ordered to send a detachment to check the credibility of this message.

"Dannail, you told me, if my memory serves me, that you know this area like your own pocket."

"Yes, sir!"

"When I freed you, I risked my reputation as an officer. I have been watching you very closely—even if you were not aware of it. My first impression proved to be right. Tonight, I am going to entrust you with the fate, not only of a regiment, but of all the people we have liberated since the beginning of the war. This is the supreme test. If you fail in any way, I'll be accused of harboring a spy. That means a military tribunal."

Danco paled. "I won't fail, sir."

Seraphimov paced the room several times before facing him again. "Something tells me that you're the best one for this mission, but I'll have to find someone that could replace you in case anything happens..." the colonel pondered.

"How 'bout two more, sir," suggested Danco.

"You have somebody in mind?" asked the colonel, eyebrows raised.

"Yes, sir. Corporal Ermin Droumev and Private Radco Boev," stated Danco while saluting.

Seraphimov smiled.

"Ahh, I think I know exactly who you are suggesting. Isn't Radco a bit too young for such a task? Maybe in this particular case his youth is a plus. We are not supposed to tolerate cronyism in the army, but under the circumstances, the end justifies the means. Take your buddies along." He began getting back into his full uniform. "The forty men downstairs are all handpicked cavalrymen. You ride with them to Arda. From that point on, you are on your own—you and those pals of yours. The soldiers will be waiting for you in the village. I have information that Arda is in no-man's land. They'll organize the Bulgarian population there without antagonizing the Mohammedans. I'll give those instructions to officer Sabev. Be sure that he follows them. He's a bit too temperamental.

Keep him cool, and don't get into a scrap with him. Let's go," he commanded as he stepped into his boots.

They went to the basement to awaken the men. The soldiers dressed in a hurry, grunting and swearing under their breath. The main cause of their complaints were the soaking wet foot wrappings. *Bay* Ivan Sullinadgiev, the owner of the house, heard the racket and came to see what was going on. When the boys took him into their confidence and told him about the wet wrappings, he ordered his elder sons to take down more than ten bales of fine cloth from the shelves and cut two yards of new wrapings for everyone. When Seraphimov finished instructing Sergeant Sabev and saw the exceptional generosity of their host, he took him in his arms and said, "If one in every hundred out here is like you, *Bay* Ivan, it makes sense to die for freedom, even to the very last one of us."

At parting, he gave Danco his full instructions and a small envelope that had the light fragrance of expensive perfume.

"Find a trusted person to deliver it to this address. Be discreet! It's in enemy's territory," said the commander, as he made the sign of the cross over him.

The outfit ambled along in silence, while a steady freezing rain drove through the bodies of the men hunched on their saddles. Through the incessant sound of falling rain, even an occasional clip-clop of hooves was hard to detect. A mud-spattered and soaked Danco rode side by side with Sergeant Sabev, with Ermin and Radco closely following them and the rest came trailing behind single file. The road, dangerous enough to follow in daylight, was almost impassable in the grayish mist of dawn. Only Danco's uncanny sense of direction kept them moving around muddy holes and edges of the road eroded by the torrents. The sergeant riding next to him thought Danco had second sight. He would lead the column around a treacherous place even when nothing was detected by the under officer. That maddened him, yet at the same time, caused him to admire the strange lad chosen by the commander to lead this special mission.

The river, swollen by heavy rain, was roaring on one side of them. Even though it was almost nine in the morning, visibility was still very poor. The distance to the village could not be too far at this point—they had to cross the bridge, then Arda was just around the hill. Suddenly, Danco made a sign to dismount. They walked the horses to the bend in the road, Where they had a clear view of the bridge. Sergeant Sabev swore almost out loud. A small Turkish detachment was preparing to dynamite the old structure.

Ismail threw the butt of his cigarette over the rail of the bridge and looked worriedly at his father. In the past three weeks the old soldier had grown visibly older.

On a day like this, thought the youth furiously as he listened to the hollow coughing eating his father's chest, a man of his age should be at home next to a hot stove. Outwardly he said, "Go to that shack, babba. I'll finish the bridge."

The old officer smiled feebly. "The place of an officer is with his soldiers, son. Don't try to order me around. We're far from home."

Ismail groped for a cigarette, but realized he had smoked the last one, making him even more nervous. An eerie premonition had haunted him since daybreak; the rain, probably. Anyway they were ready, the corporal was giving him the sign to clear the bridge.

Suddenly he was aware of some moving objects behind the rocks. Bushes? Animals? People with guns aiming at them! Before he had time to give a warning shout, there was a deafening report and most of the soldiers fell with short screams of surprise and pain. His father had both his hands pressed to his stomach. Blood streamed through the heavy coat and Arrif Agha slipped along the rail. Ismail hurled himself toward him.

"I should have sent patrols...I..." the old man groaned, choking on his own blood. Even at the last moment, he blamed himself. Death came over him like a dark wing...just a short sigh and then nothingness. His father's end galvanized Ismail into action. He had to live and kill, kill...kiiilll! Men were running toward him. He grabbed his rifle, aimed. The first one, the very first of those murderers to pay for...

The first one running was Radco! Ismail's finger froze on the trigger, paralyzed, then it was too late. They would capture him alive! With a loud shriek, he leaped over the rail into the icy waters that grabbed his body in a beastly grip. Right after him, another body plunged.

"Radcooo...nooo...Radcooo!!!" shouted Ermin in despair, leaning over the rail.

"Away, away from the bridge!" Danco yelled as he witnessed all this in the space of an instant, and as a Turk started the fuse to the explosive under the bridge. His voice did not seem to carry through the roaring of the water. None of the Bulgarians, hypnotized as they watched the struggle of the two bodies in the whirling waves, moved from the rail. There were at least six of them besides Ermin. Danco dashed toward the bridge when a hot blast threw him back to the ground.

In the raging water, Radco had secured a grip around Ismail's neck and shoulders and desperately tried to drag him out.

"You killed my father!" shouted the young Turk at the top of his lungs, wriggling to loosen Radco's hold, "Murderer! Murderer! What has he ever done...to you? Leave me alone...get your dirty hands off...me...I swear to Allah...I'll kill 'ya, Christian!"

Remnants of the bridge hung precariously on a single beam. Ermin's body was doubled over it, loud moaning coming from his bloodied mouth. Like a cat, Danco walked on the beam, swaying over the stormy river, and half dragging, half carrying Ermin, reached firm ground just a moment before the whole structure collapsed into the raging water. Ermin was silent. Under the driving rain his white face seemed to emanate a strange light. A pang broke into Danco's chest. He leaned over him, almost touching his forehead with his face.

"Ermin! Ermin!"

Ermin's lips trembled. There was a prolonged groan, then his bloody lips formed a name.

"Rossitza…"

The village of Arda had been free for a whole week. The fleeing Turkish troops just passed through. Though the police force representing the central government was still there, the villagers had thrown out the sultan's officials and had elected their own mayor, Nickola Vassilev. The policemen kept a low profile, but stayed on. At the outbreak of the war, the young Bulgarian portion of the men mobilized in the army made believe that they were going to the district town; instead they went into the hills above the village to protect against marauding Turks.

Five miles away there was a small community of several hamlets named Catoun. Those people were well known in the area as cutthroats and brigands. Lately, they had been sending messages through passing travelers that they'd soon come to set fire to Arda and take away the pretty girls. The *chetta*, civilian military, armed themselves by disarming the fleeing regular soldiers. Their leader, Tenyo Dimitrov, sent a message to the warlord of Catoun, Sadak Bey, that they were ready to take on his bastards.

Meanwhile, the youngest brother of the mayor, Gavrail, went to town with the list of new recruits and presented it to the commanding officer. When the officer asked where his people were, the young man pointed to the courtyard full of Muslims. After he was complimented for the good service, he left the barracks and joined his brother and the *chetta*. In the morning, when they went to arrest the policemen, they found the building had been vacated during the night. The Turks had taken the telephones and fled to Catoun.

The people of the village rejoiced. There was no end to the festivities. The windpipes played day and night accompanying the dancing and drinking that prevailed all over the village. Freedom...after five centuries of Turkish yoke! Only one thing bothered them. Though the cannonade from Rhojen and Carramandga was heard for days, no sign of Bulgarian troops had been seen in the vicinity. The rain came and some gloomy feelings with it. What if...

Mayor Nickola decided to visit the fabulously rich family of the Aggushevs in nearby Moguilitza. He happened to be a very close friend of the younger son. The huge portals of the castle opened to him and he was brought to the two powerful landlords. They were brothers, each one of them pushing the mid-eighties— with long, silver beards, white turbans and robes, like ancient genies out of the *Arabian Nights*, they pulled at their water pipes with impassivity.

The mayor bowed. "Chock selliam, wise men."

"Chock selliam to you, son," answered the oldest, "my son, Metyo Bey, told us you are now the commander in Arda. Afferim, Nickolcho effendi!"

"It's good to know," added the other one, "that an intelligent and just person is ruling next door at a time like this."

"Sit down with us, Nickolcho effendi," said the older brother, and ordered the servants to bring coffee, *tantoura* and sweets to the dear guest.

"Thank you, effendilar," smiled Nickola Vassilev, sitting cross-legged on the soft pillows. "Hard times have really come when a good neighbor means more than wealth."

The brandy served him was old with a touch of honey in it.

"For two hundred years," the older man spoke out again, adjusting the golden rimmed dark glasses that covered his blind eyes, "our villages have been living in peace and understanding. Our Allah and your Christian God have helped to bring prosperity and earthly riches to everybody. Now new rulers have taken over in Stanbul and Sofia and suddenly the world has become too small for them to live together in peace," he sighed.

Tears glistened in the eyes of his younger brother, who spoke in a shaken voice, "The treasure of our lives, the joy and light of our old days, young Ahmed, was taken by the Army. He is not even eighteen. We were unable to stop him from going. His pride wouldn't let him hide under the protection of our money and connections. Our only grandson! Only Allah knows if we'll ever see him again."

Nickola put his hand on the old man's knee. "God is great, Hadjy. He'll bring him back to you. But let us all stick together for good or bad. I give you my word. If the Bulgarians come to Moguilitza, as armies do, burning and rampaging, I'll stop them."

The older Bey took his hand gropingly. "If anything happens to Arda, the doors of our castle will be wide open for all the villagers, and let Allah be with us. Your enemies are our enemies."

Part Two

Heroics

BATTLEFIELD MAPS
Historic Maps Drawn by Colonel Vladimir Seraphimov

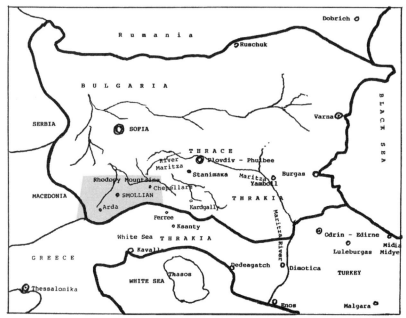

Because no accurate maps existed of Bulgaria, Col. Seraphimov pieced together the map above in mid-1912, about four months prior to First Balkan War. (Text names were typed-in later.) Grey area is detailed below.

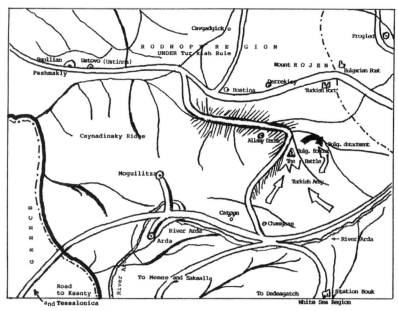

This battle-area map was sketched by Col. Seraphimov on his knee, in the fog, just before battle. His two maps differ because local sources gave him conflicting information. (Text names were added later.)

126

Chapter Six

anco was riding next to Sergeant Sabev.

"You know, Private Marrin," Sabev uttered through his teeth, trying to subdue his mounting rage, "you know that your reckless action endangered the whole mission, don't you?"

Danco struggled with his own kindling temper. "Yes, sir. But I couldn't have done anything else under the circumstances."

"You couldn't have, of course! I know your kind. You wanna run the outfit, don't you?"

"No, sir."

"Yes, you do. Well, I have a surprise for you. I am in charge of it and you stay where you belong, if you know what is good for you!" ordered Sabev gruffly.

Danco remembered what Colonel Seraphimov had told him, spat angrily and mumbled, his big fists clenched to a hurting point. "Yes, sir."

"Yes, sir...yes, sir," Sabev went on naggingly, "you know perfectly well that on a mission like this one does not take prisoners. What is that young Turk doing with us?"

Danco shrugged his shoulders. "He didn't get killed, he didn't drown either. Are we supposed to knife him to death?"

"He didn't drown because your cocky younger buddy saved him by risking his own life. I can understand doing that for a fellow Bulgarian, but for a filthy Turk! What kind of ethics does that soldier of ours have?" snarled the sergeant.

"Let's not talk about ethics," hissed Danco.

Sergeant Sabev's face became purple red. His thin moustache trembled with indignation. "In this outfit I decide what to talk about! Right?"

Danco bit his lips, the vein on his forehead throbbing heavily. "Right, sir."

The fog was getting thicker by the minute. Suddenly a strong, energetic voice shouted from behind the vague outlines of some small pine trees. "Dur asker! Evallah! Give up! You're surrounded!"

Sergeant Sabev froze. The order was in Turkish. Danco didn't waste any time. He answered flawlessly in the same language. "Shah-in-shallah, Sultan Asker! Glory to the Padishah, we are his soldiers!"

Ismail shrieked from the back, "Dushman asker, arcadash! Bulgar Asker! Enemy soldiers, friends! Bulgarians!"

The man from the pine trees exclaimed joyously in Bulgarian. "God bless you, brothers! We're the Bulgarian militia from Arda."

In a moment the two outfits were embracing and kissing each other. Tenyo Voyvoda was still shaken. "Just think...I almost gave a signal to the boys to open fire. Damn fog!"

Sergeant Sabev was mad. "I'll slash open the throat of that Turkish sonofabitch!"

Danco looked at him with scorn. "For what? For saving our lives?"

Even in the relentless rain the meeting of the first Bulgarian soldiers was triumphant. At the head of the procession were young students from the primary school in the village with their two pretty teachers, next the mayor, the priest and the school board, followed by the notables and the rest of the population of Arda.

Sergeant Sabev tried to explain that this was only a detachment, that the real army would come this way in a day or two, but the people laughed happily, telling him not to worry. They'd meet the Army as well, God bless them all.

This view of the Bulgarian cavaliers was one nobody had seen before. The nature of the terrain and the bad shape of the roads was not favorable for riding horses. Mules, donkeys and oxen were the general means of transportation. Only the Beys from the castle in Moguilitza had horses and were proud as peacocks riding on them. And now, their fellow countrymen had arrived to bring them freedom, scores riding upon those magnificent animals. The young children looked at them as if they were strange heroes from a mythical forest. "Have you ever seen a Turkish soldier on a horse?" they asked triumphantly of the equally amazed Muslim kids, "This is Bulgaria, and we're all part of it now!"

Ismail was locked in an abandoned mill. He lay doubled up in a corner in his wet clothes, his teeth chattered uncontrollably from the cold, only his fiery eyes glowed in the darkness, like the eyes of a wild beast. He stubbornly refused any food or drink and wouldn't utter so much as a word to his captors. When Radco Boev came in, alone, with dry clothes under his arm, Ismail stared at him, eyes full of murderous hatred, a low growl coming from his chest, his powerful hands convulsively tried to break the tight rope.

Radco left the clothes and kneeled down by him. "Let me untie these ropes."

Ismail recoiled from him. "Don't..." he growled, "don't touch 'em!"

Radco's knowledge of Turkish had grown over the past few weeks, and had been sufficiently augmented under Danco's patient tutoring.

"Why? Why don't you want me to unfasten your hands?" Radco asked in broken but understandable Turkish. "You'll feel much better with your hands free."

"They won't be free," hissed Ismail, not impressed by his former friend's improved speech, "They'll be locked on your throat." They both looked hard into each other's faces. Radco broke the silence, pain and desperation obvious in his big sincere eyes.

"Say, friend, you...you're not blaming me for your father's death, are you?"

"Get away from here!" shouted Ismail in a rough voice, torn with rage. "You all murdered him...don't give me that innocent look of yours! You killed my sisters, too. Murderer!"

"Ismail," said Radco pleadingly, "behave like your old self. I never blamed you for my father's death. Did I?"

Ismail breathed heavily for a while as if he had been running for his entire life; finally he uttered in a feeble voice, "That's different... You have no right to..."

"I have every right," interrupted Radco, "I don't have the time to argue with you. Your life is at stake now. The minute we leave, that bastard, Sabev, will kill you like a dog. And I and my friend have to leave pretty soon. Every moment counts."

In his excitement, Radco had switched back into his native tongue, but Ismail seemed to understand him.

"Go away...I tell you," Sadness permeated Ismail's voice, "I don't want to live anymore."

"Ismail, I fooled the sentry. I said the commanding officer ordered me to relieve him for half an hour to have some wine. A friend is covering for me, but Sabev is watching us like a hawk...he might see the sentry any moment, or drop by for a check. We have to hurry. Please...understand!"

Ismail suddenly spoke in broken Bulgarian. "I do understand, but where can I go?" Radco took out Sultana's letter.

"You go to Moguilitza and deliver this small envelope to the addressee in the castle. I can't read it. It's in Turkish. But Danco said they'd certainly take care of the messenger. It's said to be very important."

There was a brief pause, then Ismail spoke out abruptly. "Untie my hands."

Radco did it hastily. The young Turk painfully moved his badly swollen hands. Silently he accepted Radco's help in changing into the dry peasant clothes. When they finished, Ismail stood up against Radco. "You don't expect me to thank you for this."

"No, you're free to do whatever you wish. There are no strings attached. I am sorry to hear about your sisters. You should have listened to me and left."

Ismail was still immobile. He dug his moccasin into the sawdust on the floor. "What will they do to you and your friends?"

For a minute, Radco felt as if the old days, like raggedy wings, had lightly touched their foreheads. He handed him the letter with a flicker of a smile. "It's none of your business. Go!"

Ranghel Sabev had sent his junior to look for Danco. He found him at a campfire under a shed. "You have to report to the commanding post immediately."

Danco left his hot plum brandy and ran through the persistent rain to the former police station. The sergeant was alone in the low-ceilinged room, wrapped in a blanket. His uniform and underwear were drying near the fireplace. He was a big barrel-chested man, about Danco's size, perhaps two or three years older, muscular and good looking in a roguish way. He had a square face and slanted eyes set over prominent cheekbones. At the soldier's report, he threw his cigarette into the fire and drove his sharp dark eyes into Danco's. They stood for almost a minute sizing each other up, as if looking for a weak spot before falling into mortal combat. Then Ranghel Sabev coughed in a manner more like a growl and said in his low, husky voice, "Let's talk man-to-man, Private Marrin. There is no love lost between the two of us. Somehow you beat me in the wrestling. But we're in the same boat and can't get at each other's throats to solve this in a natural way. For the hell of it, we have to get along at least until this mission comes to an end."

Danco nodded silently. It had taken him almost an hour to bring that sturdy man to submission and before getting his hand in an inescapable screwdriver hold, the outcome was a toss-up. The sergeant went on, "Where is Private Boev?"

"At Corporal Droumev's bedside," Danco replied.

"Six men...well, five, dead and another crippled for life! A good start, no question about it," swore the sergeant with such vehemence and dirty language that even Danco blushed. "We have to send Ermin back to Progled first thing in the morning."

Danco suddenly appeared disturbed by the news. "Why Progled?" he nearly shouted, "That village is about a day's walk from here. Even horses can't make it in less than ten hours."

"Do you know a hospital unit any closer?" the sergeant retorted definitively.

"Send him to my sister. Derrekioy is only two hours away, well, let's say four in this kind of weather," he corrected. "The accompanying detachment could be back before day's end."

The sergeant looked at him with incredulity. "What is your sister? A nurse? He needs professional treatment. Doctors, medicine…maybe surgery."

Danco became agitated, "He does not! They might really cripple him for life. I have an uncle there. He can put together any broken bones; his knowledge of herbs and magic potions is fantastic…"

Ranghel Sabev walked slowly toward him and stopped so close that the whiff of cigarettes and wine from his mouth came to the sensitive nostrils of Danco.

"Balls!" he uttered through his teeth, fingering his large perked up cock, "Are you trying to put me on? What is your game, boy? I don't give a damn about this fucking corporal. If you aren't telling me the truth, I swear I'll send the sonofabitch to hell."

Danco felt his mind reel. Small drops of perspiration popped out on his forehead. Sergeant Sabev went on. "I don't like pansies like that fancy flute player." He giggled a bit, "You don't wish him well either, do you? You're just another bastard, and I think we're not that different, as I thought before. I might even start liking you, creep."

Danco felt sick; he wanted to beat this vile man to death, to see him bloody and scared, wriggling at his feet, pleading for his miserable life, but he couldn't budge even as much as one finger. The bum was right. He did not want Ermin sent back to Progled: Rossitza was a volunteer in the field hospital. What chance would he, Danco have with that handsome flute player under her lovely care, his big greenish-blue eyes full of magic hypnotizing her for weeks, maybe months?

The sergeant sensed his inner struggle. "I am on your side, kiddo. Let's make a deal."

"What kind of deal?"

"Now that Corporal Droumev is out, you need another man for that special mission of yours. Take me. You won't find a better fit man in the whole mountain."

"But you are the commander," Danco protested.

"Bullshit. The junior can stay with the outfit," countered Sabev.

"Why do you want to risk your life?" the suspicious youth asked.

Ranghel Sabev laughed ruggedly. "For the same reason you do, buster. If we succeed, we'll get promotions, medals. If we get killed, we just die and that's all. I am tired of being a lowly sergeant."

Something flashed through Danco's mind. If he took him along, the brute would never discover Ismail's escape. The junior wouldn't find out until morning, but he wouldn't make any fuss about it since he'd be held responsible. He'd keep silent until his superior returned, and if something happened to Sabev...

"You can come with us if I'm in charge," offered Danco.

Sabev rubbed the short stubble on his chin for a moment, then his hand went down scratching different spots on his hairy body. "Okay. If that was the colonel's wish, I wouldn't dream of going against it. For the duration of the mission, you'll be the boss," and he offered his big hand straight from his crotch.

Danco took it with a certain disgust, but no other hesitation whatsoever. "We'll start in half an hour. Get dressed and give your orders to the junior. I'll go and talk to Ermin. He won't mind going to my sister's. Under the circumstances nobody will point a finger at you. Radco Boev will follow my orders. He trusts me. Do as I say!"

A roguish smile crept over Sabev's lips. "Yes, boss, as you wish."

Ermin had emerged from the comatose state he had been in since morning. He looked from his bed at Radco and tried to smile.

"Hi, magic flute!" erupted his friend joyously. He had not budged from his bedside except for the time he took to free Ismail, "I see you're coming back."

Ermin moved a bit and his face, drained of blood, wrinkled in convulsion. His voice was hollow, almost unrecognizable. "Not quite, Rad. Tell me how badly I'm hurt. I feel there is something wrong below my waist."

Radco squatted down next to his pillow. "Does it hurt a lot?"

"Not really…if I stay still," Ermin croaked.

"Then it's probably some dislocation," said Radco with the instant authority of his young age. "They'll fix you up in a jiffy."

"Radco…" Ermin sighed weakly.

"Yes, Ermin."

"Promise me one thing, will you?"

"Tell me first," Radco insisted.

"No, you promise'!"

"Okay," mumbled Radco finally, but crossed his fingers to be on the safe side, "I promise."

"Kill me if they cut off my legs," cried his friend, clearly expecting the worst.

Now Radco was in a state of shock and panic. It took him awhile to gather himself together. "They won't cut off your legs."

"You know how it is in those field hospitals. They do what is easiest for them," Ermin stated.

"Oh, that's ridiculous! They don't unless...unless it's necessary," Radco tried to remain positive.

"They do so and you know it."

"Come on, magic flute, you know better than that. Nobody would touch your legs."

"Then why are you crying?" Ermin persisted.

"Who, me? I'm not crying. That's from the rain."

"You're a friend, aren't you?" asked Ermin.

"Of course."

"A true friend?"

"Of course, I am! What kind of questions are these?" Radco became dismissive.

"Why do you lie to me?" persisted Ermin.

"Okay...okay. You got me. I'm crying...just a little... and that's only because you're such a bastard," he admitted.

Ermin made another try for a smile. "Now say it."

"I cross my heart. I won't let you live as a cripple, but you will never become one. Take my word for it!" promised Radco.

"Thanks, pal. Did you free Ismail?" Ermin quickly changed his tone.

Radco was dumbfounded. "You just woke up. How could you know about anything that happened after the explosion?"

"That dark I came from is not that dark at all. Well, did you?" Ermin pushed.

"Yes, I did," said Radco a bit gruffly.

"I knew you would. You are such a softy."

"I am not."

"Yes you are. You can't stand to see anybody suffer."

"If only you were in your usual shape, I'd show you who the softy is," Radco laughed, feigning a threatening pose.

"Rubbish. Did it ever cross your mind that that 'escape' might backfire on Danco and even on your thick head?" Ermin turned serious.

"Don't worry about it. Danco will find a way out. He always does."

"He might not this time," cautioned Ermin.

"So what? We leave Ismail in the hands of that beast, Sabev? Is that what you're trying to say? Not if I can help it," retorted Radco.

"I didn't say he was to be abandoned," Ermin countered.

"No matter what you say, it has been done already. Ismail is free." Suddenly he became aware of the presence of someone else in the room. He turned abruptly. Thank God it was only Danco.

"Danco!"

Danco came toward the bedding. The small lamp was making his shadow hideously distorted.

"It could've been somebody else," he warned Radco. "How are you, Ermin?"

"Not too bad," the wounded youth muttered.

Radco shook his head worriedly. "He is lying. He thinks the doctors are going-to cut off his legs, so he doesn't want to go to a hospital."

Under his natural dark tan, Danco flushed lightly. "He is not going to a hospital. Early in the morning, a special unit will take him to my sister's house in Derrekioy. An uncle of mine will fix him up in no time."

Ermin's face lit up. "Thanks, Danco! And my legs?"

"You'll be good as new. I give you my word," Danco promised.

"See!" shouted Radco triumphantly. "I told you, he always finds a way out. Now, who is the cry baby?"

"Well, just...a brother wouldn't have done better, if I had one!"

Danco bit his lips. "Now you have two. Rad, let him rest and get ready for our mission. I have news for you. Sergeant Sabev is coming with us."

"He is bad news," said Ermin sleepily. "He hates your guts since you dominated him as regimental wrestling champ."

Danco shrugged his shoulders. "Better he is with us than against us."

Radco straightened up and came to him. "As you say, Dan. I hope it's for the best."

"God be with you both," uttered Ermin and drifted back into the vast empty house of many windows where he had been living since the accident.

The distance between Arda and Moguilitza isn't far for someone who knows his way around. But for Ismail, in the dead of night, with the slanting rain flicking in his eyes and patches of fog thick as a bale of cotton shrouding the landscape, it could have been as far as the end of the world.

He had lost all sense of time and distance. Only a blind instinct for survival guided him in a direction that he hoped to be right. At dawn, he vaguely made out the outskirts of a village. He prayed to Allah that it was not Arda again. He hid in the low bushes and waited for more daylight. Finally, some of the fog drifted away and, in the gray light of that dismal morning, the outlines of Agoush Beys' castle appeared in the background of tall pine trees. A slender minaret with spear headed top reached into the low clouds.

As soon as Ismail explained to the sleepy footman the purpose of his early morning visit, he was quickly ushered in. The masters were at the little mosque for their morning prayers, but a servant had told them about the letter and said they'd be with him any moment now.

Soon he was invited into the large sitting room where the dignified old men in white robes and turbans waited for him. They scolded the servants for not giving dry clothes to their guest and he was immediately placed next to a huge brazier with blazing red charcoals and served aromatic coffee and sweet cakes.

No sooner than Ismail had his cup of coffee and some sweets, the old men asked him for news about Ahmed. Ismail gave them the small envelope with a low bow, touching the Persian rug with his forehead and waited, seated on his heels, for dismissal. There was none. He seemed to be completely forgotten.

The old bony hands opened the letter gently and the gentleman who didn't wear dark glasses read it aloud, but in such a whispering voice that none of it reached the ears of the young man. It was also impossible for Ismail to tell anything from the expression on their faces. They were so white and demure. He was fascinated to a point of hypnosis by the outward impassiveness of those noble faces.

It might have been an hour; it might have been more. Ismail's legs had become numb, but he didn't dare budge in that strange room, somewhere beyond space and time, where the invisible presence of something impalpable touched his cheeks almost like the breath of a living person.

Soon, there was a sigh. Was it coming from the old men, or from that thing in the air? Ismail was unable to answer, but after that, life in the room returned to normal. One of the old men smiled at him with infinite tenderness and said kindly, "Glory to Allah! Do you know the noble lady that wrote us this letter?"

"No, Bey Effendi. I was given this letter just a few hours ago by a Christian boy in Arda."

"Let Allah put her soul in everlasting bliss in His Kingdom. She made two old people at the brink of death very proud and happy."

Ismail smiled broadly. "I am glad to be the bearer of good news."

The old man didn't seem to hear him, but was obviously deeply impressed by his handsomeness and poise. "Glory to your father, son," he said, slowly stroking his silvery white beard, "what is your name?"

"Ismail, son of Arrif Agha."

And he told them his story simply. The old men listened to him without any comment or interruption. When he was finished, they didn't utter a word for quite a while. Ismail thought that he had taken enough of their time. He got on his feet and stuttered, "I am sorry, Effendilar...somehow I got carried away. I should not have stayed for such a long time...you look so tired...it's just that I have no place to go."

The masters of the castle exchanged a few whispers; then the younger bey rose slowly from the softly cushioned sofa and approached the youth.

"I want to read you what that great lady from Phulbee has written to us at the end of her letter," he touched his gold rimmed glasses as if to make his fading eyesight stronger, perused the pages and stopped at the final sentence, "Allah takes with one hand and gives with the other."

His older brother joined him, helping himself up with a richly ornate silver stick. It was then that Ismail realized the man was blind.

"You don't have to look for a place to go, Ismail," he said, "Allah has done it for you. Your home is here."

"I hate to deprive your patients of the charming presence of their most gracious benefactress, even for a day, but I hope they'll understand and pardon my priorities," said Tzar Ferdinand.

"I'm sure they will, Your Majesty."

Ferdinand moved around his desk and bent gallantly over Sultana's armchair. "Your Majesty? When nobody's around? What happened to good old Ferdy?"

Sultana blushed, but didn't lose her poise. "Since the last time I saw you, Your Majesty. Since that last time until now, a wedge has grown between the two of us."

"A wedge? What might that be?" asked the surprised Ferdinand.

"The past, Your Majesty," Sultana said, "the past."

Ferdinand stroked his well trimmed beard thoughtfully and started walking up and down, hands locked behind his back. "Impudence, my dear lady, impudence…that's what I call bad manners."

"I am sorry, Your Majesty."

The Tzar stopped at the window and looked at the bright colors in the park. "That's all right, my dear. You can afford it." He turned around and sat on the window seat, "Robev tells me you moved from his house." Sultana nodded. "In with Madame Seraphimova?"

"Yes, Your Majesty. His information is always correct."

"Isn't it a bit too crowded in her flat?"

"It is, Your Majesty, but it is home, if you know what I mean."

The Tzar looked into her eyes, then around the enormous room—covered wall to wall, with rare paintings and objects d'art—and uttered with an almost inaudible sigh, "Yes, I know what you mean." Then, as if ashamed of the sentimentality of his remark, he added with a short laugh, "Everybody who has many homes, dreams of finding the ultimate, real home. Isn't that our case, Sultana?"

"Not quite, Your Majesty."

Ferdinand lifted his eyebrows in a sarcastic manner and went back to his desk. "I have a report on your activities right here," and he examined perfunctorily a few lines in a leather folder, "You have been giving a lot of your attention and money to help the enemy. I wonder if I ought to give you a medal or send you to prison. Many think the latter is what you deserve."

"And what is your decision, Majesty?" asked Sultana .

"Well, whatever you've done serves as good propaganda for the liberal press. The noble treatment of war prisoners in Bulgaria. I like that. Especially, when I am not paying for the extravaganza. I'll stick with the medal, then my name might be mentioned side by side with yours. Of course, that would make some people around here lose sleep in silent anger. Maybe even not so silent. I don't care. By the way, what is your husband's feeling about your humanitarian obsession?"

"His reactions are very much like yours, Majesty," she assured him.

Ferdinand laughed and continued to play with an ivory and gold letter opener. "Then, let's discuss the decoration. I suggest..."

"Pardon the interruption, Your Majesty, but if anybody deserves public recognition, it is unquestionably Madame Seraphimova. The whole project was her idea. And I just joined her in search of something to fill my time."

"Strange amusement," chided the Tzar.

Sultana disregarded the dig. "Later I was intrigued by the idea of serving people. A young man, almost a boy, changed my mind. He never got a chance in this life. He's been used and thrown out."

"Not by me, I believe," huffed Ferdinand.

Suddenly Sultana felt very tired. "What difference does that make, Your Majesty. He is dead."

The Tzar tossed the letter opener aside. "Well then, let it be Madame Seraphimova. That, at least, would not cause public outcry. May we mention you as her assistant?"

"Do as you please, Majesty." She straightened up, a bit insecure on her feet. That did not escape the watchful eye of the Tzar, who hurried to her aid. "Overworked, or getting ill?"

"I don't know. It's probably nothing."

He led her gallantly toward the door. "I just might drop by to see you at Madame Seraphimova's when I happen to be in Plovdiv."

Sultana stopped abruptly and faced him firmly. "That would cause more trouble than you expect, Majesty. You ought to have a better cause to defy public opinion... than...that."

The monarch laughed drearily.

"Seeing Rayna, for example. That might prove unwise. We certainly don't want to antagonize Commander Seraphimov any more. We need him now. By the way, how do you like my victories?"

For a moment Sultana was shocked by the lightness of His Majesty's tone. It could have been, "How do you like my horses, or my new breaches." This was a man to whom winning was something granted by birth, until now, she thought.

"The whole nation enjoys them immensely, Your Majesty," she answered with a low curtsy.

Ferdinand gave her a light caress along the side of the face. "That little velvet hat looks adorable on you. Take care of yourself and don't spoil my enemies too much."

Vladimir Chernozemsky

The 18th of October 1912
City of Plovdiv
Dear Vlad,

I wonder if I really should tell you in a letter what happened to me. I can see your bushy eyebrows coming down, your eyes scanning the lines and your low voice is almost audible: "For heavens sake, what kind of mishmash is my wife up to now?"

I have a friend, darling!

Now wipe the tiny drops of perspiration from your heavy moustache. It is a lady friend, though there is a surprise in the story, so...sit down, please.

Her name is Sultana Hadgylvanova.

I know what you have to say—of all people! Hold your horses, darling. I've never had a friend from the time I was a child. I was sixteen when I married you. You were—are everything to me. Now it's different. Sultana is something in my life that you, even you, can never be. Without her, I would have gone crazy by now. She makes everything easier. Your absence, the hospital, the Red Cross, transportation and food problems. The kids adore her. Our young patients, miserable and depressed as they are under these circumstances, brighten up and smile the moment she comes in. It's almost as if the war had never happened to them. One of them (Taxim is his name) stubbornly refused to take a bath or shave—that is, before Sultana came around. Sick with shame, he asked for a bath and his face to be clean shaven. He couldn't stand the touch of a woman without getting an awesome erection, so a couple of his mates helped and we called in a barber.

Last week we buried Ahmed, a boy hardly old enough to be a soldier. He looked much younger. I thought him sixteen or thereabouts. A very proud and talented boy. Everybody loved him. Very intelligent too. The poems he recited to Sultana were his own, and they were excellent according to her. I took Rayna with me to the funeral. I thought it important for her to see all that. It's something she

144

won't learn at the French College. The ceremony was as nice as a tragic event like that can be. And the best money can buy, Sultana paid for it. She pays for everything.

I would like to meet the person who is able to turn her down.

Rayna is not doing any better at college. She is intelligent in her own way, but certainly, school is not her cup of tea. Any school. Her painting, on the other hand, is coming along pretty well. The Maestro likes her drawings very much. Even the oil paintings. I wish he could say the same about her piano lessons. You know what a remarkable man Maestro Attanassof is. He is composing an opera now. Imagine, a Kapellmeister! *He wrote the libretto himself. He is by far the most intellectual of your friends. Of all our daughters, he thinks little Jivca is the only one with musical talent.*

So far, Elsa is the only scholar in the family. The teachers don't have enough words to praise her. Jeanna is trying just to keep up with her favorite playmate.

Assen seems to miss you a lot though, as you know, he is not the bravest man in the world and shies away even from the thought of going near the front action. The cook eats so many hot peppers that it is a miracle she is still alive. By now her guts have probably turned into glowing coals. The little puppy Jivca found on the street has a name—Teshca. Another girl. It has adjusted perfectly to the rest of the pack and runs all over the house as if she owns it.

Now about baby Lily. I left her to the very end, because she is the finest morsel, an unbelievable doll. I am sure she'll be the most spirited of our whole Amazon tribe. Her eyes dance all over the nursery, full of curiosity and personality.

Guess who I met at the hospital. Give up? You'll never figure it out. The young actor that played the part of the painter in The Lower Depths. *He is mobilized and will soon join your regiment. He'll bring you a little present from Rayna, whom he met briefly when I brought him home to give him the package and this letter. The poor young man was absolutely taken by her beauty, but Rayna, as usual, hardly paid any attention to him. By the way, his name is Ivan Zemsky. Don't be too hard on him. He is not one of your durable farm boys. He is an offspring of a very old and noble family, but treated by his own like the proverbial black sheep. He has been in a lot of trouble lately, but he will tell you more in person.*

Don't forget to wear your blue pullover under your uniform. You're not in your twenties anymore…neither am I. Oh, dear, I miss you! I miss you! I miss you!

Love and kisses, your, ELLENA

P.S. Don't be mad, dear. Sultana moved in with us. She has nobody here.

"Ivan Zemsky," said Vladimir Seraphimov, looking at the interesting face of the young man, "I remember you." He perused again the last few paragraphs of the letter, folded the pages neatly and added them to a stack of unattended papers on his desk, "I remember your performance well."

"Thank you kindly, sir. Madame Seraphimova gave me a small package also. Here it is."

Seraphimov took the package from him and placed it on his desk.

"Very good, Private Zemsky. You don't have to stand at attention all the time. Now that you have finished your task, you can relax a bit and sit closer to the fire. Do you smoke?"

"No sir."

"That comes as a surprise to me. I read a report on your activities as a student in Sofia. You were involved in some anarchistic circles and demonstrations against the monarch. You didn't volunteer for the army, did you?" Seraphimov eyed him carefully.

"No, sir. I was sent out here by the police authorities."

Vladimir Seraphimov took out his short pipe and dug the tongs into the hot ashes, poking for a piece of charred wood.

"I can't seem to get rid of this bad habit," he winked at the young man, lighting his pipe and inhaling with gusto, "but I do it only when I can afford the time, which is quite seldom...I suppose you don't drink either?"

"I don't. One glass of wine knocks me off my feet. The only indulgence I permit myself is dreaming." He stretched his long, delicate but strong hands toward the fire, "I am a dreamer."

"Do you paint?"

"How did you know?" Ivan was caught off guard.

"You remind me of my oldest daughter, Rayna. She paints too. You should see her pictures sometime."

"It would be my privilege to meet her again at any time."

Seraphimov walked to the fire and leaned over the mantelpiece. "I am afraid we'll have to wait for quite awhile, now that we have a war on our hands. I hope you are not one of those pacifists, or Tolstoists, that refuse to carry weapons, are you?"

The young man blushed. "As a matter of fact, I am."

Seraphimov shook his head without anger.

"And what shall I do with you?" he went to a portable file cabinet, took out some papers and read some of them, "According to the instructions, I am supposed to break you down...if you don't mind."

Ivan smiled again in his disarming way. "I am stubborn."

Seraphimov looked into Zemsky's mild gray eyes, which, he knew, could change to pure steel at a moment's notice.

"So am I," said he thoughtfully, "let's hope we won't be pitched against each other. What skills do you have in addition to the talents we've already mentioned?"

"Not too many, though I am good with figures."

"We have enough clerks. Are you a musician?"

"Decidedly no. I am an actor, not an entertainer."

Seraphimov, to his own astonishment, failed to get angry. "I happen to know that. Don't get upset. I am not going to impose anything on you that you dislike. If you ask me why, I have no answer. For the first time in my life, I am trying to accommodate somebody like you. I used to know your uncle, who was a fine musician. Anyway, you'll have to help me a bit."

"I wish I knew how. My family won't lift a finger for me, if that's what you mean." Offered the young man.

Finally Seraphimov felt anger coming on.

"That's not what I meant, wise guy. I know how it feels to be an intellectual thrown amidst stupid warmongers. In my younger days, I too, wanted to change the world in one day. Well, I have news for you. It doesn't happen that way."

"Sorry, Colonel...I...as a matter of fact, I am good with machinery."

Seraphimov puffed on his pipe until his temper cooled down.

"Good, that's more like it. We need technicians. I was almost ready to kick you out of here." He wrote a few words on a piece of paper and gave it to the young man, "Take this to the repair shop and ask for Sergeant Jetchev."

"Thank you, Mister Seraphimov, I certainly appreciate your understanding."

A tiny flame of merriment touched the corners of Seraphimov's eyes. "Don't mention it. Now at least I know why in the world I was so patient with you—we both have gray eyes. That means a lot, don't you think so, 'Mister' Zemsky? I haven't been that tolerant for a long time. My wife would be real proud of me. By the way, don't ever call Jetchev 'mister.' It might cost you two front teeth."

"Yes, sir."

"That sounds better. How old are you, Private Zemsky?"

"Twenty-six, sir."

"You don't look it, Gray Eyes. If the master sergeant offers you some brandy, don't be so foolish as to refuse. Spill it under the chair when he's not watching you. And don't give him any talk about Tolstoy or resistance to evil. You'll lose your job instantly. Guns are his soft spot. He loves them—he talks to them as if they were his own kids."

"Thank you…sir."

"You'll get used to it. Now go."

Ivan Zemsky gave him an awkward salute and on his way out met the huge bulk of Colonel Nedelev. He treated him to another of his awkward army salutes and left the officer completely flabbergasted.

"Where the hell do they make soldiers like that!" he exclaimed in a falsetto voice, still watching Ivan Zemsky's exit.

Seraphimov laughed heartily.

"In dreamland. Anyway, I'm glad you feel better."

For two days in a row Crown Prince Boris had been trying to see his august father face to face. No matter how hard he tried, he never got closer than General Robev's desk, and even his door was not easy to open these days. Robev had been promoted to Chief Adjutant to the Tzar, and his assets at headquarters had grown sufficiently. Boris was angry in his own quiet way. He forced himself to take a drastic step, and he accosted his father at the entrance to the palace chapel.

"You're making a spectacle of yourself, young man," the monarch hissed through his teeth while the retinue waited at a respectful distance behind them, "What is it this time?"

"Are you avoiding me, father?"

"Christ! I just don't have time for any of your brilliant ideas."

"You seem to have plenty of time for Robev's," Boris complained.

"Are you jealous?"

"It looks as if everyone around here gets promoted except me and Seraphimov."

"Oh, you and your Seraphimov. You're keeping the priest waiting. It had better be something important. Can't you postpone it until dinner?"

"You don't eat with us anymore. So when can I speak with you?"

"All right, shoot. You have two minutes."

"I want to go to the front," Boris finally demanded.

"God Almighty!" the Tzar exclaimed.

"What's so wrong with that? I am of age," Boris nearly shouted in frustration.

"Lower your voice! That's out of the question. You are the Crown Prince."

"Other youngsters out there are dying to fulfill your dreams. Who would be unhappy if I died? Mother is not alive. You and your First Adjutant consider my brother more fit to be king. Why not let me go and get rid of me?"

The Tzar snorted.

"Nonsense! Monstrous nonsense! And I am supposed to cope with it as if I don't have enough on my mind? You scrawny boy, you, of all people out *there*!!! You'll get sick on your way to the front. Now I am getting edgy and ruffled. How do you expect me to face God in such a state of mind? It might not be such a bad idea to let you go and vent your frustrations. Talk to Robev in the morning."

"Oh, my God, not up a blind alley again! Don't toss me off like a tennis ball!" pleaded the Prince.

Ferdinand looked skyward. "Isn't there anyone who will save me from my own flesh and blood!?! All right, all right. You can inspect the battle theatre at the siege of Odrin. Does that satisfy you?"

"It does not. I want to go to the mountains."

"First and Second Army do not suit you?"

"I am not interested in armies."

"Oh, you aren't?"

"I am interested in battles. And in this war, the real coup will come in the White Sea region."

"You mean that one regiment will achieve what two armies cannot?" the Tzar sneered sarcastically.

"One man, sir," added the Prince.

"Ridiculous!" exclaimed Ferdinand, but turned toward his courtiers, "You may go in to the chapel, gentlemen. I feel indisposed this morning. Don't stare at me. Go!"

The men from the retinue filed by them and closed the door. Boris grabbed the sleeve of Tzar Ferdinand's resplendent uniform.

"Don't send me away empty handed, father; give me some reinforcements for the 21st Regiment. In less than ten days, we'll be at the back of the besieged city of Odrin with the route to Istanbul wide open!"

"Did Seraphimov ask you to say that?"

"No, father, I haven't talked to him since the opening of...not even that...since Plovdiv."

"And you haven't been corresponding with him behind my back?"

"No! I swear to God. No."

"Then it's one of your strange perceptions." Impulsively he opened the door to the chapel a bit and shouted, "Robev!"

The general immediately came out, as if he had been waiting by the door for the call. He looked disturbed, but played cheerful.

"At your service, Your Majesty," he said with a curt bow.

Ferdinand examined the pale face of his son which, instead of being flushed under the emotional strain, became whiter than ever, then said to his Adjutant, "This youngster here has some strange ideas, worth exploring. I want the chief of staff immediately! Go!" With a baffled look on his face, the general left, practically on the run. Ferdinand lifted the chin of his son and smiled for the first time in days, "No tears, boy. You haven't won yet."

Chapter Seven

"**M**other gets a medal, mother gets a medal..."

In her sing-song voice, Jivca jumped around the table on one leg. Ellena was dumbfounded.

"Will you please stop!?! Sultana, there must be some mistake. Me of all people."

Sultana never got a chance to answer. Young Elsa beat her to it by a large margin.

"Oh, mother, don't try to philosophize now. Just take it like everybody does."

"Elsa, how many times do I have to tell you not to interrupt when grownups are speaking?"

"It says in the constitution that there is freedom of speech..."

"Don't give me that kind of talk, Elsa. Everyone knows that you have a big mouth..." scolded Ellena.

"But she's right, mother!" Elsa's faithful partner stomped her foot.

"You, too, Jeanna?"

Jivca stopped eating her, apple. "And me too. If I count for anything. I wonder what the baby has to say?"

"Enough is enough! Everybody out! And the dog too. I am tired of her getting under my feet. You, Rayna, stay. You haven't said anything."

The children filed out, but as Elsa passed her older sister, she stuck out her tongue, and taunted her with, "You traitor!" then banged the door shut.

Sultana almost choked with laughter. "What is this, a revolution? I thought you ran your platoon with an iron hand."

Ellena shrugged her shoulders. "Say something, Rayna."

"I think that, in a way, they feel part of this medal belongs to them. They have put up with your prolonged absences, and you haven't been much of a mother, not being around and all."

"So it was my fault. Now I have to accept this medal just to appease my children."

Sultana dried her eyes. "You don't want to cheat them. Imagine the impact on their friends at school. Many of their fathers received medals and decorations, but how many mothers? I am afraid you are the first one in this city. Besides, it is official recognition of our activities. Many similar hospitals may follow suit."

Ellena looked at the portrait of her husband above the piano and uttered, in a very low voice, "I thought about that too. Rayna, please see what the children are doing outside."

On a sudden impulse, Rayna came to her and kissed her. "Please take it, mother!" and ran out.

Ellena looked after her for a moment, then walked straight to her friend. "That medal, does it come from you, Sultana?"

The beautiful violet eyes enhanced her strength and serenity. "What do you mean?"

"You have given enough medals in this house."

Sultana blushed slightly. "Are you talking about the cardboard things I cut out for the kids?"

"No. I am talking about this particular medal."

Sultana hesitated only for an instant.

"It was the Tzar himself."

By the time the scout patrol left Arda, the rain had slowed to a drizzle. The night was foggy, cold and desolate as before, but the absence of the blinding rain was silently interpreted by the three of them as a good omen. They had changed into Turkish uniforms; two of them were fluent in colloquial Turkish, and Radco was supposed to keep his mouth shut. As the youngest, he wasn't exposed to any questions in the presence of elders, but in his heart, Radco wished he had paid more attention to his Turkish lessons.

They walked in a wide circle around Catoun and headed eastward toward Station Bouk, a small but important railway junction. At daybreak, the patrol reached the outskirts of Chamgas. One of the village houses was quite isolated in a small ravine. Ranghel banged at the door. A middle aged Turk with sallow face and angry eyes looked through a small window. "What's the racket about?"

"Excuse us, effendi," said Danco as friendly as he could. "My friend is a rowdy fellow, but he means well. Glory to the Padishah; we're his soldiers."

"If you are really the sultan's men, why aren't you fighting the damned rebels. What the hell are you doing here?"

"We got lost, effendi—separated from the main army. We are hungry and tired. Have pity on us. Let us come in and rest a bit."

The man's forehead wrinkled as he labored in thought. Finally, he conceded. "If you put your arms down, I'll let you in."

"Just as you say, *chorbadgy* effendi," said Danco peacefully handing him his gun and knife through the window and motioning for his comrades to do the same.

The house was big but poorly furnished. Their host led them to a room at the back and started building a fire. "Go out and chop some wood, boy!" he said to Radco and the lad looked helplessly at Danco. It was said in the local dialect unknown to him.

"The poor young fellow is dead on his feet, chorbadgy. Let him go to bed and this big man here will take care of the wood chopping."

The host pointed to a little door under a niche. "There is a bed in there, young man, but don't go any further. My harem is next to it."

Danco laughed. "Don't worry, chorbadgy, the boy is much too tired to even think of women. Go, little brother."

Radco understood and retired to the adjoining room. It was just a cubicle—a bed with a gaily colored quilt in the corner. Filled with much gratitude, he threw his wet clothes on the floor and was headed toward the bed stark naked when a young playful laugh, from behind a curtained door, startled and embarrassed him. The sound of women speaking quickly in Turkish had completely escaped him until that moment.

"Hi, handsome!" whispered the voice behind the curtain. "don't be afraid. I don't eat good looking boys, though I wish I could."

And the tiny ringing laugh filled the room again. In his excitement, Danco's order not to try his Turkish on natives was completely forgotten and, prudishly wrapping a blanket around himself, Radco blurted out:

"Who are you?"

"I'll tell you if you drop the blanket," the voice teased.

"I'll drop it if you come in here."

"Don't be a fool, father would kill me."

"So, you are the daughter of the house."

"There are two of us. My name is Azimee, and my young sister is Fatima. What is your name?"

"Ismail," Radco lied.

"Please, golden curled, blue eyed Ismail, let me see you again. I never thought a boy as handsome as you really existed. Never in the whole wide world, except in my dreams."

Radco hesitated for a moment, then let the blanket slip to the floor. There was a short sigh and a gasp behind the curtain and two beautiful lily like hands convulsively grasped the iron grill that barred the little window. There was a moaning behind the door that made him forget all the warnings. He grabbed at the handle with all his strength, but the solid door didn't budge. It was lined with iron nails, and bronze plated. The lock was big and heavy.

"Give me your lips, my golden boy…" sobbed Azimee from inside, with such pain and desire that Radco's heart almost broke. The curtain fell and through the grill he saw such a beauty that he thought he must be dreaming. His heart thumped so loudly that he was afraid the men in the next room might hear it. Azimee guessed at his anxiety.

"Don't worry, my darling. They are drinking out there now. Give me your lips… Oh, Allah, Allah, how honey-like they are…we are prisoners here, Ismail. We are prisoners for life. Promise me, promise me, one day you'll come back and take me away…away from here…to your native place in Bulgaria."

Radco was startled that she knew he was Bulgarian.

"Have no fear of me…you are my golden Ismail! I won't betray you for anything in the world. Would your mother accept me as her daughter?"

Radco was in a trance, his voice husky with desire. "She'd be honored to have you!"

Her arms stretched through the bars and locked behind his neck. "And I'll be free to love you…free like the wind!"

"Will you be waiting for me, Azimee? It won't be long now."

"I'll wait for you even if it is long."

"And you haven't given your word to anybody else?"

"My father promised my hand to the grandson of the Beys from Moguilitza, but Ahmed joined the army and may never come back. Oh, forgive me, Allah!"

"At any rate, I'll be back before him…" And the two youngsters drowned each other in kisses.

In the next room, the *tantoura* had brought the three men together. The rather strong brandy had loosened the tongue of their sullen and silent host, while Danco and Ranghel proved to hold the sneaky brandy pretty well. They were singing old army songs and exchanged spicy soldier's jokes with each new round. In a short time, Rashid Babba was explaining to them how to join their regiment at Bouk. He revealed how they were preparing a nasty trick, a real trap for the stupid Christians. Out there the regiment was just an outpost to engage the Bulgarian troops in mortal combat, while a whole army came right up from behind. The local forces were organizing also. The so-called *bashibouzouk*—well known for its blind fanaticism and cruelty—would close the iron circle around the Bulgarians and they'd be massacred down to the very last man. Then, the best would come, when the *bashibouzouk* rolls over all the villages which the Bulgarians had come to as liberators. The pillage and burning would have no end, especially for the renegades that had repudiated the teachings of the Holy Koran and sold themselves to the Christian faith. They'd be fastened between four horses and torn asunder. A tower to the sky would be built of their skulls—not a single head would stay on the rebels' shoulders. No prisoners. Children, women and old ones—everybody would go under the axe. Death to all infidels!

The eyes of the man bulged from their sockets, bloodthirsty and cruel beyond belief. Danco was appalled and horrified. He looked at Ranghel, whose swarthy face was flushed and covered with perspiration. Strangely, he appeared to be amused.

It had started with jokes between Christians and Muslims in the newly liberated villages.

"Let me be your godfather when you makeup your mind to accept our Christian faith."

"Why not? You gonna bring me colored eggs for Easter?"

"That's a deal! Let's handshake."

Laughter.

But soon the laughter soured.

A special delegation from the Saint-Sinnode had come to the new region with directives from the Palace to baptize all Muslims. Besides that, all the male population of Turkish origin between the ages of 16 and 50 had to be deported as prisoners of war to concentration camps in the interior of the country. The Muslim part of the population which leaned toward the new rule, now swerved back to the rebellious *hodgas* or Turkish priests, and started a mass movement into the villages still under Turkish control.

Seraphimov could do nothing but grind his teeth and cuss in every language he knew. What saved him was Colonel Nedelev's willingness to serve on those countless committees for christening or deportations, presiding and organizing those activities with utter delight, leaving Seraphimov with all the military problems. However, more often than not, a scared wailing voice would stop him on the street: "Amman-zamman, Chaush Effendi, don't send my husband to a prisoner's camp! Who will feed our eight children, all under twelve years of age? Have pity!"

Seraphimov would try to avoid the pleading eyes above the veils, but the words of the pleading women haunted his nights and chased needed sleep away.

"As far as you are concerned," said Agoush Bey to Ismail, "the war is over. I lost one son in the war with Italy, another in Asia Minor. The last one spent the best part of his life in Stanbul's dark saloons and with whores—the good for nothing. His only son, young Ahmed, died before getting married. Enough is enough. You'll enjoy life the way young people should. Tomorrow I am sending rich wedding presents to Rashid Babba, father of the most beautiful girl in the district, Azimee. She was betrothed to Ahmed. The pledge is still on. I want a wedding here while my ailing brother is still alive. Let him hold a great grandson in his arms before Allah calls him to his paradise gardens."

Ismail felt uneasy. So many things had happened in such a short time that his young mind was unable to grasp them all. He felt like he had been carried away by a powerful stream, not knowing where or why.

"Your son Mehmed Agoushev is still young, Bey Effendi."

"Grandfather."

"...grandfather?"

The old man nodded. A shadow crossed his noble forehead. "My son Mehmed has been sick. He cannot beget any more children."

"What right of succession do I have over Agoushev's family?"

"Ahmed's rights."

"Pardon me...grandfather, but aren't we forcing the will of Allah a bit?"

"Not at all, son. In his infinite wisdom, he has chosen you to take over in Ahmed's place. He has sent you to our house. We can't do anything but obey."

"One last question: how did grandfather Humayun lose his sight?"

A heavy sigh rocked the chest of the old man. "My elder brother didn't lose it. His eyes were taken out by Greek rebels."

The grounds around Railway Junction Bouk were swarming with Turkish fighting men. Hundreds of tents and piles of ammunition and equipment filled the area. It was cold and fires by the thousands sent columns of smoke into the gray sky.

Radco gasped. "That's much more than a regiment!"

"Without counting the *bashibouzouk*," growled Ranghel, squinting, " Just the regular soldiers are in the thousands."

"So far, Rashid Babba proved to be right," mumbled Danco thoughtfully, "however, we still have to verify the coming of the big army.

"Let's go and get it over with…" cursed Ranghel, "I am getting cold."

Danco blew into his hands which were turning blue from the freezing temperature.

"I agree. We two will go to the fires, you, Radco, you stay here."

The youth was seriously piqued. "Not me again! Danco…please…so far I've done nothing!"

Ranghel winked at him. "So far you've done more than any of us, fuckin' sonofabitch."

Danco laughed. "We certainly would like to leave your fiancée some chance of tasting your manhood without a door between."

Radco blushed and clenched his fists. "You big bastards! I shouldn't have told you at all!"

"Right, buster," Ranghel Sabev laughed for the first time, with no malice. "But you still have a chance. We might be killed down yonder and nobody else would know about your little dalliance. Another reason to stay put and save your pretty rump."

Radco spit on the frozen ground. "All right, wise guys. Go to hell!"

The two young men looked at each other, then Danco softened.

"You know, Ranghel, we might just be going there."

Then softly laughing, both of them crept down the hill.

Prince Boris fastened the shiny medal to her breast pocket.

"In the name of the Tzar and the Nation, I thank you, Madame Seraphimova."

Ellena stepped out of her deep curtsy, but the young prince would not let her go. "Now that the official part is over, may we have a few words, Madame?"

"Certainly, Your Highness," she curtsied.

"Of course," the prince addressed the Minister of Justice standing by, "if Mr. Hadgylvanov cares to join us for some refreshments, that would be most pleasing to us."

"If you don't mind, Your Highness, I'd be glad to," coughed the old gentleman, "I've always had a sincere admiration for Madame Seraphimova, as did your August Father from the first moment he laid eyes on her. I remember it very well. It was at a morning reception for lesser dignitaries. He was busy with a group of diplomatic small fries, when his bored eyes singled out your persona, Madame. Without excusing himself, the Monarch took me aside and whispered in my ear, 'Who is that distinguished looking foreign Dame?' I meant no offense, Your Highness."

Prince Boris blushed slightly. "Oh...my father is well known as a...connoisseur in the field. Then, it's settled. Let's go and have some tea, Madame." He offered his arm to Ellena and the three of them went to the adjoining winter garden to a little round table set for the occasion.

"Let me remind Your Highness," said the minister who sat on the comfortable, gaily upholstered chair with a painful grimace on his face, "that half a dozen reporters are waiting for Madame in the blue room."

"Marco," said the prince to the chief waiter, "serve the gentlemen in the blue room some drinks and tidbits."

"I am sure the gentlemen of the press will be delighted with your generosity, Highness," mumbled the minister, holding his cigar with an inquisitive look in his myopic eyes. "May I smoke?"

"It's all right with me," smiled the prince, "if Madame Seraphimova doesn't object."

"No objection from me, either. Light your cigar, Mr. Hadgylvanov," smiled Ellena.

"I most humbly thank you, Madame. I don't eat at this time of the day. A cigar is what I have instead of a late breakfast." He inhaled deeply on the expensive cigar with evident pleasure. "How is my wife doing out there?"

Ellena was rather emphatic in her response. "Really, Mr. Hadgylvanov, I don't know what I would have done without her. She means so much to the hospital."

The minister was thoughtful for a moment, then said gravely, "She knows how to please. Anyway, if I were you, I wouldn't trust her too far. Sultana does nothing that won't benefit her in some way."

An awkward pause followed, then the prince and Ellena laughed. "Of course you are joking, Dear Minister," said the prince.

"Of course, I am joking," nodded Hadgylvanov, without a trace of humor in his hollow voice, "Sultana is the best thing that's happened to me. No sugar in my tea, please."

They were busy with their tea cups for a while when the old man spoke again, "There are rumors around the palace, Your Highness, that you're going to visit the front."

Boris lifted his cup of tea with a slightly shaky hand.

"Yes, there were some plans, unfortunately the War Council decided that...this is not the right time for ventures of that kind." The disappointment in his young voice was overwhelming and tears of indignation glistened in his eyes. "Later perhaps, they said, when the front is stabilized and there are fewer risks." He looked at Madame Seraphimova ardently, and with respect, as if she were a judge on the Supreme Court. "The situation at the Rhodopy Mountains right now is unique, a great victory there could resolve the war in less than a month with minimum bloodshed and suffering on both sides."

Hadgylvanov shook his head. "I am sorry I said anything. You shouldn't aggravate yourself, Your Highness. There are higher authorities than our own judgment, better informed and prepared to meet a crisis."

The prince's shoulders sagged. "Pardon my outburst, Madame. This is supposed to be *your* celebration, not affirmation of my ideas. I am sorry."

Ellena fought an inner impulse to take the Prince's hand.

"We all have these moments of disappointment in our lives, Your Highness. I am sure your day of greatness will come very soon. I know a war presents an unusual opportunity in the life of a man to break the peacetime obscurity..."

The prince looked at her brusquely. "You don't really believe that, Madame. In peace and wartime, the only obscurity is in one's character. War gives more chances to opportunists."

The minister got to his feet slowly, "And heroes. I am afraid I have to leave you now. My schedule these days is simply frightening." He lifted Ellena's hand to his lips, "As a minister of justice, may I again express my admiration to you and your noble cause, Madame."

After the exit of Hadgylvanov, the prince smiled sadly. "He might have sent some regards for his wife."

"I am sure he forgot, Your Highness."

"Men like the Minister only choose to forget, Madame."

"Isn't your judgment of people a bit too harsh, Your Highness?"

"I have my own observations, Madame Seraphimova. Do you think my father would miss an occasion to deliver a medal, let's say to Madame Hadgylvanova?"

Ellena felt uncomfortable. "They are very good friends."

"I know. My opinion is that a monarch should reserve more of his feelings for his subjects."

"That's different, Your Highness," offered Ellena.

"The difference wins wars and makes great monarchs," said the young prince with bitterness, "everything now is in the hands of God and Colonel Seraphimov."

Getting into the Turkish camp proved to be easier than expected by the two fake Turkish soldiers—Danco and Ranghel. The sentinels were so few and so busy cooking their meals over the wind blown fires, that even an elephant coming out of the bushes would not have attracted their attention. The two Bulgarians appeared as if they had just relieved themselves behind the low pine trees. They came out laughing and joking with each other, joining the first campfire on the way. It was almost dark and all the faces, burly and unshaven, looked alike. The earthen pot with hot coffee was passed around and soon some bread and pieces of badly burned meat followed. The scouts helped themselves, with the rest of the soldiers sharing their merrymaking. Very little of the conversation around that fire was of any significance to them, so Danco and Ranghel moved on. At the third fire, a middle-aged man with a short curly beard came to their attention. From the reverence of the rest, he seemed to be a *hodga,* a priest, though one of minor rank. He talked about the greatness of the padishah and the wisdom of his general, Yaver Pasha.

"He expects us to engage the rebels until his army is ready to strike and destroy the unfaithful."

"But what, Holy Man, if the Christians come out with a bigger army than ours?"

"Bigger army! What are you talking about, brother? All they have is a miserable regiment that will be swept out by our mighty army like a handful of dry leaves being blown away by the mountain wind."

The man had a good voice and strong personality. His easy way with words and natural persuasiveness attracted more and more soldiers.

"Is it possible," asked Danco through the roar of approval, "that infidels might get reinforcements also? What if they are preparing a bloody trap of their own?"

The *hodga* seemed to be expecting a question of that kind. He waited long enough to focus the attention of the whole crowd gathering around him, stroking his beard and smiling mischievously. Finally he cleared his voice, looked at Danco and asked with an air of superiority, "How many soldiers are in that army of ours that's coming, soldier?"

Danco shrugged his shoulders. "I don't know, *hodga*… maybe as many as fifty thousand!"

"More, asker, more!"

Danco felt sweat trickling down his back. "Eighty thousand?"

The priest was laughing triumphantly. "More, asker, more!"

"One hundred thousand!"

"You aren't that good at guessing, soldier. Double it!"

Danco and Ranghel exchanged baffled looks. In a silence heavy with anticipation, Danco, stunned by the gigantic number, blurted out, "Two hundred thousand!?!"

There was a gasp from the crowd; then cheers erupted.

"Glory to Allah!"

"Glory to the Padishah!"

"Death to the Christians!"

"The Christians to the stakes!"

"Cut off the heads of the infidels; burn the rebels alive!"

Fanatical hatred had distorted the faces of the soldiers—eyes baleful, bloody, grim, beastly with rage.

"That's a bluff," Danco whispered to himself, "it simply cannot be true! But what if even a portion of it is, we'd better go back as soon as possible." It was just at this moment that Ranghel Sabev straightened up to his awesome height, his head sticking up over the rest, eyes blazing, his huge shoulders shuddering under the strain of an inner storm. He extended his big hand and pointed at the priest, "This man is lying!"

Danco was horrified. No possible way to stop him! All eyes were fixed on Ranghel. The crowd was momentarily silenced. It was so quiet one could hear some distant drums and the wailing of a clarinet.

There was a frightful pause; then the *hodga* bared his yellow teeth up to his infected gums. He stared at the group where the voice came from and growled, "Who said that?"

Danco stiffened. He knew that he had to find his way out of the crowd, that everything depended on him. Yet a strange force kept him from moving. The incomparable inexplicable beauty of the moment, when a single man defies a pack of bloodthirsty beasts surrounding him on all sides, ready to jump and devour, a man without a chance for survival, though calm and seemingly indestructible as if made of granite.

Now any sign of inner struggle disappeared from Ranghel's face. His voice regained its former vitality and ruggedness. "Who has ever heard of the existence of such a big army? And who is such a fool as to send it into the mountains, where it's impossible to fight on a wide front, where an army like that would be congested and paralyzed by its own gigantic power?"

Danco was dumbfounded. Where had this simple-minded sergeant, with brute instinct and little intelligence, found this brilliant thread of reasoning? Where had the strange light illuminating his face come from? There was only one answer: God! If he had had a thinking audience, he would've had a chance, but with those fanatics, he had none.

"Are you really calling the Great Padishah a fool?" screamed the *hodga*.

Ranghel calmly crossed his hands over his deep and wide chest. "I am not calling the Great Padishah a fool. It is whoever spreads those stupid rumors, I am calling a fool."

Now the *hodga* confronted him with a piece of yellowish paper.

"This is a letter from General Headquarters in Stanbul. Is it a lie? Are Yaver Pasha and the War Minister liars?" A wild roar exploded in the throats of the surrounding gray mass. "That man is a Bulgarian spy; get him!!!"

The mob piled on Ranghel, screaming and cursing, trying to get at least one bit of the prey. For a moment Danco saw a hand thrown in the air then Ranghel's head stuck on a bayonet floated over the red caps of the soldiers.

That bloody head pulled Danco out of his daze. Like a wild animal, he looked around for a way to escape. Fortunately everyone was so busy spitting and cursing at Ranghel's head that he seemed to be forgotten. Suddenly a murky voice hissed in Danco's ear, "And you, soldier, aint'cha gonna spit at the traitor?"

It was the sinister holy man.

Danco felt an overwhelming desire to lock his fingers around his throat. Then he saw the bulging eyes of the man, full of venom and cruelty. He was testing him. Almost stunned by the heavy throbbing of his heart, Danco managed to say coldly, "You bet I will!"

And he did.

Azimee stared at the pile of silver veils, purple velvet, necklaces and bracelets displayed by her father on the kitchen table, a sudden premonition thrust into her bosom like a dart.

"Has Ahmed come back, father?"

Rashid Babba's beady eyes were unable to turn from the magnificent sight. He mumbled incoherently, "Ahmed is dead, somebody else took his place…"

Azimee was stunned. "What are you talking about, father? How could anybody take his place?"

Rashid became angry, feeling as if his own daughter was trying to rob him.

"What difference does it make? It's your time to get married. You're past sixteen already. Are you going to hang on my neck forever?" he hissed.

"Is there anything wrong with me wanting to know who I am going to marry?"

"Anybody who comes from the house of Agoushev is all right with me."

Azimee felt she would die. "Even those ancient beys?"

"Allah Merciful! That would be luck! Though it is not the case. The man is young and handsome. His name is Ismail."

Azimee took a deep breath, "Help me, Allah, not to faint this very minute!" She smiled faintly, the rosy color of her cheeks returned gradually.

"Where did this Ismail come from?"

"Somewhere near the Bulgarian border. Does it matter?"

Azimee looked as if she were struck by lightning. "Was he here?"

"What's wrong with you? Of course he was here…and two more. They brought the presents. You don't expect me to introduce you to the bridegroom before the wedding, do you?"

The girl blushed, bit her lips, and tears streamed uncontrollably down her face.

"Tell Ismail, I'll take him. I'll be his until death do us part!"

Danco's face was haggard from exposure and suffering, his forehead hidden by matted hair. His beard, unshaven for days, shadowed his hollow cheeks, leaving only the bluish lips visible.

A few steps behind him, at the brink of exhaustion himself, Radco Boev closely observed the changing expression on the faces of the two commanding officers listening to Danco's report. When Danco finished his account of their findings, a lengthy silence followed. Then

Vladimir Seraphimov came forward and embraced him as if he were his own son.

"Thank you, my boy." He beckoned Radco and tousled his hair, "Barely full grown, and already a man!"

Colonel Nedelev joined the group and shook hands with the two young men.

"To tell you the truth, boys, I never believed," he paused, catching himself, "never mind. Thanks Sergeant Marrin, and to you Corporal Boev. You'll get your medals. I'll send a report to Headquarters and to the Palace about your mission. I am sure that in the near future Ranghel Sabev will be praised throughout the country as the newest national hero. You may go now and get some well deserved rest."

After the two young men saluted and left, the officers looked at each other gravely. "It doesn't matter how big that army is," said Nedelev, "we stand no chance with any army. Especially at this position. We have to return to the old border as soon as possible. There we can wait for some reinforcements."

"What about the people?"

"What people?"

"The people we liberated a few days ago."

"But Seraphimov, with all the auxiliary forces we have little more than a regiment," Nedelev protested.

Seraphimov shook his head quietly. "I can't leave those people to be massacred by the murdering Turks. It's as simple as that."

Nedelev, breathing heavily, searched for another argument. "If we're defeated here, everybody will be massacred as far down as Plovdiv. Your own family…"

"We won't be defeated," Seraphimov cut him short.

Nedelev wiped the perspiration from his forehead. Vladimir Seraphimov continued, "We'll strike quickly at Station Bouk. If we don't, their headquarters will think we're not going into their trap. Meanwhile, we'll concentrate on the path of the big army, and we'll take them by surprise."

"Where will you find all those soldiers?"

"Not from Headquarters, but I believe the population from the region will help willingly."

"That's an illusion. We can't set them up with arms. How do you expect them to fight—with bare hands?"

Seraphimov lit his pipe and blew out some smoke. "With hoes, axes, pitchforks and knives…if that is not enough, teeth and fingernails. I know what to do with their bare hands as well."

Nedelev's mouth hung open over his triple chin. "You walk in the clouds, Seraphimov, but I am not going to fall with you. I'll back you up until we receive the official directive. Then we'll follow that."

Vladimir Seraphimov shrugged in a way that could be read as yes and no at the same time. Colonel Nedelev chose to believe the first and, with a short sigh, got himself up to look for some food.

The room was bright and tidy. There were two windows decorated with blue curtains and some potted geraniums. A girl dressed in a dark a *suckman* peasant dress, needlework in her lap, kept a close watch on the restless young man in the single bed next to the fire. She never knew if he was just rambling in his dreams, or if he was actually calling. Time after time again the same name, "Rossitza! Rossitza!…"

She came to him and put her cool hand on the feverish forehead. And now the bone dry, cracked lips whispered, "Where have I seen you before?"

Thank God he was awake! She thought. But aloud she spoke, "You haven't seen me before, Ermin," smiled the girl with heart warming gentleness. She wasn't pretty but there was something different about her that attracted Ermin.

"I know your face," he insisted.

"I am Magda Marrin, Danco's younger sister."

Of course! It was Danco's face. As good looking as he was as a man, equally unbecoming was his manly beauty to a girlish face.

"How long have I been here?" he managed to ask.

"This is the fifth day."

"Have you heard from anyone?" Ermin was asking about her brother and Radco.

"Not yet, but I am sure they'll be okay. My brother is a tough guy; he's been through a lot."

"Magda."

"Yes."

"Tell me the truth. Are my legs...here?"

Magda paled a bit, but smiled bravely, getting down on her knees next to him.

"Why? Yes, of course. There were some broken bones here and there; my uncle put them together. He is as good at that as a magician."

"Magda...I don't feel them."

"It will take some time... Guess who is here?"

Ermin turned his head against the wall. "I wish Radco and Danco were back."

Magda laughed a bit forcefully. "It's somebody else that you'd wish for even more."

The youth turned his head slowly back to her. "Who could that be? I have nobody in the whole wide world... only my flute!"

A little devil danced into the girl's bright eyes. "Your cavall's here, too, all the way from your army berth in Ustovo. Somebody went to look for you there, and found it instead, but it didn't come alone."

The long sooty eyelashes closed over the strange, disturbing eyes of the young man. Two heavy tears crept underneath and rolled down his hollow cheeks. Something more like a moan than a name left his lips. "Rossitza...?"

"Yes...she's my best friend. We were at school together."

Ermin drove his eyes into her. She shuddered, never having seen eyes that could speak more clearly than the human voice.

"She wasn't looking for me there...where is she?" Ermin demanded.

"Downstairs with my elder sister. She has been here, all night long."

He struggled to get up on his elbows, but fell down with a stifled cry. "I thought it was a dream." he uttered, as if to himself.

Magda got up. "Shall I call her?"

Ermin's breathing became heavy and uneven. "Wait a minute, Magda. Be my friend, my sister. Tell me honestly, swear to God...shall I ever walk again on my own?"

Magda's voice was barely audible. "God only knows... maybe...all is in His Hands."

A deep sigh rocked the chest of the young man. It was minutes before he recovered, but his voice, when he spoke, was firm and calm, "Tell Rossitza to go back to Progled. It will be a lot easier for both of us."

Magda looked at him, dumbfounded. "Are you sure you know what you're saying."

Ermin nodded from his pillow. "Yes, Magda...and thank her for bringing me my cavall."

Magda hesitated for a moment, then shook her head slowly as she left the room. Ermin listened to her light step going down the stairs, then rolled toward the wall sobbing. When he suddenly heard the door open, he shouted roughly at the top of his lungs, "Get out, Magda! Leave me alone," still staring at the wall.

A slight touch, as if from the wing of a bird, caressed the side of his face and a voice sweeter than his flute broke his heart. "Don't chase me away, Ermin. I came so far to see you."

Ermin gathered all his courage and turned his face, bathed with tears, toward her. He looked at her with those large fluorescent eyes and spoke without bitterness. "They told you about my legs and you came out of pity."

Rossitza nodded. A wry smile touched the lips of the youth.

"Thank you, anyway. I'll remember you for that," Ermin cried.

Rossitza gently seized his shoulder. "You're my best friend, Ermin, I don't know what I would have done without the silver voice of your cavall. Remember the long hours we roamed together through the woods, my head resting on your shoulder?"

Ermin closed his eyes and spoke with sad resignation, "If you only knew… My only desire was to hold you in my arms and kiss you…kiss you…"

The noise of horse hooves and male voices came from the courtyard followed by a short commotion downstairs. Ermin and Rossitza were oblivious to the noise. They were looking into each other's eyes as the leaves of the beech trees shuffled silkily in a time gone by for ever. Their lips melted together into an iridescent substance, a flutter of wings that would never touch the sky.

A persistent knock at the door brought them slowly back to reality. A pale and distraught Magda stood at the doorframe.

"Danco is here!"

With a supreme effort, Ermin struggled to his elbows. "I knew they'd come, Rossitza…these are my brothers. Danco saved my life, and Radco is as a part of me…wait until you see him; you'll love him as much as I do…Danco! Radcooo! I am here! Come on up!"

There was the noise of a short scuffle downstairs, then the hooves of a single horse left the courtyard in a wild dash. The sound of heavy feet climbing slowly up filled the room. A downcast Radco walked to the middle of the room and looked at the couple on the bed with a mixture of sadness and reproach. It came like a sigh from the depths of his chest, "Ehhh...Ermin, Ermin!"

Chapter Eight

The detachment sent to attack the junction near Bouk consisted of four companies, sixteen hundred rifles, two machine guns and four cannons. The campaign started the same evening. Fortunately, the sky was clear and the moon almost full. The road was steep and rocky. It was a miracle that the artillery ever made it. On several occasions, the machine guns loaded on mules narrowly missed a fatal fall down the precipice. A small bridge collapsed under one of the cannons and for two hours the whole column was detained.

In the morning, a heavy fog brought the visibility to zero. It was not as cold as the past ten days, but the torrential rain that started at midday lasted all through the night into the next day. The cannons often had to be dismantled and taken by hand over extremely difficult parts of the road. The explicit instructions were not to get close to a populated area. The success of the campaign was possible only if the attack on the far larger and stronger enemy was kept secret until the very last moment. The Turkish forces at Bouk thought the Bulgarians were no further than the river Arda, and no one believed passage in such bad weather was possible. If spotted by a Turkish spy, the whole venture was doomed to tragic failure. And due to the forced christening of the Muslims, there were more than enough spies in the nearby villages.

On the third night, the Bulgarian troops concentrated on the hills overlooking the railroad junction. Almost totally exhausted by the horrible march—hungry, ragged, most of them barefooted—the Bulgarians still had the stamina to fight and win. Their incredible endurance and combativeness had gained them and their country the title of *Lion of the Balkans*.

In the early morning hours while everybody in the Turkish camp was still asleep, all four cannons, machine guns and rifles in the detachment opened fire.

The result was devastating.

Total panic spread all over the Turk's encampment. Tents caught fire, and burning men burst from them screaming at the top of their lungs. Many of their ammunition wagons exploded, catapulting limbs and heads into the air. Through the clouds of soot and sparks the silhouettes of some Turkish officers, who miraculously found their horses, desperately tried to stop the deserting soldiers and get them to fight. Those brave officers perished, easy prey for snipers. The stampede and the massacre that followed were indescribable. Thousands of voices called the name of Allah, but Allah did not hear them.

The bloody head of Ranghel Sabev, still on display in the middle of the camp, was taken off its pike and rolled in a torn flag for official burial back in his motherland.

Late in the afternoon, Lieutenant Colonel Seraphimov's courier arrived. His horse was almost dead from fatigue and the rider himself fainted in the arms of the soldiers that met him. When the rider, Sergeant Danco Marrin, regained consciousness he told the commanding officer about the imminent arrival of the huge army. One of the Bulgarian outposts had been taken by surprise and the eyes of all those captured had been gouged out. As the army advanced on the road from Ksanty, this detachment by junction Bouk would be cut off from the mainland in a matter of hours. To meet up with the rest of the Bulgarian forces, they must start immediately.

Captain Dimmitriev gave the appropriate order and the column started moving less than an hour after the arrival of the messenger. Darkness was imminent and the rain fell even harder. Going uphill was much more difficult on the slippery road that had been partially destroyed by the torrents. The soldiers had not had a hot meal since they left the regiment, yet no one complained. The proud, three-colored standard guided them ahead, and the coat-of-arms on the flag was the Bulgarian Lion.

That night, nobody slept in the village of Arda.

The *chetta*, Bulgarian home guard, guarding the village from the heights above had seen the fast retreat of the Bulgarians from Bouk, which was mistakenly interpreted as a defeat.

Encouraged by that and the arrival of their enormous army, the cut-throats from Catoun and the other Turkish hamlets in the area had organized a fighting horde. The mob, several thousands strong, had taken to the hills opposite the Bulgarian paramilitary. Even with all the volunteers from the village, the Bulgarian fighting group counted as no more than three hundred. Early in the morning, a representative of the marauders, Kell Addem, knocked at the door of Nickola Vassilev.

"Give up, Chorbadgy," he said, from the back of his mule. "Thousands of our people have you in the palm of their hands. It's all over for your rule and kingdom. An army, with as many soldiers as there are stars in the sky, will overcome and destroy the rebels. Nobody will survive unless you surrender unconditionally. Then, the lives of women and children might be spared from reprisal."

The mayor, a spare individual with a heavy featured, ruddy face, didn't waste any time considering the *bashi-bouzouk's* "generous offer." He knew very well how much their word was worth. He silenced the angry dogs, put his hand on the head of a grandson of his, who happened to be at the portal, and said softly, "Two years ago you bought the old mill at Rechany from me. You gave me half of the money, the rest you promised to deliver in the fall. This is the third fall, and I've still seen no money from you. I hear you've been doing pretty well. Anyway, I've decided, even as the new mayor under Bulgarian rule, not to ask you to repay your debt. Friendship, money cannot buy. And we were good friends through all these years. Tell me, how many of the people on the heights, ready to massacre us, have seen anything bad from us? Even when the government pressed us to make you Christians, did we force anybody to change faith?"

Kell Addem blushed deeply. He took off his red fez and scratched his head. "Not here, Chorbadgy, but other places…"

"So much the better," Nickola cut him off, "is that how you show your gratitude? Is that what Allah asks of you? And who will grant you the guarantee that things won't go the other way again?"

Kell Addem was getting apologetic. "They asked me to do it, Chorbadgy, those no good brigands from Catoun. They're armed to the teeth, and swear to kill everyone in sight. If you listen to me, you'll take all the Bulgarians away and I'll talk to the army chieftain that came to us after something terrible happened to our forces at junction Bouk. For a reason he doesn't want to discuss, he is madder than anyone I've seen before. Anyway, I'll try to negotiate with him to spare your houses from burning."

In spite of his advanced age, Nickola Vassilev was a rather strong and agile man. From the moment he saw Kell Addem off, he did not stop until the last wagon bearing frightened kids and womenfolk left the village. He sent his own prolific family away and stayed behind to burn some papers and hide valuable properties. By the time he'd finished, the strain of the day had taken its toll on him and he lay down for a few minutes.

Intense rifle shooting woke him up! It was early morning. The old man had slept through the whole night!

Instantly Nickola realized that the Turkish force was attacking and the civilian fighting force at the school was trying to fend them off.

He grabbed his rifle and ran as fast as he could toward the school, thinking that the chetniks might still be there. He had no idea that they had retreated to the hills. He rushed from one room to another calling out when, suddenly, through the windows on the second floor, he spotted a number of Turks. They crossed the old cemetery and headed for the school. One of them saw him looking out the window and warned the rest with loud shrieks.

Nickola Vassilev had little choice. He fired a few shots and by the time the Turks had run up the stairs, he had jumped out the window onto the branches of an apple tree. The branches gave way under his weight and he fell down. Luckily, even at his age, he landed safely and was able to escape under the very noses of his pursuers. By the time they'd figured out how he had disappeared, Nickola Vassilev managed to hide behind the house of Illia Ghegov and follow the trail to the Upper Mahalla, in the heights over the village.

Meanwhile, the Bulgarian fighting groups realized that the mayor was neither with the refugees who went to Moguilitza, nor had he joined with them. It occurred to them that the old man might have fallen asleep after a rough day. His youngest son, Dinno, went down to the village to look for him. He didn't find his father at home, or in the mayor's office. On the way to the school, he walked right into the same group of Turks his bubayco had fought fifteen minutes ago. Dinno managed to break away, but as he ran across the bridge, he was hit five times. Though badly wounded, the youth was able to hide behind a barn and return the fire. His older brother came to his rescue with a small group of *chetniks*. After a fierce gunfight in which both sides suffered casualties, Dinno was carried to the hills.

It was at this point that the major wave of savage Turks reached the outskirts of Arda and started burning and pillaging.

The huge massive gates of the old castle in Moguilitza were wide open to the refugees from Arda. There was room for everybody, and the food, if used sparingly, could take them through the better part of the upcoming winter. The Beys of Moguilitza did not let a single family seek asylum elsewhere.

"Don't worry about anything, good neighbors," said the oldest of the Agoushev's line. "We'll share the same food and same fate. I have word from a number of influential Muslim families in the area. They'll go to the Sultan himself if need be, so that we won't go hungry or unprotected. Allah is Great, brothers and sisters. You are welcome!"

Several days later, Danco's sisters from Derrekioy sought refuge with the Beys of Moguilitza. They were the first in the village to willingly accept Christianity and now feared for their lives and that of the young Bulgarian entrusted to them. Ermin's condition had not worsened, but after the accidental arrival of Danco and Radco in the presence of Rossitza, he seemed to drift deeper and deeper into a world of his own, hardly saying anything— even to Magda. Only his shepherd's flute gave him confidence, but the sadness and the pain in the melodies he played touched the hearts of the most rugged people in the neighborhood. Twice Magda sent word to Rossitza in Progled, but received no answer. On the other hand, her affection for the young man had grown to proportions that left no one in doubt about the nature of her feelings… save one.

Colonel Seraphimov hadn't fully explained everything about Chief Sergeant Jellyo Jetchev to Ivan Zemsky. He wasn't enamored only with firearms. He had two passions in life—guns and a book of poetry, *Epopee of the Forgotten* by Ivan Vazov, and not necessarily in that order. The arrival of Private Zemsky, who happened to share the same first name with the great poet and who also knew the whole book by memory, was an outstanding event in his lonely life. He was a big burly man in his early forties, with a somber face and a long, curly moustache like those a *voyvoda* used to wear. He drank a lot, talked little and never spoke of his private life. His helpers at the gun shop knew his temper only too well and stayed away from him. The first day Ivan Zemsky presented himself at the shop, the "master," as his subordinates called him, looked at the young man and, evidently angered by his awkward salute, roared in his usual manner, "Intelligentsia…eh?"

In his embarrassment Ivan saluted again. "Yes, sir… master!"

"Holy cats! If you give me one of those crazy salutes again, I'll kick your pretty arse out of this world. Savvy!!?"

"Yes, sir!"

"Name?"

"Ivan Zemsky, sir."

"Ivan?"

"Ivan, sir."

"You, too? He also!" The young man looked at him quizzically. Jetchev snorted and pointed at a faded picture of the poet. "I mean him."

"Oh, yeh..."

The chief sergeant bristled. "What's that *yeh*...supposed to mean?"

"I met him at the University in Sofia," declared Zemsky.

Jetchev looked at him with incredulity as if he had said he'd just met God around the corner. "You saw *him*... in person?"

"I talked to him."

"You talked to *him*!!?!"

"He complimented me on how I recited his poetry."

"The *Epopee*...?"

"The *Epopee of the Forgotten*, too," offered Ivan.

"You mean, you know some of it by memory?" stuttered Jetchev in reverence.

"All of it," smiled Ivan Zemsky.

Jetchev turned toward the rest of the mechanics working in the gun shop. "Listen to this, idiots, he knows all of IT!" He cleaned his hand on a dirty rag and offered it to the newcomer, "Me, too."

They both shook hands very seriously. "What do you do for a living in civilian life, Ivan?"

"I am an actor."

Jetchev was a bit lost. "Acting what?"

"On stage...theatre."

The chief sergeant was slightly taken aback. "Oh, I see...singing and dancing in charades...theatre?"

"Mmm...not exactly. Ivan Vazov had written three plays...dramas."

Jetchev shook his head. "Plays? For theatre? HE?"

"Of course. I participated in some of them. There are historical plays by him and a dramatization of his novel, *Under the Yoke*."

Jetchev was deeply impressed. "I know the novel… I've read it."

Again he addressed his mechanics, who were gaping at the two of them. "He has written plays for theatre also." He stroked his enormous moustache, "I've never seen a real play, but I read books, Ivan. You are most welcome here, and this calls for opening of the oldest brandy I've got."

Like a magician, he produced a small demijohn right in front of the admiring eyes of the boys. After taking a long draught himself, the brandy was passed to Ivan. Jetchev wiped his moustache and watched him as if he expected him to see the bottom of the demijohn. Ivan called upon all his acting skill and did not disappoint the *master*. He took quite a number of "gulps" before passing it to the rest. That made the old boy extremely happy, and gained him the silent respect of the crew. With another magic move of his deft hands, a brand new rifle materialized and Jetchev handed it to a confused and visibly appalled Ivan Zemsky. The chief sergeant misread the reaction of the young man for dismay at his generosity, and to the greatest amazement of all present, for the first time since they knew him, Jetchev produced a genuine, broad smile. "A present from me!"

Robev didn't wait for the secretary to announce him to the Tzar. He simply brushed him aside and closed the door behind himself. The monarch was not pleased, but no annoyance surfaced on his face, nor tainted his voice. "Oh, General, I missed your cheerful greeting."

"It's not a very good morning, Your Majesty. The Sultan has sent a very large and well-equipped army to the Rhodopy Mountains, led by his best general, Yaver Pasha!"

Ferdinand was stunned. He knew perfectly well what that meant. After an icy pause, he regained his composure and said very quietly, "So, my son, Boris, was right. And you all were against him," his lips quivered in utter scorn and disgust. "Council of War...a bunch of idiots, blind in their hatred of one man. A single man! Yes, Robev, a real man. I am sure you know who I mean."

General Robev paled and blurted into the face of his master, "But this man refused to be your friend, Majesty."

He waited for the blow, slightly bent, eyes closed, cursing himself. But the blow never came. Somehow he had failed to provoke the famous rage of the Tzar.

Ferdinand sighed and uttered, as if to himself, "I wish I knew how to gain his friendship."

"It's easy. Let him be the Tzar over you, Majesty."

Ferdinand pressed his hands to the sides of his head. The migraine was coming. Now Robev knew he had won. He had risked everything by picking at His Majesty's *amour propre*, and that masterly coup had given him an edge over the Tzar's decisions.

"He has already acted as a sovereign, Your Majesty. On his own he has defied the enemy in mortal combat."

"Explain yourself." Ferdinand sat up straighter.

"Instead of retreating to the old border, where domineering heights are the best position to hold a powerful army until reinforcement comes, the Lieutenant Colonel chose to disobey the orders of his superior commander, Nedelev, and moved on his own to fight Yaver Pasha at Allamy-Derre."

"Allamy-Derre?" repeated the Tzar, dismayed.

"Yes, Majesty. A point halfway between his actual location and the village of Arda. Extremely bad for strategic purposes, impassable for transportation of ammunition or cannons. A living hell."

Now the famous rage exploded. "Send Seraphimov a personal message from me. Retreat immediately to the old border at Rhojen, or face a Court Martial and…"

"And…?"

"A firing squad."

General Robev left the royal den with triumph written all over his face. In the waiting room, Prince Boris jumped from a chair and stopped him at the door. "What is happening, General?"

Robev smiled politely.

"Nothing very much today, Your Highness. We'll have a new national hero, a certain Sergeant Ranghel Sabev, who was cut to pieces by the Turks. He'll receive a few minor decorations—bravery in action behind the enemy lines."

Seraphimov held the Tzar's order, his eyes cold as steel.

"I'm sorry, Vladimir," said Colonel Nedelev with genuine sympathy, "we have no choice but to obey."

With an abrupt gesture Vladimir Seraphimov pulled the front flap of the tent. A crowd of several hundred women with their little children, down on their knees, wailed pleadingly, holding their babies up.

"Don't leave us, please…in the name of God, don't leave us to the savage Turks!"

"Whom?" Seraphimov turned his pale face toward his superior. "Whom do you ask me to obey, Nedelev?"

Colonel Nedelev was slightly piqued. "Stop your petty populism, Seraphimov. It won't get you anywhere. If we're defeated here, nobody can stop this gigantic army from marching up to the gates of Sofia. The whole country will be at their mercy. That could mean another yoke of slavery."

"We won't be defeated!" thundered Seraphimov. "I cannot abandon these people who met us as liberators a few days ago—I cannot allow them to be slaughtered mercilessly."

"Even if *I* ask you?"

"Even if you order me," Seraphimov advised.

Nedelev's face became crimson as he exclaimed. "That's…that's rebellion!"

"Call it what you like," Seraphimov shrugged his heavy shoulders, "I won't change my mind."

Colonel Nedelev wiped the perspiration from his pudgy face. "As a commanding officer, I'll order the rank and file to follow me. Not that I am pulling rank on you, but under the circumstances, I feel compelled to save you from your own madness. You leave me no choice but to put you under arrest."

Seraphimov smiled without malice. "The whole regiment is lined up out there. Why don't you ask them?"

Colonel Nedelev took his hat. "Let's go. Nobody is willing to die like cattle, Seraphimov. Those times are gone." He started to hurry out of the tent, tripped on his sword, and popped out like the cork of a champagne bottle.

The moment Seraphimov appeared, a voice shouted out, "Hurray…for our Commander Vladimir Seraphimov!"

A powerful cry roared from the regiment continuously until the Lieutenant Colonel raised his arm. His voice, calm and sturdy, reached the crowd of peasants far beyond the regiment's ranks.

"Dear soldiers and friends! The time has come to see where each and everyone of us stands. Headquarters has sent orders to our Commander, Colonel Nedelev, regarding the advancement in the area of a well equipped and numerous Turkish army. The orders are to retreat to Rhojen and wait for reinforcements."

A gasp came from thousands. Seraphimov continued.

"Colonel Nedelev, as a Commander in charge of 21st regiment, must obey. I choose not to. The only thing I can offer is victory. Whoever stays with me will either win or die. I give you my word of that. Nobody will live to be punished, including me. Mine is an act of insubordination against our superiors and the Tzar himself. You know very well what that means in time of war. Our chances are those of a regiment against an army, if we don't count the male population of this area, of which the great majority is on our side."

The thousands of men, women and *chetniks* from nearby villages let out such a cry that it seemed like the mountain itself had awakened.

"I give you the option of taking sides, to choose your destiny. Whoever wants to obey, let him stay in his spot; those who would follow me, three steps forward!"

The entire regiment, including Colonel Nedelev's own adjutant, marched three steps FORWARD.

Major Kerrim Abdoullah was from the Istanbul headquarters. His extreme cruelty was the primary recommendation to secure him a new appointment as commander of the *bashibouzouks*, the Turkish nonuniformed horde of the district of Arda. In previous campaigns he had received a nickname that stuck with him for life. The Vampire had a pale narrow face, with only one good eye. His thin colorless lips seldom cracked into an evil smile. And then it was considered an omen of imminent death, because only torture and death were amusing to him. As his adjutant, he chose Sadak, the infamous cutthroat from Catoun. After pillaging and burning for a whole day, the Turkish marauders established headquarters at the school in Arda.

That night Kerrim Abdoullah was in an especially bad mood. His men had found only three Christians, all in their eighties, one of them blind. They were cut to pieces, but their screams did not satisfy him. They died too fast. Then the mob went hunting for the recently christened in the Muslim part of the village. The wife of Mahmoud Hadgy Shcodrov, Stanna, had been rather active in propagating the new faith among women. When they took her out, grabbed hold of her long thick hair and dragged her toward the old cemetery, her husband Hadgy Mahmoud ran after them yelling: "If you wanna kill my wife, kill me with her!" The *bashibouzouks* stabbed them both to death, but Major Kerrim Abdoullah wasn't sure he could get away with killing the old hadgy. He was a wealthy man who had relatives in Istanbul. The local priest told him that one of Mahmoud's cousins was rather influential at the palace of the Great Vizier.

And so The Vampire stopped the killings and threatened that any further arbitrary action of that kind would be punished by death. Yet, at the same time, the drunken mob went berserk and were beyond control. He had to gun down eight of them and warn the rest that he'd send them to the front to fight the Bulgarian soldiers. He knew their kind of garbage—good at killing old men, children and women, but scared to death of the *chetnitzy* and the regular army. Hissing and grumbling, the *bashibouzouks* went back to their camps. There, until late into the night, they snarled at each other like mad dogs fighting for plunder.

The major, full of bitterness and frustration, locked himself in the school with a bottle of brandy. He banged his bony fist on the table. If only he could find a way to get his men into the castle of Moguilitza, that would be real fun. Kerrim Abdoullah laughed drearily, his hard, muscled body shuddered lustily with anticipation. He yelled at his adjutant outside, "Find me a wench, Sadak!!"

"Only ugly and old ones have chosen to remain here, master."

"Go to the castle, idiot!"

Ismail was having nightmares.

He woke up drenched with cold perspiration, a horrible taste in his mouth, as if he was choking on his own blood. He raised himself on to his elbows, his pupils wide open, adjusting to the dark, trying to remember his dream. It had a meaning, a terrible message warning him about something...but what?

Tomorrow was his wedding day.

He had tried to convince his new grandfathers to postpone it. It wasn't the right time for marriage, with war raging at their very doorstep. They had seen the smoke of burning houses in Arda. The poor refugees pulled at their hair, screaming in desperation. A wedding ceremony would be out of place amidst all this suffering...

Neither grandfather conceded. "Life and death are part of the same face," said the older, "the face of Allah. When He smiles, it means Life, when He closes His eyes, it means Death. By celebrating this wedding, we're healing wounds, not causing them."

Ismail had obeyed. And now Allah had warned him, a clear message that would help him if only he could remember! Maybe it was nothing, maybe it was his imagination at play. A result of overexcitement, perhaps he was kind of curious to see what it was like to have a wife. His first wife! The most beautiful girl in the region. Maybe in the whole wide world. He felt a hot wave in his loins and tossed about in the damp bed sheets. To hell with those stupid dreams. Come morning, come!

Suddenly it occurred to him that the message might have been from someone other than Allah. What if it was young Ahmed giving him a warning? Ismail had taken his place in this house, in the hearts of his grandfathers, laying in his bed, lusting for his girl! "Oh, Ahmed," he whispered to himself, "I know you're here, mad at me. I beg your pardon! I should have left that night in the rain, to seek my own fortune, my own destiny. Pardon me, if you can, but I was so lonely. I had lost everything of my own. I wanted to die, but I didn't. I still had one friend in this world. Radco, Radco?" It *was* him…he was lying in a pool of his own blood, his stomach torn, the golden curls covered with mud, his sunny blue eyes wide open, muddled, staring right at Ismail with silent reproach and sadness.

"Don't kill me, brother…" he uttered, "don't marry my girl…please…"

"You are mad," cried out Ismail. "She's not your girl, she's Ahmed's. You're not Ahmed Agoushev…or, are you?"

"Why not? If you took his place, and I am you…"

Ismail woke up again with another scream and jumped out of bed as if it were full of hot coals. He was breathing heavily, his still unseeing eyes wild with terror. Gradually he pulled himself together and dug his fingers into the thick mat of hair hanging over his forehead. "It makes no sense, Allah…it makes not a bit of sense," he thought, as he realized daylight was streaming through the window.

The sound of a flute, masterfully played, came from somewhere in the house, full of sadness and reproach, like a human voice.

The snow was wet and slushy. Radco and Danco were digging trenches, shoulder to shoulder. Since the incident at Derrekioy, very few words had been spoken between them. Over the backs of the digging soldiers, Radco was able to get a glimpse of Lieutenant Colonel Seraphimov, wrapped in his black mantle, guiding a bunch of villagers who were struggling to push a heavy cannon to the top of the rocky hill. Since morning, in the slippery snow, through the sharp razor-like rocks, thousands of men had dragged the bulky guns up to spots visited only by birds before. Now in the thickening darkness of the evening the youth suddenly understood why. The widely spread battery and the echo effect would create a "surround" sound and lead the enemy to the wrong conclusion. They would doubt the information of their own spies, assuming that what was in front of them was a large battalion, maybe an army.

The coarse voice of Danco broke into his thoughts abruptly. "You're resting too much, dreamer. Get back to work! Glue your hands to the shovel and forget about Azimee!"

Radco spit on his hands angrily. "I wasn't thinking any more about Azimee than you were about Rossitza."

The two exchanged murderous glances and went on digging in silence. The trenches followed an incredibly tough and rocky terrain, and the soldiers were suffering from fatigue. Even those rugged mountain men were starting to falter. They had worked since daybreak, and the strain made them irritable. There were squabbles here and there, and some of them had come to blows. By noon, their muscles were numb with exhaustion, but the digging stopped only twice in the course of the day for a brief meal. They had no need of encouragement, digging as if their lives depended on it—which was the truth.

"Danco!" Radco begged.

"Work," was Danco's terse reply.

"I can work and talk, damn it!"

"What is it?"

"I'm sorry I mentioned Rossitza."

"Forget it. That doesn't matter to me."

"You lie. It does…a lot."

"All right, all right, I'm sorry too…about Azimee. Now shovel those rocks out."

Azimee had not slept well either. She tossed and turned in her bed, but the images kept going through her head so realistically that they made her moan with desire. She was holding that shiny blond hair, feeling the warm pressure of his thighs around her own, his hands caressing her bosom, their lips devouring each other…the hot breathing, the maddening smell of male perspiration…

"Oh, Ismail! My, golden Ismail!!!"

She woke up to the sweetest cavall playing she had ever heard. That must be Ermin. If she could only walk around the house freely like that Bulgarian girl from Derrekioy! Magda had told her all about her own love for Ermin, and Azimee wished her well. She wanted everybody to be happy as she was. If she wasn't restricted to the boundaries of the harem, she would have found the flute player and told him…

Azimee's bed felt hot and uncomfortable. She got up, ran to the window and opened it. The cool morning air hit her in the face. Over her burning cheeks it felt like a hand she knew…and those hateful irons again barring a clear view of the sky. She must go into the little garden for a walk so she could stay in her right mind, she thought. She dressed in a hurry, put the veil over her flushed face and ran on tip toe down the corridor.

"Where are you going?" whispered somebody behind her.

It was Magda, fully dressed.

"Oh, Magda, you scared me," said Azimee, spitting in her bosom to ward off the fear, "I can't sleep."

Magda smiled. "I can understand that. It's your wedding day. I can't sleep either. The honey voice of the cavall chases my dream away."

"Let's go to the garden!"

Magda tightened her neckerchief around her head. "That's what I had in mind. Let's go!"

The garden was a small quadrangle with an octagonal marble pool in the middle. Now the fountain was frozen and the flowers were dead, but the outer side bordered on an old pine forest that smelled heavenly and filtered the air from the smell of a burning Arda, leaving just the scent of pine in the morning mist. The girls ran around, chasing each other with ringing laughter. Finally they stopped running, breathless and rosy cheeked. They walked along, arms intertwined around their slim waists, listening to the flute.

"I wish it was your wedding day, too, Magda."

Magda shook her head without bitterness. "I'll never get married. I am not pretty."

"Of course you will, silly. You don't give yourself enough credit. You are spirited and charming and that counts much more than beauty."

"I wish he would notice that," blushed Magda, "only yesterday Ermin asked me why I am taking such great care of him."

"And what was your answer?"

Magda dropped her head, her voice distant and sad. "I said, 'cause you're sick.' "

"And what was his reply?"

" 'I am not sick; I am crippled for life.' And then I told him, 'Your wound is healing; it is your spirit that is sick. You won't walk again unless your heart is free.' "

"Oh, Magda, his heart must be made of stone."

"Ermin's heart is the softest and most vulnerable in the world."

"Then wait until I talk to him," begged Azimee.

"For heaven's sake, no! They'll kill you if you talk to another man."

Azimee laughed happily, embracing her new found friend. "You silly, my husband will take me to his mother in Bulgaria. There we'll make our home. I'll be free to do anything there…and I'll talk to Ermin, and I'll tell him how much you love him!"

"No, you won't!" cried an alarmed Magda.

"Yes, I will. Oh, I wish we could stop going round and round like captive squirrels in a cage…"

Magda's eyes lit up. "Want to go to the pine forest?"

"You must be kidding," sighed Azimee, "With those savage Turks around, all the doors are locked and guarded day and night."

"There is a small door, Azimee, right here, behind the bushes. It's not even locked. It's just an iron bar that goes through the wall. I've been using it any time I feel depressed."

Azimee inspected the little door plated with iron. "How did you find it?"

"By accident."

"Magda."

"What?"

"I am afraid. You know what those wild *bashibouzouks* do to women."

"Rubbish. The *bashibouzouks* are busy pillaging Arda. They have no business in the pine forest. Let's go! Don't be yellow. I am going."

Chapter Nine

The repair shop for the regiment was in the small village of Allamy Derre, less than half a mile from the front line. After the heavy march and quick building of fortifications on the heights, many broken wheels and tools had piled up. Toward noon, Master Sergeant Jellyo Jetchev wiped the sweat from his bushy moustache and grumbled, "Enough is enough! At this point we're needed more at the front line than here. If we're still alive, we'll finish the work after the battle. Zemsky!" he called out.

"Yes, sir!"

"Recite for us *The Defenders of Shipka*."

The poem was about a bunch of minutemen who defended Shipka Pass in the heart of Old Mountain against an overwhelming and ferocious enemy. They fought the Turks for three days, ran out of ammunition and still didn't surrender the pass, throwing pieces of rock and the bodies of their dead comrades at the enemy until reinforcements arrived. Inspired by the patriotic poem, the greatness of the moment and the appropriate situation, Ivan Zemsky gave the performance of his life. His voice, his fiery eyes and bold gestures ignited the spirits of his highly volatile audience. Shouts of hurrah, tears, embraces and patriotic songs followed. Then, led by their "master," they took their arms and left for the front line.

Delly Hassan, the young gunsmith from Progled, stayed behind to put out the fire in the furnace and Ivan helped him. When they finished, Delly Hassan threw away his leather apron and grabbed his *berdana* from the wall rack.

"What are you waiting for, Ivan? Take your rifle from the rack and let's go!"

Ivan Zemsky opened his hands in desperation and shame.

"I am not sure I know how to handle it, Delly."

For a moment the gunsmith was lost. To the men of the mountains, handling a gun was something as natural as walking, and here was a man in his prime, older than himself, reciting poetry of battles as if he were there, yet didn't know how to operate a simple *berdana*! Then he laughed, but without mockery.

"Don't worry, man. I am an old *chetnik*. I'll teach you how. Let's go!"

The snow fell heavier than in the morning and the fog came down like a curtain before the last act. Near the top of the ridge, the two soldiers met the commander and one of his adjutants. Seraphimov recognized the youthful looking newcomer right away and held his horse back.

"What are you doing here, Zemsky?"

"I am not so sure what I am doing here, sir, but I know very well what the rest of the men are doing, so I'll try."

A tiny smile lit up the strained face of the lieutenant colonel.

"You, of all people, with a rifle in your hand? Are you going to use it or let yourself be killed by the first Turk you meet?"

Ivan lifted his eyes and met those of the older man. "I'm gonna use it, sir."

Seraphimov held his horse with a steady hand. "Thank you, Gray Eyes. I know what that means to you. God bless you. Take care, boys."

He rode away, followed by Captain Dennev.

"Are those sources really good, Dennev...I mean, reliable enough to trust them?" asked Seraphimov.

"They're villagers from Allamy Derre, sir, recruited into the Turkish army a year ago. Sergeant Marrin knows them from Istanbul. He has faith in them."

"Danco is a shrewd man. When did they desert?"

"Last night."

"Did you check with their families?"

"Yes, sir. Simple folks. Muslims, but very patriotic toward Bulgaria."

They arrived at a small stone house in the outskirts used as a commanding post. The two deserters jumped to their feet at attention, saluting the officers in the Turkish manner. Seraphimov had a quick look at their faces. Quite young, they were stiff and obviously scared.

"Very good, boys," said he, "are you brothers?"

"No, sir. Sallih is only my first cousin."

"And what is your name?"

"Radgeb, sir, effendi."

"Very good, Radgeb. Now give me this chair. I am an old man and I've been on my feet since five, not counting the riding, which is worse than walking through this rugged country of yours." Seraphimov sat heavily on the low three-legged chair brought by the soldier. "Are you older, Radgeb?"

The youth stuck out his broad chest.

"A whole year, sir."

Seraphimov arched his heavy eyebrows. "A whole year! That's quite a bit."

Sallih could hold back no longer. "He might be older by a year, sir effendi, but I am the stronger between us two."

Radgeb shot a sharp look at him. "You are not!"

"Of course I am! Ask Danco, effendi, sir. He has seen us wrestling…"

"Well, well, boys," the commander cut them off, "we'll settle this dispute another time. Now let's talk a bit about the army you just left! I've heard it's a very large army. Two hundred thousand strong."

Both youths started talking at the same time, but young Sallih out shouted his rival. "We were ordered to say that by the officers. They wanted to scare you and the population of the region."

Now Radgeb took over. "Forty thousand at most, with the auxiliary forces."

Seraphimov's face opened, a sigh of relief coming from the depths of his chest. "Very good, boys. Now tell me, if you've noticed, do they have a lot of cannon and machine guns?'"

Sallih stepped forward. "I've heard the officers complain of not having enough cannon power for the size of the army."

"So did I," added Radgeb, "and very few machine guns too."

"Is that so? I am glad you told me. But now I have a much more difficult question."

"Ask me!"

"Ask me!"

"All right, I'll ask both of you. Did you notice any movement of the troops straying from the general direction, let's say yesterday?"

The cousins looked at each other; then Radgeb spoke for the two of them.

"Of course we did. Our regiment was assigned to go around, over that ridge and come out into your back. That's when we escaped."

Seraphimov and Captain Dennev exchanged quick looks.

"You mean last night?"

"Yes, effendi. We started moving right after evening meal."

Seraphimov straightened and stood up.

"Captain Dennev, take the second and third companies and all available machine guns. Hit them in the flank and destroy 'em completely. You boys go with that captain and show him exactly where the enemy is. Would you do that for me?"

The youths nodded with eagerness and Seraphimov shook their hands.

"When we smash this army," he said, "we'll have a big celebration with medals given, eating and drinking. Then you'll wrestle for me and we'll see which one of you is telling me the truth. Now go. And God be with you!"

The matron responsible for the harem didn't look for Azimee until about ten o'clock that morning. When she found her bedroom empty, she wasn't very worried. The wedding was planned for noon time, so she looked in the huge bath, in the pool and round the little cubicles with sofas for resting. After seeing that the bride was not there either, she still didn't panic right away. She looked in the other rooms to see if the girl was visiting some of the other wives. But none of the women had seen her since dinner the night before. It was at this point, the matron decided to send the guards around the house and yards. They looked everywhere. Azimee had disappeared.

At eleven o'clock the father of the bride was asked if he knew the whereabouts of the young girl. Rashid Babba paled and went to look in Ismail's bedroom. It was empty. The bridegroom was located in the male baths, relaxing in the marble pool. When he was told that his bride was missing, he took it as a bad joke. But at that moment the matron and other women started pulling their hair and screaming and he knew that something serious must be happening. He wrapped a robe around his wet body and ran to the master's bedroom. The old men were praying in the corner and Ismail's announcement of the missing bride found them absolutely unprepared. The chief of the guard was called and he had to admit that one of his men, originally from Catoun, was missing. The previous night another guard had seen him talking through the gate hatch window to Sadak, the infamous gang leader of that hamlet. More of the guards arrived. They had found the little door of the harem garden open from inside and brought a veil and a neckerchief which were hanging over some low branches not far from the wall. Rashid Babba identified the veil immediately, but said the neckerchief did not belong to his daughter. That type of kerchief was worn mostly by Bulgarian girls. It was Magda's sister who recognized it.

Ismail's handsome face grew darker and darker by the minute. A sinister light lit up his large eyes and the pearl white teeth ground in wild anger. He asked the Beys of Agoushevo for three brave men and their blessing. At first his adoptive grandfathers were adamant about him not going, but the thousand-year-old code of honor was irrevocable: if a bride was abducted, she must be returned by the groom. Rashid Babba wanted to come along; so did Mehmed Agoushev and the Guard's Chief Roustan, who felt responsible for the happening.

While the men went to their quarters to get ready, Magda's sister knocked at Ismail's door and pleaded with him to help her sister, Magda, too. She also told him that young flute player, Ermin, was begging to see him for a minute.

"Ermin?" exclaimed the surprised youth, "I knew a soldier at Rhojen by that name. He was a cavall player, also."

Magda's sister exclaimed, "That's him. He was brought to us by a platoon of soldiers, badly hurt, almost dying. It happened at a bridge near Arda. My brother, Danco, saved his life and sent him to my house for treatment...our uncle is a sage man...he performed a miracle. The young man was brought back to life...but...he'll never walk again..."

Ismail closed his eyes for a moment as if he was recalling something painful. When he opened them they were glistening wet.

"What is your name, madam?"

"Bogdana."

"Your Turkish is flawless."

"Except for me and Magda our family is Muslim. We all have Turkish and Bulgarian names. My father wanted it that way. My husband is a Christian. He calls me nothing but Bogdana."

"Please, take me to Ermin, Bogdana."

She led him through a maze of corridors and steps, where he had never been before, to a small room in the basement. There was very little light in this room, and Ismail had to adapt his eyes to see a middle aged man sitting next to a bed. Ismail shuddered, "It's awfully damp in here."

"We're glad to have a room of our own," said Bogdana, "as this house is crowded. I pray to God to give your grandfathers a thousand years of life. We can never thank them fully for their hospitality."

Ismail shook his head. "This is no room for a sick man. It's more like a prison cell. Good day, effendi."

"This is my husband, Ignat."

"Good day, young man," the man bowed.

"We'd better leave you alone now," said Bogdana, giving a sign to her husband, and they both left.

Ismail took a few steps and sat on the low chair next to the bed. The youthful handsome face he knew had changed terribly. It was a shadow of the man he had met at Rhojen. He smiled with a heavy heart. "It's a small world, Ermin."

There was a brief silence, then the thin youth spoke in a strange hollow voice, "You look fine, Ismail."

Ismail forced a laugh. "You mean, for someone who's just lost his bride, I don't look too bad."

"You are strong, Ismail. I wish I were like you."

Ismail waved his hand. "It has very little to do with strength, Ermin. It's just that I lost so much in such a short time, I am still kind of numb."

"I saw your father..." Ermin started to say.

Ismail bit his lips. "My little sisters too...the Beys of Moguilitza sort of adopted me. They lost their only grandson in the war. So I got his bride...all in the same package."

"You don't love her?"

Ismail shrugged his shoulders. "How can I say? I've never seen her, though she has been under the same roof for the last three days. She's said to be the most beautiful girl in the region."

Ermin smiled wryly. "Lucky you!"

"Say, Ermin, at the fair on the summit of Rhojen, when we last met, you were with a girl I thought was a real beauty...I envied you...if my memory is right, her name was Rossitza."

Ermin turned his face toward the wall. Ismail took his hand, worried. "Are you in pain?"

Ermin rolled his head back to him. "No...I am all right...tell me, if you don't love this girl, why are you going to risk your life for her?"

"It's that Code of Honor of ours. Besides, if stupid tradition had not kept us apart, I might have been in love with her."

Ermin shook his head with bitterness. "Do you know what real love is?"

Ismail looked deeply into his eyes, blue-green with a golden light in them. "Is that what crushed you?"

Ermin nodded silently. "You didn't answer my question," he whispered .

Ismail buried his hot face in those big strong hands. "How is Radco?"

Ermin's hand settled on his shoulder. "He is alive and well."

Ismail got up and walked to a chest of drawers. Ermin's flute was lying on top. He took it with care and looked at it in admiration.

"I hear this magic cavall in the mornings. I should have known there was not another player like you in the whole world."

"Ismail."

"Yeh...

"I know I have no right to ask you for anything..."

Ismail came back and sat next to him with the flute in his hands. "Anything you say, Ermin."

"There is a girl out there with your bride. Magda is her name."

"Yes, I know."

"Save her life...if possible."

"I give you my word on it."

"Thank you, Ismail...but I have one last thing to ask you."

"Tell me, pal."

"If, when you come back with the girls. If I am not here—I mean if I am dead—find her a good man for husband. She is...Magda is the finest person I've ever known."

Ismail jumped to his feet. "Now you listen to me!" he thundered in his mighty voice. "I am not going anywhere until you move out of this cold, damp hole, right into my sunny spacious room. I'll make my grandfathers swear to Allah to bring the best doctors here that money can buy…from Istanbul, if necessary. But I want to see you, when I come back, standing on your feet. Promise?"

Ermin nodded with little conviction. "I promise."

The wet snow kept falling throughout the night.

The accumulation was very small, but it made the terrain even more slippery and dangerous. The soldiers from the second and third companies were told to keep physical contact with the person ahead. It was pitch dark and extremely easy to get lost in the fog. Any conversation was forbidden. The column advanced in total silence, which gave everyone an eerie feeling, as if walking in a void. Delly Hassan felt responsible for the inexperienced city boy, even though he was older. He had fastened a piece of rope from his belt to that of Ivan Zemsky. The "master" would never forgive him if he failed to bring back his actor. Besides Delly Hassan was quite impressed by the commander talking to his partner in person, as if they had known each other for years.

As happens in time of war, bonds between men were forged fast by the need to rely upon someone, through good and bad. The platoon commander, Sergeant Marrin, and his assistant, Corporal Boev, had to check on their people every once in awhile. Thank God nobody had gone astray so far.

Dennev, with his junior officer and the two deserters in tow, walked at the head of the outfit. He knew how dependent the whole plan of Lieutenant Colonel Seraphimov was on his success. That knowledge made him twice as careful. They had to move over the top of the ridge in a semi-circle and get to the flank of the Turkish troops while making the same move to the rear of the Bulgarian defense. After defeating them, he had to close the horse-shoe around the main trunk of the enemy and proceed to annihilate the captured army.

About four o'clock in the morning Captain Dennev had the feeling they had walked past the enemy. It seemed his troops had marched forever. He was ready to give an order to make a turn when the cousins from Allamy Derre stumbled over something that they recognized as being the corpse of the mule they had taken with them the previous night. The poor animal had fallen into the ravine, breaking its neck. They convinced the captain that from that point on they had to walk for at least two more hours before they would cross the enemy's path. With some misgivings, the commander agreed to it, and he wasn't a bit sorry later. At about eight in the morning, his troops almost bumped into the camp of the Turkish auxiliary forces.

The surprise was total.

It was cruel hand-to-hand combat in which the Turks did not relinquish an inch until completely defeated. Over three hundred were killed; the rest fled into the woods. Daylight and the temporary lifting of the fog helped in discovering remaining pockets of resistance.

Advancing through the bushes in search of snipers, Delly Hassan had lost sight of Ivan Zemsky. When he saw him again in a clearing a hundred yards away, a Turkish soldier who had evidently run out of ammunition, jumped from a bush on to the back of the inexperienced Ivan. With a war cry, Delly Hassan rushed to help. The Turk wrestled the young man to the ground and was grabbing for his throat, though it wasn't easy because Ivan proved to be a tough cookie. Overpowered, Ivan was still able to roll his assailant off balance, so at the moment his friend reached them, they were rolling on the ground tightly wrapped together. Delly Hassan was afraid to use his bayonet. It could easily penetrate both. His eyes fell on the knife that the attacker had dropped in the fight. In a matter of seconds, Delly grabbed the knife and plunged it deep into the base of the Turk's neck. The Turk jerked and died.

Delly Hassan helped Ivan to his feet. "Are you okay?"

"Couldn't be better," smiled Ivan, a bit pale in the face. "For a first fight, it wasn't too bad."

"No, it was not," Delly Hassan laughed with relief. "How did you ever manage to make him drop his knife?"

"Somehow, I felt him coming up behind me. A China-man used to do tricks between acts at the theatre, sliding down a rope with his hair braid fastened to it, and things like that...he taught me how to disarm an assailant."

"Allah give him a long life! You'll have to show it to me sometime."

Danco and Radco got separated also. Around noon, after everything was over, and victory complete, Sergeant Marrin looked for his friend; Radco was nowhere to be seen. Alarmed, Danco engaged the whole platoon in a search party, but to no avail. In one hour they had to move to a new position, taking their casualties along with them.

Radco Boev had disappeared.

The moment he was hit in the chest by the bullet, Radco knew it was a very serious wound. He slipped down the trunk of a huge pine tree with a low moan, the high branches of the pine danced strangely in the sky over him. The blood gushed from a wound somewhere in his midsection, and he tried to stop it by pressing his hands over it. So it wasn't his chest. It was strange how he had felt the impact at this spot. He closed his eyes to stop the tiresome dancing of the branches, round and round. Mother, flashed through his mind, I promised you I'd take good care of myself...sorry...I didn't quite make it. His thoughts raced, "And, Azimee, another promise that I have to break..." That thought gave him a sharp pain—never to be able to feel her bare silky skin next to his body! Or, maybe the pains had started. For a few minutes he was numbed by the hit, but now...suddenly he realized that somebody was speaking swiftly in Turkish! Danco? No, he wouldn't speak Turkish now. Thank God that he was not alone. He struggled to open his eyes. It took a great effort to concentrate on the faces, and recognition came slowly.

It was the brothers Metyo and Mourco from Progled. The drinking buddies of Delly Hassan Caursky in the saloon, now dressed in Turkish army clothes.

The sonofabitches! flew through his mind... pretending to be great patriots, and they were just spying for the Turks!" Radco had seen them around Delly Hassan, obviously just posing as gunsmiths in a Progled repair shop.

The men were a bit confused when they came upon Radco, but he said nothing. It was so difficult those days, to tell a friend from a foe. The two brothers recognized him too. Radco heard them talking about haydouk Dimmitar's son. Mourco, the older, wanted him finished on the spot.

"He's gonna die anyway!" he insisted.

"Don't be a fool, Mourco," argued his brother, "the boy has been promoted to a corporal. He might have some important information."

"And to whom are you going to give that information, you nut?"

"We'll join the reserve at Arda. It's not that far. Besides, later we may be able to exchange him for the hidden gold of Dimmitar, the freedom fighter. His mother, stryna Nonna, will give anything in the world to get her son back."

Mourco pondered on the subject, the strain clearly written on his blunt face. "Oh, come on, Metyo, he'll slow us down."

"And who's gonna give us a chase? The Christians have their hands full with our army. Though we were defeated, they'll hurry to help their troops. Think of the gold!"

"All right, all right. What an ass you are! He's already got one foot in the grave."

Mourco kneeled down and looked carefully at the young man.

"He really looks half dead..." he hesitated, with his usual stuttering, more pronounced when in an emotional state.

"I am...not...going to die..." blurted out Radco. If you stop the bleeding. I'll lead you...to my father's... treasure. I know where it is...it will be all yours if you...save my life..."

Then he blacked out.

Major Abdoullah was still in bed, trying to survive the aftermath of his drinking bout. He had a splitting headache, pains in his joints and was in a murderous mood. He was brooding over the events of yesterday, feeling only frustration at not fulfilling his expectations. He was not one for remorse. His father, the governor of the village of Saksalla, was also the local judge. As a judge, his word was enough to smooth out the incident with Hadgy Mahmoud Shcodrov and his wife Stanna...and many other problems should they arise. He was influential even in the capital.

The knocking at the door unleashed a volley of curses from the mayor's fetid mouth. "Go away, whoever you are, fuckin' sonofabitch! I don't want to be bothered before lunch time!"

There was a confused pause behind the door, then a cacophony of low voices. Finally, the rocky voice of his assistant, the accursed Sadak, emerged over it.

"It's me, master…Sadak. I brought you a wench from the castle as you ordered last night."

Kerrim Abdoullah licked his cracked lips. "It was for the night. Why in the name of hell so late?"

"It was not easy, master. But you should see what I brought you."

"Is she young?"

"Very young."

"Pretty?"

"Let your eyes feast on her face, master. I have no words to describe it."

Kerrim Abdoullah straightened up on his elbows, the light shining on his closely shaven head.

"Well, let me see…" The door handle cracked. "Wait a minute, idiot!" He put on the black patch over the socket of his missing eye, which he lost in a drunken fight in Izmir. "Now, come in!"

When Sadak unwrapped the burlap from Azimee's head, he covered her mouth and threw away her mantle. The Vampire jerked, as if under the lash of a whip. "Mighty Allah!"

Azimee's eyes were burning with indignation and hatred. She bit the hand of Sadak, and with her mouth free, shouted on the top of her lungs, "I am Azimee, daughter of Rashid Babba, and soon to be related to the noble house of Agoushevs. Take me immediately back to my bridegroom, or your ugly head will be thrown to the dogs in the courtyard of the Great Padishah!"

In spite of his hangover, Kerrim Abdoullah jumped out of bed with the natural ease of a wild animal.

"Major Kerrim Abdoullah from the Great Army of His Majesty, the Sultan, at your service, young lady!" He had nothing but a loin cloth around his pelvis. Though mother nature had written the value of his soul all over his face, the body he was given was wiry and tight as a whip. Azimee screamed and tried to cover her eyes. "Don't be afraid, dear, you might switch bridegrooms, but you won't be disappointed." Much as he wanted to keep her for his immediate pleasure, he was clever enough to avoid a foolish venture like this. "Take her to my father's village, Sadak!"

"Aman, please don't, Chaush Effendi," Azimee pleaded with him, "if you're taking me away for ransom, let me keep my servant girl with me!"

"What servant?" An evil flame fluttered in the Vampire's squinty eyes as he looked sharply at Sadak.

"An ugly wench for my own delight, master." Sadak muttered.

The voice of the officer squeaked with disdain. "Have I ever ordered you to hunt for yourself, bastard?"

"No, master, you did not," Sadak hissed through his teeth.

"Don't you dare to touch the servant of my bride-to-be! Take all the people involved in the abduction—use the guards from my door as an escort—and leave them to my father's disposition. I expect my future wife to be treated with the respect due to her rank."

Azimee was so horrified by the prospect of being married to this man that she was speechless. Then, her Islamic fatalism helped her regain her composure. If that was not Allah's will, Ismail would deliver her from the kidnappers!

For his own part, Major Kerrim Abdoullah was very satisfied with himself. He had second thoughts about putting Sadak in charge of transporting Azimee to his father's village and kept him back. He didn't trust him enough. Saksalla was a day and a half from Moguilitza. Hiding the girl in his father's harem would give him ample opportunity to deny any wrongdoing.

Of one thing The Vampire was sure: no news would travel that far.

October 21st, Allamy Derre
Dear Ellena,

I haven't written many letters to you and you know it is not because I'm not thinking of my loved ones. I think of you too much, and writing seems to put everything in a descriptive line. Love doesn't need description and cannot be described. I know that I miss the touch of you terribly: the touch of your skin, your hair, those full lips of yours…and still that is not love. I think love has something to do with me, you and the kids, living in the same being. Don't laugh at me. You are the staunchest zealot I have ever known, but there is a part of me in you, too, so you must understand my crazy ideas.

It's late. I cannot sleep. Not that I have a guilty con-science, or worry too much. In my mind everything is lucid. There is not a molecule of doubt that I should have done otherwise. Nedelev reproached me for risking the fate of the whole country, my own family, to protect these people out here. He calls it 'petty populism.' I've never been a gambler; you know I have never touched cards, dice, never even went near a casino. I want you to understand. I am going to save these people because I love you, because I love our country! I believe in victory. If we fail, it's going to be only by my own mistake; a miscalculation or a tactical error. And I am trying not to make even a fraction of a mistake. Fate always has a say in the course of history. For instance, I might have lost without the priceless information two deserters gave me on the eve of the battle. Now the bad surprise is reserved for Yaver Pasha and his army.

There's always a chance that I could get hit in spite of my magic mantle. I've had no premonitions; it's just a possibility. If that should happen, I pray to God that it be when everything on my side is done, and I won't be needed any more. Victory has its momentum. If the machinery is well greased, the engine set on its rails, it can arrive at its destination even without a commander. Anybody can serve as the engineer.

It won't be the same for you and the kids. You need a commander even if nobody listens to his orders. I keep that in my mind, and I'll try to dodge any bullets coming in my direction. That's a promise!

If that should happen, anyway, please find the strength to forgive me. You'll have a miserable pension and no home of your own. Try to explain to the kids that my mind was elsewhere, not on making money. I never took a bribe, never sold out on my convictions.

God bless, kiss them all!

I love you,
VLADIMIR

His binoculars were seldom aimed at the raging battle. Most of the time they were glued to the top of the ridge above. Some of the soldiers wondered if he was expecting a miracle from there. But Lieutenant Colonel Seraphimov knew better.

When, shortly after noon time, a column of gray smoke came from the ridge, the commander dropped the binoculars, made the sign of the cross over his broad chest and whispered, "Now, with God, ahead!"

For the better part of the day all his troops were engaged in a fierce battle with the enemy, greatly outnumbered, yet the psychological momentum was decisively on their side. Another factor helped as well—the devastating fire of the artillery and machine guns were situated at the most advantageous points. That gave the gunners absolute control of the gorge, producing the special effect of an enormous battery. In that narrow area, the great army of the enemy had no chance to open its forces on a wide front and make use of its numbers. Yaver Pasha could enter only a portion of it at a time.

On the opposite hill, Seraphimov had another surprise trick that he had organized the night before. Eight thousand recruits were waiting for his sign to start running downward. They were unarmed men of all ages from nearby villages, some women among them. In the falling darkness of the late afternoon, and at the right moment, they would produce a devastating moral shock to the Turkish rank and file.

Around four in the afternoon, luck smiled on the lieutenant colonel. The fog that had lifted during the day started rolling in again. He was a good showman too. Sanya, his white mare, sensed the uniqueness of the moment and danced on her hind legs, attracting the attention of the soldiers around. Seraphimov lifted his right hand, the evening breeze throwing his black mantle into the air, the silver sword reflecting the last light of day. The regiment's band started playing the National Anthem. Commander Seraphimov waved his sword high above his head and shouted at the top of his mighty voice so that every one of his five thousand men could hear him, "Attack, lads! God is with us!"

Like an angry wave, the troop rushed ahead, crushing everything in their way. The first impact on the Turkish line penetrated three levels of defense. The momentum went no further. Seraphimov signaled Captain Dennev's troop from the ridge to hit the flank. It was mayhem. The Turks vacillated. At that moment, the commander brought his villagers on the hill into action. In the falling darkness, through a thickening fog, they ran down like an avalanche with a mighty roar!"

That finished the Turks.

In front of the tent of Yaver Pasha, his whole staff was on horseback in full readiness. Next to the commander, dressed in a well tailored riding costume, with her favorite falcon on her wrist, was Zyumbul, the Pasha's one and only lover. From their vantage point it was clearly visible, that, here and there, individual soldiers were throwing down their arms and darting toward the rear. Their officers were shooting those in the back, while new ones followed.

Yaver Pasha closed his eyes and, so quietly that only Zyumbul was able to hear him, said, "This is the beginning of the end."

A liaison officer arrived on a bloodied horse. "You'll be cut off, Excellence!"

Zyumbul looked into the pale faces of the staff officers with disdain bordering on hatred. "You betrayed your Commander, yellow dogs!"

Then she set her falcon free. He hesitated for a moment, then flew into the low fog. Zyumbul stared after him with her large, fiery eyes, then grabbed the sword of the nearest officer and brandished it aloft. "Kill the infidels! Kill them all! Follow me!!!" She kicked her horse and signaled to the standby reserves, "Follow me!!!"

Everybody looked at their commander, waiting for a sign. He sat on his horse, stupefied, unable to budge. Then slowly, projecting a sense of total fatalism, he shook his head. Zyumbul kept on urging, "Follow me! Isn't there a single man behind me?!?"

Full of desperation, sobbing with rage and frustration, she again kicked her horse into a wild run ahead.

Yaver Pasha feebly tried to stop her, but to no avail. A bullet hit her straight in her full bosom, and he was hardly able to get hold of her frightened horse as she fell into his arms. The blazing eyes of so many nights, dug deeply into his soul, as if she wanted to take him along on her ride to Allah.

"Only you...only you, Yaver, followed me...it wasn't enough..." And the brave woman's eyes froze on his face, petrified with pain and misery...then nothing.

Yaver gave the signal for a total retreat.

General Robev waited respectfully until the Tzar finished reading the whole report about the battle at Allamy Derre. When Ferdinand finished the last page, he leaned back in his armchair, a thin smile on his lips.

"Incredible! That 21st regiment has defeated a whole Army! Now all Europe will sing Hosanna to me. Telegraph General Ghenev to cut the road to Yaver Pasha's retreat and capture him. Promote that Commander of the heroic 21st Regiment to the rank of General and give some promotions and medals to the rest; lots of medals, but not that many promotions. I don't want too many heads in the clouds."

Robev flushed. "I am glad about Vladimir Seraphimov," the general commented reluctantly.

The monarch raised his eyebrows. "Who said anything about Seraphimov? I was talking about the Commander Colonel Nedelev." He contemplated his well polished fingernails for a while, then said, "Oh...well, we can make the Lieutenant Colonel a full Colonel. I guess he deserves it."

Even after his many years of close service to the monarch, Robev was stunned at times by the Tzar's aristocratic lack of scruples.

"And you don't want any publicity on this battle, I presume."

"No newspapers, for Christ sake, Robev! Later, when Yaver Pasha is captured by General Ghenev, I want big headlines. Make the General a hero. I don't mind."

"As you wish, Your Majesty. And to the Crown Prince?"

Ferdinand looked over his golden pince-nez. "Not a word."

Chapter Ten

Sultan Mehmed was in a state of shock.

He looked helplessly at everyone present, especially at the British Ambassador, as if he expected him to refute the report. The Ambassador merely coughed lightly and looked at the tips of his lacquered shoes.

"Did you get this report from Yaver Pasha himself?" the mighty padishah asked in a hoarse voice that made his courtiers strain to catch the meaning of his words.

"Your Majesty," said the minister of internal affairs, "this report is not written by Yaver Pasha."

The sultan clapped his bony hands. "I knew it! In that case I categorically refuse to believe it."

"Majesty," the great vizier mumbled apologetically, "Yaver Pasha is in no condition to sign any report. The General has been captured by the rebels."

Sultan Mehmed shook his head. "Ay...ay...ay...ay, such a man! Is he dead?"

"No, Your Greatness," said the chief of protocol, "the general is alive and well. He has been seen at victory parades in Phulbee and Sofia."

The padishah lifted his hands up, his mouth open in disbelief, "He let himself be captured alive by the rebels? My best military man is exhibited at parades like...like a monkey?" he started to fall into his hysterical pattern again, screaming, his shaky finger pointing accusingly at the British Ambassador, "And you approve of that?"

The ambassador bit his lips. "No, Your Majesty, I don't approve of that, nor do I approve of a forty-thousand-strong army being taken by a single regiment."

The sultan was dumbfounded. "What regiment? There was nothing about a regiment in the report."

"That report you just heard, Your Majesty," said the Englishman, his eyes calmly fixed on the fidgety acting minister of war, "was entirely composed of articles from different newspapers. Mostly from Germany. At the time of the defeat of your army, General Ghenev and his troops were in Cardgally, at least seventy miles away. It was an unknown lieutenant colonel that did the job in the absence of his commander. A brilliant job!"

"I don't understand this at all," screeched the padishah. "Are you showing admiration for the enemy, when everything seems to be crumbling around us?"

The ambassador waved his hand in his usual pacifying manner. "Don't worry, Majesty, not all is lost... yet."

"Thank you! You've been very helpful, Ambassador. If my city of Odrin falls and the Bulgarians start marching on Istanbul, I'll ask for an armistice. Evidently, I have no generals left."

Through thick glasses, the sharp eyes studied the wrinkled, waxen face of the man who happened to be the Great Padishah of the Ottoman Empire. "Armistice?" uttered the ambassador thoughtfully, "That might not be such a bad idea."

"And if that doesn't work, shall I be paraded through the streets of Istanbul like a monkey on a leash?" whined the padishah.

"Oh, no, Majesty! Nothing that drastic. The British Crown still has diplomats with good contacts in the countries bordering Bulgaria. Although Tzar Ferdinand thinks he has formed strong alliances, he might just be in for a few bitter surprises."

Radco's mother felt strangely restless that evening. All afternoon, she had been very busy taking care of the wounded in the field hospital in Progled. Most of them were men in the prime of their lives, and she caught herself involuntarily looking for the face of her son among them. For the first time since Radco left, she felt depressed and went home earlier than usual. The night was windy and the wet snow piled over roofs, walls and roads making the way to her house on top of the hill quite a venture. Finally, she opened the gate and old Mourdgo, the huge shepherd dog that her husband had brought as a puppy when Radco was three years old, waved his tail without moving. It was a miracle he was still alive. When she entered the house, he followed her slowly, his legs shaking with the effort. It felt cold and damp inside and she got busy with the stove.

"Don't worry, old Mourdgo," she said to the dog, as he put his muzzle on her lap, "it soon will be warm and cozy in here." Mourdgo yawned. "I know you are sleepy. I am tired too. To tell you the truth, I don't feel like eating. I had something at the hospital." She caressed his back and stroked his ears with love, "I'll fix you a meal as soon as the fire gets going." The dog whined and closed his wise eyes. "You don't want to eat either…you have to…try for me, dear, please."

Mourdgo dragged himself to the sofa and lay down with a human sigh. Stryna Nonna's heart flowed with both pity and love. The once dark and shiny coat now had become silvery and matted. She gave him some milk and, as soon as the stove was stoked for the night, joined him, pulling over them a thick homemade blanket. The wind battered the house and the windows and the door creaked in their effort to keep it out.

Suddenly stryna Nonna was wakened by loud knocking at the door.

The little lamp she had left burning was dying, and in the fluttering light she saw Mourdgo jump like a young pup with joyous whining and barking. She was too stunned to think about his jumping; a paralyzing anticipation kept her on the sofa, her voice stuck in her throat. Finally she got her voice back and shouted out, "Radcooo! Come in my boy…don't stay out in the cold!"

The dog turned his eyes toward her impatiently, his tail waving frantically, the thumping at the door became heavier than before. "Pardon me, my boy, I forgot, I barred the door. I'll open it, my dearest…I'll open it as soon as I can move my damn feet!"

The knocking went on and with a superhuman effort Nonna pulled herself out of the low sofa, falling on the floor and dragging herself toward the door on knees and elbows, "I'm coming, Radco…I am coming, my boy!!!"

At last she reached the door and pulled out the bar. The heavy door flung open and the dog rushed out barking happily. Stryna Nonna was hurled back to the sofa by the power of the wind that brought inside some sort of flying pieces, like parts of a torn human body.

Late in the morning, neighbors who came to look for stryna Nonna, found a few yards from the house, the stiff corpse of a dog that very much resembled Mourdgo though that dog was young and powerful, with shiny dark fur.

Arda was on the east side of the ridge so trekking downhill, except for the slippery snow, wasn't difficult. Metyo had proven to be right; nobody had followed them.

There was time for resting, smoking, cursing as well as shifting the wounded man from one shoulder to the other, and skidding and tumbling. Finally, shortly after four o'clock, in the gray mist of approaching evening, the brothers reached the road somewhere in the vicinity of Chamgas. They stopped for a breather and to solve the problem of getting their captive uphill. By that time both brothers were tired and the dismal prospect of five more miles on a steep road outweighed even their greed for gold.

"I'm gonna go look for a mule," stuttered the younger brother, Metyo.

Mourco took a drag on his cigarette and offered one to his brother.

"Why don't you stay, and I'll look for the mule?" he said, baring his yellowish teeth.

"'Cause I am younger and wanna spare you from going astray."

"You do not, bugger," the elder forced the words through his teeth and squatted down, "you just wanna be a wise guy and leave me stranded with that dying bastard of yours."

"Mine?" Metyo protested.

"It was your idea to get rich through him, wasn't it?"

"All right." Metyo sat down by a tree trunk and crossed his short legs. "So much the better for you. I'll come back, because I don't want you to take all of haydouk Dimmitar's gold."

The sallow face of the older brother flushed with anger.

"Bullshit! You don't really believe that story, do you? If Dimmitar had been robbing people on the roads, like other outlaw commandos do, Radco and his mother would have lived in a better house than that two hundred-year-old shack, and not be working their butts off morning until night."

The round faced runt laughed derisively. "That's just to dupe sh-sheep h-heads like you," he stuttered, as he always did when under pressure, "stryna Nonna wanted her son to grow up in his native village. Then, she planned to take the earthen pot filled to the brim with golden coins to Phulbee," said Metyo.

"Did she tell you that in person, sucker, or do you just believe every bit of gossip those loud-mouthed wenches exchange over their fences? I've had enough of this mumbo jumbo! Let's cut the throat of this mother's pet and report to the officer in charge of Arda before dark," snarled Mourco.

Metyo looked stealthily at the dead white face of the wounded youth. They were about the same age. As children, they had played together at bones and marbles and fought over them. Although those battles usually ended up with Radco sitting astride his chest, the Muslim boy held no grudge against him. Radco had never cheated, never fought for a wrong cause.

"And what if I don't want him to die?" Metyo faced his older brother, hands crossed over his chest.

Mourco crushed the butt of his cigarette and straightened up on his feet, spitting in his direction. "You chicken shit, fuckin' cur! You'll do whatever I tell you to or, in the name of the prophet, I'll thrash you to death."

Metyo looked at the broad shoulders of his brother. His chances in a hand-to-hand confrontation with Mourco were practically nil and to use gun or knife on his own blood was a crime against Allah. He got up with a short sigh. "Very well. I'll do away with him, if that's what you want. He is unconscious anyway. If I press my thumbs a bit on his windpipe, he'll face the Gates of Heaven before he knows what's happening."

The runt threw away his cigarette, kneeled down by the prone Radco, and turned him over. Under the crude bandaging made from his shirt, the wound had opened again. There was a small pool of blood where he had lain and another trickle down the side of his stomach.

"It might even be better…" muttered Metyo, placing his hands round the neck of the youth, "it would save him some…"

A clear sound of riding horses came from the road. Before either one of the brothers was able to do anything, four horsemen had surrounded them. "What's happening out here, soldiers?" Ismail asked authoritatively.

The older brother rubbed his overgrown moustache, then answered the civilian with a slight bow. Though none of the men wore uniforms, something in their bearing, besides their rich clothes, told him they were big shots.

"We were trying to save the life of a young man, effendilar. He's badly wounded."

Ismail approached. "A Bulgarian?" he asked.

Mourco was confused. He didn't quite know how the bigwigs would react to such a humanitarian act. Perhaps he should tell them the truth. However, Rashid Babba's reaction made an answer unnecessary.

"Let's not waste time with these people, Ismail. Obviously they have nothing to do with the abduction."

Ismail! Both brothers looked at the handsomely chiseled face. Of course it was him! The tall youth with the rifle facing Delly Hassan Caursky in the saloon. At that moment Metyo moved aside and Radco's pale face emerged before Ismail's eyes. He gasped, jumped from his horse and threw himself on the body, to the great astonishment of his company.

"Radcooo!" cried Ismail, then he listened to his chest. "Thank Allah, he is still alive!"

Rashid Babba's thin lips quivered with poorly suppressed anger. "The enemy should be shot on the spot! Come to your senses, young man. Leave it to them. We have more pressing things to do!"

Ismail shifted his fiery eyes from Radco to his father-in-law to-be.

"You can count me out of this party, Rashid effendi." Mehmed Agoushev and Roustan—the chief of the guards—gasped as Ismail's deep voice continued. "For me nothing in this world is more important than saving the life of my brother."

Foam appeared at the mouth of Azimee's father. "You'll be dishonored!" he shrieked, "You'll exclude yourself from the Islamic Code of Honor forever!"

"I am sorry, effendilar," said Ismail, pointing at his friend. "Here lies my Code of Honor. I hope you can understand that." He took Radco's body gently and layed him across his horse. "I know the noble beys of Moguilitza would."

Metyo and Mourco ran to help him. Mehmed Agoushev looked at Ismail sadly. "What are you going to do, Ismail?"

The young man gave his purse to Metyo and climbed up behind Radco. "I'll take him to Progled, the only hospital within reach. There, he may have a chance to survive."

"Somebody's got to stop him!" shouted the chief of the guard, "he can't get through the front line without being killed!"

Ismail embraced his wounded friend with one arm and took out his gun. "Have no doubts, effendilar, anyone who tries to stop me will die first."

Mehmed Agoushev lifted his hand. He emanated some of the greatness his ancestors had passed on to him. "Let him go!" he commanded. Then he turned to Ismail, "Even if you make it through the front, you'll be arrested as a prisoner of war. Let Allah be with you and let His Will prevail!" He drew up his horse next to Ismail and kissed his forehead. "Remember, whatever happens, there is a home waiting for you in Moguilitza."

How little anyone knew about the future.

Ismail rode as fast as he could. Night had fallen and snow started coming down again. The double load on his horse took its toll, as did the slippery road. No matter how robust the animal was, it had its limits. Soon after entering the gorge, a gust of wind hit them. The horse simply refused to go any further.

Ismail got down, fastened Radco to the saddle with his belt and led the horse, tugging at its reins. Radco moaned painfully from the back of the mount, but at least Ismail knew he was alive.

Around midnight, the wind grew stronger and hurled snow into the eyes of both man and animal, driving them beyond endurance. Fortunately, Ismail was able to see the outlines of an abandoned shack just off the road. At last he made it to the shack and, once inside, they were sheltered from the wind, though the cold was biting. Ismail covered Radco with his mantle and took care of the horse. In one corner he found hay and a handful of branches. By the time he had a fire going, he felt Radco was watching him.

"Hi, brother!" said he, kneeling down, "Am I glad you're back. Knowing what a good fighter you are, I didn't doubt for a moment that you'd make it. Thank Allah that we're not too far now. A tough guy like you...please, Radco, stay with me. Don't close your eyes, I'll keep you warm."

Radco's bloodless lips moved as if he was saying something, but not a sound was heard. Ismail came as close as he could. Finally, he made out the halting words.

"Remember...the...shack...!" came weakly from Radco's lips.

"The shack in Progled?"

Radco nodded perceptibly. Ismail forced a hoarse laugh.

"It was such a crazy night! Remember the cold…and the wind, and the bastards after us? We barely made it."

In the silence that followed, the long drawn out howling of wolves was clearly audible even through the assaults of the blizzard.

"We barely made it this time, too." Ismail smiled. "We are just a couple of lucky guys, aren't we? Wherever we go, whatever we do, we have to keep saving each other. It just won't work any other way."

Now the fire really began to burn. Ismail added more branches and the flames grew taller. Strange shadows danced over the walls. The horse was restless, whining and stomping his hooves on the floor. He had heard the wolves, too.

Radco's lips moved again. Ismail bent over.

"What is it, dear friend?"

"Who is that…man?" he whispered, his eyes fixed on something behind Ismail. Ismail turned back and saw nothing. "What man?"

"The tall man…with the heavy…shepherd mantle…" Radco's eyes grew wider. He even tried to lift himself up. "He's coming…take the hood…off, Ismail…I know this man." With superhuman effort, he struggled up to his elbows, "FATHER!!!"

Ismail covered him with his arms, his own blood turning to ice. "Don't, Radco…don't!"

"Did you come to take me, father?" said Radco suddenly, loud and clear.

Now Ismail grabbed him in his strong hands. "I'll not give you up, hear me?" he shouted, tears streaming down his face. "I will not give you up to anybody! You are the last one I have in this world!" He pressed Radco's face to his chest and hollered over his shoulder, "Whoever you are,

go away! You have no more right to him! He is my brother.
Hear me? My own brother!!!"

The remnants of Yaver Pasha's army were on the run. At
Ferree their road to retreat toward the White Sea was cut
off by General Ghenev's troops and the Macedono-Odrin
Militia. Yaver Pasha was ready to surrender unconditionally.

The actual surrender took place in the tent used as a
field hospital. Yaver Pasha arrived on a black Arabian
stallion, followed by his staff officers. He had a noble face
and the erect posture of a professional soldier, something
that instantly gained him sympathy from the Bulgarian
troops who silently watched the cortege. Dismounting his
horse, Yaver Pasha entered the tent, politely greeted the
gathered officers and General Ghenev, then looked
carefully at the faces around him.

"You looking for someone in particular, Commander?"
asked his host.

A sudden smile colored the pale tired face of the
pasha. "I was just trying to guess which of these gentlemen
had defeated me."

"I am sorry, Commander," said the general, his long
face under the gray moustache expressing some surprise,
"the Colonel isn't here…but why?"

"As I thought…" muttered Yaver Pasha, "I had hoped
to surrender my sword to Colonel Seraphimov. He is the
most brilliant enemy I've ever met on a battlefield. He
made me doubt my own intelligence. I believed I was walking into a trap surrounded by an army equivalent to mine.
Against all logic…psychological strategy bordering on
self-suggestion. Admirable!" He shrugged his shoulders.
"But if he isn't here…" He took out his sword and gallantly
delivered it to his captor. "Please, General, accept my

unconditional surrender. I hope you'll be generous to my remaining troops in their captivity."

Ghenev was deeply impressed. "Of course, Excellency," he said, stumbling slightly. "I accept your surrender and guarantee you the best treatment as provided under international law, to you and your troops." He stopped for a moment as if he had run out of breath, looked at the magnificent sword covered with precious stones and, after a short hesitation, spoke confidentially, "But why? What difference does it make?"

The pasha smiled with both bitterness and sadness. "You mean, why did I want to give my sword to Colonel Seraphimov in person?" General Ghenev nodded. "Well, General, it would have made my pill a bit less bitter."

On a sudden impulse, Ghenev handed him back the sword. "Give it to the Colonel when you have the opportunity to see him in person, Excellency."

Yaver Pasha and Colonel Vladimir Seraphimov would never meet.

By this time, the heroic 21st Regiment and its newly promoted Commander, freshly washed, were marching into the liberated city of Ksanty to music and flag waving. The mixed population was as jubilant here as elsewhere. Children were singing, and young women spilled water under the hooves of Colonel Seraphimov's horse for good luck. In spite of the blackout imposed on the press, his fame had spread by word of mouth, and he was already a legendary figure.

Musicians in the band blasted their instruments full power, flowers rained, Bulgarian and Greek flags waved along the main street. It was a warm and sunny day. Seraphimov turned toward his adjutants Dennev and Dimmitriev, the sun reflecting in his steel-gray eyes, and shouted over the thunder of greeting voices and marching music, "Ready for Salonika?"

It was the finest day in his military life.

"Permission to stay, sir."

Seraphimov looked up with a smile from the arm-chair in which he was resting.

"Permission granted, Sergeant Marrin. Sit down." Danco hesitated.

"Sit down, I said...and closer. That's good. I want to express my special thanks for your outstanding service to me. No commander ever had a better orderly than lucky me." He patted the knee of the blushing, stalwart youth. "Let me tell you a secret. If I had a son—and I've always wanted one—I would've wanted him to be exactly like you—brave, clever and strong. A real man!"

"Thank you, sir."

"Now we'll be drinking some coffee and someone else is going to bring it. They make wonderful coffee in this city." He clapped his hands and the cousins, Sallih and Radgeb, entered beaming from ear to ear. Seraphimov shrugged, "I had to appoint two orderlies. After all, I think I'm entitled to splurge a bit."

Danco looked at him with shock and surprise. "I thought you were pleased with my service, sir."

Colonel Seraphimov laughed with delight. "Sorry, son. Even a big shot like me cannot keep a sergeant major as his orderly. From now on you'll have to learn to put up with your new position, Assistant to the Commander for Special Assignments. Here! Your sword is waiting for you."

For a long moment, Danco looked at his superior as if he could not believe his own ears. He swallowed and choked. Seraphimov poked at his short pipe with extra care; then remembered the cousins.

"Hey, coffee, boys. For the new non-commissioned officer and me. Two cups. And hurry up!"

"Right away, sir, Colonel, effendi!!"

"Forget the 'effendi.' "

"Yes, sir, Colonel!" they shouted in one voice and left momentarily. Seraphimov watched his new orderlies with genuine amusement.

"How do you suppose they manage to answer with one voice?" he winked at Danco, "They probably practice behind the door. As good an orderly as you were, you never were able to speak with two voices at the same time."

"Sir."

"Yes, Sergeant Major."

"You cannot be serious. There must be a mistake."

"No mistake, my boy. If we were in the Napoleonic Great Army, after the miracles of bravery you performed at Allamy Derre, you would have been at least a captain by now. The way we operate, even a lieutenant colonel barely makes it to a full colonelship."

"To be honest, sir, I didn't fight like that for the army or motherland." Danco dropped his head guiltily, "I had to avenge a friend."

"I know, Danco. Dennev told me."

Danco lifted his head with sudden hope. "That's why I came to you, sir. I beg you for a leave of absence. I want to go and look for him. He might still be alive behind the lines."

Seraphimov jumped up from his seat and walked quickly to his desk. "What was the full name of that friend of yours?"

"Corporal Radoul Boev, sir!" Danco almost shouted, getting up to his feet.

The commander dug into a pile of papers. "I had a letter from my wife...she's working in a hospital on a volunteer basis. Here it is!" He read a few lines, then looked at him. "You'd better sit down, son. Radco Boev is in Alexandrov's Hospital in Plovdiv. His body's response to a difficult surgical procedure was miraculous; he is on his way to speedy recovery."

At Saksalla, the climate was mild. One could feel the presence of the warm sea, adding to the fragrance of the lemon trees and rose bushes in the small garden beneath the wide harem windows. Beyond the tile covered roofs, a slim minaret rose into the sky, and the muezzin called the faithful to prayer. For Azimee and Magda everything was strange and unusual in this place. The oriental incense burned in small braziers, the scents from gardens where winter never had access, music of cithara—not nearly as rich and sensual as the voice of Ermin's cavall, and food consisting of sweets, syrups, dates and tangerines, rice and olives. The harem was not as large as that in the castle; the living compartments were tiny and snug. Whispers and laughs were heard, but few persons were seen, and those were mostly servants. The other wives and daughters of the house curiously spied on them in their own unobtrusive manner. Raiff Kehaya had his household well under control. Bringing up a vampire in this most idyllic atmosphere seemed incongruous...and unsavory.

Magda, accustomed to an active life, was more depressed than Azimee. She picked up a frosted date, but when it was half way to her mouth, she threw it away angrily as she jumped to her feet. "I can't lie on these soft pillows anymore. I'm so tired of it, I can't sleep! How can Turkish girls manage to go on living day after day just doing nothing? If we ever escape this paradise, I won't lie down to rest, I'll probably sleep just leaning on the frame of a door."

Azimee laughed softly. "You'll get used to it, dear."

"I'd better not," Magda stomped her foot. "Who will milk the goats and do the laundry at home? We have no servants." She kneeled down and embraced Azimee. "I'm sorry, sweetie, I got you into this and now I'm the one who's complaining. You should have me killed. If not for me you would have been in the arms of that divine Ismail of yours right now, instead of having me nag and nag some more, and rub salt in your wounds."

Azimee kissed her. "Don't blame yourself, Magda. Obviously this was the will of Allah and we can do nothing but follow it. Poor Magda, I know your heart is bleeding for your wounded hero and his magic cavall. I'm sure your sister and brother-in-law are taking good care of him. Just be patient and wait. Ismail will come and deliver us soon. The code of honor..."

"The code of honor, the code of honor. What if this Vampire comes first? What will you do, you wretched girl?"

Azimee closed her bottomless, dark-blue eyes with a heavy sigh. "Then I'll kill myself!"

Magda held her even tighter in her embrace. "No, you won't, deary. I'll kill the damn bastard first. If only that Raiff Kehaya shows up, I'll tell him a thing or two about his son. Though he runs this village with an iron hand, he's said to be fair and just. I'm sure he won't like what Kerrim Abdoullah is doing!"

"Even if the servants convey our pleas to him, do you think he'd believe one word of what you say about his son? To him he is the officer-hero, risking his life for the safety of the Empire."

"He might have asked you if you approved of this marriage, at least?" said Magda.

"Oh, Magda, you're too much of a Bulgarian. You keep forgetting our way of life. Women here have no other value...except as bed companions and entertainers."

"You should see the poor families," grunted Magda. "Women are treated worse than any animals. Everything loaded on them until the poor wrecks collapse from mere exhaustion."

"Ismail is different," sighed Azimee.

"The way you describe him, he seems to me more like a Bulgarian. Are you sure his name is Ismail?"

"I don't care, Magda. What I want is HIM!"

"Are you sure you'll recognize him after having only that one encounter?"

Azimee laughed, gently tapping Magda's nose. "You naughty girl! I see him a thousand times a day and all night long." Her enormous eyelashes closed over her eyes like veils. "He is tall, heavy boned and large muscled, seventeen or eighteen years of age. The same golden hair covers his head with a curly and unruly helmet as is sprinkled on his young brawny body, with kinky hair on his broad chest and all over his arms and groin. When he inhales deeply, his hard midriff sucks in and his muscular chest, adorned with dark nipples, rises provocatively. A fine mat of hair covers his strong heavy thighs and goes down over the powerful calves. Though his face is still boyish, it has reached an unusual beauty. Under the well outlined brows, with a curious sweep like swallow's wings in flight, two clear blue eyes peer out under long lashes. The wide cheekbones harmonize perfectly with a darling, slightly snub nose and a full sensuous mouth made for kisses. The girth of his neck is a bit too large for the proportions of his face but matches the broad sweep of his shoulders and the deepness of his chest. The smell of his body…"

Magda wriggled and put her hand over Azimee's lips. "Enough, devil's seed, you should be in hell, torturing poor girls who have never seen anything like that!"

"Wait a minute," Azimee burst into laughter, "I haven't reached the most exciting part!"

Magda flushed profusely, stopping up her ears. "I don't wanna hear anymore. Shame on you!"

Azimee tried to pull her hands off and they scuffled, laughing together.

"Don't tell me you never saw your Ermin without his clothes."

"Of course I didn't, silly. My brother-in-law gives him his baths."

"And you didn't peek?"

Magda blushed even more. "Just once, a little…but enough to tell you that he looks better than your golden curled Adonis. Besides his shepherd's flute…"

"Oh," giggled Azimee, "you saw his flute, too… shepherd's, eh? Tell me more about it. Please!"

"Shut up, you, or I'll slap your brazen face, pretty as it is! With all those fancy clothes, trinkets and rich foods, it's no wonder we're going crazy. Oh, God Almighty and you, Allah, what will happen to us?"

"Don't worry yourself to death, Magda; Ismail will come and deliver us. I know it!" promised Azimee.

"By the way," sighed Magda, "I don't want to doubt you, but I've seen your Ismail at the castle. He's handsome, no doubt about that, but his eyes are dark and so is his wavy hair."

The three horse riders from the castle passed through a dead Arda, burned to ashes, totally abandoned by everyone. In the increasing snowfall and the rising wind, there was no evidence of the army or home guard. A few homeless dogs howled and blackbirds were perched, asleep, on the still warm charred beams.

The three men, depressed by Ismail's defection, wondered what lead to take now. They missed the young man's initiative, energy and leadership. None of them wanted either the responsibility of making a decision or carrying it out. After some huffing and puffing, it was assumed that Chief of the Guard, Roustan would be able to guide the search in the most professional manner.

Since there was nothing left among the ruins of the empty village, Roustan suggested going back to the castle for the night and starting afresh the following morning. Unwilling as they were to do what they solemnly had sworn not to—come back without the bride—under the circumstances that seemed to be the only logical move, especially with the night promising an angry blizzard. So they took the lost soldiers, Mourco and Metyo, who were roaming around in search of some headquarters where they could report, and in under half an hour the sad cavalcade, enlarged by two mules that the brothers had found in the Muslim section of Arda, filed through the heavy gates of the castle.

The next day, the same group, in spite of the deep snow, found its way to Catoun. There, they met the leader, Sadak, who, impressed by the inhabitants of the castle and accompanied by two regular soldiers, told them that the Turkish detachment in Arda had gotten orders to retreat immediately to Memmee. The bashibouzouk (mercenary volunteers) were dismissed and the enemy's army were expected in the area no later than the next two or three days, and that delay only because of the heavy snow.

Emboldened by the obvious ignorance of the group about his personal involvement in the abduction, after a generous bribe, he admitted that...yes, he had seen two girls answering the general description. They were taken on horseback by a group of men in an unknown direction. He had not tried to intervene, because one of the regular guards was present and he thought the move absolutely legal. After an even larger bribe, his memory cleared a bit more, and he suggested that the most likely place to look for the girls, according to what the castle guard had told him, would be the far away village of Sacharca.

Disheartened by their new discoveries, the rescuers rode back to the castle to seek advice from the old beys.

After over four months of siege, the city of Odrin had fallen leaving the road to Istanbul wide open. The Central Railway Station in Plovdiv was congested with trains bringing in wounded by the hour. The wounded young men were everywhere—on the decks, in the waiting room, in the square in front of the building. Moaning, choking on their own blood, swearing, pleading, calling out names. The hospitals were full to bursting, as were most of the schools and many private homes. The professional staff was insufficient and overworked, the volunteers were unprepared, almost ignorant. Endless lines had formed in front of the post office and telegraph agencies. Long lists of names of those killed in action were read aloud, screams and sobs erupted here and there.

Work at the hospital was murderous. Volunteers in Alexandrov's alone had grown from fifty at the beginning to a staggering eight hundred. Most of them didn't know how to make an ordinary bandage. To show them how took more time than doing it oneself and moving on to the next case. But all human endurance has limitations. Doctors and nurses dropped from exhaustion in the middle of an operation. The long corridors leading to surgical wards were covered from wall to wall with the gravely wounded, dying and already dead soldiers. Even the most basic medications were not available.

The curse of the black market made everything disappear. Food, drugs and clothing were basic exchange, but where to find them? Overnight, fortunes were made. The owner of a struggling grocery store had buried four tin boxes with golden coins in his back yard. When he found they were stolen, he shot himself.

To save a bed in the hospital, Ellena had taken Radco Boev and his mother into her apartment. With the kids at home the rooms seemed even smaller. Under normal conditions she would have gone mad; in these crazy circumstances she managed pretty well. She even forgot to take her daily aspirins. Not that she had any, but she somehow got out of the habit. And the headaches seemed to take care of themselves.

It was after midnight. Ellena and Sultana were drinking tea in the kitchen.

"Enough is enough. I'll go to Sofia," said Sultana. They were talking in whispers so as not to disturb the rest of the household. "I'm going to the palace and I'll ask for..."

"He won't meet you in private. You might get an invitation to a public reception," Ellena interjected.

"Oh, he will!" said Sultana heatedly, "I still have some aces up my sleeve."

"Sh-h-h, you'll wake the tribe. What do you expect from this?"

"I'll tell him everything—the situation here, on the front. It's winter, Ellena. Nobody has warm clothes. The soldiers will freeze to death. I'll tell him about your husband too. What a burning shame!"

"Please, Sultana, don't. Vlado is completely happy the way things are. I know him. He doesn't give a damn about honors. If Nedelev got the highest medal for valor and he the second, that means nothing to him. I know. What he feels is important is that the people of the region are safe, that the country wasn't invaded. That's all."

"That might be enough for him; it isn't for me!" cried Sultana.

"Calm down, Sultana. You've done enough for our family," soothed Ellena.

"You mean…"

Ellena cut her off, "Everything. My medal, also. Now take it easy, will you? You're not made of iron yourself. I don't want you falling sick from exhaustion in the middle of it all. Come to think of it, you haven't had a decent meal since…I don't know when. It just can't go on this way."

"I feel fine. How's Radco doing tonight?"

"Much better. That boy has exceptional restorative powers. I think the mountain air and good food make the difference. His mother has taken excellent care of him since the operation. God bless her, only she's got me worried again with her story."

"About her dead husband?"

"Yes, about him, the blizzard, and the death of the dog."

"Do you think somebody really knocked at her door?"

"I don't know. I pleaded with her not to tell Radco about it."

"Did she?"

"She promised not to, but she might let something slip. Radco mentioned tonight something about his father coming to take him from an abandoned house along the road. He also mentioned Ismail."

"Yes, Ismail. Also the name of a girl, Azimee. Stryna Nonna seems unwilling to talk about them. Does the time you are talking about coincide?" asked Sultana

"What time? Ah, what happened to her and Radco's tale…yes. Definitely yes. Same night around midnight. He said there was a witness."

"That same Ismail that brought him to Progled and got arrested?"

"Yes, I wrote to Vlado, asking to check on him if possible," said Ellena.

"Mountain people are very superstitious," warned Sultana.

"It worries me. I wish I could talk to Ismail. Radco calls him his brother."

Ismail was locked in the same stone house in which Danco had spent three days waiting for a verdict. There were sixteen more waiting to be deported from Progled as prisoners to concentration camps in central Bulgaria.

After delivering Radco alive to the field hospital, he felt such enormous relief and gratitude toward Allah that any aggravation of his own situation was of little importance to him. He felt no bitterness. A feeling of light-heartedness and joy dominated. He had prayed to Allah to save his brother's life...no other bargains. If he had to spend the rest of his life in a Bulgarian prison, he could do it just knowing Radco was alive and well. He told Allah he would pay any price. He was ready to accept it and with no complaints. And now a voice told him that Radco would live! And for the first time in his life Ismail knew what real happiness was. The rest of the prisoners, gloomy and dark, thought him strange. Especially when he sang and laughed, telling jokes and performing funny little tricks to entertain them. They didn't know what a great feeling it was to no longer have hatred in your heart, pumping venom through one's system.

The jailer was Goran Podgorsky, Rossitza's father. He treated prisoners like dirt. There was no pity in his heart. And the wretched people subjected to his power felt the same way about him. There was such intense hatred on both sides that, at times, one could feel an electric charge in the air. Only Ismail refused to be involved in the deadly game. And Goran Podgorsky hated him even more for that.

There was one ray of sunshine in this shroud of desperation covering the prisoners. The jailer's daughter. They called her a blessing from Allah.

Rossitza was appointed by the military in the village to take care of the slightly wounded prisoners of war. Her father tried to reverse that, but to no avail. Accompanied by an older soldier, she came every other day to change bandages and treat bruises, some inflicted by her own father. Being almost fluent in Turkish, she would ask them about their families, the harvest and cattle. "There is no such thing as an endless war," she would say. "Soon you'll be back home. All of you!"

Even the old soldier shook his head at that.

"The angel is coming!" were always the words that preceded her.

"Haven't I seen you somewhere before, handsome?" she asked Ismail.

"You have," smiled Ismail, "at the fair last summer—up there, on Rhojen. You were Ermin's beautiful girl."

A fleeting shadow crossed her face. "Oh, yes, Ismail. You were with Radco Boev, weren't you?"

Ismail nodded. "I could never forget your beauty, Rossitza; as I told Ermin."

Rossitza winced. "You told him? When?"

"Just a few days ago, at my new home in Moguilitza."

The girl paled, and her hand went quickly to her mouth as if to stifle a cry. "He's alive?" she whispered.

"Yes, he is," Ismail happily told her.

"And well?"

"I would say so, though there's something crushed within him. He doesn't want to live anymore," said Ismail sadly.

Her hazel eyes filled with tears and guilt. "He will die, Ismail, won't he?"

Ismail looked straight into her eyes. "He might."

Suddenly Rossitza brushed her tears away and spoke in a firm voice. "Would you lead me to him...tonight?"

Enormous admiration glistened in Ismail's eyes. "In Allah's name, I will!"

That night, knowing her father's weakness, Rossitza made him drink to a point of unconsciousness, took his keys and set all the prisoners free.

Chapter Eleven

Shortly after the fall of Odrin, Tzar Ferdinand received a telegram from Sultan Mehmed containing an armistice offer. The truce would have initiated a peace conference, including participation of the major powers of Europe. That certainly was not a prospect Ferdinand of Bulgaria looked forward to. For three days, he kept the telegram hidden, not only from his government, but from rulers of neighboring allies. During those three days, he tried desperately to reach Istanbul, but his troops were stopped at Chattaldga. At that point, Ferdinand promptly sent a telegram accepting the truce. The Turkish government refuted it.

The war had to be continued.

Winter was well underway, the Bulgarian army was ill prepared, the supply lines badly organized, and the reserves almost depleted. The Turkish frontline was now close to major supply stores. Ammunition and food came from all over the empire.

Angered by the foolish actions of the Bulgarian Tzar, Greece, Serbia and Romania broke their alliance.

Colonel Seraphimov was unaware of the new developments. His mood was exuberant, the next day his legendary 21st regiment would march triumphantly into Solun, or Thessaloniky, as the Greeks called it. The preceding evening, Bulgarian clergymen from Cavalla had served liturgy in the open air for all the troops. They had prayed for the souls of those deceased and for the safe return of the living. With acquisition of Solun, an age old legacy would be accomplished: a strong and united nation!

"Perhaps I was wrong about wars," he wrote to Ellena, "there is death and destruction, suffering and terror, but there is greatness as well. Proof of the values of a nation, its sacred right to be. A nation without dreams is like a nation without heroes!"

It was at this moment that a dispatch from General Headquarters was delivered to him. He had to transfer his regiment immediately to Bullayr on the Eastern Front, which meant Istanbul.

Seraphimov tore up the letter to his wife.

Ermin died in the morning.

At noon a Bulgarian detachment under the command of Lieutenant Vrannev occupied Moguilitza. In retaliation for the burning of Arda by the bashibouzouk, under instructions from a Turkish major, they had set fire to predominantly Muslim Moguilitza. Refugees from Arda and elsewhere had left Agoushevitee Conatzy, or the castle, as it had been known. They were busy looking through the debris for belongings from their own homes that might have been spared by the fire. When they saw thick clouds of smoke over Moguilitza, they immediately sent a group of older boys to look in the hills for Nickola Vassilev and the chetta.

Foolishly, the guards refused to surrender the castle. Under their chief's order they opened fire against the Bulgarian soldiers. Agoush Bey and his brother, praying at the mosque, heard the commotion and tried to hurry out as quickly as they could.

It was too late.

Soldiers stormed the door after breaking it with hand grenades. In the shoot-out the blind bey was killed. His younger brother tried to pull him from under the feet of soldiers rushing in, but he was run over by their heavy boots. His golden pince-nez fell into the bloody slush, his wise, delicate face splashed with mud. A broken rib cage sent a wave of blood that gushed into his mouth, choking the last words of Agoush Bey.

On the upper floor soldiers found the body of Ermin dressed in Bulgarian uniform. Mistakenly they assumed he was a victim of torture and that started a new volley of killing and rampage. Without listening, they stabbed Bogdana and Ignat to death with their bayonets, they had been giving the last Christian rites to Ermin. In desperation, Mehmed Agoushev threw himself from the third floor into the little garden behind the house, breaking his legs. The rest of the household sought asylum in the mosque but perished in the fire. The only one who survived the debacle unscathed was the Chief of the Guards Roustan, who hid in the stable. He was the person who refused to open the gate and, defying all instructions from superiors, ordered the men to open fire. Why Allah spared him, of all people, was an enigma that only God could explain. Rashid Babba had left early in the morning after failing to convince anyone to follow him in search of his daughter.

When an hour later, Nickola Vassilev and the home guard came on the scene, they couldn't believe their own eyes. They were dumbfounded and horrified—they could only stare at the total ruination. The old mayor of Arda screamed, pulling and tearing at his hair and beard, kissing the gory faces of his protectors and friends, asking their pardon, wailing uncontrollably. Lieutenant Vrannev stopped the burning of the village, called his detachment and left in complete confusion, forgetting to take care of Ermin's body.

Late in the evening, Rossitza and Ismail reached Moguilitza, exhausted from their long walk through the mountain. For the last few miles, the young man had to carry Rossitza on his back. The devastation they saw was beyond belief.

All night long, under the sinister light of fires, half choked by acrid smoke, eyes blinded, hair singed, the home guard from Arda and villagers buried the dead. Pale morning light came as an unwanted witness. Utmost physical exhaustion brought on a stupor that dulled the pain, like a blessing at a moment when their minds were about to break under the strain.

Nature had its own way of sparing the living.

"Rossitza."

"Yes, Ismail."

"Why don't you want to go with Nickola Vassilev?"

"He might try to send me back home," she worried.

"He won't. I'll tell him. He is a good man."

"What are you going to do?"

"I...I don't know. I really don't know. It seems I am damned. Wherever I go, death and devastation follow. Now, I wonder if my father was right about that teacher and his little son. It's possible that I inherited his curse."

Rossitza looked at him with fright in her eyes. Then suddenly she embraced him. "I don't understand a bit of that nonsense..."

He locked his arms around her in desperation. "It's true, Rossitza. It makes sense...horrible sense! The old beys of Moguilitza, Radco, Azimee, even Magda. The whole castle!"

The girl buried her face deep in his chest. "You are not responsible for the destruction of the Agoushevitee Conatzy, nor for anyone else! Let me stay with you. I am not afraid of curses."

"Why?"

"Because I am damned, too!"

When Azimee was taken to Major Kerrim Abdullah's room after a brief ceremony performed by his father, she was stiff with apprehension and fear. Shortly afterward, the young man came in and matter-of-factly started taking off his clothes.

"Get out of here!" shouted Azimee from the furthest corner.

Kerrim laughed huskily and locked the door. "Why should I? We're man and wife."

"Your father has no right to perform marriages!" sneered Azimee.

"He does so. He is a Caddia."

"A wedding without a priest is not valid at all in the eyes of Allah."

"Who cares? It's good enough for me," laughed Kerrim.

He threw off the last vestige of clothing and stood in front of her stark naked. The girl screamed. He had taken off the black strap from his dead eye.

"I don't want you! Please, have pity!" she whimpered.

He came at her, sword in hand. "You'll change your mind when we get into bed."

Azimee kneeled at his feet sobbing. "Allah, have mercy!"

Kerrim's face grew uglier as lust overcame him. He grabbed her trembling body and threw it on the bed, tearing the rich clothing to shreds. She struggled fiercely, biting and driving her long sharp fingernails deep into his hard flesh. He moaned with pleasure and dug his teeth into her lips.

Azimee felt dizzy, nearly faint, the taste of her own blood filling her mouth. The horrible pain of him penetrating her drove the poor girl almost insane. She freed her mouth and shouted at the top of her lungs, "I hate you! I haaate youuuuuu!"

He laughed cruelly, purring like a happy tom cat. "Even now? Why, my dear, Azimee?"

She spit in his face. "Because you have the head of a snake, Vampire!"

Kerrim Abdoullah hissed and his iron fingers locked around her delicate throat. But at that very moment his animal instincts told him mortal danger was imminent. The door was breaking. He left Azimee half choked, and grabbed his sword.

Sergeant Major Danco Marrin was on special assignment, his newly acquired sword bouncing pleasantly at his thigh. The officer's horse trotting with vigor under his skillful horsemanship. It wasn't in vain that he was the best of his class at riding back into Istanbul. Leading a selected group of twenty-five horsemen, he had to check the villages of Memmee and Saksalla, off the flank to the main stream of the troops, continuing on to Ksanty, Mackry, through the cities of Dedeaghach and Dimotica, across the river of Maritza, along the left bank in the direction of Malghara Bullayr.

It was believed, based upon information from some villagers of Bulgarian descent, that in Memmee and Saksalla a number of Turkish officers dressed like civilians were instigating guerrilla type actions behind the lines of the Bulgarian army. According to the secret messages received from informants, a lot of arms and ammunition had been stored at certain places and the insurgents were waiting for the right moment to start their assaults. It was a dangerous mission that had to be carried out with utmost discretion by someone well versed in Turkish moral codes and Moslem ways of life.

This was Danco's first task in his new job and he wanted to do well. His men were all hand-picked by him with personal approval from Captain Dennev. They were fluent in Turkish, well mannered and physically strong. They had to keep a low profile and not invite any unnecessary trouble; therefore their number was small but their efficiency and expectations high.

"Don't forget, you'll be in enemy territory. Your actions are meant to appease, not to provoke," Captain Dennev told him at parting time.

In Memmee the action went smoothly. They assembled most of the inhabitants and told them that the new rule would protect their properties and respect their religious freedom. The only thing they were expected to do was to obey and not revolt. All arms had to be delivered to the representatives of the Bulgarian Army. Persons found hiding arms would be punished. The people—stiff and scared at first—relaxed, their confidence in the "nice young men" grew and in small groups they brought more than five hundred guns of all kinds along with lots of ammunition to the central square. While they piled it all up, Danco thought, how Colonel Seraphimov's policy toward the population was right. If they had acted like barbarians, threatening and forcing the people to give up their arms, there would have been open revolt and casualties on both sides. That's what the instigators wanted. The Bulgarian soldiers considered "good boys," loaded their rifles on mules and parted, leaving the local people on good terms.

By the time the detachment reached Saksalla, it was dark. Entering the village would have been a foolish risk. Danco selected an empty farm house on the outskirts. There were a number of barns for their horses and mules and a solid roof over the men. He ordered the privates to build a fire and sent out patrols. He wanted everyone to try and sleep right after dinner. It was important that his men be well rested for the next day's activities, although he found himself unable to follow his own orders. Turning restlessly on the mattress, his thoughts raced. Something about that village bothered him. He decided to go and check the place during the night, under cover of darkness.

He woke Delly Hassan and told him about the reconnaissance party he wanted. They looked through the closets of the house, but all they found was two pair of breeches, known as shalvary, a heavy shepherd's mantle and a short waist jacket without sleeves. The breeches were too tight for Danco, but he had no choice. He gave the jacket to Delly Hassan and wrapped the mantle around his bare shoulders. Before leaving, he woke his junior officer and asked him to wait for their return.

The village of Saksalla was unusually quiet. Even the dogs were silent. Had the villagers been warned by a messenger from Memmee about the coming of the Bulgarians, or was it these times of hardship that kept people behind locked doors in their homes? Were they preparing an ambush or sleeping peacefully in their beds?

The village was smaller than Memmee, but more prosperous by any standard. Its houses were bigger, more solid, and a whiff of late roses came from the gardens. Most of these houses were built in circles around a central square in a maze of very narrow side streets or sockaks, as they were called here. No matter how quiet everything seemed on the surface, Danco's feeling was that something bad was happening behind those walls. He took a firm hold on his sword and whispered to Delly Hassan to have his pistols ready. He had been in hostile villages before but never had the atmosphere of expectation been as thick as it was here. Thank Allah there was a full moon that lit the way for the scouts.

They were passing alongside one of the best houses in the village when suddenly the loud screams of a woman broke the silence. Danco and his companion stopped dead. They looked up at the windows. All of them were dark except one on the second floor. At this moment the heavy gate cracked and a young girl shrieking for help ran out right into their arms!

"Sister!" cried out Danco.

For an instant Magda was speechless, eyes wide open in terror and disbelief; then she grabbed at him with the force of total desperation. "Hurry, Danco…hurry, please, he's going to kill her!"

"Who?"

"The Vampire!!!" yelled she and ran back into the courtyard, followed by Danco and Delly Hassan. There were three men at the door.

"Keep them quiet!" shouted Danco at Delly Hassan as he pushed the men aside and ran into the house, sword in hand. Now the screams were even more horrifying than before. Magda led the way up a narrow staircase to a closed door. Danco promptly hurled his body against it and the door shattered.

The man was stark naked, a hard body belted with muscles, a mean sword in his hand. Magda threw herself on the seemingly lifeless body on the bed while the two men engaged each other with growls of wild beasts. Danco's eyes narrowed, almost closing. His sword hissed through the air at the head of his foe. Kerrim Abdoullah ducked, and the shining blade missed by an inch. He attacked on his own from below, aiming at the stomach, then at the throat of his opponent. Danco drove aside those blows, closing in on the man, trying to get in a good

252

thrust, but failed. The sword of his enemy cut through the air, menacing Danco's head and chest. That son of a bitch was astonishingly fast, thought Danco, as he threw off his heavy mantle. Finally he did penetrate the guard of his adversary and almost got him on the side of his stomach, striking hard and viciously, swinging with that tremendous power of his, perspiration soaking his entire body, his strength doubled by anger and frustration, all brought on by the Vampire.

It did not take him long to realize that he had met his match. They battled all over the room, swords banging at each other, carrying every attack to the utter limit, panting, intertwining, rolling back, dripping sweat and dizzy. Danco felt blood running down his face. He had lost his turban in the fight, or, perhaps, it was a blow to his head that had knocked off the turban.

Danco pressed Kerrim Abdoullah to the wall, almost driving the blade of his sword to the Vampire's throat... He pressed with all his might, their arms shaking with the effort, muscles almost bursting, teeth grinding... The major squirmed and wriggled, puffing and yelling curses. Then with the strength of a bull, he arched his body from the wall and threw back his robust adversary. Bloody, dark with rage, they beat, tore, hit and clawed at each other. The Vampire would launch an attack, howling and swearing, his face hideous with bloody foam dripping from his mouth, his dead eye almost rolling out of its socket, his body surged with fury. By now, Danco knew that he couldn't beat this demon with a sword in hand.

The Turk was the better swordsman.

Danco threw down his sword and caught Kerrim's arm that was falling over him, then grabbed his hand with both of his own. His left hand encircled the wrist and with the right he slowly bent back the fist clutching the sword until it opened and dropped the handle. Then Danco increased the pressure on his fingers as he continued to force the hand back. Kerrim Abdoullah struggled and then collapsed to his knees under the strain on his arm. Danco plunged one arm under his armpit and another between his thighs. He swung the wiry body on his back as if it was a sack of coal, feeling it tremble and squirm in his powerful hands, Kerrim's legs kicked in the air. Danco held him tight, then, with all his might, he threw the struggling body through the bay window, down to the cobblestone street. The body fell with a dull thud and did not budge again.

That was the end of the VAMPIRE.

Azimee and Magda, still stiff with horror, stood and embraced by the bed. They stared at the broken window, praying that the one-eyed man would not show up.

"Come on, girls, we have no time to lose!" Danco urged them. Magda came out of her trance and ran up to him, but Azimee was still too weak to walk. The young man had to carry her all the way, past the screaming women on the staircase, past the frightened men held at bay by Delly Hassan, and into the street where a silent crowd was gathering around the prostrate body of what used to be Major Kerrim Abdoullah.

Nobody tried to stop Danco.

From the moment she stood up from her deep curtsy, Sultana was ready to begin her long speech, drawn from her personal witness to those human tragedies caused by the vanity of a single man. That man now sat a few paces away in a deep velvet armchair, and she was speechless.

Since she had last seen him less than a month ago, the change was so drastic that she felt nothing but pity. Ferdinand had aged drastically. Heavy blue pouches had formed under his eyes inflamed by sleeplessness. New wrinkles were added between his eyebrows and along his mouth. He looked ill and exhausted.

Against her better judgment, Sultana ran to him and kneeled at his feet.

"I am sorry, Ferdy." She thrust her flushed face in his lap, "It's too late for both of us."

He put his hand over her shiny hair. "Too late for what, Sultana?"

She sighed and sat on the carpet beside him. "Too late to change," said she with bitterness. "We'll die the same old opportunists as we were born."

Ferdinand laughed a bit sarcastically. "I thought... oh, never mind!"

"Why did I go to that filthy hospital? Why did I leave the ivory tower you built around me?" Then she laughed, and her laughter was so strange and uncharacteristic that for a moment Ferdinand thought it there someone else in the room.

"I went there because I hated myself and I wanted to imitate a person you like so much. I wanted to find the difference between myself and her, though it worked in a way I hadn't anticipated. I did change a bit. Before, I hated myself, now, I despise poor me."

She laughed again huskily. "For a while I was so taken with my new part that I started applying my new code of morality. But life is not a morality play, and you are not a saint. Nor am I. I am the same sinful Sultana you used to love. Sultana the actress, Sultana the entertainer. It's no wonder you got tired of me."

Ferdinand got up slowly and walked to the window, aided by a silver cane. The damn old rheumatism in his leg...

It was snowing in the park. A roe came to the window and looked at the Tzar in an almost human way. "I didn't get tired of you, Sultana," he said quietly, "I just was not able to love anybody. I've got too much of everything...

except the only thing I want more than anything in the world."

"GLORY?"

The monarch nodded. "A nation of earth toilers and shepherds is unable to fulfill my dream."

"Oh, my God, so even if I had the purity and beauty of Rayna and the simple greatness of her mother, you still would not be able to love me!"

"Rayna is a child. Are you going back to Plovdiv?" he asked, again in a quiet voice.

Sultana felt a sudden chill. She walked to the blazing flames in the marble fireplace and almost touched them with her delicate hands.

"Even if they all died for you under the snow, you wouldn't love them, would you?" she whispered.

She wasn't sure he had heard her, but his nasal voice came across the room, "It's late...it's too damn late."

Since Radco was recovering well, and Ellena badly needed someone to substitute for Sultana, Radco's mother started helping out at the hospital while the girls cared for the house guest. There was certainly no shortage of nurses around his bed. Sometimes a dispute would arise between them as to who would give him his medicine, or tighten his dressing, leading to a temperamental exchange of most unladylike words. Taking care of a young, good looking patient was more appealing than any game.

This morning Jivca was in charge. The other girls were to be taken to the dentist by the cook. Assen, looking for food, was rummaging through the nearby villages for any kind of provisions. Jivca had never had the chance before to be in charge and was enjoying it to the hilt.

"Let me take your temperature," said the young girl, shaking the thermometer, "close your armpit and don't move. No cheating! If you only knew how busy I am!" she said with an overacted sigh, "I have the whole house to care for. The baby, the piano…and now you. You have to behave very well, or all these chores will drive me crazy."

"I'll behave, I promise," said Radco, as serious as one could be under the circumstances.

"That's good, because I don't have a knack with you like the others."

"A knack? What's that?" asked Radco.

"Well, you know what it is. When a girl sees a pretty boy she might get a knack for him, not me," she added hastily.

"Why don't you like me, princess?"

Jivca blushed. "Oh, you got that from Assen, didn't you?"

Radco nodded.

"That wily Assen! I'll tell him a thing or two."

"You didn't answer my question," Radco repeated.

"What question?"

"Why you don't like me?"

"Well, if you really wanna know, I don't like you, very much at all."

"But why?"

"Because I am too young to fall in love. Besides, I hate competition."

"Couldn't we be friends without falling in love?" asked Radco, suppressing a smile.

"No. I don't think so."

"But why?"

"Because you want to go back to the war as soon as possible and get killed," explained Jivca.

"That's ridiculous. I don't want to get killed."

"Yes, you do. I don't want a friend of mine to die. It makes me sad. When our little doggy got run over by an emergency car, I cried and cried. I still cry sometimes. I don't want another dog. Why should anybody want to go to war to be wounded, or even killed?"

"I have friends out there," Radco tried to explain.

You have friends here too," protested Jivca.

"Noooo, I am not so sure. For example, you refuse to be my friend," said Radco.

Jivca shifted her legs. "I might reconsider…if you don't go away."

"But I have to. If everybody left the front, the Turks might come and…and take your piano."

"Let them take it," replied Jivca.

"To be sure, they will do worse things than that. You don't want to be a slave, do you?"

Jivca fidgeted. "I am a slave anyway."

"Oh, come on, you know better than that."

"Well, as a matter of fact, I am a patriot like anybody else, but I don't want you to go. Turks or no Turks!" Then after a short pause, she said in a very low tone, "Are you promised to a girl out there?"

Radco whistled softly. "Whew…what do you know! As a matter of fact, I am."

Jivca sighed. "I knew it all the time. Can't you be promised to somebody here? Rayna wouldn't turn you down, I am sure."

"You promise only once, princess. Imagine that that person out there will wait and wait forever, simply because I decided to change my mind? Would you like to be in her place? Besides, your sister is a lady and I am just a country bumpkin."

"You don't look different."

"But there is a difference, princess. I know how to chop trees, turn the earth, mow the hay. I even know how to read and write, but that's about all. I don't know French, nothing about painting. I dance only rutchenitza and horro…"

"But you like her?" insisted Jivca

Now it was Radco's turn to evade her eyes.

"Everybody likes her," said Jivca with pride, "even the Tzar, but she refused him...or somebody in the family did. I heard my father shouting. Never mind."

"You see, such an important person would not pay attention to someone like me."

Jivca took his big hand and, with sincere conviction, shouted in her ringing voice, "But she does! I hear her. She talks to herself sometimes."

"You do lots of 'hearing' around this house, don't you think?" laughed Radco.

"The fact is, she likes your muscles. Last night she told me you can knock down any man. Can you?"

Radco laughed and that hurt him. "I guess, not all, but many. As you see, right now you could knock me down with a feather."

"Oh, you'll be okay...see!" she clapped her tiny hands in comic desperation. "We...forgot...the thermometer! Goodness gracious! Now it will show up at least one hundred forty degrees and I'll be held responsible for it!"

Radco pulled out the thermometer and looked at it. "Don't be silly. I have no more fever."

The girl dropped his hand and went to the door. There she waited for him to call her back, but the young man was tired and sleepy.

"Anyway," she said in a tiny voice, swallowing her pride and hurt, "If you need me, I'll be around."

The 15th of December 1912—city of Plovdiv
Dear Vlad,

We never talked about it, but somehow I don't feel that you'll be back for the holidays. And the way things are going, there'll be no reason to celebrate, and little hope, or shall I say, no hope—of having you with us at Christmas or New Years.

I get all my information from the wounded men. Recently, I've seen more limbs amputated because of frostbite than from regular combat injuries. Captain Dimmitriev is my courier, so at least I can open my heart. Is there any hope that we can survive this war? With all this talk about worsening of relations between us and our allies, it seems we're headed toward catastrophe. We are so vulnerable! Is there anything that can be done to prevent it? A growing number of soldiers are mumbling and grumbling, openly expressing their frustration.

They feel somebody up there has cheated them. They have no business at Tzarygrad. Last week three were arrested. Yesterday, two more. One of them with an amputated leg. And that's happening in a hospital!

I am worried, dear.

Ten days ago, Sultana went to Sofia. She wanted to tell the Tzar everything that we needed. Knowing the brave woman, I tried to keep her from going. It didn't work. Since then we haven't heard anything from her. I wrote the minister. He was surprised, as he knew nothing of his wife being in the capital. I don't have any reason to doubt his honesty. He called me on the phone at the hospital and asked me where she might be. I said I didn't know. Now I wonder, is discretion our best friend nowadays?

Do you think that she might have been arrested?

What else can I do?

Practically everybody around me is worried about something. In our wing of the hospital (shall I say, the prisoners' ward?), without Sultana's financial support, we're hopelessly out of money...out of everything. Moreover, the food is more scarce than ever. The kids are doing fine, except for the loss of their little dog Teshca, who was run over by a fire truck. Poor Teshca! She was like one of the family. That was the children's first encounter with death at close range. The impact was shocking and baffling, but I thought it might be even better to be prepared... Oh God!

I try to make them study their textbooks and the piano. Little success. Rayna is crazy about knitting—she's been making mittens, shawls and socks. Jeanna and Elsa write letters to the families of the wounded. Everything is for our soldiers and those at the front.

Only Jivca is unable to get over the loss of her little doggy.

In that sense, the newest member of the family, adopted after Teshca's death, is Radco Boev. I suspect that all of our daughters have secretly fallen in love with him. He's a darling boy. Even Jivca's grief for Teshca seems to be fading.

Though Radco is worried, too—about his friend, Ismail, as I wrote you in a previous letter, and something else that his mother thinks is linked to the name of Azimee. She seems to be a little unhappy with her son's inclination toward Turkish names.

Radco's mother is a wonderful woman, a character taken right out of Ivan Vasov's compositions. Since the departure of Sultana, she has been of great help to me. At first it was a shock to her, although she never complained. She started caring for the Turks with some reservations, but now stryna Nonna does everything. She does the laundry, washes floors, changes linen, dresses wounds, gives baths and talks to the boys. Makes them laugh. I wish I could speak Turkish with the fluency she has. Radco sees a radical change in her. He remembers her smiling before, but never laughing. Now she laughs. He said she seldom went to church, just on special occasions. She came with us on Sunday. Since then she goes by herself and prays, bent over on her knees, forehead touching the marble floor. Radco thinks her faith was broken after the tragic death of her husband. Now her peace with God has been restored.

The only absolutely happy person is little Lily. She giggles and coos like a turtledove. God bless her! I pray God will never let her see the horrors of war.

Donca and Assen send you their regards.

Two days ago, Assen got a notice to appear in person at the garrison headquarters. I am sorry for him. The poor boy is so scared. We'll have to get used to running things around the house without him. The cook is taking it very hard too, but there's nothing we can do about it.

Love from all of us. It hurts me to kiss you at such a long distance, always somewhere far away from me.

God be with you...all of you,

Your ELLENA

P.S. The Captain will give you a package—long underwear. Keep it for yourself, please! Don't give it to your soldiers in the trenches. They're young. You are fifty-two.

More love...Ell

The hovel of grandfather Ivvo was a low but compact structure built of stones and logs chinked with graying mortar. It stood in a clearing and was almost totally covered by snow. The wind racing over the hill drove light snow over the windows like skeins of blown cobwebs. The hut would have had an abandoned look if not for a feather of smoke whispering from its roof.

Ivvo Chichellaky was a Carracachan shepherd all his life. He didn't know his exact age. He had forgotten it. Somewhere around one hundred was his closest guess. In his younger years, during the winter he used to herd the sheep flocks to the warm fields of the White Sea Thrakia and, with the first gentle breeze of spring, return to the mountains. He had done that throughout his lifetime, because what he called younger years seemed to be just yesterday. He had been married, had sons and daughters.

Where are they now? All gone. If you asked his nationality, he would shrug his shoulders. "I am a shepherd."

When he talked about his family, he would be more discriminate. "Oh, my daughter, Ghana, she is a Bulgarian..." or "My son, Costaky, the Greek...his brother Iddris, was a Muslim and lived in Tursko..."

"How come?" you ask, perplexed.

A wily flicker would light up his ancient eyes. "That's why grandfather Ivvo lives..."

Ismail and Rossitza had found a roof to hide under from the blizzard. How they ever saw the hovel belonging to grandfather Ivvo, lost in the snow, was a mystery. It was as if an invisible hand had led them to it. "Allah be praised!" exclaimed Ismail, and "Thank God," whispered Rossitza.

The old man had a few sheep sharing the same room with him. He fed them hay and got some milk in exchange. Now Ismail hunted and they had fresh meat from time to time, but basically they shared the reserves of potatoes and cheese grandfather Ivvo had stored for himself.

The low-ceilinged room was filled with smoke from the hearth. The old man and his shepherd dog Vultcho were asleep. The rest of his companions once in a while gave out a low muffled "baa." From time to time, the man snored loudly. Ismail sat cross legged under a garland of garlic cloves, his face buried in his large hands.

"I don't really know where to go next," he moaned.

Rossitza listened to the raging wind outside, pulling the coarse blanket tighter around her shoulders. She came to him and her hand gently stroked the back of his head.

"Why go anywhere, Ismail?" She squatted next to him. "Let's stay here. I'll give our host my necklace of golden coins. The war won't last forever. Nobody will look for us up here."

Ismail turned around and took her in his arms, his dark blue, fiery eyes burning with desire.

"Rossitza…"

Still whey-faced, Azimee stared at Danco across the fire. "You are blue eyed and blond, but you are not Ismail," she said timidly.

"No, I am not," laughed Danco..

Magda, fixing the dressing around his head, joined in the laughter.

"He is my brother, Danco. The great wrestler I told you about."Azimee was in awe. "Is that why you have cauliflower ears?"

"You hit it on the nose. I like to meet the challenge of another strong guy—to find out just who's the king of the mountain."

"You were at the Sultan's palace in Stanbul?" Azimee asked.

"Yeh…for two years," Danco replied.

"But now you are a Bulgarian officer."

"Yes, ma'am." Involuntarily, his eyes followed the gracious movement of her naked body beneath the heavy shepherd mantle that he had thrown over her at the last moment before their escape from the Vampire's room.

Magda finished the bandaging, then swung her arms around the broad neck of her brother and said lovingly, "If only the Bulgarians had known that he was a damn Muslim, they would have kicked his butt right out and away from his high horse and the army before he had a chance to ask Allah for help. My presumptuous brother, Ibrahim!"

Danco raised his eyebrows. "Have you changed your faith, Magda?"

"Of course, I have! As soon as the Bulgarian troops came to our village. Me and Bogdana. Mother and father stuck to the old faith."

Now Azimee felt more at ease.

"So you have Turkish names also."

"Yes, all three of us," laughed Magda again. "My big brother Ibrahim; my sister, Ziulfiu; and I am Fatima."

"My little sister is Fatima!" Azimee clapped her hands.

"You'd better stick with Magda. I don't like to be called anything else. Against the will of our bubayco, my sister married into a Christian family. So will I, if I can."

"How about you, Ibrahim?" asked Azimee shyly, though her eyes were those of a little devil.

Danco blushed, then shrugged his shoulders. "Call me whatever you want, when…alone. And who is Ismail!"

Azimee dropped her large almond shaped eyes. "I'd rather not talk about it…"

"It was a dream," Magda interjected quickly, "just a dream of hers."

Colonel Seraphimov looked up from the pile of papers in front of him.

"Come in, Danco," he said in his usual stern voice when matters of business were concerned. "Forget the formalities; grab a chair and sit closer to my desk. It's cold outside. I wish we were still in the White Sea region."

Danco abstained from sitting. He felt something strange in the air.

"I am used to cold weather, Colonel."

Seraphimov laughed grimly. "I'd like to remind you about that when you are past fifty. By the way the chaplain told me you never join in the services." He lighted his little pipe. "Is anything wrong?"

"No, sir. I was busy."

The colonel's eyebrows moved imperceptibly. "I know, you did an excellent job. I had a bottle of raspberry wine around, but it's all gone. Sorry. The cousins are looking for firewood, so we'll have to survive without coffee too."

Danco smiled uneasily. "No problem...sir."

Vladimir Seraphimov looked at him long and hard, his gray eyes gleaming as if reflecting the blade of a sword.

"I think you should sit down now, Sergeant Major."

The young man moved mechanically to a chair and dropped in it heavily. "Yes, sir..."

"Sergeant Major, are you a Muslim?"

Beads of perspiration popped up along Danco's hairline. He opened his mouth, then looked aside and after a moment of hesitation, swallowed and said in a hollow voice, "No, sir."

"Do you happen to have names other than Dannail Marrin?"

The young man sighed and mumbled almost inaudibly, sweat drops running down his flushed face, "No, sir."

There was a heavy pause with only the sound of the fire crackling. "I had a visitor this morning, Sergeant Major," said the colonel even more sternly, "does the name Rashid Babba mean anything to you?"

"No, sir."

"He is the father of the girl who you saved last month. The Turkish girl. I think her name was Azimee."

"Yes, sir..." whispered Danco.

"He said she had been following you with a Bulgarian friend of hers. Wherever you—wherever the army goes. Is that the truth?" Seraphimov asked, eyes fixed firmly on the boy.

"Yes, sir. That's the truth, sir," Danco admitted.

"You've been living with her?"

266

"Yes, sir. The girls—one is my sister—usually take a room in a nearby village. I've been visiting."

"Do you know, Sergeant Major, how highly improper that is in the Bulgarian army, chaperon or not?"

"Yes, sir."

"And you are ready to answer to those charges?"

"Yes, sir."

"Her father says he doesn't object to marriage, provided you pay a certain amount of money and call yourself Ibrahim. My advice would be to consent to that marriage. That will spare you a court martial. Do I make myself clear?"

"Yes, sir."

"On the other hand, you cannot be a commissioned officer in the Bulgarian Army and profess to the Islamic religion. That is entirely my mistake, and I take responsibility for it. I should have asked you a few questions earlier. As to your lies of a few minutes ago, that's between the two of us. Why did you lie to me?"

"Because I want to stay with you. I love Bulgaria!"

Seraphimov coughed a bit. His voice relaxed.

"Under normal circumstances I could have done more for you. I have lots of powerful enemies. Don't ask me why because, I don't know the answer. I thought everything I've done was for the good of my country, presently my own position is rather shaky."

That came as a shock to Danco. It made him forget his own misery. "Shaky!?! People look to you as they do to God Almighty!"

"Where? At the Rhodopa Mountain? That's just a small portion of the country, regardless of what it may mean to you. The rest of the country has never heard of me." A faint smile colored his face.

"For them I am neither God, nor Allah. Ivan Zemsky, a private who used to work for the repair shop, was arrested a couple of days ago. The case against him is rather strong. Vicious propaganda attacking the authority of His Majesty, the Tzar, and his leadership. In time of war soldiers have faced a firing squad for lesser accusations. I put all the weight of my prestige behind him. I still don't know if that will help the poor dreamer or if it will precipitate ill fortune for him. In your case your life is not at stake. It is a question of religious belief. I won't impose any decision on you, but if you choose to change your faith, you'll walk out of this room as if nothing had happened. I have the power to silence any local voices of dissension, but that is as far as I can go. It's your choice."

Danco got up, slowly unbuttoned the carriage of his sword, lifted it to his lips and kissed it. He handed the shiny sword back to his beloved commander. Seraphimov straightened up and took it respectfully.

"I want you to know," he said gravely in his deep voice, "that I still would want to have a son like you, Ibrahim."

Part Three

Inferno

Chapter Twelve

The gun repair shop master, Sergeant Jellyo Jetchev, seemed terribly out of place in the improvised courtroom. It was obvious that he didn't know what to do with his overlarge heavy hands; his ever proud moustache now hung helplessly down his massive square jaw.

The presiding officer looked at the broad blunt face covered with perspiration and asked in a sharp rasping voice, "State your full name and occupation."

The middle aged man did not answer immediately. It took him quite a while to figure out exactly what these gentlemen expected of him, leaving him with the strange impression he was not quite sure of his own name. For the few people who knew him well, this miserable dull character on the witness stand bore no resemblance to the gregarious and temperamental master of the well-disciplined gun shop crew. Not that he talked a lot, but whatever was said by him had weight and authority. The Chief of the Tribunal drummed impatiently on the desk with his fingers.

"Name and occupation!" he repeated gruffly.

"Master Sergeant Jellyo Jetchev—gunsmith." Still confused, he added his serial number and that of the unit.

"Were you the immediate supervisor of the accused?"

"Yes, sir."

"For how long?"

Jetchev looked at the bench where Ivan Zemsky was seated between two soldiers. The young man smiled at him in his gentle way. "I would say four months…maybe less."

"Did you notice anything unusual about him?"

"Oh, yeh."

"Tell us."

"He has lost a lot of weight."

"Other than that."

"His face has shrunk."

The chief of the Tribunal snorted indignantly. "Concentrate on his behavior."

"He recites poetry."

"What poetry?"

"The best, *Epopee of the Forgotten*." Jetchev's eyes instinctively searched for a portrait of Ivan Vazov, but found only the kingly profile of Ferdinand. "He has met the poet in person, has talked to him and they even shook hands."

The officer bit his lips. "What else did he recite?"

Master Sergeant Jetchev scratched the bald top of his head. "He did…speeches out of theatre plays, Gorky, Hamlet, Ivanco, Pushkin."

"Revolutionary?"

"Of course." The members of the tribunal pricked up their ears. "Most revolutionary, as I told you, all of Ivan Vazov, quotations from *Under the Yoke* and…"

A member of the Tribunal cut into Jetchev's unusual eloquence. "Not that kind of revolutionary. We asked about social instigation, insinuations about the Monarch and his leadership, anti-government and army."

The gunsmith looked helpless. "I haven't read all those books, your Honor. I read *Under the Yoke* twice, but had no time to go further." Upon second thought he added apologetically, "Pardon me, if I am wrong, but did you say something about the Tzar being anti-government? Is that the sort of revolutionary you were asking me about?"

Now it was the members of the Tribunal that looked at each other helplessly. Only the presiding officer kept his eyes on Jetchev. "I am not quite sure what your game is, Sergeant," he said tartly. "Are you a natural idiot or just pretending? Anyway, I must warn you, we'll find out and you will be processed subsequently. Now step down!"

"Yes, sir!" shouted Jetchev, as he gave a perfect salute and marched out stiffly.

"You find this funny, accused?" asked the Chief of the Tribunal.

Ivan Zemsky came to his feet slowly, "I am sorry, Your Honor, really sorry about all the inconvenience I've caused. God is my witness; I tried to spare you all these tiresome proceedings, didn't deny any of the actions or quotations ascribed to me. Why bother with this endless procession of witnesses who don't even know what you are asking them to prove?"

"But you refuse to plead guilty."

Ivan Zemsky smiled with some indulgence. "Oh, that's entirely another story, Your Honor. I don't deny anything I said or did, but I refuse to be condemned on those grounds. Because all of it is true and one should not be persecuted for telling the truth. Didn't we escape a yoke of five centuries just to enjoy the freedom denied to us by the Padishah?"

At that moment, the two adjutants of Colonel Seraphimov left quickly.

Seraphimov entered the schoolyard accompanied by his orderlies, who were riding sturdy mules. When they reached the old rambling building where the court martial was held, Sallih and Radgeb dismounted hurriedly.

One of them held Sanya's reins, the other helped Colonel Seraphimov through a deep snow drift.

Captains Dennev and Dimmitriev waited for him at the school door. Seraphimov answered their salutes. "Is anything wrong?"

"Almost everything, sir," Captain Dennev shook his head, "That crazy boy is simply pushing his head into a noose."

"I gave explicit instructions to Major Andreev to…"

"Pardon my interruption, Colonel, but Major Andreev is not presiding."

Seraphimov's face paled.

"Who is presiding?"

"A special envoy from Sofia, Colonel Semerdgiev."

Seraphimov shook with surprise. "General Robev's adjutant?"

"In person, sir. He ordered all the proceedings *in camera*. I beg your pardon, sir, but you cannot testify under those circumstances. We could inform the Tribunal that important developments concerning your personal duties have prevented you from coming if you wish."

Seraphimov's eyes dilated with resentment. "Do not delude yourself, gentlemen, that I shall waive my testimony in favor of Private Zemsky."

Dimmitriev paled. "Don't you see, sir, that this whole sorrowful spectacle is aimed at discrediting you?"

"You are perfectly right, Captain. Now will you kindly let me in? I hate to be late."

Colonel Seraphimov's adjutants stepped aside and stood at attention while their commander walked briskly into the long dark corridor.

Danco made a mad dash to the nearby village. Magda opened the door and seeing his distorted face, gasped, "Oh, my God! Do you know already?"

Danco's voice was husky. "Know what?"

"Azimee's father is here."

"Where is he?"

"In the room."

"Call him out."

Magda nodded shortly and disappeared into the next room. Rashid Babba came out with a grin on his sallow face.

"Mashallah, what a pleasure to meet you again, young man. May I call you, 'son'?"

"Wait a minute, Rashid Babba. Why the hell did you go to headquarters first?"

The older man stroked his neglected beard.

"To tell you the truth, young man, I was mad at you. I thought you had abducted my daughter." He raised his arms skyward. "How was I to know that you were her savior? Last time I saw you, you pretended to be a Turkish officer."

"True...but why did you call me Ibrahim out there?"

"Shouldn't I have? My daughter called you Ibrahim Marrin, so I did, too. The news of your being of Islamic faith just warmed my heart. That's what made me decide to give you my daughter."

"How about Ismail?"

"Ismail Agoushev is as good as dead. The last I heard he was a prisoner in Bulgaria. At any rate, they've lost all their riches. After all that she has been through, Azimee thinks she dreamed about Ismail. Maybe it was the shock that this Vampire man caused her. Anyway, so much the better. She'll marry a Bulgarian officer. It was wise of you to cross over to their side. Obviously, it was Allah's will to give the infidels a victory." Now his shrewd little eyes saw the epaulets missing from Danco's shoulders. "What happened, Ibrahim? Did you lose your rank?"

Danco followed his eyes and breathed a heavy sigh.

"My sword is gone, too, Rashid Babba. I am not an officer anymore."

"Tzu-tz-tza…yazzack. You can go back to your father. I happen to know Medco Marrin. He is a good man. You can help him in his trade."

Danco shook his head, "I am staying here."

"As a soldier?"

"As a soldier."

"Vay…vay…vay… How can you support a wife?"

"You'll take Azimee and Magda to my father's house at Derrekioy. He'll give you the money you want."

Rashid Babba felt uncomfortable. "I wouldn't ask for anything if not for Azimee's younger sister and a little boy from my other wife. All my crops were lost in the war, the cattle requisitioned. I am in a bind."

"That's all right, Rashid Babba. What's fair is fair."

"I have to tell you another thing, son. I've heard the castle in Moguilitza was burned by some Bulgarian troops. I didn't tell Magda, but hardly anyone escaped."

Danco's face became wan. "You did right. Let's hope that Allah took care of my folks. There is a Bulgarian soldier with them. Now, let me have a word with Azimee."

"Madame Hadgylvanova, may I talk to you for a minute, please?"

Sultana peered into the shadows of the winter garden. No mistake. It was the voice of the crown prince. She walked around the Venetian fountain, bubbling under a bunch of resplendent palms and found Boris in the greenhouse with the orchids.

"What are you doing, Your Highness?"

"Artificial insemination."

"That's interesting, but don't you find the natural way much easier," she teased.

Prince Boris blushed profusely. "Not with some specimens, Madame. They would rather die than have it the natural way."

Sultana laughed. "You are a very sensitive young man, Highness. I find your company exceptionally charming."

Suddenly the young prince threw away his tools and stuttered with excitement, "How about telling my father that, Madame?"

Sultana's strange violet eyes rested on him. "Now, that is not in very good taste. I can see that palace intrigue has not spared even your young and innocent years."

Boris was offended. "Nobody who lives close to my august father and his courtesan can preserve his youth and purity for long."

There was an icy pause that practically touched them physically.

"Is that the message Your Highness desired to convey?" Sultana inquired.

With the desperate audacity sensitive people often exhibit when driven beyond their patience, the heir to the throne exploded quite unexpectedly. "That and much more, Madame! For a while I thought I was wrong. Especially when Madame Seraphimova told me about your highly unusual behavior in Plovdiv. I had almost forgotten the fable about the wolf and his bad habits. Who are you trying to fool with the old trick of the good Samaritan, Madame? Children? There are none left in this palace. Everybody in Sofia laughs at you and my father. At this age...at this age it cannot be love!"

"I am not so old, Your Highness," Sultana protested weakly.

"And you love my father?"

"Yes, in God's Name, I do!"

"How can you prove it?"

"I didn't come back when he was at the peak of his glory, a step from the Emperor's crown, at least in his dreams. Now, with all those dreams shattered once and for all, he needs me. Can't you understand that? This man has never been a loser. He doesn't know how to live with it."

"And are you going to teach him?"

"Yes, Your Highness. One day you'll be a loser, too, and I pray to God when that moment comes, He'll place a woman with love and understanding next to you. Then perhaps you can accept it without turning into a misanthrope, blaming everyone for your own failures."

Unexpectedly the young prince laughed. "We don't live in biblical times, Madame Hadgylvanova, and you're not Queen Esther. My father won't change his policies or his character for the love of a thousand beauties. I thought you were another opportunist, but you are nothing but a dreamer. A terribly outdated Joan of Arc. Remember just one thing: if you want to help this nation, you won't do it from the bedchamber. Not with my father."

Radco opened his eyes, though they were still heavy with sleep.

Slowly his vision focused on a silhouette set against the bright morning sun. It was a beautiful young woman at the window.

"Azimee!" slipped from his lips.

"Good morning!" cried Rayna, cheerfully.

"Good morning," smiled the still confused Radco. "Does anybody play a shepherd's flute in this house?"

"Not that I know of, but we have plenty of piano players, as you know."

"Sorry, my dreams seem to be mixed up. Yet, I am quite sure somebody woke me up playing the flute wonderfully."

The girl walked gingerly to his bedside. "Aren't you suffering from some sort of delusion, Mister Boev?"

"I don't know," said Radco, brushing back his matted hair. "When I look at you, it really seems like some kind of devilment, but when I see or hear those things, they are more real than anything in the world."

"All right, Mister Boev. Have it your way."

"You know, Miss Rayna, this is the first time in my life that anyone has called me mister."

"Don't you like it?"

"Oh, yes...I do, but it doesn't sound like me."

"Shall I call you Radco?"

"Everybody else does."

Rayna played coquettishly with her intricate hairdo. "It's okay with me. Anyway, I am two years older than you."

Radco straightened up on his pillow, obviously piqued. "Come on, Miss Rayna. You don't really mean that. We look about the same age. I've lost some weight and don't look the way I used to..."

"Oh, you look fine. Say, how come they didn't cut your hair in the army?"

"I came in late, as a volunteer. At that time they didn't have a barber in the company. Then we got too busy to fool around with haircutting. I don't care."

"But Azimee would," Rayna laughed melodiously, "wouldn't she?"

Radco blushed. "She might...women folk are rather prejudiced when it comes to looks."

"Aren't you men? Is Azimee ugly?"

Radco shifted in his bed. "Stop picking on me, Miss Rayna. It isn't fair. You know that I cannot come back at you."

"Why not?"

"Because you are a high-born girl, and I—I am simply a house guest."

Rayna laughed again, clapping her delicate hands. "And what would you do if you were not bedridden, not a house guest, and you met me somewhere up there in your mountain?"

Radco faced her, cheeks burning, eyes gleaming. "You really want me to tell you what I would have done?"

Rayna stopped laughing, dropped her eyes and nodded.

"I would've kissed you with all my heart...whether you wanted me to or not!"

Upon the entrance of Colonel Vladimir Seraphimov, all members of the Tribunal but one rose to their feet and saluted. Colonel Semerdgiev hesitated, then reluctantly joined them. It was a prickly situation.

"Good morning, Colonel," said Seraphimov. "You certainly had to travel a long way from Sofia. Is it just to help us, or is it something else that brings you to the theatre of action."

"This is the only matter I am concerned about, Colonel," answered Semerdgiev, vinegar in his high pitched voice, "at least at this moment in time."

"I am sorry," said Seraphimov, narrowing his metallic eyes, "you had to be inconvenienced with a matter that we were perfectly capable of settling."

The bird face of Semerdgiev showed silent anger, but he managed to master himself as he answered.

"No inconvenience, Seraphimov. This is my job. I fight my battles in court rooms." A thin smile spread over his even thinner lips. "I might not be as brilliant a strategist as you are; however, in my own little way I am quite useful to His Majesty, the Tzar."

Seraphimov chose to ignore the barb. "We all try to do that, Semerdgiev, though not as successfully, perhaps. How is General Robev doing these days?"

"The General sends his best regards to you. His only regret is that he could not share the burden of the front with our brave commanders."

"It's not a burden, Colonel, it's our job."

"I really appreciate your coming, Seraphimov, though I am sure you have more important business to attend."

"This may surprise you, but I consider court martialing of one of my soldiers a most important matter. So why don't you sit down, gentlemen, and let's get down to business."

"As you wish, Commander," said Semerdgiev as he made a sign to the rest, "I believe you are familiar with these reports of the extracurricular activities of Private Ivan Zemsky."

"I certainly am, Colonel, though I am surprised you had the opportunity to read them. I don't remember sending those reports to you."

The nose of Colonel Semerdgiev had to be blown at this point, and he did it rather obviously in a monogrammed handkerchief.

"You did not send them, Commander," he resumed, drying his watery eyes. "We don't blame you for that. You are a busy man. But somebody else did."

"May I know the name of that self-inspired helper?"

"The Court has the privilege of withholding names of persons involved in the current proceedings."

"I see...I am at your disposal, Your Honor."

Semerdgiev wiped his pointed nose again. It was getting very red, like the noses of addicted alcoholics.

"A bad cold..." he mumbled.

"It would be better if you stayed home."

"Thank you, Colonel. As a character witness, you can give us the details of your first impression."

"Fair. The young man has oddities, as we all do, but initially they seemed harmless."

"Have you read the file on Ivan Zemsky sent to you by Police Headquarters in Sofia?"

"Yes, I have."

"Didn't you get the impression that he was a dangerous element?"

"I sent him to the repair shop."

"That was a good measure, provided he stayed there. How come Ivan Zemsky saw action?"

"I needed every single man available. At that time, he had quite an extraordinary influence over his detail."

"What kind of influence?"

"Patriotic, Your Honor."

"Ahem, what precipitated the change to a negative influence?"

"The second phase of the war, Your Honor. During these times, it is not unusual that we have to deal with very sensitive characters, perhaps an intellectual or someone with a different level of consciousness. A whole generation of young people are trying to find a new approach to the social dilemmas that plague our times."

"I didn't know you were so well acquainted with the...hm, liberal issues of this particular moment in time."

"Let's call them humanitarian, Your Honor. I believe that moment will stay with us for an indefinite period of time. Not to recognize its ideas would be plain ignorance, inexcusable for somebody dealing with great numbers of people...and responsible, before God, for their safety and welfare."

"To whom are you referring, Colonel Searaphimov?" bristled Semerdgiev.

"Whomever it might concern, Your Honor," answered Seraphimov calmly.

"Are you relating the accused's acts of lunacy to these so-called ideas?"

"Yes, Your Honor. Except that I find nothing erratic in Private Ivan Zemsky's behavior."

"How would you suggest we designate his behavior?"

In the icy silence that followed, Colonel Seraphimov looked around at the small attendance. His adjutants faces were pale; Ivan Zemsky had tears in his eyes, but smiled; the two soldiers guarding him seemed to be listening open-mouthed, officers of the Tribunal had scared looks on their faces; and finally, the special envoy from head-quarters an air of triumphant expectation depicted. A mangy rooster, thought Seraphimov of him with derision.

"I would suggest," he said in his deep manly voice, "that we call Ivan Zemsky's behavior conscientious."

An oily smile appeared on Semerdgiev's face.

"Do you approve of such behavior in the army, Commander?"

The answer came loud and clear:

"As a commander, I don't encourage such viewpoints among the rank and file. As a human being, I don't try to play God to the rest of humanity. I let everyone decide for himself. If Private Ivan Zemsky is ready to die for his ideas, let's grant him that option. I would respect the firmness of his stand. But remember, gentlemen officers, that upon you rests the responsibility of creating a martyr through this case, and I know nothing more revered in the history of mankind than a martyr. Can we afford that under present circumstances at the front?"

Colonel Semerdgiev had a grimace on his face as if he had just bitten off a mouthful of a very tart apple and didn't know if he should spit it out or swallow it.

An army of 150,000 had been secretly gathered on the Asian side and transferred to the Gallipoli Peninsula. One group landed at the village of Sharkioy, on the Sea of Marmora, against the 7th Bulgarian division; a second occupied the heights of the Gulf of Sarrosa. In the bloodiest battle of the war, the fate of recently occupied Odrin was decided.

All dugouts were filled with water. A sudden warm wind had melted the deep snow leaving marshes and quagmires everywhere. A whole train of carts had gotten stuck in them and gradually disappeared in front of the horrified eyes of a few survivors. For three days no food had gotten through to the trenches. The hunger of the soldiers was so ferocious that a number of horses had been eaten. The perpetrators were punished by a special squad. Stripped of their clothes, they were beaten into a bloody mess with tree branches.

Danco Marrin, perched on a beam over the water, was trying to get some sleep when he felt himself being watched. A day ago, the sergeant of their platoon had drowned in the marshes and no replacement had arrived. He looked at the entrance and saw the new man looking at him.

Their eyes met. Danco jumped to his feet. Even against the light, there still was no doubt that he knew the man.

"Bravery in action," said Goran Podgorsky. "Are those medals given to anyone nowadays?"

Danco felt the blood rushing to his head.

"I am not the one to answer that question, sir. It's a matter of concern to the superiors."

"What in hell's name are you doing here?"

"I was left behind to guard the dugout."

"Some bloody guarding that was—you were asleep," said Podgorsky with indignation.

"I don't feel well, sir."

"You were not brought here to feel well, bastard," growled Sergeant Podgorsky. "There will be no delinquency in my platoon. Understood?"

"Yes, sir."

"Where are the rest of this goddam platoon?"

"In the trenches, sir. I'll lead you there."

"I don't need your fuckin' company, private," hissed the sergeant. "I am perfectly capable of finding those trenches on my own. You stay here and get all this water out of the place. What is this? A swimming hole or a dugout?"

"The water is coming from below, sir. The level cannot be reduced."

Goran's face became crimson. "No philosophizing! Work, work, work! At least that will keep you busy."

Danco felt his stomach begin to tie up in knots.

"Sir," he uttered through his teeth.

Goran, on his way out, stopped and shouted back, "What now!?!"

"There are morasses between here and the front line. Mostly unmarked. We never walk around alone."

The sergeant hesitated for a moment, then blurted out, "I want no favors from you, hear me? I don't like filthy Turks saving my life. Why are you telling me this?"

Now Danco lost control. He shouted back, "Certainly not because of you!"

Goran Podgorsky walked slowly to him, so close that their chests almost touched. A foul smell of cheap tobacco came from his mouth. "Let's get this straight, sucker! I have no daughter." Then, with a sadistic smile, he added, "She eloped with a jail bird. Some lousy Turk named Ismail!"

Until that very moment Danco had forbidden himself to think about the existence of Rossitza. Azimee had helped to reinforce this decision. But down in the core of his Muslim mind the possession of two women at a time was quite natural. And in his heart of hearts he was still madly in love with Rossitza. Goran Podgorsky saw the pain in his eyes and drove the knife in still deeper.

"The whore let out all the prisoners, but later on her choice fell to that handsome sonofabitch."

Danco drew a long breath. "How do you know?"

"I caught a couple of them," jeered Goran, "she would have slept with all those creeps if she were not smitten by the good looks of her lover boy."

Danco yelled and locked his hands around the throat of the older man. Under ordinary conditions Goran would have had no chance to escape those hands alive. But now, weakened by long starvation, Danco was easily over-powered by the well nourished, husky man. They splashed into the muddy water and rolled about, groping for each other's throats. At last Goran Podgorsky subdued the younger man, got his right arm free and drove the nozzle of his revolver to Danco's forehead.

Danco closed his eyes and waited. There was nothing but heavy panting. "Shoot, you bastard, shoot!" cried he.

"I am not going to shoot, asshole," Goran spoke haltingly, "there...is court martial for assaulting your sergeant. Why should I waste ammunition?"

He released the youth, and still shaky from the struggle, sat in a corner, mud dripping down his face, a loose hand around the revolver's butt resting in his lap. Danco, half choked from the exertion himself, came up on his elbows, brushed the mud from his blurred vision and looked at the man.

Suddenly, a strange wheezing sound came from Goran's chest; something like a spasm seized his face; then the mouth under his moustache quivered and, before Danco realized what was happening, the man covered his face with his hands, and began sobbing uncontrollably.

Danco came slowly to a kneeling position.

"Bay Goran..." he uttered, still unbelieving. He straightened to his feet and bent down to the weeping man, "Bay Goran..." he repeated, tapping Goran's shoulder. There was no answer. The heavy revolver splashed from his lap into the water.

The incident was never reported.

Soon after the arrival of Goran Podgorsky as commander of the squad, that whole regiment moved behind the lines for a brief rest.

A large, burned out Turkish village was the new location of Captain Dennev's company. All that was left of the houses were mud walls and chimneys. Even these were a welcome to the drenched men, who craved protection against a rising wind. Since morning, the weather had taken, a dramatic change. That warm, mellow weather of the past ten days had turned to bitter cold. Gusty northern winds had brought heavy rolls of clouds. Everyone felt in his bones that a new snow was coming.

There was substantial change for the better in Danco's platoon. Since the new sergeant took charge, there was little hunger. While other squads had to dig through horse and mule secretion for undigested corn, bay Goran always knew where to look for hidden flour or dry beans. He had formed a special supply committee of seven men, versatile enough to pose as Turkish soldiers left behind the lines. They had original uniforms and papers taken from dead Turkish soldiers. Danco was put in charge of it and his right hand man was Delly Hassan. This kind of foraging was absolutely forbidden by the army and severe punishment administered for it.

Around noon, an old man was discovered in the ruins of a village. He told them there was a mill about an hour's walk away. The owner, a big patriot, had hidden flour for the Turkish army. Masquerading in their Turkish uniforms, the boys found the place and took all three loads of flour, though the distance was much longer than expected—over two hours each way. A heavy snowfall started about halfway back to their quarters in the burned village. Twice they lost their direction in the blizzard and the darkness made them circle round and round the village without seeing it. When they finally made it to their quarters absolutely exhausted, another surprise awaited them. More troops moving to the east had been stranded by the snow in the same village. Now soldiers in four layers, one above the other, occupied the places behind the walls.

Danco's group had to get rid of their uniforms, get into their own, hide the flour and join the human press. When the man at the bottom was unable to take anymore living weight on top of him, he would call for a shift. The top man then would replace him and so on and so on, rotating until morning when the freezing wind, raging to gusts of some fifty miles, gradually abated.

The few remaining walls and the system of rotating the four layers had saved their lives. Most of the troops exposed to the windy positions had frozen to death. Those that tried to escape found their death in gigantic snow drifts. One resourceful commander had saved his soldiers by making them dance chorro all night long under the menace of a machine gun ready to fire.

Chapter Thirteen

Ivan Zemsky was locked in the basement of a big old house, a former palace of a pasha. It was a real old-time dungeon with damp, stone walls and rats as big as cats. In the darkness their eyes moved around like wandering flames. Sometimes they engaged in mortal combat over a piece of food and their screechy piercing voices almost drove Ivan to madness. Fortunately he was not alone in the tiny cell. A certain Roustan, former Chief of the Guards in a Rhodopian castle, was his companion. He was caught encouraging Muslims from the mountain region to rise up and to sabotage and destroy storehouses of army supplies. There could not be two more different men brought together by the same fate. A middle-aged, illiterate soldier of fortune and the offspring of an old landlord's family, a trim, spare looking intellectual with utopian ideas about life and society. They both had to face a firing squad on the same day.

Ivan Zemsky had refused to write a letter to his family. Not that he didn't care about his mother and sisters. He simply didn't want to give his father the satisfaction of pulling together the threads of the old family machinery and bringing back his life on a golden platter, a winning smile on his fat face. "Didn't I tell you, son, to stay away from trouble?" No, a thousand times no! Better death than acceptance of a life like that!

"I bet you are thinking about your family," said the Turk from his corner.

"As a matter of fact, I am," Ivan laughed nervously. "Aren't you?"

The man shrugged his heavy shoulders. "Haven't got any. Sometimes I wish I had somebody." He scratched his hairy chest, "Not now…say, you speak very good Turkish."

"I speak several languages."

Roustan was awed. "Allah be praised! Some brains you've got. Are you a teacher?"

For a moment, Ivan had the feeling that he was traveling with a bunch of curious passengers on a train. "Where are you going? What's your profession? Are you married?"

"I am sorry. No, I'm not a teacher. Just a student."

His thoughts turned inward again. At my age? I should be something more than just a student and itinerant actor. Oh, shut up! There is still time. No, there is no more time. Time is up.

"I beg your pardon, what did you say?" Ivan broke out of his daydreaming.

"I said the bugs are about to eat us alive," laughed Roustan.

"They won't have the chance. We have one more night left."

"A whole long night. What we gonna do? Sleep it off?"

"I can't, you snore too loud."

Roustan grinned, a flicker of desire lighting up his dull eyes. "How about if we make some love, arcadash?"

Ivan didn't answer. He closed his eyes with a sudden sadness that gripped at his heart like a hydra. There must be something more in this world. Freedom, Equality, Brotherhood! Freedom for whom? For tyrants like Ferdinand? Equality with whom? With the likes of his father? Brotherhood with an animal like the one in the corner? The world of Tolstoy, Gorky? How does one connect them to real life; how are they brought down to earth?

"Stay where you are, man," he said with a cold warning in his well trained voice, "don't even dare cross half of that cell."

There must have been something threatening in his eyes. Roustan crouched in his corner without uttering a single word more, and didn't dare so much as cast a look in the direction of his cellmate.

On the upper floors of that same building each room was occupied by high ranking officers and personalities of the court. Tzar Ferdinand and his son, Prince Boris, were making a personal tour of the front line. This palace was chosen as their residence during the visit.

In an unprecedented move, the Monarch cancelled his general meeting with the commanding staff. General Robev announced to those in attendance that His Majesty had retired to his private apartments with a bad headache. Another invitation would be issued the following morning.

Colonel Seraphimov bit his lip. This was his last chance to see Ferdinand before the execution. Suddenly, he stuck out his chin in that stubborn way he had when he was determined in his cause. He marched with firm steps to the group where Robev was the center of attention and put his hand on the shoulder of the general.

"Give me a minute, Robev."

The first adjutant looked back at him with slight annoyance.

"Ah...it's you, Colonel, of course...will you excuse me for a moment, gentlemen?" He fell a few steps behind. "What is it, Seraphimov?"

"I've never asked a favor of you, General, have I?"

Robev smiled a bit patronizingly. "I've never expected you to ask for a favor, you, the biggest enemy of favoritism in the whole army."

Seraphimov blushed. "Well...now I am. I have to see the Tzar in person. Tonight."

Robev looked heavenward. "As God is my witness, if I could, I would do it for you. His Majesty doesn't want to see anybody. Besides he is angry with you. Why did you pull your troops off the front line last night?"

"Most of them were 'in repose' behind the line anyway. Those at the front line would have died in the blizzard—every last one of them."

"Did you get His Majesty's explicit order to all commanders not to retreat an inch from the actual position?" Robev pushed, casting a suspicious eye on Seraphimov.

"Of course, I did, but we didn't expose any flanks, we didn't endanger the rest of our lines one bit. With this simple move behind that natural land elevation, I saved the lives of my men. In the morning we were back in our old positions. Dead men couldn't have done it, could they?"

"But, Seraphimov, what if the enemy..."

"Baloney, you know very well where the enemy was at that time. They suffered no less than we did."

"Other commanders left their troops in position."

"They are still there. I wish you could see those black and blue corpses. I wish you could hear the screams of the amputated! But you won't. You think that giving away medals makes up for everything. I have news for you, Robev. This is just the beginning."

"We have principles, Seraphimov, the prestige of an establishment, the sacred traditions that lead a Nation to greatness..."

"Robev!" thundered Vladimir Seraphimov in a voice that made everybody still in the room prick up their ears,

"The beginning of the end is always when those values cherished by leaders cease to be meaningful to the masses. And it is a catastrophe for a Nation when its leaders live in a dreamland, not the least bit aware of what is really happening."

General Robev paled as he spoke. "Calm down, Seraphimov, please, we're not alone. I swear I would arrange an audience with His Majesty if I could. It's just beyond my power. Please, believe me, that would mean complete ruin for me."

"And why not? At least it would serve an honest purpose," offered Seraphimov.

Robev's handsome features almost disintegrated. "But it would not! My interference would only destroy your cause, or...whatever it is."

"Then I'll go in myself."

"You'll be arrested."

"So much the better. I'll resist arrest. That will make noise."

"Oh, my God! Is the matter so urgent?" asked Robev.

"A human life is at stake."

That answer had a dulling effect on the "brilliant" general. He seemed unable to fully grasp the idea.

"Just one life!" he exclaimed. Then suddenly realizing the impact of his remark, he added hastily, "It comes to me, I know a person who might fall for a desperate cause without concern for what might happen in the future. The very champion of all lost causes in the palace! Come with me!"

Prince Boris opened the door himself. He was in a woolen robe embroidered with silk, a book in his hand. When he spotted Colonel Seraphimov behind Robev's shoulder, his whole attitude suddenly changed.

"Colonel! How grand of you to come and see me, General?"

Robev bowed in his distinctive manner. "Not me, Your Highness. I was just taking Colonel Seraphimov through the guards. Good night, sir."

"Good night, General. I'll remember this as a personal favor to me. Come in, Colonel Seraphimov. It has been such a long time." He closed the door tightly behind himself, his radiancy abruptly turning to affliction. "I hope you're…is everything all right?"

Seraphimov shook his head grimly.

"You can trust me, Colonel," promised the Prince.

"I wish I had a smaller problem to unload on your young shoulders, Your Highness."

"Colonel Seraphimov, I am honored to consider myself one of your friends, in spite of my youth. Please, sit down and fill me in. You have my full attention."

"It's the life of a young man, Your Highness. He'll have to face a firing squad tomorrow morning for being openly critical of your father's leadership in this war. He has a record as a troublemaker. Student nihilist circles, anarchist activities, but all just on paper. No real action. He participated in a student demonstration against your father at the new theatre. A pacifist by conviction, he was sent to the army after arrest. Instructions: break him down. He fought bravely at Allamy Derre in spite of his personal beliefs and participated in all actions until the second phase of the war. At this point, he started sharing his views and disappointments on how soldiers were treated, the reckless waste of human life, basic disregard for safety and common sense."

The prince's eyes sparkled.

"I question that kind of leadership myself, quite often, though nobody seems to take me seriously," mused the Prince.

"Discipline in the army is much different from that in a palace, Your Highness. A prince may be stripped of some of his honors, but never court martialed."

"What can I do for him?"

"Let me see His Majesty."

The prince gasped.

"Now?"

"Right now," repeated Seraphimov, those steel-gray eyes of his casting their spell over the youth." There is no more time!"

Prince Boris shook his head sadly. "Even I am not permitted to disturb His Majesty at this hour. I have no father in the sense other boys do. There is iron protocol that stands between the two of us, and certainly he doesn't do anything to alleviate it."

"Even here, far from the palace?"

Prince Boris weighed the idea.

"I don't know, I've never tried before." A sudden determination spread vividly over his pale face. "Let's go!"

The officer in charge of His Majesty's Guard stopped them at the entrance of a long obscure hallway. "I am terribly sorry, Your Highness, His Majesty is in seclusion. He does not want to see anybody."

Prince Boris brought his eyebrows together in a deprecating manner, the way his temperamental father looked at clumsy servants. "Since when am I a disturbance to His Majesty?"

The officer felt most uncomfortable. Seraphimov felt sorry for him. It was a hell of a situation to be unpleasant toward a future monarch. Who knows how long that old goat might keep the throne? Especially with things going from bad to worse.

"It's just my orders, Your Highness," he mumbled, then smiled pleadingly, "But if your august father asked you to come and see him…"

"Of course, he did," the Prince said with authority.

"And the Colonel?"

"I'll take responsibility for him."

The officer bowed and made a sign toward his guards to step back. Prince Boris walked quickly to the door.

"Stay out here," he whispered to Seraphimov, "and pray for me." He knocked at the door and without waiting for an answer opened it, then thrust his head inside as if into the mouth of a lion. "It's me, father, I heard you have a hcadache and I thought I could massage the back of your neck a bit…"

The familiar nasal voice came from inside. Thank God it didn't sound angry.

"Your mother, may she rest in peace, used to do it for me. She had patience and tolerance. A great lady she was. Don't stand in the doorway like that; there is a terrible draught. Get in and close the door."

For nearly half an hour Seraphimov waited in the dark, drafty corridor, praying to God that everything would turn out well. Suddenly the door opened and Prince Boris called for him. The room was not brightly lit, but after the darkness outside it took Seraphimov some time to adjust his eyes. Ferdinand was in bed resting on a pile of satin pillows.

"Ah, Seraphimov," he said sarcastically, "don't think I'm surprised. By now I am so used to your violating my orders that it wouldn't surprise me if you hopped into bed with me."

"Good evening, Your Majesty." Vladimir Seraphimov bowed.

"Good evening, good evening, Colonel. An old trickster you are, Seraphimov, using my own son as an envoy. Now I can see what that poor Yaver Pasha had to put up with at Allamy Derre. You are worse than a Turk, making me sympathize with the enemy. Sit down…I know there are no chairs in this damn place. Take a pillow…no, sit on the bed."

"I can stand, Your Majesty."

"I know that it pleases you to disobey me, but this time you won't get away with it. I am stubborn, too. Sit down." Seraphimov sat on the corner of the splendid bed, stifling a sigh.

"You have aged in this war, Colonel," Ferdinand went on, "it was not a pleasure ride as the gentlemen from the war ministry had promised. I am sick and tired of those sycophants." Now he realized that Boris was listening. "Thank you, young man, you had a terrific idea tonight. It worked. I feel much better. You don't have to listen to what us old people say to each other. Go back to your books about bugs and weeds, or was it machinery this time?"

The prince bowed lightly. "Good night, father. Good night, Colonel Seraphimov."

When he left, Ferdinand turned his face toward the man sitting on his bed.

"It's you, Seraphimov. You gave me the headache this afternoon. Enough is enough! You are not above me. When I ask you for something, you have to obey. Your contrariness is contagious. I can see disobedience growing in the ranks. I won't permit it! Not anymore, I swear to God. Even at the price of getting rid of you for good. I am not a fool, Seraphimov. You are my best officer. There might not be many like you in this whole wide world. But you hate me. Behind my back you encourage people to criticize me, to attack my prestige within the army. My army! I won't tolerate that—not even if it comes from God Himself! Who are you to tell me that I am wrong? Always wrong!"

"I thought you hated sycophants, Your Majesty," said Seraphimov, looking straight into Ferdinand's eyes.

Exhausted from shouting, Ferdinand dropped back on his pillows and uttered tiredly, between dry laughter, "See...even now? Can't you spare me at least tonight?"

Seraphimov saw his heaving chest, the enormous void surrounding this man and a sudden rush of pity made him feel guilty. "I am sorry, Your Majesty, I wish I knew how to help you."

Ferdinand struggled to his elbows, the labored breath making his words almost unintelligible.

"But you can...stay with me Seraphimov...it...still isn't too late...we can perform miracles together!" There was real supplication in those always imperative eyes. "Boris told me about your young friend. You can have him. I never pardoned anybody that has done wrong to me. I make no exceptions. This is a basic principle of my life. I don't admit mistakes, either. Anyone who has tried to push too hard against my will is dead, or wishes he were. I realize the differences in our upbringing. Those Russian officers have given you a taste of liberal extremities. People, earth, freedom of the individual. I am the symbol of an anti-social structure that has to be abolished! Don't forget one thing, my dear Seraphimov. The Russians have come to this country as much to liberate it as I pretended to unite the Nation in this war. Their emperor is my cousin. Basically, we have the same ideas behind our altruism: to get closer to Istanbul, possibly to take it. The accomplishment of an age-old dream, a triumphal coronation in the cathedral of Saint Sophia. Tzarygrad, the pearl of the orient, coveted by all! Nobody in modern history has been so close to it as I. I can see the outlines of its minarets from here. It's maddening to have it almost in the palm of your hand and not be able to touch it. I can't sleep, I can't eat, I have become indifferent to a woman's love. I want only one thing! Give it to me, Seraphimov, and you'll be the greatest next to me!"

Madman! flashed through Seraphimov's mind; then he said aloud, "There are other things behind a dream, Majesty. Things like people, armament and momentum. Our people have been pushed beyond endurance. The armament is outdated, insufficient and, certainly, the momentum is gone. How do you plan to overcome these limitations?"

"A miracle, Seraphimov, only a miracle! A dream needs nothing, but a miracle!"

"And you expect me to conjure up this miracle?"

"You did it once, why not again on an even grander scale? Deprivation makes a fighting spirit even more powerful. It stretches the human will to unknown dimensions. You can do it, Seraphimov. You have soldiers who are called by the world authorities on warfare—the Japanese of Europe, the Lion of the Balkans. Rise above commonplace obscurity. Be a god!"

It took just a moment for Seraphimov's eyes to become diffused, as if they had been drained of their usual vigor, as if his spiritual magnitude had lessened.

"I don't know," he vacillated. "I need time."

"Shall I call the execution off?"

"Please do."

Goran Podgorsky was visibly worried. He had sent the supply group appointed by him on a mission early that morning and by late afternoon there was still no sign of them. He lit one cigarette after another; a pile of butts lay at his feet when the worst of his fears had materialized. He saw them coming, hands fastened behind their backs, surrounded by soldiers from a special police unit. A rather young lieutenant approached Goran.

"Are these your men?" he asked, almost jumping with anger.

Goran straightened up, gave a salute and answered gloomily, "They are mine."

"Sir!"

"Sir."

"They were caught red handed in the officers' kitchen storage. Fuckin' thieves!"

"I'll punish them, sir."

"No, you won't, Sergeant. The bastards are going to be beaten in front of the whole company. Bare arsed, with branches."

"Who's order is that, sir?"

"The Captain's."

"May I have a word with them?"

The youngster was puzzled. He had not received instructions on that particular point. "What's there to talk about?"

"I want to express my personal disapproval to them."

"All right. Go ahead, Sergeant."

Goran stepped toward those arrested and they closed in around him.

"I am sorry, boys," he said in a very low voice, "it's my fault."

"Like hell it's all yours," swore Delly Hassan, "we all ate, didn't we?"

"Shut up, Delly Hassan," growled bay Goran. "If that's the case, the whole platoon should be punished. I won't permit that to happen! Marrin, you are in charge. Tomorrow when the captain asks you who sent you out, you'll point to me...and that's an order, damn it!"

"Sir, bay Goran..." he stuttered, "it's just a flogging. We won't die from it. We've certainly seen worse than that."

Goran Podgorsky, irked, spat indignantly.

"Listen to me, tough guys. It is the public humiliation of my men that I can't stand. This 'roughneck' here," he tapped Danco's forehead, "has a medal that any officer would gladly give his right arm to be wearing on his chest. No, you leave it to me, and that's that."

"What'll they do to you?" asked Danco a bit doggedly.

"That's none of your goddamn business!" shouted an angry Goran Podgorsky.

"Once Radco's mind is made up," said stryna Nonna, "nobody can change it. He is just following in the footsteps of his father. Dimmitar never said yes or no. Just went ahead and did what he felt was right. That was the way he lived; that was how he met his violent death. Sometimes I think he hung on the skirts of death since childhood. A lifelong pursuit of martyrdom, just as others pursue happiness. Not that Radco's father was a sullen fatalist. Heavens no, he was the most lovable creature I've ever known. Virile and gentle, full of joy and vitality. He would laugh, sing and horse around with his friends. But I, and only I, knew that deep inside him the omnipotent self-destruction ticked like a hidden infernal machine. God is my witness, I tried everything humanly possible to set my son on a different course." She smiled miserably. "It was futile. I failed on every count. Now I've simply gotten used to it…at least…I've stopped blaming God for it all. I have seen how He has tried very hard to protect my boy…" Sobs choked her and she stopped.

Ellena took the cold wasted hand in hers. "If I can do anything to help…"

"You've done enough. If Rayna can't help, nobody can."

Madame Seraphimova looked straight into stryna Nonna's eyes. "I want to be honest with you. I know my daughter as well as you do your son. She is not in love with him. What she likes is his body, the handsome face. An ordinary girl of eighteen doesn't see much further. And I'm afraid that's what she is. A charming, ordinary girl with extraordinary beauty. Jivca, even at her age, might go after something more than good looks…not Rayna."

301

"Don't get me wrong, Madame Seraphimova. I am very much aware of your position in the world. Rayna is too good even for an officer..."

Ellena felt uncomfortable. "No, Mrs. Boeva...that is not what I meant. I would love to have Radco in my family. My husband is from a village in the central part of the country. Very small and very poor. His father was beheaded by the Turks when Vlado was six years old. At the age of eight, he started working as a hired hand; at ten, he was in Anatola, far away in Turkey, learning handicraft at the workshops there. At fifteen he came back here barefooted with three leva in his pocket. Vlad would be only too happy to have a son-in-law from a common background. He is a very proud man, Mrs. Boeva, very proud of his past."

Stryna Nonna's prematurely aged face brightened. "If that is true," she said in a voice shaky with supplication, "let's get the youngsters together. See what a good pair they are, made for each other. That might strike down the black magic of Azimee, and I could live to see grandchildren on my lap."

"It's not that simple, Mrs. Boeva. Times have changed. We do not decide if they are made for each other. It's up to them...their lives...their future..."

"What do children know about life and future?" grunted stryna Nonna.

"What do we know? It's generally accepted that older people know better about such matters...about any matters. I wouldn't like my daughter pointing at me one day and saying, 'She messed up my life!' I don't know a great many things. Every new day shows me how ill prepared I was to take on my responsibilities as a parent. It takes time to outlive the old clichés; it takes courage to go on living without establishing new ones."

Young voices singing and laughing came from the adjoining room. Someone was playing The *Blue Danube*

Waltz on the old piano, feet were shuffling on the bare floor.

"Mrs. Boeva, you are a naturally intelligent woman. You speak of self-destruction, infernal machines. I saw you reading magazines in the kitchen. You understand me perfectly well. Let's not spoil Radco's farewell party with any interference from us. You have my word that I won't try to influence Rayna one way or the other. Let Radco go to the front with an open mind. If he wants to come back one day, he will be gladly accepted as one of us."

Stryna Nonna dried her eyes and smiled bravely.

"Radco is my only son. My family disowned me after I eloped with a Christian refugee from the village of Batack. Somebody brought Dimmitar as a child to Progled. His folks were massacred by the Turks in a small church, before the liberation. Women and children, all stuck in there. He was found amidst the corpses. When he grew old enough, he took this terrible oath to avenge what was done to his people. Thus he became a freedom fighter." A deep sigh left her lips. "It's a great relief to know that if anything happens to me, Radco will have a home. I never told my son that I was born a Muslim."

"Now, don't start crying again, Nonna, 'cause I don't know how I can hold back my tears," confessed Madame Seraphimova, and the two women fell into a warm embrace.

In the next room, Radco waltzed again and again with all the "mademoiselles" of Seraphimov's family. He was a natural dancer. Rayna had shown him the city dances just ten days before and now, smartly dressed in the cadet's uniform of Vladimir Seraphimov, he seemed as if he had danced them all his life. The table was pushed into a corner, the carpet rolled back…bright eyes, flushed faces, quick feet glided over the smooth parquet. Nobody even noticed when Ellena and stryna Nonna joined the party, still holding hands.

"Ya...hoooo, it's great to be alive again!" yelled Radco.

"Only four months," sighed Ellena, "it feels like we've always been together. Hey, girls don't wear out our only gentleman even before he goes to the front!"

"Nothing to me..." shouted back the ruddy cheeked youth. It's like being in paradise with all these angels around. It will have to keep me going for a long time."

Stryna Nonna wiped her eyes with the handkerchief Madame Seraphimova offered her.

"It's hard to believe that he was brought to me half dead just a few months ago. Seems like it never happened at all! Thank God!"

The dancing was at its peak, dancers huffing and puffing, radiant with pleasure and youth. Piano players rotated, mercilessly butchering the same old waltz. At that moment, to everyone's surprise, a most familiar alto voice drowned out the hullabaloo.

"I'm afraid the gentleman will have to brace himself for another dance!"

"Aunt Sultana!!!"

A chorus of joyful screams greeted her. In just moments she had the girls hanging all over her elegant dress. Ellena gasped at first, then pressed her hand to her heart, and finally ran to help out her friend who was being smothered with kisses from all sides.

"What happened? Where have you been?"

"Nothing happened." Sultana burst into her contagious laughter, as if she had just come back from shopping. "I am back home, that's all!"

When Ivan Zemsky awoke in the morning, he had to admit, to his own great surprise, that he had slept soundly all through his last night. A gray misty light filtered through the iron grill, barring the outer world. Muffled voices came from the courtyard above.

His cellmate wriggled over in his corner. He coughed and spat on the floor. His voice came out gruffly, full of reproach, "You slept all night, soldier boy."

In spite of their clash the night before, Ivan felt pity for him. Anyway, they were going to die together.

"My conscience is clear," he said almost cheerfully, "I had no guilt feelings to keep me awake."

Ivan was not religious, but somewhere deep in himself he believed in God. Shortly before waking he had dreamt of being a little boy. His mother was lighting the candle in front of a Christ icon.

"Why do you light the little oil lamp, mom?"

"It's for the dead, my dear!"

He felt perturbed. At this stage he had never seen death.

"You shouldn't. Nobody has died yet."

His mother pointed at Jesus. "He died so that no one would really die anymore."

"How?"

"From His Cross He gave us hope."

Roustan was asking him something and he had to cut himself off, almost physically, from remembering his dream.

"Do you think they're gonna feed us before?"

"I don't know," laughed Ivan a bit sourly, "our jailers might be frugal; food is short nowadays."

"I'm hungry," complained the older man. "Don't you wanna eat a good meal and smoke a narghile before you go to Allah?"

"Well, first, I am not so sure about my appointment with Allah and, second, what differences does it make?"

Roustan shook his head. "There must be something you would like to have for the last time."

Ivan looked at the long leathery face with those empty popping eyes and tried to imagine what kind of a young man the former Chief of the Guard had been. Maybe he had some ambitions of his own, had fought, loved, drunk and hoped. Maybe Allah would not be too harsh on him and would spare a tiny spot in his gardens for his enjoyment.

"Do you believe Allah will pardon you for your sins?" asked Ivan.

The man seemed quite surprised. "I have no sins. I belong to the right faith, have always said my prayers..."

"Never killed a man?"

"I have killed many men...enemies. That should count in my favor up in the heavens."

"I hope Allah has a special liking for murderers."

"To kill on behalf of your faith or country, isn't murder."

"What is it then?"

"You put your life against that of your enemy in the hands of Allah. He is the one who decides who should live and who should die."

Ivan leaned his head back on the cold and damp stones. "It sounds very sensible, practical too."

"It's the only rightful thing between Heaven and Earth. Allah never makes mistakes."

"Why didn't you sleep through the night then? It seems as if everything is in order for your passport to Heaven."

Roustan licked his full lips voluptuously. "I couldn't sleep because I wanted you."

Suddenly the absurdity of the whole situation dawned on Ivan. He—who had imagined so many times dying for his ideals, freedom, social justice, self sacrifice—in his last hours had served as a bait to the beastly instincts of a Turkish ruffian. He burst out laughing.

"Holy cats, isn't that a sin?" mocked Ivan.

The man was so shocked by his laughter, he neglected to respond. In the silence that followed, Ivan closed his eyes and tried to concentrate on something worthwhile. There was nothing in his head. It was like a blank page, as if he was dead already.

He was the first to hear the distant steps coming down the corridor. A sudden pang of almost beastly terror, bordering on total panic, seized him. It clouded his mind, took hold on his throat, squeezed his heart and simply devoured his stomach. A wave of self-pity came in its aftermath. He felt terribly sorry for having missed what he had never tried, never said, never tasted...for those fiery nights spent with girls, for those special moments before dawn after a night of lovemaking, the piercing regret of never really being in love, never to have found a person to love more than anything in the world...to abandon himself in this overwhelming craziness called *Love*.

He almost screamed out that he was not ready to die. He wanted a last chance to have his head at his mother's bosom, her loving, all-redeeming hands stroking him gently. There was nothing more terrifying than those inexorable steps nearing the ingress, reaching possessively for his innermost being. He didn't want to die! Go away steps! Go away!!! He caught himself praying... "Please, God...dear God...make them go away...please, give me another hour...half an hour...ten minutes more...I am not ready to die yet!" Something deep inside him was sobbing, screaming, breaking into pieces. Outwardly he was calm, though all the blood had left his face.

Now the other man had heard them too.

He rose to his feet shakily, eyes bulging with animal fear, hands outstretched, as if he wanted to keep out the approaching men by force of dark magic.

"They're coming," he whispered, drained of blood too, "Allah have mercy on me!"

"They" were unlocking the door. No mistake; it was for them. The hinges screeched loudly, almost like a human scream. Suddenly the tiny cell was full of people.

Ivan got up slowly, his knees giving in as if made of clay. Two soldiers grabbed Roustan. He did not resist. They led him past Ivan as he started to join them. A hand pushed him back roughly.

Roustan stopped. "Why?" We were going to die together!"

The soldiers got a better hold on him.

"It's none of your business," the officer butted him with his gun, "go!"

"It is my business," shouted Roustan, digging his heels into the earthen floor, "why are you holding him back?"

"Ivan Zemsky has been pardoned by His Majesty."

"Then, I am pardoned, too!" cried the older man.

"No. You are not! Go!"

Now the man was putting up a real struggle. Writhing, scratching, biting, foam running from the corners of his ugly mouth, he sobbed and yelled in total despair. "Why...fuckin' swines? 'Cause I am a TURK and he is one of yours? It's not fair. Let me go! Allah, why do you let them do this to me???"

When they dragged him through the door, he turned his face, distorted with rage and fear, and spat at Ivan. "Be damned, bastard! For the rest of your life, be damned!"

Ivan stood, absolutely numb, listening to the screams dying away. His hot breath came from his mouth with a strange wheezing sound that made him sick. The cold, damp air around him turned into clouds of vapor. Suddenly, he felt freezing inside and out, although something warm was running down his thighs and calves at the same time.

He had wet himself.

The sky was clear. Festive sunlight blazed over snow spattered with frozen mud. Everyone in the company was lined up around a group of naked men. Danco and his comrades stood at the center, stripped of their uniforms, bodies blue with cold, shivering and red faced with shame and humiliation.

A number of freshly cut branches waited at the feet of Captain Dennev. He coughed a bit to ease his voice, then announced to the surrounding men, "Attention, company! You are called upon here to witness the punishment of a bunch...I won't say soldiers, because that would further tarnish the honor of our army and flag. I don't want to even mention the sacred name of our Fatherland. These people are thieves and they have been thieving right out of the mouths of their own brothers in arms. Therefore, in the name of His Majesty, I inflict upon them this severe punishment, flogging their bare skins with raw branches."

He read the names of all accused and asked them, one by one, if they assumed their guilt. The bluish lips formed something that could be read as guilty.

"Who sent you out to steal?" asked Captain Dennev in the deadly silence. He waited a bit, then asked again, "Was the crime committed entirely on your own?" Dennev scrutinized each face. "I am asking you, because if you acted under the orders of a superior rank, according to army discipline, you are not to be held responsible. He and only he would be punished. Therefore, I am asking you for the last time—were you under orders?"

Danco lifted up his head and uttered. "Yes, sir...we were."

The silence was so deep that even those furthest away could hear it. There was a gasp from the troops.

Captain Dennev, without forsaking his integrity, with austerity, asked once more of the wretched men in the square, "Under whose orders?"

"The platoon chief's, Sergeant Goran Podgorsky," mumbled Danco through his chattering teeth.

"Sergeant Goran Podgorsky," shouted the captain, "step out here!"

There was no answer. A corporal stepped forward, "Our Sergeant is not here, sir."

"Where is he, Corporal?"

"I think he stayed behind in the dugout, sir."

Captain Dennev turned to his junior officer, "Go and get him!"

The officer took a patrol with him, and briskly walked out to the dugouts. "Give these men some coats!" cried Dennev at the gaping soldiers.

Sergeant Goran Podgorsky was found dead. He had shot himself in the mouth. All charges against his soldiers were dismissed.

Chapter Fourteen

Delly Hassan Caursky was at the observation post when the cortege of dignitaries arrived. A company lined up at the foot of the knoll where the platform stood and started to shout "hurrah" and a band played the Tzar's Anthem. At first Delly Hassan was amused by the tiny moving figurines. He even turned the portable telescope in their direction and saw the glitter of His Majesty's medals. Soon, he realized that they were moving in his direction and his amusement turned to bemusement.

The hill proved to be too steep for the Monarch. It was General Robev and the Crown Prince who helped him up. When the party reached the top, they were all flushed with excitement and short of breath. A cold breeze from the Sea of Marmora slammed in their sweaty faces. Panting and laughing, the small group climbed up a few wooden steps. On the platform, stiff with bewilderment, Delly Hassan met them with his best salute.

"Welcome to observation post number thirty nine, Your Majesty!" he shouted.

"Oh, brother," laughed Ferdinand, "you speak with a thicker accent than mine. What is your name, young man?"

"Private Delly Hassan Caursky, Your Majesty!"

"Are you sure we are on the right side of Marmora, Seraphimov?"

Delly Hassan was sort of relieved to see a familiar face among all those strangers, though there was something odd in it at the same time. Seraphimov's face was drained of its usual vitality, eyes vacant, staring at a seagull floating on the crest of a wave.

Prince Boris filled the silent gap. "Can we really see Tzarygrad from here?"

"What do you say, soldier," the Tzar asked sharply, "it seems you're the only one paying attention to what I'm saying."

"You cannot see Stanbul from here, Majesty, though you can observe a cavalry drill on the Turkish side through the telescope."

"Sounds interesting," mumbled Ferdinand. His attention still on Vladimir Seraphimov, he took the instrument absentmindedly, "let's see what the enemy is doing. Well, I see some dots moving out there. Though not very clear, definitely a better day for bird watching."

The festive mood had dissipated.

Everyone in the retinue now acted like marionettes, worried that their threads might get tangled. Each one of them took the telescope and made some stupid comment on that "war game." Boris approached Colonel Seraphimov. "Are you expecting a storm, Colonel?"

Seraphimov tore his eyes from the bird flying over the high waves. "On an overcast day the sea turns to a dull gray. Those waves keep on coming and coming in the same monotonous way, until a heavy storm links the elements into a magic, flaming circle…"

"Are you all right, Colonel Seraphimov?" Boris was suddenly concerned with what was taking place in Vladimir's mind.

Two tired gray eyes focused on the gentle young face of the Prince. "It's poetry, Your Highness. The words of an old Turkish song I learned in Anatolia. It popped into my head from nowhere—maybe from the sea itself." A heavy sigh rocked his chest. "The enemies will keep on coming at us like those waves...come and die...come and die... until the last big storm."

"It doesn't sound very optimistic, sir."

"It's not meant to be, my dear Prince. One day when you take over the helm of our nation, try to rule the way nature rules the world, then you'll last until the Big Storm. Don't try to play God, even for a moment."

Tzar Ferdinand joined Seraphimov and the Prince. "It's very unkind of you, Seraphimov. As host you're supposed to share your precious company with *everyone*. What has the Prince done to deserve so much?" He swung an arm around the narrow shoulders of Boris. "Don't make me jealous of my own son, Colonel."

"Aren't you tired, Father, of calling him a colonel?"

"Not a bit, son. This man has given colonel a title of distinction compared to..." his eyes wandered and stopped on Robev, "some generals, like Robev here..." he giggled, "I wonder if he doesn't ever pull his rank over mine. However, it's getting too cold for me on this open platform. A touch of pneumonia is all I need now. Soldier, come here!" He pulled off one of the minor medals from his chest and hung it on Delly Hassan's. "Remember me with good thoughts, young man."

On a sudden impulse, Delly Hassan grabbed his hand and kissed it. That was not missed by the two photographers. Quick snapshots were made of the touching scene and this picture was published on the front page of all major newspapers.

When the procession filed downhill, another "hurrah" was heard from the lined troops, and there was a replay of the Anthem. All rank and file expected the Monarch to give a speech, to thank them for their courage and good service. Ferdinand, deeply absorbed by his own thoughts, didn't seem to notice them at all. Gradually the greeting died away and an uncomfortable pause hung in the air. Robev approached the Tzar.

"Your Majesty…"

Ferdinand hesitated for a moment, then walked a few steps toward the troops. "Young heroes! One day when you recall the time you fought between the Gulf of Sarrosa and Marmora, tell your children that Tzar Ferdinand, your father, came as far as the position at Bullayr, just to see his sons."

That speech did not live up to the expectations of the men. A short, disheartened "hooray" greeted the end of that handful of pompous words.

That night, after a horrible artillery cannonade, the giant Turkish army made two landings; at Bullayr and Sharkioy. A couple of auxiliary companies guarding the beaches at Sharkioy had found some vats full of wine at a nearby village and had drunk themselves into oblivion. Some informants later reported that the wine had been brought on barges directly from Istanbul. Sadly, those Bulgarian troops were caught sound asleep and never woke to tell their story.

The situation for all troops in this sector was beyond desperation. The 7th division had to absorb a powerful blow from three Turkish dreadnoughts and continuous attacks of advancing infantry. The 2nd division had been called from the rear in a relentless march. Those Bulgarian troops barely made it by morning, arriving hungry and on the brink of exhaustion.

The major Turkish forces were concentrated at Ursha, just a few miles inland. Only the mist hanging over the shore had saved the 13th Bulgarian regiment from a sight that could have brought them a sound psychological defeat. There was no formation, just a giant mass of humanity shouting Yurush, totally unconcerned about life and death.

During that endless night, the flag of the 13th regiment had been in Turkish hands several times. All ranks fought the invading forces. Even General Todorov, the division commander, engaged in hand-to-hand combat in the trenches on several occasions.

During that phase, Bulgarians found an unlikely ally in the face of their most dreadful enemy—a Turkish battleship. The battleship guns were set to fire at a range bordering the Bulgarian positions. Poor visibility prevented them from seeing their own troops had arrived at that range. It was a terrible scene to witness—an enormous mass of humanity under relentless fire of heavy artillery. There was no place for them to hide from the steady onslaught. Bloody pieces of dismembered bodies flew sky high. At this point, in an attempt to lift the spirits of their soldiers, Bulgarian officers were instructed to announce that the 50th regiment was coming. Both sides, engaged in ferocious hand-to-hand battle, heard the announcement. Not understanding the Bulgarian language that well, the Turkish interpreted it to mean: "Hold on brothers, fifty regiments are coming!!!"

That was the turning point.

The rumor spread with lightning speed. In less than an hour, the Turkish troops from Mount Sivryteppe to Bullayr Heights, ran back to the anchored ships in Sarrosa. When the 2nd division arrived there were very few Turks left along the beaches.

This last great effort of the Padishah's army to take initiative and surround all Bulgarian forces at Odrin ended in a complete failure. Sultan Mehmed was forced to ask for a negotiated peace.

Radco Boev traveled with his mother to Progled along one of the regular supply routes. By the end of February, there were few points of resistance left in that area. Many villages had suffered the fallout of two fighting armies. Very little was left for a new start—houses burned to ashes, cattle confiscated or killed, crops destroyed. General famine visited this formerly self-sufficient population. Fortunately, the second half of February was unusually mild and that saved a lot of people from freezing to death.

Progled was one of the few villages along the border left intact by the raging war. As a military hub, Progled's significance had been augmented. Quite a number of new buildings and other structures had been built for military use. With a constant influx of refugees, the population nearly tripled. The busy traffic on its only road, leading to the heart of Bulgaria, gave an air of importance to that forgotten sleepy village of the past.

It was quite a disappointing shock for Radco to discover that his outfit had moved to Bullayr in Turkey. He was invited to join the local garrison, but he preferred to join his friends, and his mother's silent reproach only reinforced his decision.

One day, as Radco was getting ready to leave, he walked around just to say goodbye to the old places. Rossitza's house was closed and boarded up. He listened to different stories but, on the whole, it amounted to a rather sad ending. Rossitza had freed the prisoners and escaped with one of them. If the description was accurate, that man was Ismail. On one hand Radco rejoiced at his good luck; on the other, he couldn't stop thinking about the tragic circumstances that might follow. The whole situation had backfired on Rossitza's father. He was sent to the front as punishment for his drinking at a time when he was supposed to be watching the prisoners. "There, he'll be cured of his bad habits," laughed the villagers, not without malice, "his captain won't wake him up with a bottle of tantoura!"

However, Radco was more concerned about Azimee. None of his inquiries among the local people had given him any worthwhile clues, so he planned to visit Chamgas. On his way out of the local *lazaretto*, a traveling, temporary hospital, he bumped into Magda Marrin. After the initial emotional outburst, he took her to his mother's house. She filled him in on everything that happened after he was wounded at Allamy Derre. When she got to the death of Ermin, her self-control left her. She had also lost her sister and her brother-in-law.

Radco took the sobbing girl in his arms. "I really don't know what to tell you, Magda," he choked with tears as he tried to swallow. "Ermin was a great guy—the best, we won't forget him."

"He was so lonely. Nobody claimed his body. He was hastily buried by the back wall of the castle in Moguilitza," she explained sadly to Radco.

"I'd have liked his place to be here, Magda, among us, but he is out in the woods, where the wind still carries his tunes. You shouldn't be sorry about his burial place. Right there, in the age old pine forest—that's where he belongs."

Then Radco told her about himself and Azimee. Magda could not quite get over that.

"So you were Ismail! Jesus Christ, that never crossed my mind. What my wretched brother has done to you! If only he knew…"

"But he knew, quite well, dear Magda, all the way. What he did was done willfully." Radco was shaking with anger, struggling with the deep feeling of a brother's betrayal. After awhile, he took control of himself. "What's done is done…but you've got to help me see her before I leave."

"That's a difficult one, Radco. Azimee is my brother's wife. For now she is convinced that your brief appearance was only a dream. Why reopen old wounds? Danco will make her happy if only God brings him back. She is with our parents. They watch her day and night like hawks. After everything that's happened, I am not welcome there. I came here to find some kind of work in the military *lazaretto*. I have no other place to go. Don't worry about Azimee. Danco'll take good care of her."

"How about Rossitza?" Radco bristled.

"Nobody knows where she is. She is as good as dead by now, I suppose."

"And how about me?" asked the young man with bitterness in his voice, "am I as good as dead as well?"

Magda gently put her hand on his tousled head. "You are like a brother to Danco. You can't let a woman come between you two. Please understand. You have all my sympathy. My father is a Muslim. He won't let you see her before Danco returns. You know the tradition. After Bogdana and I became Christians, father disowned us. For him, Allah punished us. I told you. He doesn't want me in his house. I wish I could help you."

"Don't worry, my mother will take care of you. That way she will feel less lonely when I...she'll find something for you in the hospital. She works there."

The silence fell over them like a shroud. Magda felt uneasy. "Radco."

"Yeah?"

"You'll come back soon, won't you? There is a lot of talk that the war is over...or almost over."

"I don't know, Magda. If that comes to pass, I might go back to Plovdiv, maybe try my luck at the military school there."

"You have no high school diploma. How can you ever make it?"

"I know somebody that made it in spite of that. I'll try as hard as he did!" promised Radco.

Danco had not been feeling well for quite a while, and the day after the battle of Sharkioy, he felt extremely tired. He had been tired before, but usually his youth and strong restorative powers quickly took care of that. Now the fatigue wouldn't go away. His head was heavy, vision blurred and everything kept going round and round. His stomach gave him pains and nausea. His mouth burned. When he dragged himself behind a wall, it was as if his blood was running out.

Dysentery!

Loaded onto an oxcart, Danco was sent along with many others to a *lazaretto* some twenty miles away. The weather had turned mild again, yet a slanting rain, driven by gusty winds, splashed over them all the way. On arrival, seven were already dead and the rest unable to get out of the cart.

A large private house served as a *lazaretto* for the whole division. After a long wait, Danco's turn finally came. At first he didn't see anybody in the room, but at last found a doctor sitting behind a high porcelain stove. He was a fat stately man with a goatee that seemed glued to one of his many chins.

"Read your papers!" he ordered. Danco read as well as he could and the fatso behind the nice warm stove took some notes. "Go to the dispensary," said he, sullenly, "they'll give you some medication. Come back tomorrow."

"But, I can't, sir," mumbled Danco, "my company is twenty miles away."

"Then don't come." He looked at him through his golden framed glasses. This "doctor," who was later appointed Minister of Social Care and Health for his exceptional duties at the front, added, "we're full to bursting."

Danco thought he must be dreaming. He simply did not know what to do, but stood, swaying back and forth on his feet. Then the fat man got really mad. He approached Danco and started poking at his ribs with a walking stick.

"Go! Go! Go!"

Danco made it outside.

It was raining even harder. On the opposite side of the courtyard he saw a wooden outhouse. He gathered what was left of his formerly great strength and dragged himself across the muddy puddles. A bloody stinking mess covered the floor inside, but at least the rain was not falling as hard, and the wind was less bitter. He crouched in a corner and, for the first time in his life, began weeping uncontrollably. His medal for bravery in action broke loose and fell into the hole. It splashed into the gooky mess and disappeared as if it had never existed. It hit him as something very funny, and he laughed, and laughed, and laughed...

Morning found him still alive. Danco was carried to a small room where twenty more like him were infirmed. For two days, they got no attention whatsoever. Only a patrol checked from time to time to remove the dead. On the third day, the survivors were fed raw chickpeas.

A week passed and not a person from the medical staff had visited that narrow unheated room. It was full of stench, lice and misery. About that time, Danco made a startling discovery. The stretcher bearers were bringing in typhus cases. He recognized the colored spots on those half decomposed bodies. Sudden panic struck him. He had to get the hell out of there. Still very sick, he had some chance to survive, but only if he could avoid that dreadful disease.

Around noon, Danco slipped out of the death trap. Once outside he tried to run, but his weakness made him feel faint. His feet felt like they were made of lead, taking orders from nobody. Danco tried to plead with them. It worked a bit, and he was able to reach the few huts spread around a low hill. He knocked at the closest door. A little girl opened it just a crack.

"What do you want?"

"Let me in, tiny bird, please!" he swayed and leaned on the door frame.

"You're funny," said the girl, her large hazel eyes studying him with profound attention, "I am not a bird, but *you* look like a skeleton."

"I am very sick. I may die if you don't let me in. Please!" The girl put her tiny finger into her rosy mouth.

"Father told me not to let in any soldiers. I am afraid of you."

"You don't have to be. You could knock me down with that little finger of yours."

She opened the door hesitantly. "Father will tear my ears off. Anyway, you can stay inside until he comes."

Danco entered and collapsed in the furthest corner.

"Thank you, little bird," he groaned, "it's warm in here. What's your name?"

"Orrania," she replied.

"I thought you were Turkish," whispered Danco.

"We're Greeks. What are you?"

Danco closed his eyes and tried to muster a miserable smile. "I wish I knew. To Turks, I am Bulgarian; to Bulgarians, a Turk. I really don't know what Greeks would call me."

Orrania sat beside the hearth. "Well, it depends on you. How do you feel?"

"I feel like a hunted animal. Nobody seems to want me," Danco croaked nervously.

The girl took a baby doll made of rags and kissed it gently. "What is your name?"

"Dannail."

"Well, don't worry about what other people take you for. You are Dannail."

"It's not that easy. I have one more name. Ibrahim. Ibrahim Marrin."

Orrania pondered over that new found problem for a while, cuddling her baby and looking at the stranger with her big thoughtful eyes. A moment later her delicate face, unusually mature for her age, reflected the solution of that puzzle.

"Then you are all of that. Dannail-Ibrahim Marrin!"

"Isn't that a bit too long for one ordinary person like me?"

"No," Orrania shook her curly head, "I've heard longer names."

"Well...that seems to take care of me. You've been very helpful."

"I know...my grandfather is a Carracachan shepherd, my aunt a Bulgarian, uncle Idris is a Turk...my father says I am a Greek like him, but I haven't quite decided yet."

Danco's head was reeling. The warm cozy air was making him terribly sleepy.

"Let me know when you make up your mind."

"What shall I call you?"

"You can call me anything you like, I am not fussy."

Orrania pondered a bit, "Then I will call you Danby—Dannail and Ibrahim together." After a pause, she questioned, "Tell me, Danby, do you have a little girl of your own?"

"No, Orry—could I call you Orry?—I haven't had a chance yet...why?"

"You won't laugh at me if I tell you, will you?"

"Certainly not."

"My father thinks I am crazy and has forbidden me to talk about those pictures."

"What pictures?"

"They are pictures I see about people just out of nowhere. When my mother was struck by lightning...

"Did you see me in those pictures of yours?" Danco asked.

"Not exactly, it's blurred somehow. But I see the girl very well, she is about my age and very pretty. She's not dressed in rags and barefoot like me. Her name is Ji...va. No...yes! I know...Jivca. She is sitting next to an empty bed, caressing the pillow as if it were somebody. Now she says, 'come back, come back, I love you!' and she cries."

Startled by the expression on Orrania's face, Danco did not quite feel like laughing. "She is not calling me, sweetheart."

"No, it's another stranger, though you know him. You've done him wrong."

"Who could it be. There are plenty of people that have done wrong to me, but I can't think who I have done anything to," protested Danco.

"But you did, and you know what you did!" Orrania cried.

"Who knows...I..." and Danco fell asleep.

Orrania took a blanket from a chest and spread it over the sleeping man. When her father came back in the evening, she put a finger across her lips.

"Shush, don't wake him up. He is sick."

Her father was flabbergasted but spoke in a hushed voice, "Who is he?"

"Danby. Nobody wants him," Orrania affixed a stubborn line between her pretty eyebrows.

"Including me. I'll get him out of here."

"No, you can't, father! He is too big, and you have only one hand."

"Is that so? Who's gonna stop me?"

"If you touch him, I'll leave you forever," Orrania threatened.

"Where will you go?"

"To the mountains. I'll live with grandfather Ivvo, and you'll never see me again."

"Like mother, like daughter! God give peace to her soul," sighed Costaky, her father. He was quite a young man but, the very lightning that had taken his wife's life had dried up his right hand. For two days he had been in a coma, then life came back to him little by little. Use of his hand was lost. That saved him from army service but was of no solace to him.

"What if he has typhus?" asked Costaky his daughter.

"We'll take care of him," Orrania suggested.

"He belongs in a hospital."

"That is not so. You told me yourself that no one comes out of there alive." She began to sob, shaking, "I don't want him to die!"

"All right! All right! You win. I give up, evallah. Peace!"

"I don't know why you always make things so hard for both of us," said Orrania, tears running down her dainty face, "even though we never end in disagreement."

"That's because I hope just once to win, angel. You have no heart for me."

"But I do," she cried out, hanging on to his neck, smothering him with kisses, "You'll see, next time I promise to step down, even if I am right...as usual."

Her cry woke Danco. He tried to get up.

"I am sorry, I feel much better now. In a minute, I'll be on my way."

Costaky came to him and kneeled down. "Please stay, whoever you are. I don't want to lose my daughter. Say, young man, you don't have typhus, do you?"

"No...dysentery," croaked Danco.

"God be blessed! My father Ivvo taught me how to cure that sickness." He straightened up briskly on his legs and was all business.

"Orrania, put a tile on the hearth. Where is the Stanbul sugar?"

"At the false bottom of the food chest, father. I'll get it. You just tell me how to use it."

"Fill a pot with the sugar, about two pounds of it, and let it melt slowly over the fire. Then let him drink it while it's still hot. The tile has to be under him in bed. Lie in my bed over there, young man. I'll sleep with my daughter."

Danco looked at his gentle face, eyes overflowing with tears. "How can I ever thank you…"

"Spirridon-Constantin is my name. Costaky for short."

"God bless you, Costaky."

"Thank my daughter."

"…and her, that little bird of yours."

"What did she say your name was…Danby?"

"Well…Danby is fine with me."

"You can do something for me, Danby. I have two younger kids staying with my sister Ghana in Chepellare. If you happen to go there, tell 'em that we're still alive," pleaded Costaky, taking a serious tone.

"I certainly will, if I ever make it back home. It's only a half a day distance from my village."

"Oh, you'll be fine," smiled Orrania's father, "in three days, you'll be as good as new."

The news of an armistice came over a devastated land. Thousands and thousands of corpses lay unburied after the last battle. Some efforts to bury the dead were made, but it was hard to dig in that frozen rocky ground. The work commandos were distraught with moral despair and physical exhaustion. Malnutrition and constant strain prevailed. Battlefields along the Sea of Marmora were strewn with piles of broken and abandoned warfare. Here and there, portions of decomposed bodies stuck out—a hand pointing at the sky in silent accusation, or legs spread apart in a mock sign of victory. Soon, the rising temperature brought a new menace. A reek of death floated over the carnage.

And riding on the wings of countless birds of prey came CHOLERA!

Ferdinand wouldn't look at any faces.

"I had to accept the terms because of the overwhelming pressure coming from everywhere. The Great Powers, our ex-allies...even our own Parliament. Gentlemen of the War Council, you were my only constant support and inspiration. Thank you."

The oldest general rose from his chair and bowed respectfully. "Is there anything we can do for Your Majesty?"

The Monarch turned his sharp impatient eyes toward him as if he had been waiting for that question a long time. "There is, gentlemen. I want your honest opinion. Can we count on our army for a last great effort?"

"A blitzkrieg?"

"A blitzkrieg. *De facto in bona fide*, I accepted a demarcation line at Media-Enos, but that armistice can be broken...for a week or ten days. Before the Great Powers realize what we're up to, Tzarygrad can be ours. Then we'll dictate our own terms."

A heavy pause followed his feverish speech. The War Council was stunned.

"Gentlemen," said Ferdinand derisively, "I was not hoping for general applause, but at least I expected partial approval."

General Robev made an effort. A few others followed hesitantly, but the same old general spoke out again.

"We have quite a number of commanders that excelled in this war, some defensively, others in the siege and attacking a stronger enemy. But blitzkrieg is not a battle, Your Majesty. It's a whole war of a different nature. Do we have a person able to lead this sort of warfare?"

Ferdinand was not bemused even for a moment. "If that is your only concern, General Jallov, I have somebody in mind. Anything else?"

"Do we have any guarantee that our former allies, in event of an unexpected attack on Tzarygrad, would, shall I say, morally support us?"

"We won't give them time for such decisions," asserted Ferdinand.

"There is already a widening breach between all nations in the Balkans. A slight reversal of that delicate balance might invite unfortunate developments," complained the general.

"After a great triumph, the eyes of all mankind will be focused on us in admiration. Under those circumstances our neighbors won't have the courage to attack the invincible Lion of the Balkans!"

Jallov cocked his eyebrows. "I hope so, Your Majesty, One last question, if I may. Where do we find the resources?"

"We'll use all available resources, General."

"We will need some well rested, well equipped divisions. To my knowledge, we've already used all our reserves."

"How do you know what we need to win, General?" smiled Ferdinand derogatorily, "As far as I know, you've never won a battle except in the field of poetry."

Some sharp biting laughter erupted around the oval table. Jallov's face remained impassive. He said calmly, "If Your Majesty is alluding to my poem written in honor of Vladimir Seraphimov's victory at Allamy Derre, it's only a stanza, but I humbly accept the compliment. Your Majesty is a well known connoisseur."

Ferdinand sized up the white haired man, his Greek profile, erect posture and proud behavior, then said sarcastically, "You might have a better chance of pleasing us, General Jallov, by writing a whole book of poetry on that same person."

The faded blue eyes dilated with surprise. "Are you saying the Colonel is your choice, Majesty?"

"I haven't quite made up my mind," said the Tzar provocatively, "but Colonel Seraphimov is being considered." He looked at all present. Their reaction seemed to be more of shock than opposition. Only the War Minister emitted a terse comment, "I hope you're finally satisfied, Jallov."

The old man sat down resignedly, staring at a point far beyond the palace walls. "I can't believe it, Your Majesty," he intoned, "I am sorry, but it sounds utterly irrational."

A light tumult of hushed voices spread around the table.

"Get rid of Socrates!" hissed Ferdinand in the ear of his First Adjutant General Robev.

Ellena was adamant.

"I won't let you go home without washing your hands in the medicated solution."

"You must be out of your mind," objected Sultana, "that strong disinfectant will ruin my skin."

"You're worse than a child. You don't wear your mask, your white robe is all the way open to show off that pretty dress of yours and now you refuse to disinfect your hands. There are cases of cholera in this hospital, in case you've forgotten, Madame Hadgylvanova."

"I have not forgotten. I didn't want to tell you, but Assen is one of them. He was brought in early this afternoon."

Madame Seraphimova leaned against the wall. "You saw him?"

"I talked to him before he died."

Ellena buried her face in her shaking hands. "Oh, my God! That poor boy…he was so afraid of death." Then she grasped Sultana's shoulders. "Why did you go? I ordered you to stay away from that ward!"

"He sent for me," she said, pulling back from her friend.

"You should have told me," accused Ellena.

"Assen didn't want you to get close to him because of the kids. He is very…he was very fond of them. He sent his special regards to you and the master, begs you to kiss that little princess of his and buy her a beautiful dress with the money he left with you. He left all his worldly possessions to the cook. Nothing to his family. They didn't care about him, nor he them. You were his only family and to you, he sends his last love and affection."

Ellena sat at her little desk and wept in abandonment. Sultana came to the weeping woman and touched her head with infinite tenderness.

"I am not coming with you, Ellena."

Madame Seraphimova looked up at her in surprise. "Where are you going this time?"

Sultana smiled sadly. "Not to the palace any more. I have no further illusions about changing the fate of this country. I'll stay in a hotel room for a while. I was a bit incautious this afternoon."

Ellena straightened up, all the blood drained from her face.

"What have you done, Sultana?"

"I am sorry, dear, you have every right to be mad at me, but he was talking in such a feeble voice, I had to get very close to his mouth. I couldn't catch what he was saying…and then…then…he vomited in my face."

The armistice announcement found Radco Boev still in Progled.

Even for someone as stubborn as he, it didn't make much sense to go to the front at this point in time. He decided to stay home, at least temporarily, and watch for further developments. There was a lot of talk about a new war, this time against the former allies.

Stryna Nonna went to church and lit the largest candle available.

It was about this time, that a Carracachan shepherd, passing through the village, spread the word about Rossitza Podgorska living with a young Turk in the mountain sheepfold of grandfather Ivvo. The population was outraged. For some unknown reason the not-so-*heroic* death of her father was blamed on Rossitza. She was openly referred to as the *bitch* and labeled a traitor. There was talk of sending out a posse to punish her for debauchery.

Radco knew his fellow villagers only too well, so he wasted no time. That same afternoon he hit the road toward Moguilitza and Arda. Shortly after passing the crossroad to Derrekioy, his eye caught a solitary figure ahead of him. As he was riding their house mule, Mancho, there was no difficulty catching up to the lonely pedestrian. At about a hundred yards distance the stranger realized Radco's coming from behind and dashed into the bushes.

It was a veiled woman. No doubt about that.

But what on earth was a *cadana* doing alone on this road? Radco's curiosity was awakened. He poked at Mancho and made him trot a bit. When they arrived at the spot, Radco looked around. The woman was hiding behind some low pine trees.

"Hello there," he shouted. "Need some help?"

A short scream came to him, then the woman started running toward him, arms outstretched. Even under the loose robes he could tell that it was a young and beautiful body. Halfway, the veil fell from her face. For a moment, Radco was paralyzed with surprise. Then he jumped down and ran toward her.

"Azimee!!!"

"Ismail!"

They flew into each other's arms.

The impact was so strong that they both tumbled on the thick carpet of dry leaves. For a while their lips were so tightly pressed that it seemed nothing in the whole universe would separate them again. It was a heavenly delirium, delicious agony. Radco's hand found the silky warm touch of her heaving bosom, his mouth slipping over enticing flesh and shiny dark hair, then meeting her full lips again in breathtaking kisses. They'd caress, tease, adore...writhe in wild desire. Offering, forcing, taking, urging, rolling in the dry pine needles and small green cones—laughing, dizzy, tickling each other, trembling with happiness, fingers finding the most excitable zones.

Then he was inside her, penetrating deeply, Azimee gasped and moaned in ecstasy.

When they came back to reality, it was like spring had flown over the bare woods. They could smell the aroma of strange, exotic flowers, a tantalizing taste of wild berries in their mouths.

"Don't ever leave me, Ismail," whispered Azimee, her deep passionate eyes burning into his very soul. "Don't disappear, my sweet dream-come-true!"

"Oh, Azimee..." moaned Radco, "I swear, I won't, even if I have to commit a crime. God Himself wants us together!"

Violet twilight hung over the branches like torn veils. It was time to find a roof under which to pass that coming night. It felt cold and damp. Soon Azimee mounted the mule and Radco led it looking for a coal burner's hut.

"Where were you going, Azimee?"

"Back home. Or wherever, but not to that jail."

"The old man Marrin wasn't good to you?"

"Oh, they were both sweet. He and his wife. They pampered me like a child, but wouldn't let me go as far as the garden. I'm not even married to their son yet!"

"You're not!!!" Radco cried out. "Magda said you were legally wed."

"If she said that, she was lying just as they all lied to me that you never existed, that you were only a figment of my imagination." Then she told him about her abduction, that real nightmare in the bloody hands of a man called "Vampire," the miraculous deliverance, how nice and tender Danco was with her after the shock she suffered. Her tale differed little from Magda's except for the last part. "We lived together almost a month, but we never got married. His father paid for me, but I am not for sale."

Round the bend an abandoned shack loomed in front of their eyes. There was no way Radco could remember that this was the same shelter where he and the real Ismail had passed a memorable night a few months ago, a night between life and death for him.

Chapter Fifteen

Ivan Zemsky was released from prison and the army—
a dishonorable discharge. He got a ride on a military
echelon train to Plovdiv and underwent a brief
medical examination on arrival. After the medical officer
signed his free pass, excluding the capital city of Sofia and
other major cities, he felt lost in his native town. He simply
didn't know where to go next.

His old friends had gone to the front, and a relative
was the last person he wanted to meet. There was no
money left on him to buy a railway ticket, any ticket for
that matter, and using army transportation was not
possible. Besides, Sofia was specifically indicated on his
civilian passport as a forbidden destination for him.

He had to find a job. Any kind of job, just to keep
himself going. The young man was leaning on one of the
four wooden columns in the station's lobby, when a lady
from the receiving committee approached him. She was
young and exceptionally beautiful. "Welcome to our town,
soldier," she smiled, "I guess this is your first time in
Plovdiv."

Holy cow! It was Rayna Seraphimova in person, of all
people!!! Obviously she didn't recognize him. He had lost
a third of his weight, his moustache was unkempt and he
wore a raggedy uniform. For all the tea in China, he didn't

want any recognition under these present circumstances. On the other hand, he didn't want to lose her company.

"Don't know the city very well," he mumbled, trying to disguise his voice, "I do seem to have some problems."

"We're here to help…"

"Ivan Zemsky," saluted the young man, "at your service."

"Did you say Zemsky? The name sounds familiar. Anyway, Mr. Zemsky, what brought you here?"

"I was just discharged from the army," he answered.

"Discharged?"

Ivan blushed. "Dishonorable, I am afraid."

"Oh…I am sorry."

"I presume you are not supposed to tell me about a job. Any job."

"I don't know. I'll have to ask the lady in charge."

"Sorry, please, don't go! The old lady will just tell me to go to hell, anyway. You…you forgot to tell me your name."

"Oh…sorry…Rayna Seraphimova."

He felt embarrassed by his own double play. "You're not by any chance related to Colonel Seraphimov, are you?"

"Vladimir Seraphimov is my father. Do you know him?"

"Do I know him! Holy mackerel, who doesn't know Colonel Seraphimov?!? He is a legendary figure. The black mantle commander and so forth. Besides, he saved my neck from the gallows."

Rayna looked at him with those magic eyes of hers and smiled pleasantly. "Then you cannot be so bad. My father wouldn't lift a finger for a dishonest person."

"No I am not…sooo bad."

"You are right about the ladies here, Mr. Zemsky, but I'll ask my mother. I am sure she'll be able to find you something suitable. What is your profession, by the way?"

Ivan bowed elegantly. "Everywhere I go it seems that my best known profession is that of black sheep, but my second best is acting in the theatre."

At that, a light of remembrance came to her eyes. Rayna clapped her pretty hands.

"But, of course! 'My hands are always dirty...' or something like that," she recited imitating his voice, "the artist from the play, *The Lower Depths* by Gorky. I saw you on stage only a year ago. You were very good. What a coincidence."

Ivan Zemsky blushed to the roots of his hair. His attempt to remain incognito had failed miserably.

"I most humbly thank you. It's very kind of you to remember, though that certainly was just a small part, by far not my best."

"Which one is your best?"

"*Hamlet*, of course." In his mind Ivan swore at himself, impostor and liar, that's what you are! You have never even been an extra in that play. Out loud he went on, "I hope you can see me sometime when theatres resume their activities."

"I'd be happy to. I am sure my mother will be delighted to see you."

"We've already met, at the hospital. I had a medical examination there before going to my toy soldier appointment. At least, that's what I thought then."

Was it just an illusion, or did her cheeks look rosier than before?

"That's even better, Mr. Zemsky. Why don't you come and have a cup of tea with us this coming Sunday at five o'clock. Do you know our address?"

"As a matter of fact I do. I accompanied Madame Seraphimova to your place by the public gardens. I had the honor to meet you for a moment or two. You gave me a small package for Colonel Seraphimov, while your mother wrote a few lines."

"How extraordinary! And I had forgotten all about it. It must have been the shawl I knitted for him that took a number of years! Did he wear it?"

"I wouldn't know that, but I'd bet my last fiver he did. It was extremely cold out there."

"Then it's a deal. We'll see you Sunday at five."

"My pleasure, Mademoiselle, *et que Dieu vous guarde! A bientot!*" said Ivan Zemsky gallantly, kissing her exquisite hand with all the sentiment he could muster.

He was foolishly and hopelessly in love for the first time in his life.

"Going back to the front," insisted Costaky, "makes no sense at all. An armistice is on the way, cholera's raging. What are you going to do there? You're still weak, your chances of surviving are rather slim. Who is going to profit from it? Be reasonable, Danby, come with us. We need you. I would like to take along as much of my worldly possessions as I can load on the wagon. We're poor people and can't afford to leave things behind. The road to my father's place is steep. That poor mule must be helped. I really can't do much with my single hand, but together we can make it. There's plenty of room in grandfather Ivvo's hut. Rest a bit until the situation improves and then go home."

"Please, Danby," pleaded Orrania again in the thin helpless voice that Danco was not able to resist, "don't turn us down. Come along. It would just kill me to know you were left behind, an easy prey to that awful cholera."

Danco vacillated.

The rest of his platoon would think him dead. A new commander would not even be aware of his absence. Delly Hassan was not an informer. He'd keep his mouth shut. So would the rest, if they were still alive. And Danco really was still kind of shaky. Costaky's medicine had worked a miracle on him, but his health was far from restored. He had lost at least half of his normal weight, and his large bones, in spite of that thick layer of muscle, protruded everywhere. Even his once fabulous muscles were emaciated. Contracting cholera in this condition would mean sure death. Only the clean mountain air and healthy nourishment could put him back in shape. Besides, in spite of the sickness that drained him and all the horrors he had been through, his young body yearned for Azimee…his soul bled for Rossitza. He must go back even if he'd despise himself for the rest of his life.

"All right," sighed Danco, "let's get going. Because of my illness, you stayed behind longer than anyone else around."

The little girl jumped with joy. "Hurray! You'll come with us to grandfather Ivvo's place?"

"You have my word on it Orry."

"May I hug and kiss Danby, father?" pleaded Orrania. "He's quite well now."

"Be patient a bit more, my dear," Costaky smiled gently, "you'll have plenty of time to hug and kiss him."

Suddenly the beaming face of Orrania was contorted. "Oy…oh, my God!" she whispered, plainly scared.

Both men exchanged worried glances.

"What is it, little bird?" asked Danco.

"Don't you feel well?" her father asked almost at the same time.

Orrania opened her eyes and looked at them as if she just had come from far away.

"It's nothing," she said in a tired voice, "just one of my silly pictures. We better start moving. What will be, will be…"

Rossitza was running toward Ismail, radiant with happiness, her honey colored hair waving in the air, long and silky, her eyes gleamed with love, a handful of snowdrops in her apron. Ismail let the shiny axe bite deep into the pine trunk he was cutting and waited, his heart beating like a crazy drum.

"Look, Ismail," she cried with excitement, "the first snowdrops. They have never been around so early!" Ismail took the running woman in his arms, "Watch it, roughneck, you'll crush them all," she giggled, abandoning herself to his fiery kisses.

"I'll crush all of you," he whispered into Rossitza's ear. "You turn my blood into fire…" He peeked at grandfather Ivvo sunning out front and then pleaded with her, "let's go behind those pine trees, my love!"

Rossitza pried herself free from his embrace, the devil danced in her gold-flecked eyes. "Oh, noooo…shame on you, Ismail…so early in the morning!" She laughed a bit forcefully, her whole body craving his touch. Then unexpectedly, she dropped the snowdrops from her apron. "You'll have to catch me first, wise guy!" And she darted in the opposite direction. Ismail gave a mock bear's growl and pounded his fist on his bare chest.

"I'll catch you, little roe, and Allah is my witness, I'll eat you alive."

Rossitza taunted him from afar, putting her thumb to her adorable snub nose. "Don't call Allah after us if you know what's good for you!"

It was a wild chase amidst the stalwart pine trees, through thick layers of ferns and veils of cobwebs still glistening with dew. Finally he tackled her next to a bubbling little stream, and they crashed down in a roar of laughter, tussling around happily.

"You big bear…" Rossitza wriggled underneath him "Let me up or you'll be sorry. I won't let you in on my very special secret!"

"Oh, you and your secrets," huffed Ismail, red faced, "I'll let myself in on your very special secret, like it or not!"

Now suddenly she became quite serious. "Ismail, dear, listen to me for a moment. Don't play rough with me, it might hurt him."

The young man looked at her flabbergasted. "Hurt whom?"

"The little one that is coming, silly."

He remained motionless like a dummy, speechless, staring at her in disbelief. The next moment he let out a yell of joy and triumph that shook the old forest. "I'm going to have a son!!!"

Rossitza burst out laughing.

"I don't want to aggravate you, dear, but with our double curse, it could just turn out to be a daughter."

"I am not Ismail," said Radco early the next morning, when he and Azimee were getting ready. "My name is Radoul Boev, but everyone calls me Radco."

Azimee swung her arms around his neck and kissed him gently. After all the kisses of last night, their lips were kind of sore.

"To me you'll always be my sweet Ismail!"

"I hope not...'cause where we're going now, you'll be facing the real Ismail—a hell of a good looker, and I don't relish the idea of you comparing us. The original might prove better. So, I strongly advise you to accept me for what I am, a Bulgarian lad and a Christian too," he said tipping her small gracefully formed nose. "My name is Radco, Radco, Radco!"

"Don't worry, beloved. I don't care what your faith is, or your nationality. There won't be any competition, because for me you are, and forever will be, the original, no matter how many good looking young Ismails happen to be around."

"Even if he is your first husband-to-be?"

"Even if he is the last husband-to-be in the whole wide world! Kiss me, kiss me, falcon beloved. Now that I know you're a Christian, are your kisses any different? Oh Allah, I swear in Thy Shiny Name, they are even sweeter!"

Out on the road, Radco and Azimee met the first crowds of refugees chased away by cholera from White Sea Thrakia. Close to Moguilitza, they had formed shanty hamlets of branches, rugs and boards left intact after the fire. Their stories about the merciless disease were blood curdling. Further on, the two travelers entered a village they had known since their childhood; now Moguilitza was a ghost of its former self. When Azimee saw the blackened walls of the Agoushevitee Castle, she bent down and wept over the ruins as if they were her own mother's tomb.

"Save some of your tears, Azimee," Radco said embracing her, "for that poor young man, the flute player."

The harem garden had not been destroyed by fire and some of the rose bushes circling round the fountain were already covered with buds. First, Radco and Azimee kneeled at the graves of Bogdana and Ignat. Radco made the sign of the cross, and his companion prayed to Allah. When they turned to the third grave, there was a figure dressed in man's clothing prostrate over it.

"Who in the world can that be?" whispered Radco to Azimee. "Ermin had nobody that would care to come here." He kneeled down by the man and put a gentle hand on his shoulder. The head, clad in a heavy fur cap, turned slowly. A square but feminine face, drained of blood, showed itself under the hat. Two deeply shadowed eyes, full of tears, glared up. Magda! Radco withdrew his hand instinctively. The hatred in her eyes moved from the confused youth to a frightened Azimee and back to him.

"Oh, you made it, cheater!" she snarled. "Everybody but him, and he was the best!"

"I'm sorry, Magda..." Radco started.

"Like hell you are! He's dead and all you can think of is how to curl up next to someone's wife. You even have the nerve to come out here with that insatiable bitch. Don't you have any shame? Why, oh God, should he be dead and the likes of you enjoying yourselves to the hilt? Where is the fairness? No, don't touch me! I need no pity from you!"

"Magda!" Radco pleaded, reaching for her.

"Don't touch me, jerk! Go touch that wench out there. She'll like it!"

Radco straightened up, his eyes sparkling with offense and indignation. "And what right do you have to lie on Ermin's grave, the gentlest of all men, splashing venom and frustration in the face of the others?"

Azimee took him from behind and tried to pull his big body away.

"Let me be, Azimee!" Radco shook her off. "I don't want that bag of hatred on my friend's grave. He was like a brother to me and who is she?"

Magda hissed and spat at him, throwing clods of earth at him. Radco swore and pushed her toward the wall. Her body hit the stones and slid down, totally spent, foam dripping from a half-opened mouth.

Azimee, shocked by this ugly scene, stifled a scream, shaking like a leaf. Then on a sudden impulse, she ran to Magda and embraced her, caressing her face and kissing her with affection.

"Oh, dear soul," she cried out, choking with tears, "how much you have suffered!"

Now Magda broke down and they wept together.

"Forgive me, Azimee dear," sobbed Magda bitterly, "I didn't mean to hurt you—either of you...I must've gone out of my mind..."

Radco squatted down by them, still red faced, and took Magda's hand in his. "I treated you dastardly, Magda. I never thought of myself as such a ruffian—it's just this temper of mine that I can't control. It flares up and goes its own way. Please forgive me!"

"I am the one to blame, Radco," sighed Magda, her sobbing abating gradually, "everything you said is true. I have no right to be here. Ermin never told me I was anything more than a nurse to him. The rest is my imagination. I should have known better than to follow you."

"That is not true, Magda. I am his friend; I know his tender heart. I am sure he did…"

Magda interrupted, "Shush, Radco. What's the use of pretending? It's enough to look at me. How could an angel like Ermin…"

"Oh, he wasn't that much of an angel, Magda. "He was a full-blooded man like everyone else."

"What could a man like in me, my lovely face, or my good character?"

"You look great dressed as a boy, sister," said Azimee, kissing her. "After seeing you, I might just leave this rough-neck for you."

Madame Seraphimova crossed Main Street at the Central Post Office and entered the spacious lobby of Hotel United Bulgaria. Sultana had not come to work and the telephone at the reception desk in her hotel was either busy or off the hook. Toward noon Ellena was so worried that she could not concentrate on anything else. She was of little use at the hospital in her state of mind, so she left and looked for a phaeton for hire. Not many of them were left in the city now; most of the drivers had been recruited and their horses requisitioned by the army. Finally one of the doctors took her in his own cabriolet.

The hotel lobby was unusually quiet—no guests sitting on the comfortable arm chairs reading newspapers, no elegant ladies, no hurrying bellhops. Ellena approached the reservation desk with a sinking heart. The old Frenchman bowed to her stiffly and said in his strongly accented voice.

"I am sorry, Madame, no reservations today. We'll be closed until further notice."

Ellena felt like the marble floor was swaying under her feet.

"Is anything wrong..." she halted, "...anything wrong with the lady in suite #14?"

The man looked at her through his steel rimmed glasses, a nervous tick twitching his flabby left cheek. "Madame Hadgylvanova was taken by an ambulance this morning."

Ellena had to grab hold of the desk to keep herself upright. "Where?"

"To Djendem Teppe's barracks."

"The *lazaretto*?"

The old man nodded with some compassion. On her way out she saw a policeman putting up a big Red Cross poster on the front door. It read, "Do not enter! To be disinfected!" The sound of his hammer sounded like the nailing of a coffin.

Colonel Vladimir Seraphimov waited all morning.

The antechamber of His Majesty's den was a small room stuffed with files and bulky furniture. High ranking officers and members of the cabinet went in and out in a hurry, worried expressions on their faces. Nobody seemed to pay the slightest attention to him.

Around noon, one of the very young and smartly dressed secretaries approached him. He snapped his heels, medals bouncing on his protruding chest. "We're sorry to keep you waiting, sir…"

"You're not keeping me waiting, Lieutenant. I was called by His Majesty."

The young man blushed. "My mistake, sir. His Majesty sends you his apologies. He'll be able to see you in the next half hour. Unexpected developments have delayed him."

"What has happened, Lieutenant, if it's not a state secret?"

"General Jallov of the War Council, committed suicide last night."

Seraphimov nodded slowly. "You may go, Lieutenant," He said quietly as he slowly sat back down.

The youngster saluted smartly and ran off, deeply impressed with his own importance.

Vladimir Seraphimov closed his eyes. The finely-chiseled face of Jallov came to him as he had seen him at his graduation ceremony. He was the senior officer who had taken his oath. How long ago that had been! They had not met for many years.

Jallov was in the diplomatic service. Vladimir Sera-phimov did his time the hard way—routine service. Day by day. Family, duty, maneuvers, drills, petty intrigues and clashes in the officers' club. And daughter after daughter was born into his family. What if that ugly war had not happened? No, it wasn't ugly at the beginning, it became so. But isn't it the same with all wars? War, good or bad, made him somebody, or was it so? He was a nobody, an unknown aging officer, but he had strong principles. Now he had disregarded them. Was compromise the only way to become somebody? Was that flashy newcomer *Somebody* in him killing his own real identity? And how could one restore it afterwards? Perhaps the way General Jallov did last night.

Maybe that was the only way!

The mountains brought a striking change in Danco's appearance. His ashen gray facial tone dissolved into a healthy dark tan. His strength seemed to grow by the hour, his spirits soared as high as the still distant ridges. He started singing. His rich powerful baritone sounded as if it were made for the old folk songs. Orrania wanted him to teach her each and every one of them. An avid sharp-shooter, he kept their small company well provided with fresh meat. By the end of their third day on the road, he was able to do all the pushing of the wagon through steep and tricky spots by himself. Danco's appetite grew rapidly. His two companions wondered how he could eat all that meat without bursting wide open.

On the fourth day, they came upon a big brown bear. He paid little attention to the passing strangers, and kept on eating young buds. Obviously just out of his winter slumber, his appetite was about the same as Danco's. When the stalwart youth challenged him to a wrestling match, he only growled disdainfully, but the daring young man went on teasing him, "Come on, old fart, come wrestle me. Show me your strength!"

The bear growled at him contemptuously, but Danco doggedly kept his challenge. "Afraid of me, eh, weakling?"

Finally, the bear, actually young and virile, shook his head angrily, straightened to his hind legs, extended his front paws fearsomely and let out a loud growl. Danco immediately jumped at the opportunity. He grabbed his neck and tripped him over. Both of them rolled on the ground wrapped together tightly, grumbling and puffing.

"Oh, father," Orrania cried out, "Do something, pull them apart. The bear will tear him to pieces and eat him up!"

Costaky laughed with merriment.

"It's not clear yet who's gonna eat whom. Our friend seems to be doing very well." But when he saw her still frightened eyes, he added hastily, "Don't worry, my dear, that bear is not a man eater. I know his kind. He feeds on berries and honey. Danby knows who to wrestle."

After a while both opponents, obviously out of shape, short of breath and muscle weary, consented to a draw. They stood apart, chests heaving, still distrustful of each other. The bear roared, baring his big yellowish teeth.

"Don't swear at me, buster," grunted Danco. "You're lucky to get off today without a broken neck. But just you wait a bit. I'll find you some other time, and you won't get off so easily!"

The bear gave another ear rending growl and left the battleground.

Costaky warned, almost choked with laughter. "You better quit bragging, champ, or you'll find your match some day…more than you bargain for."

"Bah, give me ten days more and I'll take on anyone, two or four legged. You just name him."

Orrania accepted this to the letter. She looked at him with deep respect and admiration, as she would a favorite hero from the fairy tales and legends told to her by grandfather Ivvo.

"I want a house with forty windows and many porches," said Rossitza dreamily, "with garlands of red peppers strung from side to side on the balconies, a garden full of peonies and junipers, a small fountain offering a drink to the birds in cool evenings."

"How about some clucking chickens and grunting pigs? We won't get fat in your garden without vegetables and stockyard, I am afraid," laughed Ismail.

"Oh, Ismail, how can you even mention pigs. The Great Warrior of the Islam!" Rossitza beat him on the broad chest with her little fists, "How can you shatter my dreams like that?"

"Well," Ismail laughed again, "if you don't mind, I have some dreams of my own: I want a house full of kids and a lot of fertile soil around that will give us plenty of food for any army of noisy pugnacious boys and a daughter exactly like you." His face darkened, "Where on earth will we find our dreamland?"

Rossitza put her head on his strong shoulder.

"Remember what that visiting Carracachan shepherd said last week. It's armistice! The war is over, or almost. We are free to go wherever we want."

Ismail stroked her shiny hair thoughtfully. "I don't want to clip your wings, but let's face the truth. I am not a citizen of this country, and you are not of mine. After that cruel war, peace between our two nations won't come over-night. There will be lasting enmity, not only professed by the authorities but in the hearts and minds of people. It has been stored there by centuries of misunderstanding and violence. You don't expect that to be erased with a magic stroke. Good genies don't mix with people anymore. They are banished from their hearts."

"Why so?"

"Because, people have sold their souls to the demons," Ismail mused.

"Come on, Ismail! Don't drop into that gloomy chasm of yours. I thought during these months we've spent together you were cured of that. Open you soul to the sun."

The young man swung his arms around her and pressed her body to his heart as if she were a sacred object.

"Let's hope the world has changed," he whispered, "you are the only bright, sunny spot in my life. I don't know what I would have done without you.

"Don't be afraid, dearest, nothing can come between us. I love you!"

A posse to hunt down Rossitza and Ismail was formed in Progled on the morning after Radco's departure—fifteen men of all ages, mostly refugees who had lost everything in the war, embittered and desperate. They were riding sturdy mountain mules and, with the silent approval of the garrison commander, had armed themselves at the local military depot. Crowds of refugees who had settled on Stronghel's Meadows came out to see them off.

Radco Boev's head start of a day had disappeared with his meeting Azimee, spending the night in the hut and visiting Ermin's grave. The girls slowed him down as well. Magda had asked to accompany them and although she had a mule of her own, Radco still had to lead the animals by walking alongside them.

Another problem held back their small group. To start with, Radco had taken enough food for himself. He shared it with Azimee; then came Magda. So they had to stop now and then to look for food. In that part of the mountain, game was not easy to find. Hunger had depleted the once rich reserves. The same with crops. Providing for themselves was time-consuming and, before long, the posse after Ismail and Rossitza was on their heels.

"I don't want to open old wounds, Magda," said Radco while walking ahead, "but of all people, why do you insist on seeing Rossitza? I thought you hated her after what she did to Ermin, God give him peace."

Magda rode in silence for about a minute, then spoke out.

"She didn't do it to him. He did it to himself. Bless his soul, he was that kind of a man. Always running after the shadow of a cloud. He would never take what was at hand, only what was unreachable and distant."

"Didn't she extend hope to two men at the same time?" Radco continued to doubt her.

Magda shook her head. "At the time my brother was as good as dead. He had gone to Stanbul years before and never wrote back. I think, at that point, he didn't quite know what real love was. Like many men, he learned the hard way. Maybe you're right to take Azimee from him. He still does not fully appreciate the love of a woman."

"It's our way of life," sighed Azimee. "Our men should keep in mind that one can't carry two melons under the same arm."

"That's a good old saying," smiled Radco, "though men will usually give it a try from time to time."

As happens in March, rain appeared from nowhere. Radco took in his hand the red and white good luck tassels his mother had made for him and sang out in his ringing tenor:

> *"Spring rain falls in vain,*
> *Wash my feet in the mead,*
> *Make my head soaking wet,*
> *Come in spree, go in glee,*
> *Let me grow, svelte as thou!"*

Ferdinand looked much better.

Part of his nervousness had eased and his eyes were watching Colonel Seraphimov with slight amusement. Even his taunting smile was the same. There was an obvious discrepancy between his mood and what he was saying—quite usual for His Majesty's personality.

"I am so sorry about my old friend Jallov. Did you know, Seraphimov, that this rather unusual general was one of your most ardent admirers? Here is a little poem he wrote about you after the battle of Allamy Derre. Let me read it to you." He fixed his glasses, found a small piece of paper, cleared his throat and read with a bit more pathos than necessary:

> *"There is greatness*
> *born in palaces,*
> *cut out of gold,*
> *molded by sycophants,*
> *sold on the streets*
> *two cents per piece.*
> *There is Greatness*
> *born in the wind,*
> *worn like a mantle*
> *over the shoulders*
> *of coming centuries.*
> *Don't try to buy it,*
> *Its not for sale!"*

After a pause—Ferdinand seemed to be rereading the poem—he took off his glasses and looked at Vladimir Seraphimov.

"What do you think, Colonel! It doesn't do very well in the rhyme department, as modern poetry goes, but the man had some talent. If not on a battlefield, at least on paper. Here," he handed it to Seraphimov and walked to the window. "You can have it. There is a dedication and all, as you can see." He laughed a bit through his nose. "My friend, Sultana Hadgylvanova, says whenever I get emotional I walk to the window to air out my feelings. She might be right. Isn't she a good friend of your wife's, Colonel?"

"Yes, Your Majesty. They are very good friends."

Ferdinand's attention was drawn to a gathering of noisy sparrows quarreling with a squirrel over some nuts.

"You, you didn't see her when you stopped in Plovdiv on the way up here, did you?"

"No, Majesty. I didn't have the time. My family came to the railway station to visit during the half hour layover of my train to Sofia."

"I thought, by now, she was one of your family. Sultana is like a cat. She makes her nest wherever she feels comfortable. Last night, I had a dream about her. She was wearing a scarlet velvet dress—hat and feathers, gloves and shoes, everything red. She wanted to tell me something, but there was a funny looking oxcart passing between us. It was so long, almost endless, stacked with corpses four or five high. Finally the oxcart was gone, and so was Sultana."

"If Your Majesty thinks something has happened to Madame Hadgylvanova, I can ask my wife."

Ferdinand turned from the window, and with a slight limp, walked back to his desk.

"No need, Seraphimov, Sultana is indestructible," he replied as his eyes followed the colonel's movement to fold Jallov's poem into his pocket. "Sit down, my friend. You may be wondering why I gave you the poem?"

"You gave it to me because you don't want anyone else to do it. This way you could observe my reactions first hand," Seraphimov answered matter-of-factly.

The Monarch was obviously pleased.

"My honest friend Seraphimov! You will never learn the 'good' manners of a courtier. When His Majesty asks a question like that, you are expected to say, "I don't know, sir," thus providing me the pleasure of proving one more time how dumb you really are."

"Though, I'm fuzzy on one point, sir. Why this particular timing? You could have given it to me after…after…"

"My, my, Colonel Seraphimov. You don't actually think the devil is as bad as his worst enemies depict him," he smiled with overt disappointment. "I wanted to read you this poem before the bargain for a number of reasons. First, to see if you have a natural appetite for greatness; second, to prove to you that I pay for honesty with honesty; and, third, I had in mind to ask you openly what your definition is for greatness, to probe your eagerness for it and the goal of your ambition."

"Do you want my answers, Majesty?"

"Nooo, I already have them. You have a remarkably open face, Seraphimov. I wonder how you ever manage to…ahem, converse and deal with women other than your wife."

"I don't have to, sir. My wife has every quality I like and want in a woman."

"But sometimes you are separated for months," challenged his Highness

"That makes our love even stronger," Vladimir answered without hesitation.

"I see, you're a one-woman man," sighed Ferdinand. "I envy your moral equilibrium. Presumably, that is what sustains the extraordinary spiritual strength you are able to inspire in your troops. Some simply lead by charisma that instills trust."

"I have no divine powers, Your Majesty."

"Holy Mother, am I happy to hear that! As an old autocrat, I believe in absolute monarchy; but as ruler of a constitutional kingdom, I have to surrender my divine rights and powers. Certainly, I wouldn't like to see my army commanders using them," he chuckled.

The guards at the portal stopped Ellena.

"Sorry, Madame. Nobody gets beyond this point without special permission."

"I am on medical service with the Red Cross. Who is in charge here?"

"Lieutenant Illiev."

"I want to see him."

The reservist scratched behind his ear. "I don't know. Well, it won't hurt to ask him. Gherro, take this lady to the office."

Lieutenant Illiev was congenial and accommodating. All smiles, he invited Ellena to sit on the only chair in the room—his. Yes, he had heard of Madame Seraphimova. Who hadn't? He would be glad to oblige, but it was beyond his authority. Nobody is admitted as a visitor to the barracks.

Ellena was desperate. "There must be some way for me to see her, Lieutenant!" she begged.

"If I get an authorization from the head doctor at City Hall, I might let you in after getting you to sign a few papers."

"May I use your phone?"

"Of course, Madame. Anything I can do to help you."

It took half an hour to reach Dr. Michailov. When he finally answered, he listened to Ellena patiently, then responded in a very tired voice, "Are you sure you want to visit with your friend? Think of your family, if you are not concerned about yourself. It is a highly contagious disease."

"I know, Doctor, I am fully aware of the risks I am taking. I'll sign the necessary papers and accept any kind of restrictive measure," answered a very distraught Ellena.

"We're trying to keep the disease from spreading to epidemic proportions."

"I can understand that Dr. Michailov."

"Ask for a white robe and a mask," Dr. Michailov advised.

"Yes, Doctor."

"You may talk only through the window. Madame Hadgylvanova is alone in a private room."

"Yes, Doctor."

"I've seen Madame Hadgylvanova on many occasions... such beauty and poise! Brace yourself for an unpleasant sight."

"Thank you, Doctor. Has her next of kin been informed?"

"No. Madame Hadgylvanova insisted that we not do so."

In another half hour Ellena was walking through the makeshift encampment grounds with an elderly aide. The afternoon sun was extremely bright. A volcano shaped hill straight ahead was the ominous Infernal Hill, *Djendem Teppe*.

Ellena waited outside a window on a rocky patch of ground. Not a single strip of grass, shrubbery or tree in sight. Only dry yellow earth, cracked and desolate. The large rocks in the background were equally forbidding.

"You can talk now," said the fat aide who sat on a chair next to the window she had just opened.

"Sultana, I can't see you!" cried Ellena.

"There is a screen between you and her," mumbled the fat woman, munching on sunflower seeds. "She wanted it that way."

"Sultana, can you hear me?" breathed Ellena. "Are you there?"

"Yes..." said a feeble, unfamiliar voice.

For a moment Ellena was stunned. That can't be Sultana! Mother of God, please make me wake up from this nightmare!

Ellena quickly came back to herself. "Sultana, darling, it's me, Ellena."

"How did you get in, Ellena?"

"It wasn't easy. They make it practically impossible. Your coming down with cholera sobered them up. Now every patient coming in from the front, even the unidentified ones, are separated."

To speak privately they began conversing in French. "Ellena, I am going to die."

"That won't come to pass, my dear. You are strong."

Cela va sans dire...cela m'est egal...apres tout. "Of course, I don't care...after all."

The fatso was disappointed. She couldn't catch a single word.

Sultana continued speaking in French. "How's everyone at home?"

"Fine, just fine...they ask about you every day. I haven't told them..."

"You did well."

"Yesterday we went to the station. We saw Vlad for almost thirty minutes. He had lost lots of weight. I wanted to tell him so many things and then I was in his arms with all the kids hanging around. Like an absolute dummy, I didn't remember a single thing I had to tell him, I couldn't understand what he was talking to me about. I just cried and cried like a stupid debutante. When I was able to speak, he was gone. I had to ask the kids to tell me where he was going."

"I bet he went to see His Majesty."

"Why, yes, he did."

"Yes, he needs him now, although it is too late. Ellena, dear, I am leaving you all my money. Do with it whatever you think best."

"Sultana, you must believe you'll get better."

"I am sorry, Ellena, I don't believe in the absurd. I hate disillusionment. I have tried to keep it to myself and not spread it to others."

"Have you succeeded?"

"I really don't think so, but I did try. It's all my fault. I've always lived at my own risk and expense."

"Sultana, what kind of medical care are you getting in this slum?" Ellena asked as she looked about the room.

"Don't worry. Every kind money can buy. You have to see the rest of it. No…you don't."

"But that horrible woman…"

"Oh, she's fine. She seems to be immune to all microbes and fears known to the human race. She even eats my food. Anyway I can't eat," she said as her voice grew weaker.

There was a short pause. Ellena could hear the painful breathing behind that screen.

"Sultana, I'll come and take care of you!"

The voice from the corner came unusually strong, almost like in the old days.

"No, you won't! I forbid it! In the name of your children, if God's name is not enough to stop you! Please, don't cry. I can hear you. It arouses my own self-pity, too. I've had a good life—a bit lonely, but generally good."

"Sultana, you are in pain!"

"I just pray not to get delirious again. It's coming. I have to hurry. Ellena, on my death bed, I swear I am not a courtesan. I love him. As gaudy and selfish as he is, there is something in him that I love. In some way, he is like a child…*enfant gate*…*enfant terrible*…a very naughty child. I tried to make him better, but failed. I didn't succeed in changing myself, either, but here I am—part good, part bad and ready to go."

"Sultana!"

"Go…go away, please! It's here, that hairy thing in the corner. I am scared…don't let it come, please, don't let it commme!!! God, have pity on me, don't let it swallow me…please, God…please…please…"

Then nothing.

Chapter Sixteen

Spring came unusually early in the Rhodopy Mountains. The wrinkled ridges were green with new grass and its endless softly molded hills came alive with yellow and blue splashes of blossoming wild flowers and sage.

It was a fine morning, sunny and clear.

A number of tiny rounded clouds scattered over a dark blue sky, like a celestial herd. Grandfather Ivvo sat in his usual place on his porch, his callous-hardened fingers effortlessly rolling a cigarette. There was a bit of a stoop in his stance, his little eyes beneath a sweat stained fur cap, held a mixture of shrewdness and natural goodness. The face was tanned, weathered by years in the sun and wind, in contrast to a white brow covered with a fine cobweb of wrinkles. That brow, under the heavy cap, seldom saw daylight. His brown leather tobacco pouch was not fancy, but always full of aromatic chopped leaves. Even on the hottest days he dressed as if it were winter time. His shirt was buttoned to the neck, thick woolen socks were pulled over breeches made of such coarse fabric that they could stand upright by themselves, as if made of cardboard. Those trousers matched perfectly with his jacket and the heavy coat trimmed with sheep's fur.

The youngsters had disappeared into the pine trees, chasing each other like lovebirds. A broad smile settled over Ivvo's face. He stroked the head of his old shepherd dog and took a drag of his cigarette, eyes focused on the glistening blade that a minute ago had been brandished by Ismail and now rested deep in the trunk of a tree. Was grandfather Ivvo following the young couple in his mind or were his own memories knitting a capful of dreams in his head? It was hard to tell.

His dog suddenly became restless, jumped to its feet and growled. The movement and noise snapped Ivvo back from some distance in time and space. He stroked the bristling hair on the dog's furry back.

"Easy, Vultcho, easy, my boy, what is it? Travelers don't come out this way, but could it be guests or enemies. Can it be my daughter Ghana from Chepellare? No, you wouldn't bark at her, would you, old boy? Who else? My son Costaky? He would come from the opposite direction. Now I see, two men and a woman. Never saw them before. Very young, probably lost in the wilderness. Knock it off, Vultcho. Quit barking. Be nice to these people. Can't you see they're not brigands. Come here, down…down, I said, there's a fine fellow."

"Good morning, grandfather Ivvo!" Radco greeted him politely and took off his fur cap, the bright sunlight nested in his gold curls. "My name is Radoul Boev from Progled."

"Well, I'll be damned," exclaimed Ivvo in an agitated voice unusual for him, "if you're not the son of haydouk Dimmitar! Same handsome devil. I was thinking of him just a minute ago."

"You knew my father?" asked a surprised Radco.

"Did I know your father! God give peace to his noble spirit. He was ambushed right over there at that tree with the ax carved in its trunk. Those worthless scoundrels cut him to pieces right behind my fold. Then roasted two of my sheep and ate and drank. I wish I had never lived to see that day." A heavy sigh rocked his old chest. "I shouldn't talk about it right now. I can see how scared the young ones are. Are they your brother and sister?"

"No grandfather Ivvo. This one is also a girl, dressed like a boy for traveling purposes. She is Magda Marrin from Derrekioy, and the young lady is my fiancée, Azimee."

"God be praised! Such a beauty. Brother could turn against brother for a woman like her, young man."

Radco paled a bit, but tried to laugh it off. "I'll keep her face veiled, grandfather."

"All right, all right, I was just kidding. You must be tired and starved. Get them down from those mules."

Radco helped Azimee, while Magda made it down on her own.

The rifle across her back impressed grandfather Ivvo. "Can you handle this carbine, maiden?"

"Compare me with any man you know," Magda said self-assuredly. "I'm a great shot. My brother taught me. I went hunting with him."

Grandfather Ivvo shook his head. "No kidding! Obviously I missed something. A new spirit has grown in the old mountain. Brave children...I talk and talk like a chatterbox. You must be starving."

"We slept nearby," Azimee explained, "in a little shack three miles away, next to an abandoned fold. We're not too tired, but we are as hungry as a pack of wolves. We haven't had a decent meal since we left home."

"I see, I see, poor children. I'll give you milk and cheese right away. Ismail will be back any moment now. He'll roast some meat for you. Lead the animals behind and fasten them to the fold. There's plenty of grass, let them nibble."

"We're sorry to impose on you, grandfather," said Azimee in her sweet and melodic voice.

"No imposition at all, make yourself at home. Come on in, girls, and take whatever you like. The cheese is in that pouch hanging over the beam. Milk, you'll find in the skin back a bit further over."

Azimee and Magda ran into the house, followed by an already friendly Vultcho. Radco came back and sat on the porch steps.

"A beautiful place you've got here, grandfather Ivvo, a nice sturdy house and, from this spot, one can see as far as the world goes."

Ivvo laughed, evidently pleased. "I built this house myself, strong as a block house. Every famous freedom fighter has found shelter here one time or another. See, those marks on the front are from bullets. So far it has never been taken by siege. If your father had made it inside, he would have still been alive. Hey, girls, bring out something for this young man. Don't leave him to survive on my tittle-tattle alone."

Azimee came out with some cheese and milk for Radco.

"Sorry, grandfather Ivvo," Radco said through a mouth full of cheese; "we dropped in on you uninvited..."

"Good Heavens!!! What kind of talk is that? Haydouk Dimmitar's son does not need an invitation to my home. You and your friends are welcome at any time."

"I know, grandfather, and I thank you from the bottom of my heart. Though this may not be the right time for a visit, something very urgent brought me here. You had a guest last week?"

"Right, son we did. Nikodim, the shepherd, dropped by to say hello."

"That man came through Progled and told everyone about Rossitza and Ismail."

"So what?" smiled grandfather Ivvo kindly, "very nice youngsters. What could be wrong with them?"

Radco sighed and told him the whole story. "Goran Podgorsky is dead now but the hatred he espoused is still alive and thriving, mainly among the refugees. In Progled, there are other people, too, who would kill a man just because he's wearing a turban or a fez. Ismail and Rossitza must go into hiding right away. A posse might be here anytime this afternoon."

Grandfather Ivvo shook his head slowly. "How could anyone in this world..."

"Here they are!" shouted Azimee.

Magda came running out. "Is the posse coming?"

"Not yet," smiled Radco. "It's Rossitza and Ismail."

"Oh, Azimee," Magda spat in her bosom against fright. "You scared the hell out of me!"

At that very moment, the young couple recognized them and ran toward home. Radco and Magda rushed to meet them halfway. Soon, they were in each other's arms.

"Allah be blessed, Radco," said Ismail, still panting from the run, "I am so happy to see you back good as new. Didn't I tell you?"

"You sure did, brother," laughed Radco, tears in his eyes. "But if not for you, Allah wouldn't have moved a small finger to help me out."

"Shush, you infidel," Ismail scolded him, "don't fool around with Allah! We might need him again very soon."

Radco looked at him open mouthed. "You don't know how right you are, Ismail!"

"What do you mean?" asked Rossitza, seized by a premonition.

Quickly Radco told them about the unfortunate developments of the last few days.

"I thought it was a good wind that brought you here," Ismail frowned, lowering his well outlined eyebrows. "But thank you anyway, brother. Now you are saving not only my life, but that of Rossitza and...I'll tell you later."

"Oh, my God!" Rossitza cried out, "if this had not come from you and Magda, I wouldn't have believed it. People that I knew! What have I ever done to them, Radco?"

"No time for this now, Rossitza," Ismail embraced her with love and concern.

"Oh, my, my" teased Azimee in a sing-song voice, her keen eyes sizing up the powerfully built nude torso of her fellow countryman. "Darned if that's not my intended husband!"

"What do you want of me, Your Majesty?" asked Vladimir Seraphimov, finally reaching the very limit of tolerance for Tzar Ferdinand's Machiavellian ways.

His Majesty walked slowly around the desk, his limp more pronounced than ever, and stopped at arm's length from Seraphimov.

"I've been waiting for that question, Colonel," he said very quietly, "I've waited a long time. It has cost me more than you think. I've lost almost every chance of achieving true greatness. Give me Tzarygrad, Seraphimov!"

The silence was so profound that the noises from outside grew to dramatic proportions. The rhythmic clatter of a typewriter, the clip-clopping of horse's hooves beyond the park, a distant melody from an Italian barrel organ…

Colonel Seraphimov met the expectant eyes of his Tzar. They were eyes abnormally dilated and filled with insane desire and supplication.

"I am not a conjurer, Your Majesty. I work with people and I have to be able to give a reasonable explanation as to why I want them to die."

Ferdinand brought his eyebrows together, "What do you mean, Colonel?"

"Peter has a wife and three kids. He has borrowed money from a lender to buy seeds and a new plough. He owes many years of taxes to the state. It might rain in time this year, it may not. Hail might fall. His ox Sivcho is too old, he may not survive until spring. Those are his problems and perhaps more, the health of his family, the children to come. Now, you want me to tell him that he needs to fight for Tzarygrad. Why, Your Majesty? To achieve Greatness for you? Or for me? He doesn't give a damn about that. Those are our problems. We have to solve them. But I don't have the answer. Teach me how to answer, and I'll give you whatever it is you want of me."

The Monarch's eyes became coolly deprecating. "Well, Seraphimov. It's not only me and you in this game. Something older and greater than us two, greater than our conscience and remorse—Bulgaria. It's *her* greatness we fight for. It is for her that Peter must die. That happens to be my dream also!"

Seraphimov shook his head with bitterness. "Peter has been dying for his country's greatness time after time. We keep repeating the same old song like that broken barrel organ outside: Fatherland, Freedom, Well-being, Prosperity. So Peter survives the INFERNO, comes back home, hungry, ragged, full of lice…and finds the same old problems have grown even worse. His oxen has died, his wife has gotten consumption, the lender has taken over his land. He doesn't believe us anymore, Majesty. We have to tell him the truth at least once. Then, he'll fight for us; he'll die for our ideals."

"You put everything on a rather selfish basis, Colonel."

"How many times have you fought for his ideals and dreams, Majesty? They are small and unimportant to you, but they are the whole universe to him. And that is where *real greatness* begins. You want some of it. Fight for it. You don't have to look for it in Tzarygrad. It's here, in this country. Right at your doorstep!"

Ferdinand had turned aloof and vindictive again. "You can leave, Colonel. I don't need you anymore," and waved him out.

In the aftermath of Sultana's sickness and death, Rayna completely forgot about her invitation to the young man she met at the railway station.

That certainly was not the case with Ivan Zemsky. He went through a number of complicated maneuvers to get himself a decent suit of civilian clothes without letting anyone at home know that he was in the city. Finally one of the old servants agreed to commit this "crime" just for the love of him. It was not exactly what Ivan had requested, but under the circumstances anything was better than his old ragged uniform. To obtain money for a bouquet of white roses and a box of chocolates was a bit more complicated. He went to Djumaya Djammia Square and joined a line-up along the mosque wall to "manpower" transportation of loads throughout the city, which was very much in demand. With horses and wagons virtually absent from the streets, porters were the only alternative left. Under ordinary conditions, competing with all these young husky men from nearby villages would have been out of the question for the likes of Ivan Zemsky. Now, compared to a bunch of aged men, not good for the army and a gang of noisy gypsies, he was preferred, if not for his strength, at least for his good looks and pleasant manners.

However, to gain respect from the gypsy gang took something else. He had to fight their gang leader, Sellym, a mere teenager, undernourished like the rest, but wiry and quick. He fought dirty, kicking biting and scratching. No one tried to stop them. The porters' fights on the square were a central attraction and passers-by trooped to watch.

Ivan's experience in this field wasn't rich, except for Delly-Hassan's lessons in fist fighting and wrestling. That, somehow did the job. He threw the gypsy boy on the sidewalk, sat on his chest and started pounding. The youth cried out something in gypsy slang and his friends saved him, but proclaimed Ivan as the new boss and showed him due respect.

Two old men even taught him how to balance loads on his back, how to manage the binding ropes and all the techniques of unloading. After a few unfortunate starts, Ivan got used to it, but at the end of the first day, he found that the cramped, sore muscles all over his untrained body kept him awake. However, his youth came to his rescue and in a couple of days, Ivan was able to pay the rent for a small basement room. His only problem now was to avoid recognition by any of his father's numerous associates around the city or, even worse, by Rayna. So, every morning, he smeared his face with soot and tried to talk the coarse language of "The Lower Depths." In his ragged uniform and army boots, unshaven, spitting all over the sidewalk with elaborate curses, there was not one bit of resemblance to the handsome young man who, before his fall from grace, was a sweetheart to all the leading beauties of Plovdiv. He still preserved some of his good manners for customers who didn't know him personally because it earned him extra sympathy. He brilliantly played a bright young man stricken with bad luck and misery.

On Sunday morning, Ivan Zemsky went to the best Turkish Bath and spent over two hours washing the accumulated dirt from his body and relaxing in the warm pool. By about 3:00 p.m., the metamorphosis was striking. He came out of a barber shop with the most handsomely trimmed moustache one could dream of. A dashing, youthful gentleman dressed in a custom-made black suit, top hat, gloves, a slender cane and a white flower in his buttonhole, matching the bouquet of long stemmed roses. He couldn't spare the money for a box of chocolates, but had enough time to walk around the Public Garden and try the effect of his persona on a number of well-chaperoned mademoiselles. As a result, his confidence grew sky high...but Rayna was something else.

When Ivan Zemsky rang the doorbell at Seraphimov's, his heart was thumping heavily, he found a house in deep mourning. The young girl who answered had eyes red and swollen from crying.

"Who are you?" asked Jivca sullenly.

The young man was flabbergasted. "I...I forgot my calling cards..." Ivan stammered.

"Never mind. The casket isn't here. Take your flowers to..."

"Don't tell me she is dead!" Ivan said in a shaken voice.

"Of course she is dead...aren't you a mourner?"

"Not exactly..." he uttered, a scene from *Romeo and Juliet* flashing through his mind.

Impressed by his distorted face, Jivca opened the door another inch. "You must be a close relative of hers," she ventured a guess.

Ivan shook his head sadly. "We met several months ago. When did she die?"

"This morning...at dawn."

Ivan's eyes filled with tears. "I can't believe it...I talked to her only..." he started.

Jivca hurried on, "You'd better believe it, 'cause she's absolutely dead."

It was an effort for Ivan to stand up. His knees were giving in. "Where can I see her?"

Jivca opened the door another inch.

"I am afraid you cannot see her, she is locked in a leaden casket."

Ivan felt the hair on the back of his head stand up. "What did she die of?" he almost whispered.

"Cholera," said Jivca in a subdued tone.

Cold sweat ran down the young man's forehead. "Oh, my God! " he moaned. "I still can't believe it!"

"Jivca!" called a voice from inside, "whom are you talking to?"

"A mourner!" shouted back the girl.

"For Heavens sake! Why do you keep him standing at the door?"

Jivca shrugged her delicate shoulders. "I don't know him...he's a stranger!"

Madame Seraphimova appeared at the door, pale, dressed all in black.

"Oh, Mister Zemsky! Please do come in. This unexpected death has driven us out of our minds. I beg your pardon for my young daughter's behavior; she doesn't know you. Please do sit down. I had no idea you knew each other so well. How nice of you to get dressed in mourning clothes, top hat...and the flowers..."

"I loved her," said Ivan, tears running down his face. "It was love at first...second sight. How could I have known that in just a few days..."

Ellena broke into tears, covering her face with a wet handkerchief. "I don't know, I still see her everywhere..."

Ivan's eyes stared transfixed at the open door behind Madame Seraphimova, visibly paling.

"Me, too...I can see her right this minute," he managed, open-mouthed.

At first Ellena was too horrified even to look behind her. "Are you sure you see her, Mr. Zemsky?"

Ivan nodded, wiping the cold sweat from his eyebrow with the flower from his buttonhole instead of the white handkerchief from his breast pocket.

"As sure as one can be," he whispered. "She is even smiling at me."

"What are you two plotting out there?" said Rayna jovially, walking toward them, "I haven't gotten cholera yet."

"Now, that was in very bad taste, Rayna," Madame Seraphimova reproached her. "My friend is not even buried, and you have the heart for jokes. I can imagine what an impression you've made upon our guest. This is my oldest, but not wisest daughter, Mr. Zemsky."

"That presentation is absurd, mother. We've already met."

Ivan jumped to his feet and kissed the generously offered hand. Ellena Seraphimova was in shock. "Where did you meet Mr. Zemsky?"

"The first time, you brought him here; the second time, we met by pure coincidence at the railway station. I invited him to come and visit us."

"Splendid! But you...you...could've at least told me" admonished her mother.

"I intended to, but then Madame Hadgylvanova was sick. I cried and cried and just simply forgot. I am sorry I laughed, but you two looked so spooky. Aunt Sultana would have died again of laughter if she could see you two *tete a tete*, whispering to each other."

"I don't understand anything," said young Jivca, "but I don't count for beans as usual."

"Well, there was a little, ahem, confusion," said Madame Seraphimova sternly. "Of course, all because of you, Rayna, and my preoccupation with..." She looked at the young man and there was an immediate tacit understanding not to mention the incident in front of her children. "As you see, Mr. Zemsky, we lost a very dear friend, and we just can't think straight. I hope you haven't gotten a wrong impression of our family. We're not this crazy all the time."

"Oh, mother, we do act like..."

Madame Seraphimova lost her patience. "Not if I can help it! Enough on that subject!"

Ivan Zemsky got up. "This is not the best time for a visit. Perhaps it would be better if I visited another time…"

"No," Rayna cut in swiftly, "the roses will die."

"That's very kind of you, Mr. Zemsky," sighed Madame Seraphimova. "Stay with us. You don't have to go through the same expense again. I know that your family is quite wealthy, but…"

"Wealthy? But, mother, he was looking for a job at the station. I thought you might be able to do something about it. Anyway, he did find something by himself. I saw him working as a porter on the street. The poor man, his face was all smeared with black. It's kind of a dirty job, isn't it?"

Ivan Zemsky looked for a hole to hide in. There was none in the room.

"What a remarkably brave young man!" exclaimed Ellena in sincere admiration. "But if you ask me, you should let your mother know that you're all right. I am sure she's worrying herself to death on your account. I know you have differences with your father, but why torture your mother? Want me to do it for you?"

Ivan, who during this speech, had blushed to the roots of his hair, nodded silently.

"Why do we all stand? Take your jacket off and sit down, Mr. Zemsky, I can see you are rather warm. Make yourself at home. Do you want a drink? I am afraid I can't offer you much of a choice. My husband never drinks, but we still have some brandy for medicinal purposes. Sultana is our purveyor. I'll have to ask her…" She put a trembling hand over her mouth, tears dimming the swollen eyes. "I am sorry, Mr. Zemsky…I'll bring some tea and brandy…"

She left hurriedly.

An uneasy silence filled the room. Rayna buried her lovely face in the bouquet of roses.

"I guess Aunt Sultana will be with us forever. May I have your handkerchief, please. Mine are all wet. Thank you. She used to play games with us, give us presents. Now everything is gone."

Ivan Zemsky gathered all his courage and looked for the first time straight into her beautiful eyes.

"Not everything," he said and took her hand with a sudden impulse that surprised even him. "There is much yet to come."

"Now listen to me," said grandfather Ivvo, poking at his short neglected beard. "Why don't you all go to my son Costaky, by the White Sea, in Thrakia? He's quite lonely after God took his wife and left him with three kids and one hand. He'll be only too glad to have you for a while. When the storm passes, you can come back here."

"That's real nice of you, grandfather," Radco spoke for the rest. "But it seems that everyone's fleeing that part of the country. I wonder why your son hasn't come here yet? He might be on his way."

"That's very possible," said the old man, rolling a cigarette for himself and passing his pouch to Ismail. "This sonofabitch, Nikodim, mentioned something about cholera last week. I thought it was only in Tursko."

Ismail and Ivvo lit their cigarettes with a flint and steel; then smoked in silence. Azimee came to them and sat on the step next to the youth.

"May I have a drag of your cigarette?"

Ismail looked at her without surprise and gave her his cigarette. "Keep it, Azimee. I'll roll another one for myself," he said pleasantly.

Azimee inhaled deeply and closed her eyes. "Glory to Allah! It feels good."

The Bulgarians in their small company were shocked but silent, except for Radco. He sat on the other side of Azimee, moping.

"I don't like you smoking, Azimee. Throw it away."

Azimee gave a short giggle and tickled him. "Don't be such a sourpuss, darling. Just one cigarette for my enjoyment."

"It's not becoming to a woman," grumbled Radco. "Do me a favor, please, throw it away."

"Let her be," laughed Ismail, "a cigarette won't kill her. She's used to it from childhood."

"You stay out of this," Radco snapped at him. "You started it!"

"Mind your own business," said Azimee doggedly. "We're not married yet. Don't assume the part of my master. I have no masters and I don't intend to."

Radco's face flushed with anger. He pulled the cigarette from Azimee's fingers and tore it to pieces. The young woman bit back a scream of rage and turned toward Ismail.

"Make me another."

"Mind yourself, Ismail!" shouted Radco.

"Don't you tell me what to do," bristled the young Turk, "I don't take orders from anybody."

Radco jumped to his feet, fists clenched, eyes hard on Ismail. "Don't you stand between me and this girl!"

Ismail straightened up slowly, his own eyes burning. "So what? You gonna teach me how to live?"

"Ismail!" Rossitza called pleadingly, getting between the two.

"Let them fight it out," laughed Magda tensely, "only one cock can crow in the same hen coop."

"Put that boys' stuff aside, young'uns," Ivvo scolded them, "you've got more important things to do right now."

"What's more important, old man?" sighed Azimee, "To keep running like a wild beast until they catch up to you?"

"You have something else to offer?" asked Rossitza with alacrity.

"No, I don't, but that's what men are all about. Men don't take hints from wenches."

"Snapping at each other won't get us very far," intervened Magda, obviously sobered by the rising crisis. "We're all tired and nervous. Let's resolve our differences another time. Shake hands, men."

Radco and Ismail peered at each other from under their lowered eyebrows.

"I didn't really mean that," muttered Ismail, extending his hand half way. "Though I won't say I'm sorry for what I said, because...because I am not."

"Okay," agreed Radco, taking his hand, "that's good enough for now. We'll settle this some other time. No hard feelings."

"Same here, but if you're eager for a fight, I'll be sticking around."

Azimee did not want to lose face, but without her sole supporter, she felt she was on shaky ground. "You expect me to apologize? Well, I'm sorry I set you two against each other, but I am not apologetic about what started the argument in the first place."

"Oh, she is a bitch!" mumbled Magda to herself, "but then, so am I, in a way."

At this point Vultcho started barking loudly and ran toward the trees. Everyone except Ivvo was alarmed.

"The posse!!!" exclaimed Rossitza.

"No, kids," said the old man, a broad toothless smile on his kind face, "Vultcho is barking at somebody he knows and loves very well."

A cart full of household stuff appeared around the bend, a tired mule pulling it, two men behind were helping it along. An ecstatic little girl was waving her hands from the top, shouting, "Grandfather Ivvo-o-o-o! Grandfather Ivvo-o-o-o!!!"

The old man got up shakily but smiling, "Orrania, my angel...my little angel!"

The men were out of sight behind the carriage though there was no doubt one of them was Ivvo's son, Costaky. Radco and Ismail ran down to help and as soon as they reached the back of the cart, a joyful cry created echoes, "Dancoooo!!!"

Azimee made a move toward the house.

Rossitza swayed, all the blood drained from her face.

Magda sobbed, pressing her hand to her breast, "Dear Lord!"

Grandfather Ivvo was too busy embracing and kissing his beloved granddaughter to notice any of it. Then the cart made a squeaky stop in front of them, Costaky ran to kiss his father's hand and Danco came around, big and handsome, like the mountain itself. Out of breath and flushed by the effort, perspiration dripping, an ear-to-ear smile blooming on his ruddy face, he confronted the three young women. Instant joy and perplexity struggled to possess him.

Magda hung over his broad neck.

"Brother!" she cried. "Dear brother!"

Danco kissed her cheeks and stepped toward the two beautiful women in his life. There was no feeling of guilt, he just did not know whom he should honor first.

"Chock selliam!" he stammered a bit, still not aware of the present circumstances, "long time no see. I hope you haven't cried out your eyes for me..." the young man laughed, trying to look at both of them at the same time.

"Ibrahim!"

"Danco!"

Radco bit his lips. He was totally unprepared for such an early confrontation. Ismail, completely unaware of what was going on, seemed slightly amused. Danco, unable to decide if he should embrace them both at the same time, or one after the other, chose to wait for them to hug him. So, he just opened his arms in expectation, but neither of the girls even came near their former lover. That puzzled him a bit. "Aren't you ever going to come and give me a 'welcome' kiss, girls?"

Now for the first time, Azimee and Rossitza sensed something fishy on his part. They exchanged swift glances of surprise and bewilderment. Magda stepped aside, aware of the awkward situation. Only Ivvo and his children, chatting happily, were unsuspecting of the brewing storm.

"Just what do you mean by that, Ibrahim?" asked Azimee belligerently, hands on hips.

Danco licked his dry lips and muttered in a thick and raspy voice, "In Allah's name, aren't you both my girls?"

Rossitza was too shocked for so much as a word for him, but that certainly was not the case with Azimee. "You never told me you had another girl."

Now Ismail was stark raving mad. He grabbed Danco's arm roughly and shouted in his face, "How dare you call Rossitza your girl, bastard!"

Danco felt more at ease dealing with men. "I called her that because she's mine!" he hissed back.

Grandfather Ivvo and his family were startled to discover the new development. Ismail pulled out his knife.

"Got a knife?" he asked viciously.

Danco drew out a short dagger. "I knew we were going to clash sooner or later!" he snarled. "Defend yourself, bastard!"

General commotion followed. Women screaming, men cursing. Radco and Costaky tried to wrestle the blood-thirsty rivals apart. Orrania hung on Danco's arm.

"Danby, please...don't! This is not a bear..." she cried in desperation, "you might stab each other to death ! I don't want you to die, hear me! I love you, I love you so much!"

"Leave me alone...will ya?" Danco uttered through his clenched teeth.

"Get lost, Radco," raged Ismail, "let me cut open the guts of this mother-fucker!"

Rossitza threw herself at Ismail. "You mustn't do that. If you love me. I beg you, don't!"

Tears of fury and bitterness popped into Ismail's eyes. "You still have a soft spot for him, admit it!"

"No, silly," cried Rossitza in a frenzy. "It's because I bear your child. I don't want him to be an orphan before he's even born into this cruel world!"

A beastly shriek of exasperation came from Danco. "You bitch!" and he lunged at Ismail.

Even over the loud hubbub of the fighting, Ivvo sensed something peculiar in Vultcho's barking. In the next moment he spotted the riders filing over a ridge, less than a mile from where they were.

"The posse is coming!" he shouted. His desperate cry penetrated even the fogged brains of Danco and his opponent. They stopped charging at each other and looked around as if just coming out of a bad dream. Reality was not any better. The women stifled their screams and everyone's eyes concentrated on Ivvo. He had proven to be the only sensible man. He, therefore, instantly became the unquestionable leader of this small unruly clan.

"How many rifles do we have?" he asked, suddenly rejuvenated. All the men had pistols, but only Costaky and Magda carried rifles. "That's fine. I have three rifles and a small arsenal of ammunition. Ismail, get out the rifles and arm the men!"

"Aye, aye, sir!" shouted Ismail as he ran behind the house.

"Are you really good with that rifle, girl?" Ivvo turned to Magda.

"Pretty good, sir. Ask my brother."

"She's okay," Danco admitted grudgingly, "in a sharp shooting contest she could beat most of us."

"How about you, girls?"

"I can handle a pistol," said Rossitza, "father taught me."

"I am not able to operate firearms," sighed Azimee, "but I can pass along the ammunition."

"I can do that too!" cut in little Orrania excitedly.

"You stay out of it," her grandfather chided. "You are under age."

"So what?" revolted his granddaughter. "You are over age and I trust you as a commander. Is that any way to repay me for my confidence?" She stomped her foot, on the verge of tears, "You should be ashamed of yourself!"

Ismail brought the rifles. He thrust one in Danco's hands.

"I haven't forgotten you, jerk," he grunted, making sure that Ivvo wasn't listening, "I'm gonna cut you to ribbons. Pray Allah we survive."

"Better pray to Him to give you an easier death than the one you'll get at my hands," parried his worthy rival.

Radco took a rifle from Ismail, his smile tinged with bitterness.

"Eye for an eye, tooth for a tooth...eh, brothers?"

Chapter Seventeen

General Robev paused for only a moment on his way to Ferdinand's working den.

"Wait for me, Colonel. I won't be long."

Seraphimov sat in the corner, perfectly calm, his usual integrity restored.

"Tea or coffee, sir?" asked the same young officer politely.

"How about a vodka?" winked Vladimir Seraphimov.

"I don't know, sir, but I'll try."

The clock standing in the opposite corner measured out three prolonged chimes, "So it is done..." thought Seraphimov crossing his legs and groping for his short pipe. "I am done, and I feel nothing but hunger. I could eat at the officer's club, something real good...if I am still an officer. I am sure Ellena would approve of what I said. She'll be proud of me, and she'd love Jallov's poem. I wonder if I can smoke in here? Why not? What have I got to lose?"

"Here's your vodka, sir."

"Thank you, young man. You have distinguished yourself. What is your name?"

"Lieutenant Semerdgiev, sir, at your service."

"Let me guess who your father is," said Seraphimov sipping his drink. "I am not an experienced drinker...just to mark a special occasion, to your health and quick promotion, Lieutenant."

"Thank you, sir."

"Can't you steal another glass of vodka for yourself? I'd love company."

The officer blushed. "I'd be discharged, sir."

Seraphimov waved his hand. "No, you won't. I am sure your papa can arrange something. He presided over a court martial in my outfit recently."

"A kangaroo court, I presume."

Seraphimov held back a belch. "How do you know?" he stammered slightly. "It hasn't been in the newspapers."

"I know my father, sir."

"You do? You're an awfully good guy, Lieutenant... handsome too..."

"Thank you, sir."

"Just one thing. You'll never move any further up in the service if you don't know how to keep your mouth shut. Ask me...I should have kept mine under lock all my life; then I would've been a god. A lesser god...but a god. If you don't believe me, ask His Majesty..."

The young officer threw a glance over his shoulder. They were alone.

"I am an admirer of yours, Colonel Seraphimov," he said in a hushed voice, "there are a lot of us who think the same, even in the palace."

"No kidding!" exclaimed the older man, losing his battle of the belch. "Pardon me, son, I am not quite used to drinking. It goes to my head right off. I haven't had anything to eat since last night—I shouldn't have had this drink, but after all...why not? Will you do me a favor, my boy?"

"Certainly, sir."

"If I have trouble getting out of this damn chair, will you help me to the street? I'd never find my way out of this warren."

"Of course, sir."

"Even if you get a kick in the arse for it?"

The boy smiled. "Even if I lose my job in the palace."

Seraphimov finished his drink in one huge gulp. "Bottoms up! Bottoms up!" he sang. "Wonderful!...has anybody told you, you have a great smile? Women would like it, it's a good thing you took after your mother; she's a fine lady because, with all due respect to your father, his bird face is only good for a hen house. No offense, eh? My tongue is so thick, it hardly fits in my mouth. Soon I'll have to let it hang...all the way out!" He began laughing heartily.

General Robev appeared at the Tzar's doorway. Seraphimov made an heroic effort to regroup.

"Now, son, help me just a bit."

Lieutenant Semerdgiev helped Seraphimov to his feet.

"You are excused, Lieutenant!" said Robev coldly.

"I am sorry, General, but this youngster is like a part of me, if he goes, I go..."

Robev shook his head desperately. He took Seraphimov by the arm. "I'll take care of you, Colonel. Go, officer, go!"

The young man hesitated for a second, then left hurriedly.

"For Christ sake, what did you tell the Monarch, Seraphimov?"

"Nothing very much, dear General...you know me... I am the world's worst speaker. Oh, I remember now. I told His Majesty I am not a warlock. And I swear I am not. Have I ever lied?"

"Not that I know of."

"What's gonna happen to me?"

"You are going directly from here to Dobrudga as commander of the garrison of Dobritch."

Seraphimov laughed. "As my wife would say: *"C'est magnifique, mais ce ne pas la guerre!"*

379

"No, there is no war out there," said Robev suavely. "His Majesty doesn't consider you fit for that purpose anymore."

"Extraordinary, Robev! For the first time in my long military career, His Majesty and I are of one mind. Tell me one thing, Robev.

"What?"

Seraphimov made a cross over his own mouth. "I most solemnly promise I won't spill the beans!"

"What is it?" asked the general impatiently.

Seraphimov looked straight into his eyes. "Did you shoot Jallov in the back or did you have the nerve to face him?"

Robev lost every drop of blood from his cocky face. For almost a minute he was absolutely speechless, unable to take his eyes from Seraphimov's, whose were steel gray and pitiless.

"You forget yourself, Colonel!" Robev was shocked into saying.

"I wish I could," sighed Seraphimov. "Now, you take care of this empty glass, and I'll take care of myself."

From the balcony of Topkapi Palace, Lord Covington could see the minarets and domes of Istanbul, thrusting their silhouettes through the fine mist that came from the long stretch of Golden Horn. He knew the structures by their outlines. Yani Mosque right beneath, Hagia Sophia and the Blue Mosque a bit further on. Scores of seagulls flew over the seemingly motionless barges. The lights of Uscudar beyond Bosporus were merging with the bright stars of a magnificent violet sky. A powerful, mysterious and sensual charm arose from the darkened city below. A cool, gentle breeze brought thousands of spicy scents weaving the mantle of night that the "old empress" spread over the two continents.

"What are you thinking, Ambassador?" The screechy voice of Sultan Mehmed tore the Englishman's eyes from the enchanting panorama. He thoughtfully took a sip from the crystal champagne glass and observed the hunched skeletal figure with a narrow cruel face under a turban adorned with precious stones and gold.

"I was thinking how much Lady Covington would have enjoyed this magnificent view."

"Why don't you bring her out here, Ambassador? Now that the war is almost over, there is little reason to keep her away."

"Your Majesty is right, as usual. Though the war is far from over."

The Padishah looked at him in distress and surprise. "What do you mean, not over? Didn't we, according to this miserable peace treaty, give enough territory to the rebels? The demarcation line is drawn almost to the doorstep of my palace!"

"That's exactly what we must not accept, Majesty. Under pressure from Germany and France and, of course, the Russian Emperor, we had to agree on those boundaries. But that certainly was not our last word."

"What next?"

"During the second half of May, Serbia and Romania will declare war on their former good neighbor and ally. Upon the intervention of those combined forces, the Bulgarians will have no other choice but to leave Your Majesty's borders almost unguarded. The Great Army just needs to move silently and take back what belongs to the Padishah. I hope your troops will be able to do at least that without any hitches. We'll give the Romanians Northeast Bulgaria, called Dobrudga, and the Serbians a fat piece of Southwest. Greece will receive the White Sea Thrakia.

That will leave the Lion of the Balkans in no position to be of any further threat to your crown, Majesty."

"You don't expect me to say 'thank you,' Ambassador, do you? You brought me to this; it's up to you to deliver me."

Lord Covington had another sip of the good wine, as he deprecatingly sized up the spiteful little man beside him. Then he said coldly. "We don't expect any gratitude from you, Your Majesty. Though, we do have one condition."

The tiny evil eyes of Mehmed pierced the Englishman. "I knew it! What is it?"

"According to our information, a lot of the population in those territories has converted to Christianity. His Majesty, the King of the British Empire, does not want another Armenian genocide in the Balkans this time."

Mehmed's teeth were heard grinding in the tense pause. "And what if I refuse to obey?"

"There will be a democratic revolution in this country and the last Padishah will say adieu forever to his Empire and the Throne of Bayazid."

Early in the evening, two men from the posse arrived in front of grandfather Ivvo's homestead and waved a white piece of fabric. Radco peered through the thickening darkness. He knew them from Progled and more… Mourco and Metyo…but he said nothing.

"We wanna talk to the owner of this place!" shouted the younger one.

"I own this house and all the grounds around it," Ivvo shouted back. "Whoever wants to see me, can enter. Though your intentions do not look good, I guarantee you a safe return if you promise to behave yourself, and lay down your arms."

The messengers put their heads together and talked among themselves a bit. "All right!" spoke out the same man. "We'll come to the porch. We carry no guns."

"How do we know?" demanded Ivvo.

"You can see, we're leaving everything out here."

"I see nothing. It's too dark."

"Take our word for it, as we do yours."

"You know who I am. Who the hell are you, night stalkers?"

The men consulted each other, then spoke out again. "My name is Metyo, and this one here is my brother Mourco, born in Baroutin, but later moved to Progled."

Ivvo turned to Radco Boev. "Do you know them, boy?"

Radco nodded shortly. "I can't see them very well, but the voice is well known to me and corresponds to the name."

"Okay, you come with me. Ismail and Danco will cover us from behind. Leave your gun and knife here, and let's meet the bastards."

The brothers were already at the steps. When they recognized Radco, their mouths gaped, and then their eyes dilated with horror. Obviously, they hadn't come from Progled, otherwise they would've known about him.

"Are you alive, R-radco?" Metyo stuttered pitifully.

"As you see me," Radco cut him coldly. "You didn't kill me then, it won't be now, either."

Mourco was hesitant also. "We…are just soldiers of fortune, Radco."

Grandfather Ivvo glanced angrily at them. "Good evening, soldiers of fortune. What do you expect of us?"

"The j-judge of P-progled asked us to b-bring back t-two of your g-guests," Metyo stuttered again, "he wants t-to ask 'em a few q-questions."

"Is that so?" the old man was holding his wrath, "And which of my guests are sought, may I ask you? What is the accusation? I harbor no criminals under my roof."

Mourco answered, "There is a Turkish lad with you, Ismail is his name. He escaped from jail some two months ago. That man is a spy."

"What proof do you have?" Ivvo demanded

"We don't have it; the caddia has it."

Grandfather Ivvo smiled mischievously. "How do you expect me to believe that? Do I look like some kind of sucker?"

Metyo was offended. His comely round face assumed a dogged expression." "We d-don't lie. Tell him, R-radco. You know me."

"I certainly do," grinned Radco, "last time we played backgammon, you cheated twice. I caught you, didn't I? And gave you a bit of a spanking for it. Remember?"

Metyo bit his lips and stammered. "That…that was just…a g-game."

"Everything's a game the way we look at it. If you're honest, you are honest all the time. Part time honesty is for the birds. As for your brother Mourco, everyone in Progled knows he is a snake in the grass." Radco was full of contempt.

Mourco growled with rage. "Come to think of it we saved your life, bastard!"

"Not from the goodness of your hearts. You got paid for it. Last time I saw you both, you were dressed in Turkish uniforms. What are you doing now in a Bulgarian posse …and expecting to be trusted?"

"How about yourself. Do you tell the truth all the time?"

"I try," countered Radco.

"Okay, try hard, because I'm gonna ask you a few questions," Metyo growled.

"Try me," Radco challenged.

"Did Ismail sneak behind the Bulgarian lines without permission?"

"You know better than anybody else why; he brought me half-dead to the *lazaretto*."

"That doesn't matter," insisted Mourco.

"It matters very much to me."

"Well, if he wasn't doing anything wrong, why was he arrested and make an escape?"

"He shouldn't have been arrested in the first place. For bringing back a wounded Bulgarian, he should have been given praise, plus a medal."

"Are you out of your mind?" yelped Mourco at the top of his voice, "To him...a Turk?"

"What difference does that make, if he is on our side? You took his Turkish golden coins, didn't you?"

"He isn't on anybody's side! He is a traitor!" roared Mourco, "You are a liar!"

"Mind your tongue, man!" said Radco menacingly. "The last time you called me that, you got a split upper lip and two broken teeth!"

"That's what you are good at, one to one, but there are fifteen of us around this place."

"It takes more than that number of cowards to take us," Radco spat at his feet. "And who is the other person sought by your gang of no goods?"

"Easy, easy, boy," Ivvo said, leaning heavily on his long shepherd stick. "You heard his question, messengers. Answer."

"There is a girl from Progled," said Metyo sullenly. "She stole the jail keys from her father and set free twenty prisoners. Rossitza Podgorska is her name. Ismail has been her lover ever since then."

"And how would you know, creep?" Radco angrily asked. "You haven't held a candle over their bed, have you?"

At this moment, a deep voice came from the dark porch. It sounded like Allah almighty speaking in person. "You two miscreants squandered my purse of golden coins in a great hurry. If you had to sell your services to that motley posse you must be penniless." The stalwart figure of Ismail lightly descended the steps and joined the small group.

The brothers recognized him and lost even more of their composure. The heir of Moguilitza!

Metyo shook with fear. "B-b-bey ef-fendi, excellency, your honor paid us g-generously. My good-for-nothing brother spent it *all* on bad wenches, wine and roulette."

"Shush, runt!" Mourco bared his yellow teeth, "I'll disembowel you for those words!"

Metyo shouted back, "Eat your own sh-shit, bastard! Because I'm staying here w-with my good friend Radco. He knows me."

"Shut up, shorty," Mourco threatened. Metyo stepped next to Radco.

"Leave him in peace, bully!" Radco exploded, "I'm running out of patience. I'll break your neck like a match-stick!"

Metyo spoke from behind the protection of Radco's broad back, "Take heed, Radco! The b-brigand is armed with a pistol and a long knife."

Old Ivvo frowned and sharply commanded, "Run to the fence, Ismail, and gather their arms!" Ismail quickly obeyed. "Surrender your pistol and knife, liar!" Ivvo ordered Mourco.

Radco grabbed Mourco Bachov from behind, while Metyo deftly relieved his brother of his hidden weapons.

Ismail came back carrying the rifles and ammunition. "Regular Bulgarian carbines," he stated.

With a worried look, the old man shook his head. "Let him go, Radco. If it's so, they would have been given hand-bombs, too."

Mourco licked his bluish lips and said, "We have machine guns, also!"

"Hah!" Metyo blurted. "There's not a single machine gun."

Old Ivvo gave Mourco a derisive look.

Radco suddenly spoke, "And what do you intend to do with us if we refuse to surrender, bastard?"

Grandfather Ivvo winced and ordered, "Keep quiet, Radco! Let him talk."

Mourco scratched his curly head and chewed on the end of his moustache. "I guess...I guess we'll have to kill you all," he finally threatened sneeringly.

"You don't take prisoners, do you?"

"It depends," purred Mourco Bachov slyly. "If you surrender...you have some young women, too, don't ya?"

Now grandfather Ivvo blew his top. "Don't be so quick to lick your chops, scoundrel. You'll touch our women over our dead bodies."

"So that's your answer? How about the Turk and his wench?"

Radco showed him his middle finger. "Come and get 'em, if you can. There is not a single tree or bush around this house. Nothing to hide behind. We have plenty of ammunition and a good number of sharpshooters. The night will be of little protection to you rascals. There is a full moon. This is no game. Each one of us will aim to kill, so you'd better go back to your devil's seed and tell the bastards we have nothing to negotiate."

"Hell's fire!" shrieked Mourco Bachov. "You'll be bloody sorry for those words. You're gonna regret them... there won't be any pity for you or your pack! The old scoundrel, too."

"Now my patience is completely gone, you bastard," shouted Radco. "Get the hell out of here before I make you real sorry for talking like that about a brave and noble old man. Now scram!"

Grandfather Ivvo patted Radco's square shoulder. "You said it all, son. Your dad would've been proud of you."

Mourco was mad. He had lost the weapons and his brother, who represented half of his delegation. The leader of the posse would hold him responsible. "You'll be tortured to death for revolting against the State!" he shrieked insanely. "You'll be bloody sorry. Especially you, old fart."

Radco's blood boiled. His right fist squashed the nose and fetid mouth of the gangster. The punch threw Mourco on his back. When he insecurely rose to his knees, he was spitting teeth and curses.

"That should be a lesson to you, fucking soldier of fortune. Now scram, before I hit you again!" Radco threatened.

Shakily, Mourco straightened to his feet, threw them all a poisonous glance, wiped the blood from his mouth with his sleeve, but had run out of courage to speak further. He swayed on his feet, then feebly darted toward the ominous pine forest.

Metyo danced around Radco, clapping his hands. "All my life I've wanted to see that happen to my brother, Radco!" He wasn't even stammering. "Glory to you! How much I've had to put up with from that bully! He deserves much more, but what a bang it was, wow!"

"If that is their shrewdest man," laughed Danco scornfully, "I am not worried at all."

"Don't be too sure, pal," Radco said as he massaged the knuckles on his right hand. "That bum is pretty ruthless when he goes into action, a true fanatic."

"Come on, brother," said Ismail with a coolly deprecating face, "remember that night at the saloon? They acted like fools. Nobody started chasing us until we were safely ahead of them."

"Not exactly. If not for that old shack appearing at the right moment, I would say our goose would have been cooked."

"All right, all right, you guys! A victory is not a matter of opinion, but planning and more planning," said grandfather Ivvo, twisting the ends of his long moustache, his age-old commando blood brought to life again. "What do you suggest? Who's the eldest of you boys?"

"I'm almost twenty one," exclaimed Danco, obviously piqued.

"Pardon me, *old man*," grandfather Ivvo began facetiously, "I should have looked a little closer. No offense, my son and Orrania told me about your heroics. Now don't blush. A man should be proud of himself no matter how short his stay on Earth is. Tell me, how would you build our defense if you were the commander?"

Danco leaned on his long rifle, "I believe," said he, coughing a bit, "the best defense is to attack from the rear. Colonel Seraphimov defeated a much greater foe at Allamy Derre by sending a detachment in a semi-circle to the rear of that gigantic army."

"I heard about that," nodded Ivvo, rolling a cigarette. "You think we can beat them that way?"

"I don't think," responded Danco enthusiastically, "I am positive, if you, Costaky and the womenfolk keep our enemies at a distance, I and these two lads here will crawl behind them and hit them hard. They don't really know our numbers."

"We can make some bombs," added Ismail heatedly, his eyes burning with anticipation of the fight. "We certainly have all the ingredients, thanks to old man Ivvo's farsightedness."

"What if they circle around us?" challenged Radco, no resentment in his voice.

"So we break that damn circle," Danco banged on the rail. "It's made of people, not iron!"

Old man Ivvo laughed happily, his eyes gleaming softly in the moonlight. "I thought the old spirit had died with the last of those great freedom fighters of my youth. I was wrong. God bless you, lads!"

Colonel Vladimir Seraphimov left the palace and walked alongside the high wall. Soon he was at the public gardens in front of the National Theatre. The lofty statues of Triumph and Victory, perched on top of the theatre towers made him sick. He imagined himself stranded up there, with people passing by and only glancing at him from time to time. Then, one stops suddenly and points at him.

"Look out men! The statue of Colonel Seraphimov is swaying!"

"Oh, my God," screamed a fat woman, "can't you see. The Colonel is drunk. He's falling off his platform; he'll break into pieces on the hard pavement!"

A gusty wind coming down off the massive Vitosha Mountain almost knocked Vladimir off his feet. There was practically nobody in the little city garden except for an old man who was staring at him. Older than Seraphimov, he had a heavy moustache streaked with white and deep kind eyes.

"Are you all right, Vlado?" asked the man, real concern in the familiar voice. It was that great poet and writer, *deity* to Master Sergeant Jellyo Jetchev, Ivan Vazov.

"No, I am not all right," groaned Seraphimov, suddenly aware of who the man was, "drunk as a Cossack, Vazov, that's what I am. Just one glass of vodka and I'm all finished."

"I was going to the club; why don't you come with me?" said the older man, trying to hold onto his Homburg against the wind.

"Well, I was going nowhere, so why not to the club? I was terribly hungry, but now it's gone, though I could stand some strong coffee. It will do me good."

They walked slowly across the garden in silence. Ivan Vazov, cane behind his back, would stop every once in a while to smell the rose bushes.

"How is your poetry, grandfather Vazov?" asked the Colonel.

"Don't ask," smiled the old poet, without displaying bitterness. "In the last reviews, they called me '...the rusty barrel grinder...' and said my poetry's good for fourth graders in elementary school; the theatre plays, ridiculously naive and uncouth. Times have changed," he said with a short sigh, "new people, ideas, ideals...if any."

"Come on, you know how much the real folks love you. You don't have to pay any attention to those fresh new esthetes."

"I know, but it hurts anyway," Vazov replied sadly. "There are rumors around that you're finally moving up the ladder."

"It didn't happen that way. I am stuck at a dead end, grandfather. Tonight, I leave for my new destination—Dobritch."

"It's none of my business, Vlado, but I think any punishment imposed on you is a sign of distinction. One day your monument will stand higher than those silly allegorical figures, because you built it in the hearts of a whole nation, impenetrable to a jealous monarch who might wish to desecrate it."

"I am sorry, Your Highness, His Majesty wishes to see no one."

"General Robev," declared Prince Boris in a deadly calm voice, "I won't allow you to stand between me and my father any longer. If you dare to do this one more time, I'll take steps to have you totally discredited and...yes, put away for good."

For the first time in his long career, Robev was really frightened of the young prince. There was something inside him that said his days in the palace were numbered.

"You know, Highness, that I am just a tool at the hands of His Majesty," Robev tried to placate.

"Then pretty soon His Majesty won't need any such tools to make His decisions."

"That's not fair, Your Highness..."

The Prince arched his eyebrows. "You and fairness, General?"

Robev squirmed. "I was used...used for all sorts of dubious enterprises. You don't expect me, Highness, to forget my long years of service here overnight, do you?"

"Are those your sharp teeth you're showing, General? If so, I must remind you of what happens to courtiers with long memories...or maybe I don't have to. Perhaps, you've already helped some of them through Hades? Now get out of my way and, next time you see me coming, simply disappear."

Robev bowed humbly and stepped back in the shadows of a colonnade.

Ferdinand did not answer the knock on his door. Prince Boris pressed the handle. The elaborately polished and lacquered door opened noiselessly. The Tzar was sitting in a deep armchair facing a window, peering into the thickening darkness outside as if expecting something to materialize. Two crystal lamps on the mantelpiece provided very little light in the immense room whose walls were covered with rare books and priceless paintings.

"I don't need anybody," said he quietly, but firmly.

Boris still wasn't sure if, by some uncanny sensitivity, his father had felt another presence in the room or if he was just talking to himself.

"I had to see you, Father."

The Tzar didn't show any surprise or disapproval. His royal profile kept its deeply imprinted impassiveness. Prince Boris came up from behind; the soft Persian carpet absorbing the sound of his footsteps. He stopped at the back of the great chair, a feeling of disconnection draining his initial courage. It was as if that man in the chair was a complete stranger to him—as if he had nothing to do with, or say to him. All he could think of were banal words and meaningless expressions. The aura of this stranger seemed to be filled with solitude and isolation. Boris had to push himself to overcome a strong desire to leave. He walked around to the side and almost touched the hand of his august father.

"What is it, son?" Ferdinand asked suddenly without moving his head. "More bad news?"

"I am afraid you are right, sir, much as I hate to be the bearer of it."

The Prince wanted to kneel beside his father, but he never acted on impulse, and he distrusted any manifestation of feelings not publicly acceptable.

"It's about Madame Hadgylvanova."

For a moment Ferdinand lost the iron grip on his own emotions. He turned to his son with almost human concern. "You have news from Sultana?"

"I had a telegram from Madame Seraphimova," Boris explained more gently.

"You had a telegram? I don't understand. Why you? Is there anything wrong with her?"

Boris' hands were wet with perspiration. "She is dead, father."

The meaning of his son's words did not seem to penetrate. Then, "You never approved of her, Boris," he finally spoke very quietly. "I wonder why? She is your type of a person—abstract, emotional, devoted. She is the only one that loved me the way I am."

"I know, Father. I got to know her real self, only too late."

"She never asks me for anything, and I treat her like...but, she is a very decent woman, my boy." His eyes were pleading, desperate. "So you won't object anymore... if I ask her to come and live with us?"

Boris felt like his his blood was freezing. "Father..." he stammered, "Sultana is dead."

There was a long pause, with only the sound of the night wind from Vitosha drumming on the window pane. Ferdinand got up quickly, walked to the window and opened it brusquely. The gust knocked down a vase and threw the velvet curtains high up in the air. All the crystal chandeliers sang in the blowing wind.

"I thought I saw her a few minutes ago," he whispered, staring off into the void, "right there, between those two birch trees. She was waving at me. She wanted to tell me something. I wasn't sure, it was like a scarf in the wind, caught in the branches. It was a full moon and I saw the moonlight shining in her long hair." He turned his deadly white face toward Boris. "You think we should look around? She might still be hiding behind a tree. She might be cold?"

Prince Boris ran to his father and grabbed him at the very minute he was about to fall down. Calling up all his strength, the frightened young man dragged the heavy, gasping body back to the armchair.

"Father, you are not well!" he cried alarmed.

"No...I am not...well," uttered the man who seemed to have turned much older.

"I'll call a physician!"

"No, please don't. That would cause political aggravation everywhere. This is not the time for me to be sick. Sultana wouldn't like that. She would have liked me to be strong, energetic...and to save the pieces...if still possible."

Plovdiv, 15th of May 1913
Dear Vlad,

I don't know your current address, so I am sending this letter c/o General Headquarters. It will take some time for a letter of yours to reach me, and I need a shoulder to cry on.

Sultana is dead!

A dreadful death it was. As I told you at the station, Assen had called for her. The cholera took him and a couple of days later, Sultana…Darling, I was there! Don't be angry. I simply had to go. I took every precaution in the world, talked to her from a window, and haven't touched the kids since then. Now, thank God, I am out of danger and the girls seem to be all right. Of course, we are still under that great shock, and I doubt if we ever will be able to get over it completely. Especially Jivca, hypersensitive and sentimental as she is. I had to tell her of Assen's death in order to fulfill his last wish. The end of her beloved Aunt Sultana put her in a horrendous state. She sleepwalks at night and talks to the dead. There was a wounded boy in our house, as you remember. She calls to him too and I am not quite sure if she sees him dead or alive. That girl always has been fragile, and now she's lost so much weight that there's nothing left of her but a pair of enormous eyes. I am afraid things got out of hand for all of us and only the coming of a young man, Ivan Zemsky, took some of the sting out of it. Rayna had met him a few days ago when he arrived from the front. She invited him to a five o'clock party on Sunday and, as could be expected of her, totally forgot about it. He came dressed in black suit, top hat, white gloves and a bunch of roses in his hand. My mind was so obsessed by Sultana that I took him for a mourner. On his part, he thought Rayna had died, so it was very much like a vaudevillian type situation comedy, except for the real tragedy surrounding us. Mr. Zemsky is a rather brave young man. He did not beg his family to take him back, but has been working as a porter around the city. I must admit that I was deeply impressed by this.

Oh, my dear, I miss you more than ever!

There are persistent rumors: a peace treaty will be signed this week in London that will make Bulgaria sprawl from Black to White Sea. I hope that will appease the insatiable appetites of some rulers. If it is true and you're sent to a garrison, we'll join you as soon as possible. No matter how small and far away it is. I only pray to God that it happens before I go out of my mind.

We all love you and kiss you. Take good care of yourself. Don't worry about anything. The money you left will take care of us for quite a while, and what Sultana left will keep the hospital wing going.

Have all my love, my only one!

Ellena

The clear moonlit night was protection to the besieged, but it hampered Danco's action plan as well. Until midnight an attack had been expected, but no assault of any kind came and old man Ivvo sent everyone to rest except for three men. They kept watch with him on each side of the house. Then, to stay awake, they busied themselves making hand grenades.

"It's good that I always keep empty shells," muttered the old man, inhaling his pungent tobacco, "I thought the day might come when I'd need them, and it did."

"Even with grenades," smiled Costaky, operating deftly with his single hand, "you think we'll last until morning?"

"Wash your mouth, boy," scolded his father. "One does not joke about things like this!"

"Who said I was joking," Costaky shook his head. "I wish I could believe there is a chance for survival."

"You are not only softhearted, but softheaded as well, son! In a real battle, if one fights like a man, only God knows who will survive."

"Well, I might not be the fighting kind, but I am not a coward either," protested the young man, "I was just being realistic."

Ismail took a drag on his cigarette. "Maybe Costaky is right, grandfather Ivvo. What right have we to endanger the lives of everyone here, especially a child? Why don't we try to escape before dawn. I mean, Rossitza and me. We have some chance of getting by unnoticed if you divert their attention away from us."

Old man Ivvo thrust a murderous glance in his son's direction. "You see what you've done, bungler? You should feel very proud of yourself."

Costaky reddened to the tip of his ears. "I didn't mean that, Ismail. Please don't make me ashamed of myself. If Orrania hears about this, she will never forgive me even if it wasn't what I meant."

Ismail swung an arm around his shoulders. "Rubbish! I didn't misunderstand your intentions. It just gave me the idea."

"I won't listen to ideas like that any more," grunted Ivvo. "Nobody leaves my house in that fashion without insulting me."

"All right, no harm done," cut in Danco, "don't blow your top for nothing, grandfather Ivvo. I might have a grudge against this guy here, but it's strictly between us two. I won't let him pull a stupid trick on himself and…and Rossitza, even if I have to hold him pinned down with my own hands for the rest of the night."

"Good enough," approved the old man, "you're getting tired, Costaky. Go and wake Radco. He's had two hours of sleep."

At this point Magda joined them. "You two go and get some rest, grandfather Ivvo," she said as she checked out her rifle. "I am used to getting along with little sleep. These young ones will be more important in a fight. Let them rest. Go, Danco."

"Let Ismail go. I won't be able to fall asleep anyway," Danco added to the mix.

"What makes you think *I* will?" Ismail put out his cigarette butt. "I have more on my mind than you do."

"Okay, don't start that again." Old man Ivvo got up. "I'll go and take a snooze if you two promise not to fight each other."

Magda laughed. "Don't worry. Radco will keep them apart."

After old man Ivvo and his son left, Magda kept on talking. "You boys have to show me how you make those bombs."

There was no answer from the boys—they both pretended to be very busy.

"Very well," pouted Magda, "Is that the way you entertain a girl?"

"Hold your horses, sister," said Danco, "Radco will be getting up in a minute; he's the professional entertainer. Just be patient."

"No wonder women don't stay with you," teased Magda.

"Don't throw grease on the fire, girl!" Radco reprimanded her as he came out from behind the partition, his eyes still heavy with sleep. "You might burn your own fingers too."

"Oh, look who's here!" jeered Magda. "Hello, happy face!"

"Happy face, my foot, I have a toothache," Radco complained.

"Come on, a great entertainer should know how to hide pain with a smile."

"Who said that?"

"My brother."

Radco waved his fist at Danco. Danco smiled. "Don't listen to her. She's crazy."

Radco slapped his forehead. "Holy cats! He cracked a smile. Did you see that, Ismail? The stone face, himself!"

"Shut up, clown, or you'll get one in the mouth," grumbled Danco, most of the former resentment and bitterness gone. "Don't fool yourself into thinking you can get away with my girl. Nobody takes from me without getting punished."

Magda was not amused. "Girls are not objects to be taken or given, brother."

"Leave me alone, will ya? I don't mess in your…in…" Danco started.

"In my what, brother? In my dead love?"

Danco threw the empty shell and knocked down the keg of gunpowder. "Hell's fire! It seems everything I do is wrong."

"At least there is some change. Now you are aware of it," said Radco trying to sweep the spilled powder back into the keg.

They worked for about ten minutes in silence, listening to all the animal noises coming from outside.

"Never thought there were so many birds and animal movements at night," muttered Magda, leaning on the porch rail. Ismail left his tool and joined her swiftly. He listened carefully, then looked at Radco and Danco gravely. "Those noises are make-believe, just to distract attention and cover their real movements. I think our assailants are coming from the opposite side."

Part Four

Epitaph for the Heroes

Chapter Eighteen

In the early hours of May 20th, 1913, Bulgaria was attacked on two fronts. Romania and Serbia had declared war. Greece silently occupied the White Sea Thrakia. Shortly afterward, Turkey broke the London Peace Treaty of May 17th, 1913, by passing the line Midia-Ennos. Though attacked on all sides, exhausted in a total war against a much bigger and more powerful enemy, the Bulgarians still fought with pathetic and desperate courage. Hungry, plagued by mortal epidemics, short of supplies and arms, outnumbered by well-rested, well-equipped armies, a handful of heroes battled almost bare handed. The Lion of the Balkans was going to be torn to pieces by a pack of mad dogs!

The shelling of Colonel Seraphimov's troops was mercilessly cruel. Because they were lined up against a mass of rocks, he was losing dozens of men by the minute. Each explosion in the rocks turned into thousands of ricochets, killing and crippling soldiers by the hundreds. There were numerous cases of madness brought on by the horrendous effect of detonations and the sinister whistling of projectiles. Three times, their commander tried to obtain permission from headquarters to retreat behind this rocky ridge where they'd be protected instead of devastated by that natural wall. Three times, he got the same laconic response: "Bulgarian soldiers—not one step back!"

Under a pitilessly hot scorching sun, under piles of dust and fragments, lay hundreds of dead, dying or condemned to die. The eyes of dead and still living followed Colonel Seraphimov in silent reproach. He knew that their retreat was not going to expose any flank of neighboring troops, or create a bad example to the rest. It was senseless obstinacy of a blind command that kept them exposed to complete annihilation.

"Water...water, please..." moaned many cracked lips under eyes filled with horror and desperation.

Vladimir Seraphimov's own lips were parched with thirst and heat, his grimy face smeared with blood from a deep scratch on his forehead. Throughout the morning, he had been at the most badly hit places—encouraging, reprimanding, helping the stretcher bearers.

Finally, the endless day was over and the thundering cannonade gradually ceased. The night came, balmy and soothing, over a theatre of agony. Now that the immediate threat to the soldiers' lives had diminished, every other pain gripped their bodies and minds. Flocks of memories of loved ones, of their native homes, and the almost physical realization that they would never see them again.

Seraphimov had no time to get to know his new outfit personally, though basically they were no different from the boys he had before. New to this distant post only a few days or weeks, all the men, of various ages and occupations, felt terribly lost and out of place in the endless plains of Dobrudga.

Now it seemed they had to die a senseless, cruel death...not even sure what they were fighting for.

"Not if I can help it, God!" Seraphimov caught himself talking aloud. "No matter what the cost to me."

His old friends, the stars, seemed to have heard him. Suddenly they loomed brighter. And the blood-curdling moans from the shallow trenches had a note of hope, ringing somewhere in the depths of desperation.

At the end of that rocky range, began a field of wheat with no limit in sight. Seraphimov kneeled amidst the young crop and caressed the silky heads gently.

"Same wheat as ours..." said a feeble voice very close to him. It was as if earth itself was talking. The Colonel looked around. Then he discovered the body. Under the silvery moonlight, a man was prostrate among the short stems. Seraphimov bent over to take a closer look. The face was broad with high cheek bones and a daredevil moustache—he knew the man, one of his own old timers. Then it came to him; the gun shop master, Sergeant Jellyo Jetchev.

The man's dimmed eyes flared in recognition. "It's you, Colonel..."

"Yes, Sergeant. Are you hit badly?"

"You know me...sir!"

"Of course, I know you, Sergeant Jetchev."

"I am dying, sir...I didn't want to part with my soul on those infernal rocks, so I crawled out here. It's nice...it smells like home. No, Colonel, please don't. I am beyond any help."

"What happened to the old company?" asked Seraphimov, sitting next to the dying man.

"We were all dispersed...we knew too much."

A slight breeze came from the plains like an inaudible sigh.

"Do you want me to write to somebody for you, Jellyo?"

"You remember my name...thank you, Colonel. You're my favorite hero—like those from the *Epopee of the Forgotten...*

Three days since a handful of heroes
defend Shipka Pass...Mounts and forests
repeating the thunder
of that raging battle.
Assault, after assault...'

"Tomorrow everybody at this position will be dead, sir..." Jellyo whispered.

Seraphimov took his big rugged hand. "No, Jellyo. I'll move them tonight behind the range."

"On whose orders?"

"On my own."

Jetchev choked on his own blood, coughing as he managed to get out, "I knew it! What will they do to you, Colonel?"

"I don't know," Seraphimov answered in an even voice, devoid of inflection.

"God bless you, sir. You're the last of the forgotten..." a last sighing breath and Jellyo died.

A tiny cricket jumped on the forehead crusted with blood and dirt, and chirped sadly as if he knew the dead man from home.

The assailants had reached grandfather Ivvo's house almost unseen.

They had set fire to the tool shed and an old outhouse. Under the protection of a low stone wall, they started an intense fusillade.

Inside, the surprised comrades tried to organize an effective response. Costaky and old man Ivvo had not yet fully drifted into sleep, so they were able to wake up the women. There was no panic. Everyone seemed to know what to do. Costaky and Rossitza were at the front porch; Magda, grandfather Ivvo and Metyo took care of the sides; Ismail, Radco and Danco had the back, where every assault bordered on frenzy.

"Holy cats!" exclaimed Danco, "what's that Satan doing here?"

"Who do you see?" asked Radco, recharging his rifle.

"That man with a black, closely cropped beard, piggy eyes and fat face."

"Who is he?" shouted Radco over the volley of fire.

"It's that three-times-cursed evil creature who set the Turks against Ranghel Sabev at junction Bouk."

Ismail waited for a pause in the shooting.

"Are you sure? That's the 'would-be-priest' from Catoun. I've seen him with Sadak."

"I could never forget that pig's snout!" Danco spat out in rage. "That filthy gang cut a friend of mine to pieces; I wish I could get my hands on him!"

"I don't mind rendering you that service," Ismail cursed. "What is a 'priest' of ours doing in a Bulgarian posse?"

"Some holy man!" grumbled Radco and he aimed his gun at the priest. It was close, but not close enough. "I am sure he started the fire. It's written on his ugly face."

Several bullets splashed at the beams over their heads. Azimee and Orrania came around with a basket full of ammunition. Danco was furious. "Didn't I tell you, devilish girl, to stay behind that partition with the little one?"

"Don't be mad at her, Danby." Orrania embraced him from behind. "There are plenty of bullets flying around at the back."

"Get off my back, Orry," Danco pleaded with her. "Go lie down on the floor, sweetheart. Take Azimee with you. Will you do it for me, please?"

A new salvo exploded and a score of bullets crashed around them. The little girl came even closer to him.

"I can't Danby," she whispered in his ear sadly, "I *have* to be with you.

It happened at that very moment.

The bullet went through Danco's chest and nested in Orrania's stomach. In the heat of the fight nobody was aware of it.

"Are you hit, little bird?" coughed Danco, blood trickling from the corners of his mouth.

"Yes, I am..." moaned Orrania, bravely struggling with the growing pain. It hurts, Danby. It hurts more than...I can take..." she gasped as she slid into his arms.

"What's happening out here?" Azimee crawled toward them.

"Leave us...alone...Azimee..." said little Orrania haltingly, her delicate face distorted by the cruel pain. "Danby will take care of me. He is so strong..."

"Oh, Allah!" screamed Azimee. "They are hit!"

"Who's hit?" yelled Radco above the thundering reports.

"Danco and Orrania!" Azimee shouted back, trying to help out the wounded.

Grandfather Ivvo saw the commotion, but kept on firing.

"It's all right, Costaky!" he cried to his son. "They'll be all right...don't stop!"

Radco shook his fist at the dark heads behind the wall. "You murderers!" he yelled, tears streaking down his grimy cheeks, "Come out here. I'll split you open!"

As if they had heard him, the attackers left the protection of the shallow stone wall and charged toward the house. It was now the homemade bombs came in handy. Two of them sent the assailants rushing back, three bodies wriggling and thrashing around on the ground.

"Die, bastards, die!" roared Ismail hurling another bomb after them, the explosion almost destroying a portion of the low stone wall.

"We have bombs, too!" shouted someone from the corner of the burning outhouse, as he threw a heavy grenade on the roof of grandfather Ivvo's rough cabin.

The detonation broke four supporting beams and a rainfall of stone slates crashed to the floor. One of them knocked old man Ivvo unconscious and another opened a bloody gash in Ismail's arm. Rossitza left her post to help the old man, but Ismail hollered at her to keep on shooting. Radco fired at a man that was trying to throw a flaming torch on the broken roof. Light from the burning shed spread on the face—it was Mourco Bachov. He dropped the torch, grasped his throat and tumbled down with a short scream.

"Brother!" Metyo cried out. Radco looked sharply at him. Metyo was torn by conflicting feelings but said, "Nothing to me, Radco." His voice lacked conviction. Radco turned away and went on shooting.

Now, obviously, the priest had taken over. He shouted something to the rest; as he gestured toward the house. A new attack was launched on the flank defended by Rossitza. Magda and Ismail hurried to her support...

"How are you, little bird?" asked Danco in a choking voice, his big hand tenderly stroking the cooling forehead. "Does it still hurt a lot?"

"No...Danby," whispered Orrania, mustering a smile, "very little...now...I just feel sleepy. Stay with me..." she said dreamily, a single tear making its way down the hollow cheek, "...are you still strong enough, Danby?"

"Yes, Orry...I'll last a bit more."

"Take me in...your arms, like...in a cradle and rock me to sleep...please."

Danco took her in his embrace and rocked the fragile body gently, some of his blood trickling over her.

"I am happy, Danby..." Orrania muttered sleepily, "I love you...so much..."

"I love you too, little bird. From the very moment you saved my life."

"It didn't last long…Danby…"

"It wasn't…for long…really, but we met each other, didn't we?"

"Yes Danby…we did…and you would've waited…for me…yes?"

"Yes, little bird…as you will…for me now…"

"Thank you, Danby. Even if you don't come, thank you…"

A light shadow passed like a caress over her face. Although the gentle, lovely eyes were still open, Danco knew she was gone. He kissed her fading lips until the end of life, and beyond.

Colonel Seraphimov was arrested early in the morning. By that time, the movement of his troops to behind the rocky range had been accomplished. The enemy had started firing its heavy guns at daybreak, but with little success. A new commander was sent to replace Vladimir Seraphimov.

The Colonel was the first one to notice the cavalcade. It wasn't difficult to pick out among the riders the bird face of Colonel Semerdgiev. The officers got off their horses and approached Vladimir Seraphimov on foot.

"I am under orders, Colonel…" began Semerdgiev, his arrogance running short as he confronted the noble and severe face of the legendary commander.

"I am fully aware of that , Colonel Semerdgiev. Please, proceed," Seraphimov said calmly.

Semerdgiev pointed at the officer next to him. "Lieutenant Colonel Vrannev, will take over your obligations."

Seraphimov sized up the young man humorously. "Lieutenant Colonel!?! I had to wait twenty-five years for that promotion. You do quite well at thirty. I do remember you. The hero that burned the village of Moguilitza—under orders of course. The castle and its inhabitants, too. Remarkable."

Vrannev defensively came back with, "I do only my best for His Majesty and the Fatherland."

"I know that much, Lieutenant Colonel," Vladimir retorted dryly.

There was an uneasy silent pause. It was as if even the enemy was listening to the conversation and had put his artillery pieces to rest. But breaking into that dead silence were disturbing growls that emanated from the circle of soldiers tightly enclosing the officers.

"What is that?" said Semerdgiev, obviously agitated. Are we going to have a riot? I am vested with authority to discharge the whole regiment. You'll all be court martialed. Do you hear me? Step back immediately!"

The soldiers centered their bayonets at him and steadily advanced with cool determination in their eyes. Young Lieutenant Colonel Vrannev's face paled, but he tried, his voice shaking badly, "Fall back in Line! Hear me, soldiers! I'm your new commander. Insubordination in action is a very serious crime. I order you back to your given position in front of this ridge!"

The bayonets were closing inexorably.

Semerdgiev turned to Vladimir Seraphimov pleadingly, "Colonel, do something...I beg you..."

"On whose authority?"

"You are still the Commander of the Regiment."

Seraphimov stepped forward.

"Fall in Line!" he bellowed. His soldiers stopped instantly and followed his command. Vladimir Seraphimov went on gravely, "You have a new Commander. He's young and needs your help. He doesn't have any idea what's behind this ridge. He's been ordered. But now I have the belief that he won't try to push you back into the inferno where only death is in command. For good or bad, we're all representing the Army for the Honor of Mother Bulgaria. The Lion of the Balkans! These fields are covered with our blood—over the mountains, to The White Sea and Marmora. I have to leave you now—not in shame and dishonor, but in eternal Triumph and Glory. Forever together! Nobody will be able to part us. In this sense we'll march shoulder-to-shoulder into history."

He pulled out his sword, kissed the blade glistening in the morning sun and handed it to Colonel Semerdgiev.

Four stalwart soldiers grabbed Seraphimov and set him on their powerful shoulders. The regiment parted in two formations, the path leading to his white mare Sanya. An earsplitting "Hurray!!!" left the parched lips of every man in the regiment and made the very earth tremble.

After a short hesitation, Colonel Semerdgiev gave a salute and followed. Thus, the arresting outfit turned out to be Seraphimov's Guard of Honor. The riders took out their swords, holding them in attitudes of honor.

Everybody stepped out of rank, running alongside the procession, like a river in the midst of the wheat fields, their faces streaked with tears.

Everyone shouldered their way closer to their beloved Commander. To kiss his hand; to throw handfuls of young wheat over him, to touch his horse or at least the hoof prints left behind for GOOD LUCK and because they were HIS soldiers, FOREVER.

May 26, 1913, City of Plovdiv
Dear Vlad,
    I don't really know where to send this letter.
    At Headquarters, everybody shrugs their shoulders and evades my eyes. I know something has happened. I do not

permit myself to think the worst, but if it comes to that, I am not scared. I have been ready for it all my life. We two are so much the same person. Nothing can make you disappear from my life. You believe more in life than in death, but you'll see the difference is only the way we accept reality. A reality we touch and a reality we feel are two estranged dimensions. I'm sure one day we'll talk it all over with Sultana. She was another disbeliever.

Please don't worry about us. Yesterday Dr. Michailov offered me a full time job at Alexander's Hospital. A salary and other benefits included. Rayna is taking courses in typewriting. It's the new craze among young people, but one day it might come in handy. Her painting and music won't get her far and rich husbands, in the immediate future, will be as rare as a meteorite in the back yard. Jeanna still lingers in dreamland, but Elsa definitely wants to be a teacher of mathematics. Jivca, for the time being, will stick with the piano. She is a true artist. Your friend, the Maestro, before dying in Italy, sent me a postcard asking us to pursue her talent. Baby Lillie will be a ballerina. She started dancing even before she learned to walk. Don't laugh at me. You should see her graceful movements while Jivca plays the piano.

My dearest one, something tells me that you are more alive than ever, that you'll be in my arms very soon. I pray to God every night to watch over you because…because you are a good man, and very few of that kind were spared by the war.

Please, Dear Christ, let him come back as soon as possible!!!

Have our love and my kisses,
Your ELLENA

At sun-up grandfather Ivvo's cabin was still holding. Like a flock of blackbirds, the handful of assailants took their wounded and retreated to the pine forest, disappearing as if they could exist only in darkness. One of them was taken prisoner. Nobody tried to get him back.

In his last desperate effort to lead his gang to a successful assault, the priest had walked right into the trap Radco and Ismail had set for him. The spiteful man was tied in a package on the floor amid piles of debris. His doleful eyes, red and watery, scrounged around as if he were a burglar caught while still undecided on what to pilfer first.

Radco looked at him as a dangerous beast brought to final judgment. He did not even want to guess how many murders were committed by this man, how many crimes were on his conscience. But to his own great disappointment, Radco was unable to hate him the way he should! Even with his best friend and that sweet little girl slain, he didn't feel bloodthirsty, his soul did not crave revenge. He caught himself wishing he had never taken that scoundrel prisoner. Now everyone expected him to tear the man to pieces, to drink his blood. And all Radco wanted was to lament the death of Danco and Orrania. The still shaky voice of old man Ivvo pierced his thoughts.

Supported by Magda and Costaky, the old man had come to see the murderer. He took a long hard look at the priest, who cringed like the coward he really was.

"You know who I am, Ramadan." he said, his voice gathering strength.

The man nodded shortly.

"You've met that man before?" asked Radco.

Grandfather Ivvo closed his tired eyes for a moment as if reliving something very painful. "I met this Turkish priest ten years ago. So help me God! After a horrible night like this, he was one of the ambushers that cut your father, Dimmitar, to pieces."

Radco bit back a scream, his eyes not on the man that massacred his father, but firmly fixed on Ismail. In his mind, his mother's anguished face appeared before him. "Please, ma...I...I know...what you said is true. It's horrible...I wish I could explain it to you..."

Stryna Nonna spoke in his mind as if she was present and interrupted him. "You cannot, my son. You can't explain five centuries of slavery, humiliation, lawlessness and barbarity. You can't erase all memories, the bitterness, the suffering of your people in the name of *any* God. It just has to be forgotten, buried in the past."

"You tell me, ma, and I'll do whatever you say." Radco said mentally. "Do you want this Turk to suffer just as my father did? I can take him to the woods and carve him with my father's knife."

Rossitza shook his shoulder, a look of sympathy and understanding in the depths of her gold-flecked eyes. "Radco, dear, it's decided. You'll have him. Nobody else has as much right to revenge as you do."

"Take that beast to the woods, where he belongs," said Costaky overwhelmed with bereavement, "and do to him what was done to your father. I wish I had my two hands to do that."

"Go, take him, my son," old man Ivvo embraced the youth. "Take him away, so his filthy screams won't disturb the peace of our dead."

Under a clear blue sky, from the centuries old pine forest, emanated a thin healthy fragrance that made breathing easier. A tiny breeze hid amidst the tall ferns. Birds exchanged love calls. Bees busied themselves around the streaks of multi-colored flowers spread over clearings and the singing banks of streams.

Radco's heart was heavy.

Walking behind the bound man gave him the same feeling as walking to his own funeral. He tried to think of all the good times he had had with his dead friend. There were not too many. It seems they had endured mostly hard times together. Did Azimee still stand between them? Radco felt like spitting in his own face. Wasn't his indignation a bit exaggerated? Hadn't he experienced a kind of relief? He knew Azimee had. She was disturbed by Danco's death, but there was something else in her eyes...a kind of relief.

Did Ismail and Rossitza feel the same way? Were they just better actors? Was Magda the only one that cared about her brother? ...or maybe she was pretending too? She lay unconscious for two hours, but when she came to, she didn't cry at all.

How horrible!

Radco tried to remember the face of the man he used to call his brother. It escaped him. He could see the body. But a face? What was his face like?

"Oh, my God!" he cried out so loud that even the prisoner turned back for a moment. That man...that evil man, thought Radco. He killed my father, many others... and now Danco and Orrania. What has Orrania ever done to him? But then again who has seen him killing them? Maybe the real murderer just got away. Radco's perspiration ran cold. Maybe I am as much a murderer as he is. Last night I killed a man cold-bloodedly who I used to play backgammon with—and many others. Was it only in self-defense? I think I enjoyed it, and I would do it again. How does Metyo feel about it—his only brother, his only family, dead by my hand. I killed and killed. *Is the war a valid excuse?*

Radco felt so bad he wanted to put a bullet through his own forehead.

"Stop, you bastard!" he called to his prisoner. The priest obeyed and turned a pox marked face toward his young executioner.

"You gonna slash my throat here, pup?" There was quiet defiance in his half mocking smile.

Radco felt uneasy. Was this man really so cool, or was life as dear to him as to anybody else? Was he a pretender, too? Or perhaps he was just tired of life and didn't give a damn. Was he just a beast without feelings? A poisonous snake whose head should be smashed as soon as possible?

Radco leaned over a fallen tree.

"It's none of your goddamn business what I'm going to do with you, priest," he muttered, sucking on a blade of grass. His father's knife poked at his ribs as if wanting to jump out of his belt and, on its own, do away with the murderer.

"Are you chicken, or what?" laughed the man huskily. "Do you want me to show you how I cut off the genitals of your father, boy?"

Radco screamed as if the knife had gotten him. He took it out of its sheath with a smooth movement, his teeth grinding, blue eyes turned to ice spears.

"Why do you want me to kill you, beast?" he hissed.

"You won't kill a man with hands tied behind his back, will ya, pup?"

"Did you unfasten my father's hands?"

"No," said the priest quietly, "but you're different. You'll set me free before trying to kill me."

"Why?"

"To ease your conscience."

"Did you read that in your holy Koran?"

"No, I read it in your eyes, sucker. You are not a murderer."

Radco walked behind him and silently cut his ropes. The man charged immediately, strong as a bull. He caught the wrist of the youth's hand and tried to wrench the knife out, his other hand groping for a choke-hold. A vile stench came from his mouth. Radco wrestled his arm with the knife free, but lost his balance, and they both tumbled on the ground. At this point, he got a cruel kick in the groin that doubled him with pain and a chop in the windpipe that left him breathless.

It was like a black curtain falling over him.

Long formations of troops were traveling in the opposite direction. Loose, ragged men, unshaven and dirty, with grim faces and hopeless eyes. As they headed for the front, they had to tow all sorts of objects pilfered from nearby Romanian towns and villages—portable sewing machines, bundles of fabrics and linens. Whatever they were unable to take along, they destroyed. In minutes, furniture and belongings stored for a lifetime were made completely useless. Grand pianos were chopped to pieces, Brussels mirrors broken to smithereens, and velvet chairs cut to ribbons, just for a piece of cloth to shine a pair of dirty boots. And officers of all ranks deliberately closed their eyes to this despicable looting.

It's not the same Army, thought Seraphimov with bitterness. Maybe God wants to spare me this cup.

He turned his head from those endless lines enveloped in dust.

"May I be of help to you, sir?" asked one of his escorts.

"I guess so, Lieutenant. Let's step up these horses and get to the railway junction fast."

"I know a short cut through the fields, Colonel, but it's a bumpy ride."

"Excellent, my friend. That's exactly what I need. Let's go!"

Every morning on her way to her typing class Rayna crossed Dgoumaya Square. This time she stopped at the line of gaping and jeering porters. Ivan Zemsky's face was carefully washed and smoothly shaven. He threw an angry look at his colleagues and flashed a charming smile towards Rayna even though he felt bashful and awkward.

"Don't pay any attention to these vulgar guys, Ms. Seraphimova. Their only excuse is, well, perhaps that none of them has ever seen such a beautiful and elegant young lady."

"Oh, you're not one of them, Mr. Zemsky," Rayna cut in swiftly, giving him a smile that made his knees shaky. "You are a gentleman, no matter what you do for a living." She played a bit with her little umbrella, then glanced at him under the protection of a flowery straw hat. "What a pity we can't go for a stroll along the river. I have my classes," she sighed dramatically, "and you have to work."

Ivan looked at her, enchanted. "You have the most lovely eyes I've seen in my whole life!"

"Others have said that before, Mr. Zemsky," laughed the young lady coquettishly.

"Forget the courses! I can quit here any time!"

"You know we can't do that, silly man."

Ivan lowered his head. "You are ashamed of my dirty, ragged clothes."

"No, not that!" Rayna quickly interposed. "If you'd like, you can accompany me to the office building past Courshoum Han."

The young man threw a triumphant look at his comrades along the wall, who had been closely watching them. Ivan and Rayna left, leaving Ivan's compatriots open mouthed, still skeptical that a miracle such as this could happen to one of them.

"An angel fallen right from the blue," sighed the young gypsy, Sellym. "I would give half my life just to touch her hand. Oh, brother, she hardly touches the ground when she walks. She might take off any moment back to the sky. Lucky Vantcho!"

"Wake up, Sellym," his older buddy laughed at him, "or you may take off into the sky yourself."

Radco pulled himself together. The pudgy hands of his enemy werc still on his throat, though they were now stiff and lifeless. A glossy, yellowish light had frozen in the little evil eyes, and a gush of blood coming from his wide miasmatic mouth, trickled down through the unkempt beard. His dead weight pressed on Radco. It was suffocating. Radco struggled to free himself from Ramadan's death embrace. When he finally got rid of it and crawled aside still stunned by the choking hold, he stared back at the prostrate man. Suddenly a mind-boggling realization came to him.

His father's long knife was driven right through the back of Ramadan Hodga.

Epilogue

After some initial successes against the former allies, Bulgaria was attacked by the Turks and Greeks and slowly bled to death. Eventually, an unconditional surrender was signed and big chunks of Bulgarian territory were taken away forever. Occupation forces settled in Sofia. Bulgaria was poorer and smaller than ever, and had been ravaged by burned villages, lost crops, depleted resources, raging epidemics and sky-high reparations to be paid. Hundreds of thousands died for no reason. Millions of dollars wasted in a greedy gamble for power.

The victorious countries were merciless. They were like birds of prey over the body of a dead hero. A marching song expressed the bitterness and growing spirit of vengeance characteristic of those days and represents part of what brought us down—

> *Allies—brigands*
> *stormed us with meanness,*
> *our former brothers*
> *stuck a knife in us,*
> *sucked from our blood,*
> *ate from our flesh.*
> *Choked by all sides,*
> *brought to our knees*
> *we swear to God*

to be proud and free.
Vengeance is the word,
hatred—our sword.
Allies—brigands
stormed from behind,
our flag is down
and we have no rights.
But The Day is near,
tremble, foes, and fear!

In those simple unpolished verses, people sought a bit of hope and reliance on their own forces. The frantic hatred of neighboring nations was well used by official propaganda dispensers to distract attention from social issues and intentionally mislead. The principal culprit, hidden in his palace, went unpunished. In spite of numerous voices uttering accusations in the Parliament and in some newspapers, Ferdinand survived almost unscathed. A number of student demonstrations were dealt with mercilessly. Prisons were filled to the brim, opposition stifled. Once again Bulgaria rode precariously on a tidal wave toward a new war.

Colonel Vladimir Seraphimov was dismissed with a pension and to oblivion. Any thought of a trial against him was wisely abandoned. A public martyr of his magnitude could unite all opposition forces behind him. And this scenario was not wanted by a shaky government—an undesirable risk for the palace. Ferdinand had to put aside his hatred toward the man.

The heroes of the day were the likes of Sergeant Ranghel Sabev. Portraits of him were printed, and dozens of idealistic heroic stories told about him. Neither the portraits nor the stories bore any likeness to the original. Anyone that really knew him was dead or reduced to total apathy. When Radco Boev heard the local teacher describe Ranghel as a gentle, modest person, devoted only to his

Fatherland, sacrificing his youth for the freedom of the people, he merely shrugged his shoulders. A hero is a hero.

In 1914 World War I erupted.

Once again Bulgaria joined in with hopes of restoring her prestige and territorial unity.

Shortly before that outbreak, Ismail had been apprehended by a posse of vigilantes, accused of being a spy and executed. Rossitza gave birth to his son, Ismail, Jr. She left the mountain forever and disappeared into one of the large cities. Grandfather Ivvo died of a heart attack a year after his beloved little angel was killed. Costaky joined his family at Chepellare. Magda never married. She worked in hospitals to the end of her days.

Radco Boev and Azimee were wed and had a daughter, a sweet little girl they called Jivca. He was killed in a soldiers' riot in 1916. Azimee remarried and left her mother-in-law's house.

Stryna Nonna went on living by herself like a hermit. It was said that she was visited by spirits, and strange stories were told about unnatural apparitions around her little house. She was generally feared, and meeting her was considered a bad omen.

The village of Progled was swallowed up by obscurity.

Ivan Zemsky didn't marry Rayna Seraphimova, but her younger sister, Jivca. She shared his life, in love, joys and sorrows to the very last. From poverty, he managed to emerge as one of the leading pioneers of a young and struggling Bulgarian industry. Later in life, blind communist hatred and his stupid and ignorant treatment by The Party led him to his grave.

The First World War was longer and costlier than the Balkan War. Hunger and disease plagued not only the front, but the whole country as well. It was obvious that Bulgaria was fighting on the losing side again. Suddenly, the troops rebelled, left the front and angrily headed for the Capital City of Sofia. They wanted the heads of those responsible for two national catastrophes.

Tzar Ferdinand asked Colonel Seraphimov to use his enormous prestige with the Army to stop the rebels. Seraphimov flatly refused. Trembling for his life, the Tzar left Sofia and hid in an iron-clad train, waiting for a verdict from the Parliament. It was delivered to him by the Prime Minister. Abdication in favor of his son, Boris. He signed and fled to Vienna.

About that time another monarch was leaving the city of Istanbul by ship. Livid with fear and fury, Sultan Mehmed watched his Topkapi Palace melt into the mist forever. The revolution of the Young Turks had sent him to a life in exile. This time, he had fought on the wrong side, too.

Tzar Boris III proved to be a wise ruler and a fine diplomat, but had no chance with the strong and well organized pro-German clique, bequeathed to him by his father, and led by Prince Cyril. He could not stand up to the political complications when his old mentor, Colonel Vladimir Seraphimov, returned to public life. He chose to forget about him.

But the people didn't.

A new epoch had come. Nations were no longer going to tolerate the whims and the irresponsible, costly mistakes of their masters. In 1935 a beautiful mausoleum monument was built by the people of Rhodopa Mountain. It was dedicated with love and gratitude to Colonel Vladimir Seraphimov and his brave soldiers. It was on the side where Allamy Derre's battle was fought over two decades ago. The top of the monument, at the insistence of the old commander, was left unfinished, as a proud symbol to a lost dream—unification of the whole country.

The Black Mantle Commander did not live to see it. But he is still there. Waiting. Who knows? Maybe he can see it coming from his post. Until then and beyond, let's leave him, engraved upon the never-ending monolith of eternity, those few unprepossessive lines:

> *There is greatness*
> *born in palaces,*
> *cut out of gold,*
> *molded by sycophants,*
> *sold on the streets*
> *two cents a piece.*
> *There is Greatness*
> *born in the wind,*
> *worn like a mantle*
> *over the shoulders*
> *of coming centuries.*
> *Don't try to buy it,*
> *IT'S NOT FOR SALE!*

Lion of the Balkans and other books by Vladimir Chernozemsky are available through your favorite book dealer or from the publisher:

Triumvirate Publications
497 West Avenue 44
Los Angeles, CA 90065-3917

Phone/Fax: (818) 340-6770
E-Mail: Triumpub@aol.com
SAN: 255-6480

Lion of the Balkans **(ISBN: 1-932656-01-4)**
$24.95 Hardbound.

A Continent Adrift **(ISBN: 1-932656-00-6)**
Science Fiction Novel, $24.95 Hardbound.

Please add
$4.50 shipping for first copy
($1.50 each additional copy)
and sales tax for CA orders.